LORI FOSTER

Charade

Recycling programs for this product may not exist in your area.

ISBN-13: 978-0-373-77922-2

Charade

Copyright © 2014 by Harlequin Books S.A.

The publisher acknowledges the copyright holder of the individual works as follows:

Impetuous
Copyright © 1995 by Lori Foster

Outrageous
Copyright © 1997 by Lori Foster

Printed in U.S.A.

™ www.Harlequin.com

CONTENTS

Dear Reader,

I very much hope you enjoy this 2-in-1 reissue that includes the first two stories that started my writing career, *Impetuous* and *Outrageous*. As you read them, please keep in mind that these originally came out in 1995 and 1997. I hope you find that they withstand the test of time!

Although I now write many connected stories, both of these stories stand alone.

You can see all my books with their new and original covers, and a brief description, on my website at www.lorifoster.com/bookshelf.

All my best,

Lori Foster

www.LoriFoster.com

Impetuous

Chapter One

"YOU CAN'T BE a coward forever."

Carlie chuckled, despite her nervousness. "Quit pushing, Bren. You're not going to provoke me into rushing out into the party dressed like this."

"Rushing? You're already ten minutes late." She had parked in the back of the house, away from the main flow of human traffic entering the party. Small, twinkling lights surrounded the pool and pool house, even though the weather was too brisk for swimming.

"And that's *your* fault. What were you thinking, to pick me a costume that was so...so..." Carlie couldn't quite find the words to describe the skimpy harem outfit her best friend had chosen for her. If she had to go to Brenda's stupid Halloween party at all, she would have preferred to be a pumpkin or a witch. Anything that was less revealing.

"So...what? You look fantastic. What's wrong with that? I want you to have fun tonight. I want you to loosen up a little and try socializing. Talk to people."

"You mean men, don't you?" Carlie shook her head. "I'm

not a hermit, Bren. I have my students and more than enough school activities to keep me busy." Then she glanced down at herself. "What *were* you thinking?"

"You said you didn't have time to pick out an outfit yourself." Brenda lifted one shoulder in a halfhearted shrug. "Besides, you make a very sexy harem girl. All the single men here tonight will drool. It'll do you good to realize how attractive you can be when you aren't hiding behind those hideous suits."

Carlie winced. She was feeling far from attractive. Exhibited, displayed and downright exposed was more accurate. She was pretty certain she looked ridiculous more than anything else. "Which single men, exactly, did you invite?"

Brenda waved her hand in dismissal. "You've met almost everyone, I think. Some of Jason's associates, a few neighbors, friends...Tyler."

Carlie went perfectly still for a heartbeat, then frowned at Brenda. "Tyler Ramsey at a costume party? I didn't think your notorious brother-in-law would bother with something so—"

"Don't make fun of my party, Carlie."

"I wasn't. I just thought fancy banquets were more his speed." Carlie couldn't imagine Tyler dressed in a costume. He always seemed so...suave. And he always had a very sophisticated, very elegant woman on his arm.

"Tyler came because Jason asked him, and he would never let his brother down. You know how close they are." Brenda shook her head and added, "You know, you and Tyler actually have a few things in common."

Carlie turned away. "You're dreaming, Bren. We live in different worlds."

"You just don't understand Tyler. He had it pretty rough growing up, too." Then she touched Carlie's arm. "But at least Jason was always there for him."

"My brother had his own life," Carlie said. "And he was right, my problems were my own."

"Jason would never turn Tyler away if he needed help."

"Jason's a terrific guy. But he and Tyler are nothing alike."

"Not now, maybe, but they used to be," Brenda said with a grin. "But then, Jason met me. I think Tyler will be the same. When he finds someone he cares about…"

Carlie narrowed her eyes and stiffened her shoulders. "That will be a little hard for him to do when his relationships rarely last long enough to get to know a woman."

Brenda stared at Carlie, her eyebrows raised. "You seem to be keeping pretty close track of my young brother-in-law."

"He's not that young." But Carlie flushed at being caught. "I mean, he's a grown man. He must be in his early thirties… oh, never mind."

"Tyler's a good guy, Carlie. He may change dates a lot, but that's because the women he usually hooks up with are only impressed by his status in the community and his expanding financial portfolio. Tyler *thinks* he wants a no-strings attachment, but he's never satisfied with it."

Carlie had a feeling it was Tyler's looks and outrageous charm that really attracted women, but she kept her mouth shut. She certainly didn't want Brenda to get the idea she had a crush on Tyler Ramsey.

Good grief. A *crush!* No, she didn't. Certainly not.

Carlie was shaking her head at her errant thoughts, even as she said, "You don't have to defend Tyler to me, Bren. What he does is no concern of mine."

"Fine. Then if you're done stalling, can we get back to the party now? I think it's about to rain."

Carlie glanced up at the dark sky and smelled the moisture thick in the air. "You go on, Bren. I think I'll just wait a few more minutes."

Brenda hesitated, then she nodded. "Don't be too long."

Too long? Carlie wondered if another hour or so would be too long. She truly didn't relish the idea of going inside, not that anyone would recognize her. Dressed so differently, no one would see her as Carlie McDaniels, grade-school teacher and spinster extraordinaire. Her persona this evening was as far from her usual self as a woman could get. Even her hair and eyes were different, thanks to the wig that came with the costume, and the colored contacts she was wearing.

She was a coward, true, but it had been two long years since her divorce, and though that had been enough time for her to gain her independence and put some order to her life, it hadn't been time enough to repair her confidence in herself as a woman. Brenda claimed Carlie was attractive and appealing. Carlie's ex had made an entirely different claim.

Shivering, she forced her mind away from the disturbing memories, mustered her courage and started toward the door. She could make Brenda happy by mingling for an hour or so, then she could make her escape. The thought of her small, tidy, *empty* house seemed very nice all of a sudden.

Tyler Ramsey hated parties.

Looking around in mild amusement, he tried not to appear bored. Everything was the same—the ritual, the games. There were several women, alone and obviously on the hunt, who had been eyeing him since he'd entered. A Cleopatra, an elf, an Indian maiden—they all were playing their phoney roles to the hilt. They were drawn to his reputation, he knew. The funny part was, most of it wasn't even true.

Turning away, he wondered why he'd allowed Brenda to talk him into coming. True, he'd been bored for a while, at loose ends with himself. He needed a spark; he needed someone who could make him laugh.

His brother laughed a lot these days.

Not that Tyler wanted to settle down. He hadn't met a woman yet with whom he could consider spending the rest of his life. Jason was lucky to have found Brenda; she was the best. But women like her were rare. Glancing around the room again, Tyler realized just what a find Brenda was. The house was filled with females, but none of them held his attention. They were all...the same. Laughing, flirting, drinking. They stood poised to best advantage, their gestures predictable.

He'd been told more than once now how dashing he looked in his pirate costume. Everyone knew it was him. He wasn't wearing makeup as some of the other guests did. His only concession was an eye patch, worn rakishly over his left eye. A billowing white shirt that he found extremely comfortable, and tight black trousers completed the costume. His belt— wide, with a huge brass buckle— held a scabbard, with a sword resting inside it. His black boots came to his knees.

He sat in a chair, observing the crowd dispassionately. Immediately, a blond Valkyrie, brass breastplate shining in the glow of party lights, came to perch on his knee, and gave him a sly smile. He recognized that smile. It belonged to his ex-companion, Valerie. It was a smile that signaled her intent, and he used to respond to it appropriately. All he felt now was irritation. She leaned close, and he forced a polite expression to his features. They'd shared something brief, and by her insistence, with no strings attached. The outcome had been predictable.

She'd wanted a man who knew the score, who could afford the best, who moved in certain circles—her circles. She liked his sports car, his professional connections, and sex. In that order.

And he'd needed someone to help him fill his time, to give him something to think about other than his legal cases and the fact that his personal life was basically...empty. But it was over.

He knew it. Why didn't she?

"Don't you recognize me, Tyler?"

There was no place to put his hands, so he rested one on her back, the other on her naked thigh. "Of course. You're a beautiful Norse goddess." His legendary innate charm surfaced through his impatience.

Valerie chuckled throatily. "You make a very believable pirate. Have you made any plans to plunder the party and steal away with female captives?"

He didn't feel like playing, so he conjured the lie without hesitation. "Actually, sweetheart, I have."

She pouted, and ran her fingers through his hair. "You look so dashing, Tyler."

He barely restrained himself from rolling his eyes. He thought of going home to his empty house—and the thought no longer seemed so unappealing.

He glanced up, and saw his sister-in-law, Brenda, standing by the kitchen door, talking with a man dressed as a Roman general. Tyler was just deciding to go home and nurse his discontent in the privacy of his own home, when Brenda turned toward the kitchen with an expectant look on her face. She gave a wide smile, and the Roman nearly dropped his glass of liquor.

Tyler felt anticipation for the first time that night. He stared, waiting. Brenda suddenly appeared to be very delighted, and he wondered why. She seemed every bit as impish as the fairy she was dressed to be.

Slowly disengaging himself from Valerie's clinging hold, Tyler stood, his curiosity swelling. He was so intent on watching Brenda, he didn't hear Valerie's complaints. His eyes were glued to the kitchen doorway.

And then he saw her.

His knees locked and he felt his thighs tense. The woman stood uncertainly by Brenda, apparently oblivious to the stares she was drawing. She was magnificent.

Long, dark curly hair fell to her shoulders, and her costume left little to the imagination. Lush, was the first thought to come to mind.

She wasn't slim, but her curves were in all the right places. Her long legs were beautifully shaped, lightly muscled, teasingly displayed in the wispy, transparent harem pants. Her waist was trim, her navel a soft shadow in the gentle swell of her belly. Her shoulders, straight and broad for a woman, were held proudly, despite her obvious reluctance, and her pale breasts were very full, firm and high. She was wearing an ornate mask, that covered her face from her nose to her hairline. He didn't care.

She bent and whispered something in Brenda's ear. Brenda lost her smile, and looked around the room as if seeking encouragement. Her eyes passed over Tyler, then seeing his rapt stare, she turned to the harem girl. *Her eyes* soon followed.

He caught her gaze, literally. Even from the distance that separated them, Tyler could feel her nervousness. She seemed startled by his awareness, and displeased. She was poised for flight.

He didn't smile. He pulled off his eye patch and started toward her. She seemed unable to move, her eyes widening. As he came closer, he saw that she was very pale and that her eyes were a startling, unnatural shade of vivid blue. Contacts? As part of her costume?

He was intrigued.

With only a few feet separating them, he was pulled to an abrupt stop by Valerie.

He glanced at Valerie with stark impatience. "I have to go."

"Tyler, wait! I wanted to talk to you." Her hand slid up his arm to grip his shirt. Her voice lowered to a purr. "I need a date tomorrow. For a banquet. It will be...fun."

He didn't have time for this. Valerie always came around

when she wanted something from him. He had no doubt she needed him to gain entrée into the charity banquet. With plates going at a thousand dollars apiece, she knew there would be influential people there.

He wasn't interested.

Shaking his head, he turned back toward the woman in the harem costume...but she was gone. He moved to the kitchen in time to see her ducking out the back door. A hundred thoughts flew through his mind.

She was exquisite, exciting, and she was evidently running. From him?

He didn't want to lose sight of her, didn't want to take the chance that he wouldn't be able to find her again later. It was ridiculous, really, the urgency he felt, but he acted on it, anyway.

Brenda caught his arm as he tried to go past her.

"Tyler!" Her grip was firm, effectively stopping him. "Aren't you going to say hi?"

"What?" His question was a bark, filled with impatience.

Brenda stared at him. "What's the matter with you?"

"Who was she?"

Her eyebrows arching, Brenda looked behind her. "Oh... just one of the guests."

Tyler narrowed his eyes. "She's leaving already?"

"No, she..." Brenda shook her head. "She's a little shy. I had to talk her into coming tonight and now she's having second thoughts."

"I think I'll go get some fresh air."

Her smile slipping, Brenda seemed startled by his abrupt statement. "It's starting to rain, Tyler. Why would you...?"

Starting to walk away, but at a more reasonable pace, he said, "Don't worry about it, Brenda. I promise not to track in any mud." Then he stepped out the back door and peered through the cloudy night, trying to catch sight of her. A lighted path led to the pool house, and more lights, in an array of party colors, circled the small building. Through the smattering of raindrops falling on his face, Tyler was able to see a flash of movement. Ignoring the rain, he followed.

His heart was hammering heavily, his stride rapid on the wet flagstone walk. His muscles were so tight, his movements seemed rough and jerky. He couldn't remember the last time he'd felt so anxious to meet a woman.

Impatience and anticipation were riding him, and he forced himself to stop outside the door of the small house. He tilted his head back, letting the rain cool his face. He was overreacting. She was only a woman, after all, he told himself.

But then he remembered her wide, startled eyes and felt his stomach clench.

He put his hand on the doorknob, half expecting it to be locked. It opened silently, allowing the muted sounds of the party to intrude.

Colored light filtered through the windows in diminished shades, elongating shadows and playing over various forms and furnishings. He gave his eyes a moment to adjust to the dim interior, and then he saw her.

She had been standing turned away from him, one hand pressed to her forehead, the other knotted at her side. But when the door closed with a soft click behind him, she jerked, then swung around to face him. Her hand fluttered to her chest and she took a hasty step backward, then halted, staring.

Tyler swallowed heavily. He could feel her nervousness, her uncertainty, and something very basic, very male, erupted inside him. He'd never known a woman to be this way, had never before felt the overwhelming urge to offer comfort, to ease a woman with assurances. He wanted—right this minute—to hold her, to touch her...to make love to her. He sucked in a deep breath, leaned back against the closed door and forced a gentle smile. "Hello."

★ ★ ★

Carlie felt frozen in place. She could feel his eyes drifting over her body, could hear every breath he took. She didn't know what to do. He couldn't have recognized her, yet he obviously liked what he saw. She'd never seen a man react that way—not to her. She couldn't speak, her voice was trapped in her throat.

He whispered softly, "You're beautiful."

Her eyes shifted nervously with the racing of her heart. Brenda had said men would find her attractive, but.... She hadn't believed her, not really. Usually, Tyler never looked at her twice, but then, he'd never seen her dressed like this.

The costume was definitely a mistake.

Tyler was still watching her, and she inhaled. She had to say something. "You look...dangerous."

His teeth flashed in a quick grin. "Not dashing?"

Confused, she shook her head. In an even lower tone, sounding of accusation and anticipation, she asked, "What happened to your date?"

He tipped his head, as if he was straining to hear her, then carefully stepped away from the door. "She wasn't my date."

Liar, she thought. A man like him wouldn't come to a party alone. He attracted beautiful women without even trying. And Valerie Rush was certainly that—beautiful, chic, sophisticated and very sure of her own appeal. She was everything Carlie was not.

So why was Tyler here now? She'd always been aware of him; he was impossible to ignore. Dark, charming, a devastating man. But completely unattainable. At least for her.

Of course, after her disastrous marriage, she didn't want any man, not even Tyler Ramsey.

He took another step forward when she remained silent, and she went back one, bumping into the wall.

He was watching her so very closely, almost stalking her, and she could feel her chest shuddering, straining for air. She trembled inside, feeling light-headed and so conscious of him as a male. She didn't dare take her eyes off him.

He took another step.

The rain was coming down more heavily now, tapping against the windows and the wind had begun to whistle. Carlie was glad for the darkness. She didn't want reality to intrude too quickly. She didn't want him to recognize her. Not yet.

Maybe not ever.

He started to reach for her, then dropped his hand. "Do you know who I am?"

She shook her head. "No." She didn't know this man at all, so intense and attentive, exuding raw sexuality. The air was filled with his scent, his purpose.

His eyes drifted over her body again, then he stared intently into hers.

She didn't dare say anything. What was there to say? He wasn't reacting to Carlie McDaniels. He was reacting to the night; to the atmosphere and the mystery of a masquerade. If he knew who she was, he'd lose interest quickly enough. He'd give her that same polite nod she'd always received from him, then go on his way.

Tyler stepped toward her and she balked, feeling her back against the wall. It would be mortifying for him to realize her identity now, with her acting like such a ninny. She was a professional woman, a teacher, mature and capable. And here she was, behaving like a coward. A virgin coward.

She knew in that instant, she wouldn't tell him. He would never find out who she was. She had to leave, had to...

His hand caught her arm. "Wait. Please."

She trembled, trying to pull loose, stunned by the strength of his grasp.

He released her instantly. Holding his hands out to the sides, he tried to softly reassure her. "It's okay. I'm sorry." She trembled again, and he said, "You're cold."

Swamped with uncertainty, wanting to do one thing, but knowing she should do another, Carlie turned away. Then Tyler was behind her, not touching her, but the warmth of his body surrounded her. She felt a pulse beat of heat run through her, swirling in her belly. The feeling was unfamiliar…and exciting. As his breath brushed her nape, she shivered with growing sensation.

His palms grazed her shoulders, smoothing away the chills and the dampness from the rain, warming her. She was surrounded by him, by his scent.

His touch was tentative, careful, and when she didn't move, he leaned closer, his chest barely touching her back, his thighs brushing her own. She shuddered.

His fingers continued to stroke, feather-light, up and down her arms. He drew in a slow, rough breath, then molded his hands over her shoulders, holding her. She felt his suspended breathing, his hesitation. And when he finally spoke, his voice was low and unsteady.

"*I want you.* I think I wanted you the moment I saw you."

She stilled as his lips very lightly touched the side of her neck. Slowly, he drew her toward him, her back against his chest, then waited, keeping her pressed close to his solid length.

"I want you," he repeated. "*Stay with me.*"

Only in her wildest imaginings had she ever considered Tyler saying such a thing to her. It was unbelievable. It was outrageous.

It was her own private fantasy.

She swallowed hard, squeezed her eyes shut, then whispered, "I want you, too."

Chapter Two

TILTING HIS HEAD BACK, Tyler exhaled slowly, then tried to relax. It was unbelievable how much her answer meant to him. *She was staying.*

He didn't understand his own reaction, or hers, for that matter. He only knew he needed to get closer to her. She'd stood there in the doorway earlier, looking feminine, yet so unsure. Unlike the other women in the room, she hadn't flaunted her assets; she hadn't even seemed aware of them, despite the provocative harem costume that left her more bare than not. Even now, she seemed so vulnerable, so wary.

He leaned down, inhaling her fragrance, then touched his open palm to her soft belly. She jerked and pulled away.

He was surprised by her reaction, and forced himself to go perfectly still. He squeezed her shoulders again. "Shh. I'm not going to hurt you." She remained strangely quiet, her body trembling, and then it hit him just how innocent she truly was. Suddenly, it made sense—the way she'd reacted to his interest. She was wary, and with good reason. He felt confusion first, then the unfamiliar stirring of protectiveness. He didn't want to frighten her, didn't want her to be uncomfortable with him. He closed his eyes and wrapped his arms around her, hugging her carefully.

"I would never hurt you."

Her hands came up to clasp his arms where they crossed her chest, giving him her silent trust.

His chest squeezed tight. It was remarkable how she affected him. Smiling, he rubbed his chin against her temple, then turned her to face him.

He cupped her jaw, tilting her chin toward him. He could see the scant light reflected in her wide eyes. Slowly, tentatively, he bent and put his lips to hers. It wasn't a devouring kiss, but tender and sweet. She seemed unsure of where to put her hands, then laid them lightly on his chest.

He groaned quietly, tugging her closer. "Open your mouth," he urged, continuing to nibble at her lips.

She did, gasping, and he teased her, stroking her mouth, licking carefully at her lips, touching her tongue with his own.

After a few moments, he pulled back. Her fingers had curled tight against him, and she was panting softly. Instinctively, he pressed his arousal, full and hard, against her belly. She seemed stunned by his blatant need, and he relished her reaction to it, watching her eyes slowly close. Nothing had ever made him feel so wild or urgent, so alive with sensation, as her innocent acceptance.

Her mask was in the way and he touched his fingers to it. Instantly, she jerked back, her hand coming up to cover her mouth.

His muscles grew taut. "I didn't..." Tyler hesitated, then shook his head. "I'm sorry. I just...it seems so...right."

She shook her head. "You can't take off my mask."

His eyebrows shot up.

"I don't want you to know...who I am."

He stepped closer to her, feeling the heat build under his skin. She was the most fascinating woman he'd ever met. He tried to get her to look at him, but she turned away. It was unbelievably erotic, a woman appearing so demure, but wearing such an enticing costume. He touched her chin, bringing her face back toward him. "What do you want?"

Swallowing hard, she whispered, "You. This." And she leaned toward him.

Tyler caught his breath, and then he was kissing her again. He stroked his tongue deep in her mouth, drawing her closer, feeling his urgency swell. He was no longer thinking of his own consuming desire, not entirely. Now he was driven by a need to give her everything she asked for, everything she could possibly hope for. He didn't want her to regret trusting him.

He didn't want her to regret anything.

When he lifted his head, she was breathless and trembling, her small hands clasping his shirt in a death grip. Moving slowly, he touched the buttons on her skimpy jacket, for the moment ignoring her mask. "A mystery lady."

His words were deep and husky and she trembled as he undid the first button. As soon as it slid free, he raised his gaze to her face, judging her reaction.

She flattened her hands on the wall beside her hips, but she didn't protest. Tyler smiled, then looked down to watch the slow unveiling of her breasts.

The second button was undone, and still he didn't touch her in any other way. He was only using one hand, being careful not to startle her. The third button was straining at the material. With one finger, he traced her cleavage, over the swell of each breast, then up her throat. He looked at her lips, then traced the fullness of her mouth, pressing slightly to glide over the inside of her bottom lip.

Her lips parted and she instinctively curled her tongue

around the tip of his finger. His eyes closed and he drew a slow, painful breath. When he looked at her again, she was watching him cautiously, her eyes dark in the dim shadows. He leaned forward and kissed her very gently, tenderly, his lips moving over her chin, to her collarbone, then her breasts.

The third button held, and Tyler found her nipple through the cloth. She moaned. Even through the material he could feel the heat of her body as he drew upon her, his teeth carefully nipping.

The last button opened, and he covered each breast with a warm palm, cradling her lush weight, shaping her with his hands. He pressed her breasts together and nuzzled her cleavage before moving his mouth to a nipple, licking and plucking with his lips, then finally taking her inside, suckling strongly. A sound of raw hunger escaped her, and he felt the impact of that small sound deep in his belly.

Her fingers sank into his hair, pulling him away. But he didn't leave her. Instead, he slipped to his knees, his mouth against her ribs. Closing his eyes and locking his arms around her hips, he rubbed his face against her skin, breathing in her heated scent, tasting her.

He savored her, taking his time to explore each facet of his senses; touch and taste and smell. And sight. He enjoyed looking at her; he enjoyed her pleasure and her surprise as he found a particularly sensitive spot.

His hands cupped her buttocks, startling her. Then slowly, he removed her slippers, his fingers lingering on her slim ankles. His palms coasted up her calves, over her thighs, and to her buttocks again, squeezing and cuddling. Then his fingers hooked in the waistband of her harem pants and, still watching her, he started sliding them down.

Tyler saw her embarrassment, and he leaned forward, kissing her navel, dipping his tongue teasingly inside. He wanted to reassure her, wanted her to understand how unique this was for him. But at the moment, words escaped him.

She stepped out of the pants as he directed, then remained silent while he looked his fill.

Oh God, what she did to him.

Gazing at her from his position on his knees, he had to call upon all his restraint to keep from rushing her. He wasn't himself. Feelings he hadn't known existed washed over him in hot, insistent waves.

The small jacket hung from her shoulders, serving more as ornamentation than covering since her breasts were freed. The shadowy room only enhanced her curves and made the moment more intimate. He could see the darkness of her nipples, her navel, the soft feminine curls between her thighs. He lightly brushed his fingers over her, finding her wet and hot. He delved deeper, stroking her, his breaths coming fast and low.

She gasped, and her hand clasped his wrist.

He turned his palm so he was holding hers, then took her other hand also, pinning her arms gently to her sides. He leaned forward, and this time it was his tongue that stroked her. She reacted immediately, pulling away, staring at him in appalled fascination.

Again, he felt that possessiveness, that need to protect her.

Tyler came slowly to his feet, his face flushed, his chest rising and falling quickly. He kept his tone gentle and quiet. "What's wrong?"

Her voice emerged as a dry croak. "It's...you can't."

Since he now understood her innocence, Tyler didn't press her. But he wanted her to realize the depth of her own allure. "I understand, but honey, I want to kiss you there. I want to kiss you everywhere." He held her eyes, refusing to let her look away, then added in a husky whisper, "You taste like a woman should, very sweet and sexy."

She shivered, then pressed her right hand over his chest, near where his heart was thundering. He covered her hand with his own, then began unbuttoning his shirt. He felt her nails as she flexed her fingers into his flesh. He'd never had a woman watch him with such intent curiosity. His body reacted to her interest, tightening and swelling. His gaze never left her face.

He removed his trousers quickly, hearing her low, fast breathing. He found a condom in his wallet, then tossed his pants aside. He laid the protection on the table.

When he turned to her again, he saw her uncertainty, and pulled her close, relishing the feel of her naked skin. Kissing her throat and shoulder, his hands curved around her body, his fingers splayed warm and firm on her sensitive belly.

He was patient and gently persuasive, but he was also very aroused. Deliberately, he nestled his fullness against her buttocks. He needed her to know the effect she had on him.

He kissed her for a few moments, and when he finally slid his fingers down her belly and into the soft curls between her legs, she didn't draw away. His fingers delved deeper, and she moaned.

His heart thundered at the small sound. "That's it. Relax, sweetheart." He slid a finger inside her, and she quivered, letting out a short cry. "You're wet," he said, softly stroking her, bringing his other hand up to hold a heavy breast, idly plying the nipple with his thumb. She leaned back on him, gasping, and he smiled.

She clutched at his hard thighs, her fingers biting deep into his muscles. Her legs stiffened, and soft, hungry sounds escaped her throat.

Close to losing what was left of his control, Tyler lifted her into his arms and carried her quickly to the narrow couch. He laid her down, coming over her and pulling her close.

She moaned as his mouth closed over her nipple, then moaned again when he smoothed his hand over her soft belly and into her feminine curls. His fingers stroked, dipped, plucked lightly, making her squirm. He lowered his mouth to her nipple and toyed with it, teasing her with his tongue and teeth.

Her climax took him by surprise. It gripped her body, forcing her to arch wildly, her eyes closed, her mouth open as she gasped and gave low, throaty moans. Enthralled, Tyler watched her, feeling her pleasure and her loss of control. Seeing her shock.

And when the rushing sensations would have ended, Tyler bent to taste her, crushing down on her with renewed urgency, his hand holding her face still for his kiss. She was crying, unable to help herself, and he kissed her jaw, undone by her soft, breathy sighs.

"It's all right now. Shh."

She shook her head. With tears clogging her throat and reflecting in her voice, she whispered brokenly, "I've never..."

"Shh. I know." His mouth skimmed hers, his eyes alight with satisfaction and possession.

He couldn't wait any longer.

Lifting slightly away from her, he reached for the condom and slid it on. She didn't watch him, but he didn't think it was embarrassment now, so much as repletion. Her breasts, heaving still, showed soft and white, reflecting the scant light. Her belly still quivered. But there was a small, awed smile on her lips, a look of wonder that filled him.

Thunder clapped loudly outside, and the storm picked up tempo, mirroring his explosive emotions.

He began kissing her again, light, biting kisses that made

her smile and open her eyes. His muscles were taut, straining for release. She laid her palm to his cheek.

He sat back to look at her, running his fingers through her hair. It was then he realized she was wearing a wig. The hair was too coarse, too dense to be real. The fact that she had taken such pains to conceal herself only added to her intrigue. His mystery woman.

She pulled him closer in silent demand.

He reached down and parted her with his fingers, then gently pushed inside. His groan was long and ragged. Gasping, she twisted against him, her arms tightening, her hips lifting to his. He pressed her knees wider, giving himself more access to her body, then clenched his jaw as he sank deeper. "There we go. All the way."

She shuddered as her body adjusted to his length and thickness. It was pure fantasy, he thought, wishing he could stay like this forever. She squirmed beneath him in delicious sensation.

Tyler shuddered, pressing his hips to hers to still her movements, trying to maintain his barely leashed control, but it was too late. He reared up, his arms stiffened on either side of her, his eyes hot and probing, holding her gaze. Then he began to move.

The friction was exquisite, and she lifted her hips toward him, taking more, her legs wrapping around him. His gaze dropped to her breasts, to her tightened nipples. He was enthralled, watching her full breasts sway as each of his thrusts rocked her body.

He threw his head back, biting off a groan. His jaw was tense, his words a growled whisper. "I don't believe this!"

He felt her tighten around him, felt the pulsing of her climax. He groaned heavily, and his body went rigid as he climaxed. Then he stilled.

His weight was now fully upon her and his heartbeat rocked

his body with its uneven cadence. He stroked her idly, without thought, without even knowing what he was doing. She smelled so good, and he *felt* so good.

She stirred beneath him, and he obligingly raised himself to his elbows. Her mask was askew, and he smiled at the picture she made, tousled innocence, sensual lure. He didn't want the night to end.

"Do you have to go anytime soon?"

That surprised her.

Smiling, Tyler stroked her cheek. "Will you stay with me for a while longer?"

Her smile was shaky, a bit uncertain, but it was a smile.

Laughing, feeling incredibly lighthearted, he held her tight as he turned on the couch, putting her on top of him. She came up on her elbows, her heavy breasts swaying over his chest.

"Now, this is nice." His hands cupped her, his thumbs flicking over her soft, dusky nipples until they drew tight.

"Can you scoot up just a bit?" he growled. "I want you in my mouth."

Her lips parted, but she complied, her breath already thickening. Tyler swept his hands down her back and spread them wide over the buttocks, pressing her close.

"I'm going to make love to you all night, honey. I want to show you all the different ways to enjoy yourself. I'm going to see to it that you're so overwhelmed with pleasure, you won't be able to resist seeing me again." He said the words quietly just before he took her nipple in his mouth, licking and teasing and making her shudder. His hands moved over her bottom to the back of her thighs, then parted her legs so she was draped over him. "You'll wake up at night and think of me touching you." His finger slid inside her and she tensed, her hips pressing hard against him.

"I want you to think of me," he explained, loving her with his fingers until she trembled uncontrollably, "because I know I'll be thinking of you."

Tyler held to his promise, exhausting both himself and Carlie with pleasure.

Hours later, long after midnight, he slept, still holding her close. Carlie was stunned by all that had happened, never having imagined that such complete satisfaction was possible.

Tyler lay relaxed beside her, one heavy muscled arm circling her belly, his hand splayed over her hip. He was even beautiful when he slept, she thought, when the lines of his face softened, making him look almost vulnerable.

Of course, he could never know the truth. She would be mortified if Tyler ever discovered he'd made love with his sister-in-law's dumpy best friend. Tyler didn't even *look* at women like her, let alone sleep with them.

Not that she wanted it any other way. She was dumpy by design, choosing her clothes with an eye for concealment, rather than enticement. She didn't want a man, any man— not now, not ever.

Relationships hurt. She'd learned that lesson after her marriage failed. And she'd also learned she could rely on no one but herself. Not on the grandfather who'd raised her after her parents' death, treating her more like a burden than a grandchild, nor on her brother, who'd made it clear she was to deal with her mistakes on her own.

But marriage had been her biggest mistake. One she wasn't likely to forget.

She could never tell Tyler the truth, but at least she'd learned something valuable; she wasn't frigid. Her husband had been wrong, his accusations unjust. Probably, it had just been another of his attempts to destroy her self-confidence. But now she knew the truth, and for that, if nothing else, she was glad she'd stayed with Tyler.

He shifted in his sleep, and she stilled, watching him closely, but he didn't awaken. She leaned down and very gently kissed him on the corner of his mouth, then slipped from the couch.

By the time Tyler woke, a smile of anticipation on his face, Carlie was gone.

Chapter Three

"YOU CAN'T TELL anyone I was at the party."

Brenda tugged Carlie through the kitchen door and then quickly shut it. "I wondered all night what happened to you. Where did you go? Why did you leave so soon? I thought for sure you were going to enjoy yourself."

Wincing, Carlie gave Brenda an apologetic look. She had enjoyed herself, all right, just not the way Brenda had expected. She pulled out a chair at the round wooden table and slumped into it. "I didn't mean to worry you. I'm sorry."

"So what happened? Why did you run off?"

Hesitating, Carlie tried to decide how much to tell her friend. It wouldn't be the whole truth, that was for certain. Somehow, the night seemed...magical, something she could tuck away and keep to herself. She couldn't share it, not even with Brenda. But she had to tell her something....

"Brenda...I felt really foolish...in the costume. Maybe if I hadn't been wearing something so..."

"Sexy?"

Carlie spared her friend a quick look, and saw Brenda was

smiling. "Yeah, well, maybe. I just couldn't face all those people looking like that."

"I'm sorry I pushed, Carlie. I just wanted you to realize how attractive you are. Those damn baggy suits you wear make you look fat." Brenda pursed her lips, then idly traced the wood grain in the table with a fingertip. "Tyler noticed you."

Carlie felt her heartbeat race. "I... Did he say something to you?"

"He asked who you were."

"You didn't tell him!" Carlie nearly choked on her embarrassment, waiting for Brenda's reply.

"No. I just told him you were a guest." Then she patted Carlie's arm. "Hey, calm down. It wouldn't be the end of the world if Tyler took a liking to you. You have to admit, he's gorgeous."

Oh, yeah, he was gorgeous. Carlie licked her lips, then said carefully, "He, ah, approached me."

"He did?"

"Yes." Carlie cleared her throat, then immediately launched into her rehearsed story. "We talked for a while. In, ah, the pool house."

When Brenda's eyes widened, Carlie reminded her, "It was raining, remember? And we went inside to stay dry. He, well, he was attracted to me."

"No kidding?"

Carlie hated the note of fascination in her friend's tone. She also hated lying to her, but she didn't see any way around it. Brenda leaned forward. "So, what happened?"

Carlie shrugged. "He didn't recognize me."

"Well, of course he didn't! He's used to seeing you looking like this!" Brenda indicated Carlie's dark, frumpy suit. With her honey blond hair in a tight braid and a pair of glasses perched on her nose, she looked nothing like the harem girl of the night before.

"This isn't funny, Brenda!" Carlie felt like strangling her. "And you can't ever tell him, either. I don't want him to know it was me he was…flirting with."

Brenda looked skeptical. "Ah, Carlie, don't you think—"

Whatever Brenda was going to say was cut off by a loud voice from the living room. Seconds later, Jason and Tyler strode into the kitchen. Carlie stiffened, all her defenses jerking into place. But her face remained impassive. Almost painfully so. There was absolutely no way she would let Tyler know she was the woman he'd spent the night with. She didn't even want to think about how mortifying that would be.

Brenda didn't miss a beat after shooting Carlie an I'm-not-responsible-for-this look. "I thought you fellas were going fishing. What happened?"

Tyler reached Brenda first. He leaned down and lifted her from her chair, giving her a tight bear hug and a kiss on the cheek.

Brenda's face turned pink. "What did I do to deserve that?"

Tyler's smile was so warm and sincere, Carlie had to look away. "You invited me to your party." Then he added softly, "Thanks."

Jason shook his head, and Carlie had the horrifying suspicion that Tyler had confided to him what had happened. *Don't blush, don't blush!* She glanced at Jason, but he was looking at his wife.

Leaning down, he kissed Brenda, then nodded briefly to Carlie. "The fish weren't biting and it's damned cold out there. Besides, Tyler can't seem to sit still today."

Tyler pulled out a chair and straddled it, crossing his arms over the chair back. "Could I have some coffee, Bren? Then

I need to talk to you." He glanced at Carlie, and smiled. "Hi. Ah, Carlie, isn't it?"

"Hello." Carlie mentally applauded her calm response. She was more than a little surprised Tyler remembered her name. She prayed it was all he remembered. And then she looked at him, and despite herself, she remembered lying beside him in the pool house, remembered that magnificent body of his leaning toward her... She looked away, trying to collect her thoughts. Good looks only took a person so far, and from what she knew of Tyler, his had taken him around the block more than a few times. Last night had been a milestone in her life; to Tyler, it had probably been no more than a good time.

Carlie breathed a sigh of relief when she realized he hadn't connected her to the party. His expression had been friendly, nothing more. Already he was ignoring her, dismissing her easily.

"I'll have the coffee ready in just a minute." Brenda was grinning affectionately at Tyler, obviously more than pleased to cater to him.

Tyler tapped his fingers on the table with an excess of energy. His gaze took a turn around the room, then settled on Carlie again. "So. What are you ladies up to today?"

She felt her heart flutter and color rise to her cheeks. Carlie wanted to smack herself. Enough was enough. She would not be an idiot around this man. She composed her features and met his look squarely. "We were talking about the new sports program I'm working on for the school." She paused, then decided to elaborate. "It's a way to help the kids who have trouble socializing. They're not bad kids but they just aren't sure how to conduct themselves with their peers. They need guidance and a chance to interact, with supervision. If they're playing a sport, they'll be getting exercise, burning off energy and learning to work together. I think the program will go over pretty good. I thought I'd try basketball first. The kids have to play together, but since it's not really a contact sport, tussles ought to be kept to a minimum. Brenda and I were just discussing how great it is that Jason has agreed to be an instructor."

Tyler listened, his eyes intent on Carlie's face, watching her so closely she felt herself near to blushing again. "Sounds like you really care about these kids."

His tone was soft, almost disbelieving, and Carlie stiffened. "Of course I do. I care very much about all my students."

Tyler rubbed his chin, still watching her. "And you really think you can make a difference?"

Carlie leaned back in her chair, forgetting her embarrassment, forgetting last night. The gall of the man, to question her like this! With her hands in fists, she replied, "I'll certainly do my best to. At least *I'm* trying to do something to help."

Jason looked at Carlie, then Tyler. A smile appeared. "I, ah, suppose I should tell you something, Carlie. I won't be able to help you, after all. Some things came up at the office." His grin widened, and he shrugged. "I talked to Tyler this morning, and he agreed to do the project with you, instead."

Carlie closed her eyes for a heartbeat, praying she hadn't heard that. But when she opened her eyes, Tyler was still watching her, his smile now smug.

She cleared her throat and shoved her glasses needlessly up the bridge of her nose. "I don't know, Jason." What excuse could she use after practically challenging the man to help? "Maybe that wouldn't be a good idea."

It was Tyler who answered her. "Why not?"

Floundering, she racked her brain, but couldn't come up with a valid reason. "You understand, it will be three or four nights a week? And we need someone who will set a good example for the kids. Someone patient."

Tyler raised his eyebrow, looking affronted. "I'd be a good example. Hell, I'm a lawyer, same as Jason. I've been to college. I'm articulate."

"You're even housebroken," Brenda added, seeming to enjoy the situation.

He nodded. "Damn right." Then to Carlie, "You see? I'll be perfect for the job."

"But..." The truth was, she simply didn't want to work with Tyler. Not now, not after last night. "I don't know. Have you ever worked with kids? And remember, these kids can be a little...difficult."

Jason interrupted. "Tyler should understand them on a gut level, because he was always damned difficult, too."

Tyler laughed. "So it's settled. When do we start?"

Carlie stood with as much aplomb as she could muster. Tyler's eyes drifted over her body, almost out of habit, it seemed, but there was no sign of recognition in his expression. It rankled, even while she prayed he wouldn't make the connection. She tugged at the bottom of her tailored suit coat, smoothing it over her slacks. Then she used a tactic that had worked with many rebellious students. She deliberately looked down her nose at him. "I'll have to let you know."

Tyler merely nodded. "You do that."

Brenda rushed forward to give Carlie a hug. "Give me a call later. Promise?"

"Of course. And thanks for the company, Bren. See ya' later, Jason." She ignored Tyler, not feeling the least bit guilty about it, and exited the room, her back stiff, her tight braid pulling at her temples. She wasn't entirely out of the house when she heard Tyler say, "That has to be the prickliest woman I've ever met. I got the distinct impression she didn't like me. Can you imagine?"

Jason's laugh was sharp. "Unheard of, isn't it?"

There was a shrug in his tone when Tyler replied, "There's just no figuring some women."

Carlie allowed the door to slam just a bit too hard behind her.

It was a very neat, utilitarian office. Carlie was surprised at how functional each piece of furniture was, with only a modicum of necessary decorations. The walls were beige, the carpet a swirling mixture of blues and creams. The sofa and two chairs were upholstered in a rough nubby fabric of a deep blue, and the wooden end tables were light oak. It was a comfortable room, without any indication of Tyler's personal style, which she'd assumed to be rather flamboyant.

The office door opened and Tyler stepped out, accompanied by the secretary who had first greeted Carlie. His smile was warm, a natural smile that Carlie knew he bestowed on almost every female he encountered. Beyond him, she could see into his office, and noticed his desk strewn with papers and files. Suddenly, she realized how disruptive, and presumptuous, her visit was, but she also knew if she hadn't come today, she wouldn't have come at all. Brenda had told her he'd been asking about the harem girl from the party. He wanted to know who she was.

Carlie hoped he would eventually give up and forget about that night...but then, she also knew how badly it would hurt her if he was able to do just that.

Lately, she felt awfully confused.

"I'm sorry I kept you waiting, Carlie. I didn't realize it was you. I'm not familiar with the name McDaniels."

Of course, he wouldn't be. Carlie took his hand. Very briefly. "I hope I'm not interrupting. I can see you're busy. I just wanted to stop by and tell you I'd like to accept your offer of assistance for our new sports program." She was rushing through her words, but she couldn't seem to stop herself. She'd spent three days stewing over what to do, and finally decided that her personal embarrassment had to take a back seat to the kids' problems. She was the only one who knew she had reason to be embarrassed, and since no one else had agreed to help, Tyler was her only option.

"We hope to start next week, so I wanted to drop off the material I've put together. You might want to look it over before meeting the children."

Tyler accepted the papers she thrust toward him, then motioned her into his office. "Come on in and have a seat."

"I don't want to take up too much of your time." And she wanted to get away from him as quickly as possible.

He lifted one shoulder in an exaggerated shrug. "I needed a break, anyway."

Carlie followed him into his office and sat on the edge of a straight-back, narrow leather chair. Tyler went behind his desk, seating himself with all the officious attitude of any good lawyer.

After skimming through the papers she'd given him, he looked at her again. "You're very thorough."

She blushed and she hated herself for it. "It's just a basic overview of the children who will begin in the program. I thought it would help if you knew what kind of problem each child was having and what their backgrounds were like. The idea is that any child who collects more than three after-school detentions or in-school suspensions will have the choice of joining the team or having their misconduct shown in their grades. Of course, if they choose to join the team, they'll have to contribute wholeheartedly and follow instructions to the letter. In other words, they'll have to work together and get along. They'll have to accept that rules have a purpose, and everyone has to follow them. The program had been used in several schools. So far, it's been very promising."

Tyler nodded, then gave her another of his intent, probing stares. "How many children will we be starting with?"

Carlie cleared her throat and looked away. She let her eyes roam around his office while she spoke, pretending an interest in his bookshelves, but really trying to avoid his stare. "The list I've given you has nine kids. Of course, that number can change daily. And the children will be released from their obligation whenever they show an improved attitude toward school. But no child will ever be forced to quit the team."

"Will we get to compete against other teams?"

Carlie didn't answer right away. Tyler's genuine interest amazed and confused her. She had half expected him to give only a show of concern. But he was studying the list, all signs of the womanizer gone while he perused her notes. She was looking at the top of his head, at how thick and dark his hair was, how it curled just the tiniest bit. He glanced up and caught her staring. At his *hair* for crying out loud.

He ran his fingers through it negligently. "What's the matter? Have I sprung a streak of gray?"

Carlie folded her arms defensively. "No, I…no. I was just thinking."

Tyler laid the file down, once again giving her his full attention. "About what?"

"About…whether or not we'd be playing other schools, of course," she said quickly. Then, taking a deep breath, she continued. "I don't believe so, at least not at first. If after a time the team shapes up, that would be entirely your decision how far to carry it." Carlie forced herself to stare at him directly, though she felt a faint blush on her cheeks.

Tyler smiled at her again, leaning back in his chair and folding his hands across his stomach. "You have the most unusual eyes. Very intense. Especially now, while we're talking about the children. I don't believe I've ever seen that exact shade of hazel."

She stiffened. "Thank you, but I don't think the color of my eyes has any bearing on this program."

"It was just an observation."

He was still leaning back in his chair, his posture relaxed, his gaze lazy, and Carlie realized he was deliberately provoking her. She decided not to oblige him. She came to her feet, still holding his gaze, and stared down at him. "Personal observations aside, do you have anything else you'd like to discuss?"

Carlie watched as he struggled to stifle his amusement. He stood behind his desk, his dark eyes warm and smiling. Then, leisurely, he began looking her over. She tolerated his perusal, trying to keep her expression blank, even while her pulse raced and her palms grew damp. She was well aware of what she looked like. Her suit was a deep, dark green, almost brown, and it was cut in straight lines, effectively hiding any signs of her figure.

"You're tall for a woman."

What an inane comment. But true. Carlie's head was just about even with his nose, and she was wearing flats. She glanced down at her shoes when he did. They were ugly, round-toed, and extremely comfortable.

She drew on disdain to hide her sudden discomfort. "If you don't have any other questions about the program, I'll be on my way. I wouldn't want to keep you from anything… important." She turned, and headed for the door without another word.

Tyler came around his desk and stepped in front of her, blocking her exit. He wasn't grinning now, but she could still see the humor in his eyes. "Forgive me, Carlie. I didn't mean to be rude." Before she could reply, he lifted the folder in his hand. "May I keep this?"

She watched him warily. His apology sounded genuine, but she still felt he was laughing at her. She gritted her teeth, wishing she could rid her mind of intimate thoughts concerning Tyler Ramsey. She hadn't thought of a man that way in a very long time.

She was determined to stop right now. She didn't return his smile, or acknowledge his apology. "Of course. I have my own copy."

Tyler gave her an amused, mischievous grin, almost as if he'd read her thoughts. "Excellent. When do we start?"

"How soon can you start? I'll send home the notices to the parents as soon as you give me a schedule that suits you."

"Tell you what. Let me check things over and I'll get back to you tomorrow. What time do you leave the school?"

Carlie hesitated. "Around four."

"I'll come by then. Maybe we could go somewhere and work out a schedule that will suit us both." He indicated his cluttered desk. "Unfortunately, I don't have the time right now to take care of it."

"I..." Carlie mentally scurried for excuses. She did not want to go anywhere with Tyler Ramsey. The man had a chaotic effect on her senses. He had only to smile at her, and memories came rushing back, so intense, so powerful, that her stomach clenched and her nerve endings rioted. She hoped her thoughts of him would fade with time; she hoped she could eventually forget him completely.

It wouldn't happen today. Though she hated to admit it, even to herself, he rattled her as few people could. But she refused to be a coward about the situation. The best way to deal with a problem was to face it head-on, she reminded herself. Summoning a bland smile, she nodded. "That would be fine, Tyler. Thank you."

She was standing at her desk, stacking papers, when Tyler walked in. Her door was open, so he took a moment to simply look at her. Dressed in another of her prim, spinsterish outfits, her hair pulled back in a braid, she looked like the epitome of the perfect schoolmarm. And she was humming softly.

He felt something shift inside him. Never in his own school days could he remember a teacher like her, someone who actually wanted to help. He'd always thought of Carlie as simply Brenda's friend, a little odd, a lot frumpy, but nice enough.

Now he had to look at her with new respect.

Raising a hand, he gave two sharp knocks on the open door. She jerked, looking up with wide eyes and peering at him through the lenses of her glasses.

"They told me at the office where I could find you." He stepped in, looking around the room with interest. "Very nice."

She smiled with an obvious touch of pride. "Thank you. I try to make the classroom nice. It should be a comfortable place to be, an *easy* place to be. Do you know what I mean?"

Strangely enough, he did. The room was decorated in bright colors with plenty of the children's artwork hanging on the walls. It was a thought-provoking room. He walked toward a workstation that was filled with hands-on activities. There were dominoes, rubber stamps and numerous math games. The room gave an overall appearance of bustling activity. He smiled at her, seeing that she was watching him cautiously. "You like to teach."

She straightened. "Yes. And I'm good at it. Children respond well to me."

She could be so damned bristly, with no real provocation. "I'm sure you are. You're authoritative, but gently so. Children wouldn't be afraid of you."

Lowering her eyebrows, she gave him a ferocious look, as if she didn't trust the sincerity of his words. He smiled back, and waited.

Finally, she nodded. "No child should ever be afraid. Certainly not of their teacher. I do my best to make sure they're at ease, to let them know they can talk to me if they need to."

Tyler turned away. He didn't want her to see how she affected him. He could still remember being a kid himself, feeling defensive and hurt because his dad wasn't around, and his mother couldn't be bothered. His teachers hadn't cared about a kid with problems. Their idea of understanding was to send him to the office whenever he upset their lessons.

He certainly hadn't had a teacher like Carlie.

"What is it, Tyler? What's wrong?"

Her perception was uncanny. He realized he was holding a math paper one student had left on a desk, and he slowly laid it down and turned to her. "I have the greatest respect for teachers. For anyone having a gift with children. There are too many people out there who don't care about kids, even their own."

He knew he shouldn't have said so much the minute the words were out of his mouth. Carlie was scrutinizing him carefully. He shook his head and wandered around the room, surveying all the desks, laughing when he saw one that was overflowing with old papers. He straightened a chair, centered a book, replaced a pencil that had fallen on the floor.

Carlie began helping him tidy up. "The children may like me, but they're always in a hurry to leave when the bell rings." She indicated the disheveled desks. "They tend to be a little sloppy at times."

Tyler refocused on her. "Do you have children of your own?" He discovered he was suddenly very interested in her.

"No."

Just that one curt word. He crossed his arms over his chest. "You're not married?"

"Mr. Ramsey..."

He smiled. "Do you want children of your own someday?"

Lowering her gaze, she ignored his question and pulled her purse from beneath her desk. "We'd better be going. I have tests to grade tonight and lessons to prepare for the morning."

He accepted her change of subject without comment, and motioned for her to lead the way. They'd be spending a lot of time together, several nights a week. He'd get to know her better, and she would eventually warm up to him.

That thought brought with it images of another woman, a woman who had warmed up to him, only to leave him. He still felt irritated when he thought of how he'd woken up alone, a stupid smile on his face. But even then, he hadn't considered that was the end of it. He'd assumed he'd find out who she was from Brenda, then have the pleasure of getting to know his harem girl better.

But Brenda said the woman didn't want to be identified, and short of telling her *why* he wanted to know, he couldn't very well demand the mystery woman's name. But he hated the thought he might never see her again, and he hated even more that the night had evidently meant so little to her. It had been special to him, a night to cherish.

And the woman didn't want anything to do with him.

Carlie was halfway to the door when Tyler caught up with her, automatically taking her arm. "Let's take my car, and I'll bring you back here when we're finished."

"I'd prefer to drive."

Bristly. She was stiff, her arm rigid in his grasp. He had the distinct notion she resented his touch, though he hadn't a clue why. He was getting a little disgruntled with female rejection, and the question came out a little sharper than he'd intended. "Why?"

She didn't look at him, but he saw her pull her bottom lip between her teeth. She had a nice profile, he realized, and the lip she was punishing was soft and full. Then she nodded. "Very well. You may drive."

Chapter Four

TYLER HAD VERY large hands.

Carlie stared, without meaning to, as he cut into a piece of peach pie, then put the bite in his mouth and chewed. His jaw was strong, lean and hard, with only a slight shadow of dark beard stubble. His nose, straight and high-bridged, would appear aristocratic but for the lump where he had broken it in a fight when he was younger. Bren had told her the story, about how Jason had joined in and the two brothers had ended up defeating four other kids.

His eyebrows were straight and dark. His lashes thick and long. His cheekbones high and sculpted. There was a healthy color to his skin, not a dark-baked tan, but definitely the added color of outdoor activities.

Carlie sipped her coffee, her gaze going again to his hands. She remembered those hands so well, the way they had touched her, their strength, their gentleness. The memory gave her an odd tingle.

"Aren't you going to eat your pie?" he asked.

Carlie pulled her eyes away from his hands. She nodded and

took a large mouthful to give her something to do, namely chew, while Tyler filled the silence with questions.

"I could come to the school Friday, around four again, if you want me to do some sort of sign-up, or make a roster. What about you? Can you make it, or is that too soon?"

"Friday would be terrific. I'll put out a few calls tomorrow during lunch to see who can stay over. The ones who can't make it can have a schedule Monday."

Tyler pulled a piece of paper from his pocket. "These are my best times to get together. I tried to make them as regular as possible, so the kids can know what to expect. You can look that over then let me know if you'll have a problem with any of those dates."

She tucked the paper into her purse. "It'll be fine."

"You didn't even look at it. How do you know it won't interrupt your plans?"

Carlie gave him a quick smile. "We're glad to have your help. Whatever works for you is fine with me."

Tyler laid his fork by his plate and shook his head. "You know the saying about all work and no play? You have to take time for a social life, too."

"Why don't you let me worry about my social life, all right?" she said, annoyed with his persistence.

"What social life? It doesn't sound to me as if you have one."

That was entirely too close to the truth, and rubbed Carlie the wrong way. "Look, Mr. Ramsey. You may be the authority on having a good time, but I take my commitments seriously."

She watched Tyler's face go rigid, and then he leaned toward her. "And I don't?"

"Not from what I hear."

Leaning back, Tyler observed Carlie thoughtfully. "You know, if we're going to work together, you'll have to get over your attitude. I don't know why you dislike me so much, but it's not something I'm used to. Nor do I intend to get used to it." He waited a heartbeat, and Carlie felt his annoyance wash over her before he added, "I'd really like to work with you and the kids. But if you would rather find someone else to help you with your project, I'll drop out."

It was plain, by his tone and expression, he didn't want to do that. He wanted to be involved, for whatever reasons, and Carlie *did* need him. She hated to admit the truth, but it was her own personal conflict that was causing the problems. What she needed was an emotional compromise.

After adjusting her glasses, she straightened. "I think we can manage to get along if we keep it on a business level."

Tyler shook his head. "No go. I don't have a 'business level.' You're going to have to get your little nose out of the air and be friendly."

Her compromise exploded into oblivion. Did everything have to be his way? "You're an extremely arrogant person!"

His chuckle was warm and husky. "Bren says the same thing regularly. Funny, it sounds almost affectionate coming from her."

"She's too softhearted."

"Yes, she is. It's amazing you two are friends."

Uh-oh. Dangerous territory. Carlie held his gaze with an effort, the implied insult overlooked entirely. "We've known each other for a long time."

Tyler considered that. "Do you know many of her other friends?"

"A few."

"Who?"

Ah, so that was it. He didn't for one minute suspect her as the mystery woman from the other night; she was too unlikely to even be considered. But he was fishing to find out who the woman was. She hesitated just long enough, pretending deep thought, until he cleared his throat.

Several names came to mind, most of the women quite attractive, and Carlie named them, watching as he pondered each one. She was ready to laugh, when a familiar voice interrupted them.

"Ms. McDaniels! How nice to see you here. And how is my boy doing?"

Carlie smiled, and turned in her seat to face Mr. Briant.

She was totally at ease as a teacher dealing with a parent, and invited him to join their table. She reassured the anxious father, taking a few minutes to go over things he could do at home that would help his son improve his skills even more. She was specific, but very patient with the man's concerns. She was also aware that Tyler was watching her, sipping his coffee and listening to their conversation intently. He looked almost…impressed by her.

When the father finally left, Tyler lifted his coffee cup in a salute to her. "Does that happen often?"

"Yes. This is a small town, and thankfully the parents are, for the most part, very involved with their children's education."

"Your Mr. Briant seemed to hang on your every word."

Carlie smiled crookedly. "We had a misunderstanding of sorts with the first failing grade I sent home with his son. You see, he decided it was my fault, and came to the school to tell me so."

"Let me guess. You chewed him up and spit him out, right?"

Carlie's smile froze. "I'm not an ogre. He was upset, so I tried to explain. I pulled out all the papers I had been keeping on his son, Brady, and showed them to him. I went over the procedure we used with new materials, and I told him his son was distracted and not paying attention in class."

"Carlie, I didn't mean—"

She shook her head. "It's all right. I know what you meant." Idly stirring her coffee, she whispered, "It was such a sad situation. Mr. Briant had just lost his wife. He was very withdrawn and angry. He hadn't been able to concentrate on his son yet, who was having his own problems adjusting." She sighed, remembering how difficult it had been to see the father and son together, each struggling with his loss. "We spent a lot of time together after class. Sometimes we worked on lessons, but a lot of the time we just talked. I...I lost my parents when I was young, so I knew how Brady must have felt. At a time like that, school work kind of takes a backseat to trying to survive the emotional pain."

Tyler was studying his coffee cup. "It must have been rough for you."

His quiet words, filled with understanding and sympathy surprised her.

She nodded. "Everything worked out, though. After Brady started catching up, Mr. Briant joined us in our after-school lessons. I think he was lonely, too, and looking for some direction. He wanted to learn how to help his son study, so for a few weeks I helped him do that. Now they're on their own, and Brady Briant is earning A's."

Tyler stared at her, and Carlie could feel him looking beneath her calm control, trying to read her thoughts. "You're very dedicated," he said quietly.

"You have to be dedicated, to any job, if you want to do it well." Then she smiled, curious over Tyler's distracted expression. "That's no reason to be so solemn, though."

"I was just wondering how dedicated I am to my job, to handling the small load of petty cases that land on my desk each month."

"And?"

"Oh, I'd say...not very."

"That can't be true. Jason says you do a wonderful job."

"I'm a good lawyer." It was a statement of fact, with no fringe of lace to pretty it up. Abruptly, he reached across the table and took her hand.

Carlie tried to pull away, but he held her firm. "I'm sorry if I inadvertently insulted you. I only meant that you're very sure of yourself and you appear to be able to handle any situation. Including irascible fathers."

It was more difficult than she'd expected, because Tyler wasn't what she'd expected. At least, not completely. There were too many facets to his personality, and now he seemed genuinely thoughtful, interested in the children and concerned that he might have hurt her feelings. And he'd been very patient while she'd talked to Mr. Briant.

His hand was warm and strong, feeling exactly as she remembered. But her reaction wasn't dulled by familiarity.

"I'm not invincible, Mr. Ramsey. I simply don't believe in allowing myself to be trod upon."

"You've done that before, you know. Called me mister when you're agitated. I think we know each other well enough to dispense with mister and Ms., don't you?"

She managed to slip her hand free, but only because Tyler allowed it. She needed to regather her defenses; Tyler was a devastating man when he was being the seducer. But as a caring, considerate man, he was downright potent. "I don't really know you at all, but I think I know your type, and I'm not all that impressed by it. That's one of the reasons I hesitated to involve you in this program. But I'll be honest with you... Tyler. There was no one else to take Jason's place, and—"

He interrupted her long enough to say facetiously, "Stop, Carlie. You'll swell my ego with all this praise."

Carlie heaved a disgruntled sigh, and saw Tyler's eyes go

automatically to her breasts as she inhaled. He wouldn't be able to tell a damned thing, though, other than the fact that she did have them. Her shirt was buttoned to the throat and her suit coat was bulky, concealing any dimensions or shape. Carlie glared at him.

Still not looking at her face, he said, "You've made quite a few assumptions about me, haven't you? Did you ever consider you might be wrong?"

"No. I hadn't considered that."

"Well maybe you should."

When he finally looked up, appearing totally unrepentant, she frowned at him in exasperation. "I think it would be better if you kept your hands to yourself."

Tyler did a double take. "All I did was hold your hand. I didn't make an indecent proposal."

His blunt speech could easily rattle her, but still her tone was brisk and confident. "This is a very small town," she said. "People love to gossip. I don't want to give anyone reason to speculate."

Tyler blinked, completely incredulous, a small, uncertain smile playing about his mouth. Then the smile broke, and he indulged in unrestrained laughter. Carlie immediately felt like a fool. Her remark had been totally asinine. No one would ever assume Tyler Ramsey was romantically involved with her. Secret rendezvous in disguise aside, the idea was too absurd.

Tyler shook his head, still chuckling and watching Carlie with an air of expectation, as if he was waiting for another joke. She knew her face was red, and she hated it. She reached into her purse, blindly searching for her wallet, then threw a couple of bills on the table and stood. She slipped her purse over her shoulder and walked away.

"Carlie! Wait a minute."

She ignored him.

Tyler cursed as she walked out the door. When Carlie glanced back, he was hurrying after her.

It was a beautiful autumn day outside, with only a hint of chill in the air to suggest that winter was approaching. The sun was a hazy tangerine glow dipping low on the horizon. And beneath it, her sturdy shoes clapping loudly on the pavement, stomped Carlie. She was intent on marching back to the school to retrieve her car.

She heard Tyler jogging after her.

"Leave me alone," she said succinctly as he reached her side and tried to grasp her arm.

"Be reasonable, Carlie. You can't walk all the way back to the school."

"Of course I can. We didn't go that far."

"I'd rather drive you."

"*I'd* rather walk."

Growling, Tyler grabbed her arms, despite her resistance, then shook her gently. "Will you stop being so contrary? You were worried about causing speculation? Well, what do you think it will do if I carry you back to my car?"

"You wouldn't dare."

"Take one more step and you'll find out what I dare."

It was a standoff, and they glared at each other until finally Carlie did an about-face and, without a word to Tyler, stalked over to his car. She stood by the passenger door, impatiently waiting for him to unlock it. But before he opened the door, he caught her shoulders again.

"Carlie, I didn't mean to…that is… Oh, hell, I'm sorry, all right?"

Carlie faced him, hard as that was to do. She felt thoroughly humiliated and had no problem blaming Tyler for her discomfort. She may have memories to cherish, but Tyler would obviously be appalled to learn the true identity of his mystery woman.

Straightening her shoulders to hide her hurt, she stared at him with cold indifference. "Do a good job with the children. That's all I ask. Beyond that, you don't concern me."

Tyler nodded stiffly, then walked to his own side of the car. His hands flexed on the wheel twice before he started the engine.

"Doesn't anything rattle that damned calm reserve of yours?"

Carlie stared out her window. "Is that what your insult was meant to do? Rattle me?"

"Actually, I didn't mean to insult you at all."

Carlie snorted. "I'm not an idiot, Tyler. I understand how ridiculous I must have sounded. Certainly no one would ever think... I mean, the idea of me and you..."

"That's not why I laughed, Carlie."

She snorted again, and he grinned. "There, you see?" he said. "You just never say or do what I expect. You were sitting back there all prim and proper, your pretty hazel eyes all disapproving, and it just struck me funny. You seem too much of a modern woman to be so prudish."

Carlie felt mortified. "I'm not prudish," she mumbled, memories of a few nights ago tumbling about in her mind. Then she told the necessary lie. "Just circumspect."

They stopped at a red light, and he turned toward her, scrutinizing her. She stubbornly ignored him, only briefly glancing his way. But it was enough to see his smile. She had the vague suspicion that he felt challenged. And an even worse suspicion that if it came to a battle of wills, she'd lose. Hands down.

Tyler certainly had more experience sparring words. A thrill of trepidation ran down her spine, and then her reason for that trepidation was verified.

"Your lips are nice. Full and soft, but not a hint of a smile. And I like your small, stubborn chin."

He was teasing, she could tell. And she almost grinned at his underhanded tactics. Almost.

"Does it hurt?"

That gained her reluctant attention, and a quizzical frown. "What?"

"Wearing your hair so tight. It gives me a headache just to look at it."

She should never have looked at him. His dark eyes were shining and his firm lips were tilted in a boyish grin. He appeared totally harmless. But she wasn't buying it.

"How long is it?" Tyler moved when the traffic light turned green and drove smoothly down the uncrowded street. "Shoulder-length? Longer?"

"I can't see where my hair could possibly interest you, Tyler. But to end your juvenile tactics to annoy me, I'll tell you. It reaches my shoulder blades, is a very mousy brownish blond, and I wear it this way because I don't have time to fuss with fancy hairdos. As long as a person's hair is clean, what should it matter to anyone else how it's worn?"

Very softly, but with devastating sincerity, he said, "I don't think your hair is mousy."

Her head swiveled so sharply to look at him, she winced.

"I think it's a nice color, especially with the sun on it. I see shades of red—which suits you—but also blond and dark brown. It's very nice. You should wear it loose."

"I don't know what game you're playing, but I'm not interested. I'm not a teenager to be flattered by comments on my hair or eyes. I want to do a job here, Tyler. I'm very serious about it, even if you aren't."

"You are so damned defensive."

With reason, she wanted to scream. If he found out…. She sucked in a calming breath and stared at his profile. Her voice was patience personified, and filled with sane reasoning. "I'm not defensive. Just realistic. As you already made clear, there's very little about me that would ever entice you. I'm not naive. I'm aware of how I look. Why don't we talk about something important now? Like the students."

"I was only being honest with you, Carlie."

She gave him her patented teacher's look, reserved for students who had pushed her past the line. He shrugged, then returned his attention to the road.

She felt oddly deflated.

As he pulled into the school parking lot a few minutes later, he asked, "Were you at Bren's Halloween party?"

Coming out of left field like that, the question left her temporarily routed. Then she gathered her wits, opened the door and stepped out. Tyler left the car also, the consummate gentleman, and walked her to her own car, opening her door.

Carlie wasn't certain if it was just an innocent question, or if he was guessing at the identity of the masked lady again. She hesitated.

"Carlie?"

She saw no way around the lie. "No, I didn't go. There's always a lot happening at school this time of year. We had our own class party, you know. For the students, I mean. And we've already started practicing for the Thanksgiving play. And then, with the new project I've been working on…" Carlie came to a fast stop, appalled at her rambling. She looked into his eyes as she added truthfully, "I don't go to parties very often."

"Why not? You don't have a steady date?"

Carlie rolled her eyes, leaning back on the car. She adjusted her glasses carefully on the bridge of her nose. "I most certainly don't need a man to take me to a party if I wish to go."

"Of course not. I was only going to say that I didn't have a date, either, but I...well, I had a...terrific time. You should have come. I think you would have enjoyed yourself." He grinned. "I went as a pirate."

"How appropriate. Did you rape and pillage your way through the party?"

It was a lousy jest, and Tyler made certain she instantly regretted it.

"I wouldn't do something as reprehensible as rape, Carlie. As for pillaging, I would never steal from my brother. Now, if it was at your house...do you own anything worth stealing?"

She should have known better than to throw that verbal punch, but she hadn't been able to resist. She didn't have an answer to his facetious question, so she settled for a look of disdain. Tyler only smiled.

Carlie turned away and climbed into her car. She needed to get away. She couldn't remember the last time she'd felt so emotionally drained. Or so invigorated.

That personal acknowledgment angered her even more, and she tried to slam her car door. But Tyler got in her way, gripping the window frame and holding the door open.

"You should go out more, Carlie. It might do you some good to socialize, I think."

"Then you probably shouldn't think. You might damage something vital, and then what would the female population do?" She smiled with false sweetness, slammed the door and immediately pulled away.

She glanced in her rearview mirror and saw Tyler still standing there, watching after her. Even from a distance, she could see he was smiling. And then Carlie realized she was smiling also. She shook her head, bemused. She couldn't recall the last

time she'd actually had fun with a man. Even arguing with
Tyler was somehow fun.

Maybe she had been missing out and didn't even know it.

On her drive home, she thought about seeing Tyler again.
She was actually anticipating it. He didn't seem to be at all
deterred by the cold shoulder she was giving him. In fact, she
believed it amused him. He smiled often enough to give her
that impression.

The very last thing she wanted to do was amuse Tyler. She
had to maintain an emotional distance; she had to keep herself
safe. It certainly wouldn't be easy, but she'd just have to try
harder not to react to his little provocations. The only problem was, Tyler could be very provoking even when he wasn't
trying. All the man had to do was stand there, and women
fawned all over him.

But Carlie wouldn't be like other women. He'd find that
out soon enough. She'd see to it.

Tyler bounced the basketball, feeling impatient. Where was
Carlie? He was anxious to see her again, which surprised him
to no end. He'd decided he must be a glutton for punishment,
because as much as she seemed to look down on him and his
life-style, he still enjoyed every minute he spent with her.
Even when they were arguing.

The woman had a real flair for putting him in what she
considered his place. She was fun.

He heard a sudden squeaking of gym shoes and looked up,
a huge grin spreading across his face when he saw her. Carlie
was waltzing onto the gym floor, looking as if she wore the
comfortable, baggy sweatpants and thigh-length sweatshirt
every day. She couldn't quite stop her nervous hands, how-

ever, from tugging on the hem of the shirt, trying to pull it farther over her thighs.

He couldn't resist teasing her. "Well, Ms. McDaniels! You have very long legs. I hadn't realized."

She held his steady gaze and Tyler found himself anticipating what she might say. She never reacted as he expected her to. She never reacted as most other women would.

She was definitely unique.

"There was no need, nor will there ever be a need, for you to notice my legs, Tyler."

His grin never slipped. He enjoyed baiting her, watching her struggle with her temper. "Is every damned thing you own the same shade of mud? Don't you have anything blue or yellow?" He smacked his forehead, as if struck by a thought. "Red! You might look...nice, in red."

Her teeth snapped together in a loud click. "Watch your language. There are children present, and no, I have no desire..."

"None at all?"

"...to *wear red!* We're only playing basketball, for goodness' sake, and I hardly think the occasion warrants dressing up."

"It doesn't warrant dressing down, either. Is your body actually in there somewhere?" He leaned back, his gaze ranging slowly over her. "There's enough extra material there to clothe three women."

"Not that it's necessary for me to explain myself to you," she told him, starting to lose that steady, rock-solid calm, "but I thought I should wear clothes that were loose to allow for freedom of movement. I always wore something similar when I was a child and played basketball. I believe in being comfortable."

Tyler paused with interest. "You have some experience with the game then?"

"A little."

He chuckled. Knowing Carlie, and he *was* getting to know her, despite her efforts to remain aloof, "a little" probably meant she was very proficient at the game. "Excellent. We'll start by outlining the rules to the children, then we'll choose sides. I'll lead one team, you can lead the other."

Carlie nodded, but put in, "After warm-ups. I don't want to take a chance on anybody getting hurt."

"Whatever you say. But you'll have to lead those. I don't know any, other than sit-ups and such, and I'm not certain what kids this age are used to."

Tyler watched Carlie as she rounded up the kids and introduced them to him. As he spoke with each child, taking the time to joke and put them at ease, he caught Carlie staring. He winked at her, and she favored him with a genuine smile.

He wasn't used to her doing that, and for a second there, it threw him. Then he realized she was merely pleased that he was taking the time to really *talk* with the children. What had she thought he'd do? Bark at them?

The exercises she'd chosen were simple, but she challenged the children to keep up, to do each individual stretch properly. Throughout it all, Tyler watched her, and he grew increasingly curious.

Her breasts bounced. He'd never really noticed how amply endowed she was until now, but Mother Nature had treated her generously. And from what he could tell, she was totally unaware of it.

Unfortunately, he wasn't.

After helping a little girl catch the rhythm of the exercise, he wandered between all the children, checking to see if anyone else needed help. But even as he did that, he kept his gaze on Carlie, watching her every move.

When they finally broke up into teams, Carlie taking four

girls and the biggest boy, Tyler with four boys, he announced they would play "shirts and skins." He led the boys in stripping off their shirts, then noticed Carlie staring. She tightened her mouth and blushed bright red when he caught her eye. He was amused, but he also liked the idea of her liking his body. Walking toward her, seeing her back up a step before she could stop herself, Tyler grinned. When he reached her, he slipped a fingertip over her lips, then chucked her chin, all without a single word. She closed her mouth with a snap, stomping to the other side of the hoop. But still, she looked her fill.

Later, after each of the children had taken a few practice shots, Tyler pulled Carlie aside. "They're well-behaved. Only a few of them are a little rambunctious." He laughed. "I heard one of the boys daring another to do a few...indiscreet things. They saw me looking and changed their minds."

"Just remember that when the novelty wears off and they get used to you. They can become a little more than rambunctious."

There were several occasions to point out misconduct, ranging from offensive language to shoving. Once, Tyler had to break up a skirmish between two of the boys. By the time six o'clock rolled around, Tyler was beat and Carlie looked exhausted.

But still, she took the time to make certain each child was bundled up properly. She helped with tying shoes, answered numerous questions and convinced one little boy that he didn't really want to hit another, just because the child had sneezed on him.

Then she gave the sneezer a tissue.

"I'm impressed," Tyler told her, his eyes on her flushed face. "You're really good with kids. You never once lost your temper."

She shrugged off his compliment. "I enjoy them. They're fun, and honest to a fault."

Tyler felt a tug on his hand, and looked down at a little girl named Lucy. She was smiling at him, showing him the stuck zipper on her coat. He helped her get her coat closed, then tweaked her nose. As he started to stand, she threw her skinny arms around his neck and squeezed him tight. "Thank you, Mr. Ramsey. I had fun."

Surprised, he looked toward Carlie, then ruffled the girl's tangled hair. "I did too, Lucy." She giggled, and Tyler grinned at her. "You'll be here Monday?"

"Yes, sir." She skipped away, leaving Tyler to stare after her.

"Whatever could that little girl have done to deserve detention? She's a doll."

Carlie waved goodbye to the last little boy, watching as he climbed into his parent's car, before allowing the heavy gym door to close. She turned to Tyler, chuckling softly. "Lucy has a problem with her language. She could make a sailor blush when she puts her mind to it. Personally, I think she just wants attention. Her father took off about a year ago, and her mother has her hands full trying to take care of five kids, all under the age of fifteen. Lucy sort of falls into the middle of the group."

Tyler turned away, his left hand rubbing the muscles of his neck. "I hate hearing stories like that. They make me want to strangle somebody." He began idly bouncing the ball, just to give his hands something to do and his mind something to focus on other than the problems of innocent children. But it didn't work. The issue was a sensitive one with him. "Why is it the kids who have to get hurt?"

"It's always the ones who are most vulnerable. That's simply human nature." She shrugged philosophically, then took him by surprise, snatching the basketball out of his hands and dribbling it across the court.

Tyler watched her antics, knowing she was trying to distract him, and appreciating her efforts. Being with the children today reminded him of his own childhood. It had been rough for him and Jason, and when they'd become teenagers it had only gotten worse. Tyler had always pretended with his friends, bragging about the freedom he and Jason had, making it sound as if raising themselves had been a lark. And he had refused to admit to the embarrassment of having a mother who was the town "lightskirt."

God, it had been hard. Luckily, he'd had Jason. But it wasn't the same. Children needed an adult to look up to, someone they respected and who cared about them.

These kids had Carlie, but he wanted to help, too, wanted to make a difference.

"All right, Tyler," she said, breaking into his thoughts. "Enough moping over things you can't change. I hereby challenge you to a little one-on-one. The first to make ten baskets wins."

His grin was slow and filled with wicked delight. He put his hands on his hips, watching Carlie as she continued to expertly dribble the ball. "What are we betting?"

"That I can beat the pants off you." Her tone was smug and taunting. And then she understood exactly what she'd said. She flushed scarlet.

"My pants? Well, Ms. McDaniels! It wasn't enough to ogle me without my shirt? You want to strip me of all modesty?"

"That would be impossible." Her face was still hot, but she began dribbling the ball again. "You don't possess any modesty and probably never have."

His grin widened. He approached her slowly, his eyes never leaving her face. "I'm ready when you are, sweetheart. But the stakes have to be worthwhile. Say...dinner? At the winner's choice of place?"

Carlie gave him a confident smile. She did a fancy little feat of bouncing the ball behind her back, then between her knees, before shouting suddenly, "You're on." She raced down the court, scoring the first basket before he realized the game had started.

"Oh, ho! Getting tricky on me, huh? I like a woman who can take me by surprise." Carlie faltered at his words, nearly losing the ball. Tyler lunged, staying right on her, his body looming over hers, his arms outreaching her, his legs able to cover the same amount of ground more quickly. Carlie claimed it was an even match.

She was good, real good. She dunked the ball three times before he had a chance to score. Then he got serious. But all the while, he grinned. He felt better than he had in a very long time.

They were both sweaty by the time the score was evened up, eight all. Tendrils of hair had come loose around Carlie's face, sticking to her forehead and flushed cheeks. She looked done in, but still very determined to win. And she was laughing, obviously enjoying herself.

Then Tyler accidentally hit her. He made to jump for the ball, and his elbow smacked against her temple. Stumbling backward, she landed on her butt, her glasses slipping off her nose and dropping into her lap.

Tyler was horrified. "Oh, God, Carlie. I'm sorry!" He knelt beside her, taking her face in his hands, staring into her dazed eyes. Wide, hazel eyes. "Are you all right?"

She managed a slight, shaky smile. "I'm okay." Then she looked up at him.

His eyes locked with hers, and his fingers moved an almost imperceptible amount. As he studied her, something seemed familiar, some memory tickling at the back of his mind. Those wide eyes....

Then Carlie broke the contact, pulling away from his hands.

"You knew you were about to lose, right? That's why you belted me?" Her voice shook, and she tried another grin, but it was a weak attempt. Tyler wondered how badly she was hurt.

He was too busy trying to analyze the situation to answer right away. Carlie stuck her glasses firmly back on her nose, then called, "Yoo-hoo? Anybody home? Tyler?"

Finally, he shook his head, chasing away the errant confusion. "Sorry. Here, let me help you up."

"I'm fine, Tyler. I don't need any help." He helped, anyway, giving Carlie no choice in the matter.

He turned her, holding her chin in his palm. "Let me look at you. I think you have a lump coming up already."

She jerked away. "I told you, I'm fine. Quit fussing."

Tyler propped his hands on his hips, worried and filled with guilt. "I'll concede the game. Dinner is on me."

Carlie looked down at herself, then shook her head. "Dressed like this? I don't think so, but thanks, anyway."

Her refusal didn't surprise him, but it did annoy him. "You have to eat. It's been a long day."

"I have stew in the Crock-Pot at home. You're free and clear."

He picked up his shirt, drying the sweat from his chest and arms with it. He didn't particularly want to be free. "Stew sounds good. We bachelors don't get a home-cooked meal all that often."

Carlie raised her eyes to his, a look of disbelief mirroring her thoughts.

As hints went, his was blatantly clear and he held his breath while waiting to see what she would say.

"*You* are wrangling *me* for an invite?"

He shrugged, but the movement felt stiff. "I figure anyone

who can play basketball as good as you, must surely be able to cook, too."

"Your logic escapes me, and besides, I don't think I made enough."

It was almost as if she was challenging him. He wanted to spend more time with her, but she was determined to put him off. He didn't like it, not one little bit. They *would* spend the evening together, despite the woman's ridiculous reservations. "I'll stop at the bakery and pick up some sourdough bread to go with it."

Carlie narrowed her eyes at his persistence. "Don't you have some female somewhere waiting for you to call and check in?"

"Nope. And I'm hopelessly lonely. Be kind, Carlie. Take me home."

"Like a stray dog? If I feed you once, will I have trouble getting rid of you?"

He managed to look hurt. Shrugging his bare shoulders, he said, "Never mind. I didn't mean to intrude. I just thought since we were both going home alone, we could share a meal. I had fun today. I don't get to goof off all that often anymore, regardless of what you think."

Carlie froze. He knew she wouldn't be able to handle hurting his feelings. Carlie was, despite her efforts to prove otherwise, a real softie. He watched her out of the corner of his eye and knew the moment she relented.

"I had fun, too, Tyler. And I suppose it would be nice to have someone to chat with over dinner."

Tyler raised his head, all remnants of self-pity disappearing. "Terrific! I knew you could be reasonable."

"Why, you big fraud!"

He simply laughed, not the least bit concerned with his deception. "Go get your things. I'll follow you to your house."

He watched Carlie stomp away. He could see her silently

fuming. Damn, but he enjoyed her company. She was prickly, independent, determined to do things her way. She didn't pout, didn't treat him to the silent bit. No, when Carlie had something to say—and she usually did—she said it. She was so unpredictable, so *unexpected,* she chased boredom right out the door.

Chapter Five

TYLER DROVE BEHIND Carlie, noting the slow, careful way she maneuvered her car. He was on the verge of laughing out loud. He shook his head, bemused. He couldn't recall ever having such verbal skirmishes with a woman. Women didn't react to him that way. But damned if he didn't like it. It was fun.

For that matter, Carlie was fun.

And he'd never thought of a woman that way before. She appeared totally immune to his flirting, but it wasn't because she was shy or withdrawn.

On the contrary. She was one of the most outspoken women he'd ever met. And intelligent. He enjoyed her company.

It was like having a pal, someone he could exchange mild insults with and still smile. But it was so utterly different with her being female. It was as if a whole new facet had been added to the relationship. It went a long way toward relieving his distraction over the mysterious—and missing—masked lady. And that in itself was a major feat.

Carlie pulled into her driveway and parked beneath a carport. Tyler pulled up to the curb out front, then he stared. He wasn't sure what he'd expected, probably a mud-colored house with a barren expanse of lawn and not a single speck of color. She took him by surprise. Again.

Her house was a small Cape Cod cottage nestled at the end of a narrow side street. A farmer's fields were on the right side of the house, a heavily wooded area to the left. Behind and in front of the white-and-yellow wooden structure was a well-tended lawn. Daisies were blooming everywhere, and her mailbox was designed to look like a small, colorful barn.

Tyler looked around, captivated. There was a tire swing hanging from the gnarled branch of an ancient oak off the back corner of the house. A curving porch circling to the right of the front door had a rattan porch swing attached to the overhang.

"A real swinger, aren't you?"

Carlie shrugged as she dug her key from her purse. "I'm not an idle person. I don't like to be still, even when I'm relaxing."

Tyler tried to imagine the classic picture of a woman superimposed with Carlie in a flowery dress, her hair loose, swaying in the breeze and humming softly while her bare feet maintained the gentle motion of the swing.

He wasn't quite that imaginative.

The inside of her house was also a contrast, so different from the woman he was getting to know. There was little furniture, only the basic necessities. It was an eclectic mix of modern and antique, light oak and glass, chintz material and delicate doilies. There were no photographs, but there were framed prints of the most outrageous things. Each room appeared to have a theme.

The living room was spring, with a large, brass-framed picture of a bee, busily collecting pollen from a daisy. Porcelain flowers decorated each tabletop and filled one curio cabinet.

The dining room, which was minuscule, was decorated with birds. A border of them circled the room, a dainty, delicate figure sat looking over every corner, and in each plant, one peeked from between the leaves.

The kitchen was whales.

He raised his eyebrows at her in question. "How did you choose whales, may I ask?"

Carlie had been busily putting their jackets on the coat tree and checking the stew. She looked at him over her shoulder as she lifted the Crock-Pot lid. "One of the children at school gave me one, once. I said I liked it, and…" She smiled.

"They all decided to give you one?"

"Each class seems to take it into their head that I need a new collection of something. But I don't mind. It makes for consistent Christmas presents. There are bunnies in the bathroom and cats in my bedroom."

"What are you going to do when you run out of rooms?"

She tilted her head. "Mix and match?"

He smiled at her wit. "Can I help you set the table or something?"

"No. You can turn on the television if you like. I'm just going to heat the bread and set the table."

Tyler wandered into the living room again. His attention was drawn to the television set and an array of DVDs sitting on top. He looked through them, and stopped when he spotted a "Work Out With the Oldies," video. He carried it with him into the kitchen. "Whose is this?"

Carlie paused in the process of serving the stew. "Mine. Who else would it belong to?"

"You work out to the oldies?"

"I like older music. It's more fun than this new stuff kids listen to."

"So do you hop and jostle around in a pair of tights?"

She smirked at his expression. "You're looking at my work-out clothes." She spread her arms in the air. The shirt raised a bit and he caught a glimpse of the pale flesh of her belly.

To his disbelief, and annoyance, he felt a brief spurt of interest. It had only been a flash, an instant of white skin, gone too quickly to really appreciate, if indeed, there had been anything there to appreciate.

With the clothes she favored, it was hard to tell for certain. But she definitely had a large bosom. He'd established that today when she was exercising, her body bouncing in all the right places. And from that prominent point, her clothes fell almost straight down, giving no hint of curves or dips and hollows.

But her arms had felt slim when he'd shaken her the other day. And when she'd come into the house, she'd kicked off her shoes, showing narrow feet and trim ankles.

It was simple curiosity, he decided, that was making him react to her. Not that he would ever consider doing anything about it. She was a schoolteacher, which was bad enough as far as dalliance went, but on top of that she was too damn prickly, and was his sister-in-law's best friend, to boot. She was so far off the scale of available females, he knew he didn't have to concern himself. But he did, anyway.

He'd never met a woman so dedicated to a cause, so at ease with children and so giving. She was totally disinterested in his supposed prowess, in his community standing, in his reputation. All she wanted from him was his help in achieving a worthwhile goal.

Disgruntled with his thoughts, and his overactive imagination that kept him guessing at her elusive figure, he stalked toward her and asked bluntly, "How much do you weigh?"

Carlie halted in the middle of opening a package of butter. "That's none of your business!"

"You're working out, so you must feel you need to lose some weight, right?"

"Wrong. I work out to keep in shape. Everybody should." She poked him in the middle. "Don't you?"

"Of course. But that's different."

"Why?"

"I go to a gym. I'm a man."

"Well, I can't afford to go to some fancy gym. And no one ever told me being a man was synonymous with being outrageously snoopy and impertinent. I would have thought a man your age would have learned some manners by now."

It was her teacher's voice again, and Tyler saw that he'd made her truly angry, though she was trying to hide it. He watched as she slammed bowls onto the table, then practically threw the spoons next to them.

"What are you drinking?" he asked cautiously, waiting to see if she would end up throwing something at him.

"I'm drinking milk. You can find yourself something in the refrigerator."

He did. Milk.

After sitting down to eat in perfect, strained silence, he ventured, "I'm sorry...?"

"You're not sure?"

"Of course I'm sure. I just didn't know if you would want me to speak to you. I, ah, seemed to have hit a nerve."

Carlie sighed, dropping her face into her hands.

Tyler had the awful suspicion she was going to cry. In a near whisper, he asked, "Carlie?"

Her shoulders shook, and Tyler's heart stopped. "Aw, Carlie don't. Sometimes I just stick my foot in it. You shouldn't pay any attention to me. Really. Carlie?"

She slowly raised her head. A wicked grin spread across her

features. One look at Tyler and she broke into peals of laughter. He fell back against his chair, glaring at her.

"Oh, Tyler. You didn't hit a nerve, honestly." She chuckled again, then removed her glasses to wipe her eyes. "Actually," she put in, obviously intent on controlling her hilarity and not entirely succeeding, "you're finally acting exactly as I thought you would."

"Is that right?"

"Yes, it is."

He felt the sting of her insult, deliberate, he was certain. "So, you assumed all along that I was a jerk? Is that it?"

"Not a jerk. Not really. You're an okay guy. But you think you can make up your own rules and everyone, especially females, will abide by them. You deliberately provoke me, and you're purposely outrageous. You don't even try to follow normal codes of manners or behavior. And why should you? Women relentlessly fall at your feet, despite your attitude, so why should you change to accommodate polite society?"

He didn't like having her categorize and analyze his faults as if he fell into an expected mode of "male behavior." "All this lecturing simply because I commented on your weight?"

"Because you felt it didn't matter if you were rude. After all, I'm not a woman you'd aspire to sleep with. You have no personal, sexual interest in me, so why go out of your way to be charming? There wouldn't be any benefit, now, would there?"

He studied her, his eyes probing. Damned if he wasn't letting her get the best of him, again. So far, that was how it had been. She consistently sliced him up, verbally at least, while he was sitting there admiring her. Laughing with him was one thing, but Carlie was actually laughing *at* him. It was intolerable. "I'll be honest with you. For some inexplicable reason, I'm intrigued by you."

Her eyes widened enormously, and she choked on a breath. Her amusement was instantly, and completely, gone.

He waited impassively until she'd regained her breath. "I've decided it's because you're so damned mysterious."

She sent him a wary look, then shook her head, refusing to meet his eyes. "No. No, I'm not. I'm an open book. You simply refuse to accept there's a woman who isn't bowled over by your charm."

He pretended she hadn't spoken. "What does your body look like? That's what I'm wondering. How plump are you? How big are your breasts, how bountiful is your bottom? I'm used to looking at a woman and seeing what's there, be it attractive or not, not this infuriating guessing game, trying to see beneath layers of ugly clothing."

Very slowly, Carlie laid her spoon by her bowl. She stared at him, then tightened her mouth. "You're terribly spoiled. You think nothing of going for the jugular just so you can win. All right. So I'm overweight." She lifted one shoulder in a stiff shrug, holding his gaze. "It runs in my family. And flaunting my body would be a bigger crime than hiding it. But so what? I don't need a man's approval to feel good about myself. I'm a very nice person, and I do a very good job, and I *care*. About this community, about the children, about people in general. Can you say the same, Tyler? So you're handsome. So what? What real contribution have you ever made to your own small part of the world?"

He spooned up a bite of stew, saluting her with it before putting it in his mouth. He chewed thoughtfully, feeling her simmer beside him, her anger growing with his nonchalance. Finally, knowing he'd pushed her far enough and sensing that she was ready to throw her stew at his head, he said, "You do a good job of going for the jugular, as well. I can't think of a single important thing I've ever done in my life. But I don't do bad things, either, discounting my comment on your weight, of course. I pay my taxes on time, I don't drink and drive, I donate to charities—although, only when they actually catch me. I'm a gentleman and I'm kind to older people. Surely all that counts for something?"

"Not much."

"Come on, Carlie. Can't you forgive me? I was only curious, after all, not being deliberately insulting. If I was too nosy, well it's only because I think you could be very attractive. No, don't make rude noises at me again. You are intelligent, very intelligent. That's something to be admired. If you made a little effort with your appearance, you might have plenty of equally intelligent men knocking your door down. You would probably have a very busy social schedule."

"I don't have time for a...busy social schedule."

"It's not a disease, you know. You're a fun person to be with. You should be involved with someone special."

Carlie tilted her head back to survey the ceiling. Without looking at him, she asked, "Why do you care, Tyler? I'm not some bird with a broken wing you need to teach to fly. I don't want to fly. Walking is much more my speed."

"I have an idea," he announced, very pleased with himself.

"Oh, no. Now we're in it deep."

He laid his palms flat on the table, and raised himself out of his chair to loom toward her. "Date me."

Carlie eyed him as if he'd grown a second head. As she kept him waiting, he reseated himself, tapping his fingers on the table. "Well?"

"I'm waiting for the punch line."

"All right. Here it is. You might like it. You might enjoy my company."

She made a show of stifling her laughter. "You should get paid. You're a professional."

"Professional what? Or should I ask?"

"Comedian, of course."

"I'm being serious here. The least you could do is listen to me."

"No, the least I could do is make you go home and take your insanity with you." She seemed almost angry—and flustered. Her cheeks were a warm, rosy pink, and her hands trembled just the tiniest bit. Then she widened her eyes comically, gasping. "You don't think it's catching, do you?" She shoved her chair back, holding her hands up in a defensive gesture.

Tyler slowly rose from his seat. "All right, you. I think I ought to take you in hand. Talk about *my* manners!" As he advanced on her, circling the table with a menacing stride, Carlie shrieked and jumped to her feet, moving quickly to keep the table between them.

"All right! All right! Tell me what you have to say."

Tyler advanced. "Too late. You've challenged my masculinity. And with my ego as enormous as you claim, that must surely be grounds for assault. Now you'll have to pay."

She was trying not to laugh. He watched the grin grow on her face, and felt satisfaction. Chuckles emerged from between her tightly drawn lips. She clapped a hand over her mouth, still moving cautiously. He followed.

Then Tyler lunged across the table, grabbing for her. She screeched in surprise, but it was already too late. He had her.

Hauling her body across the table, his grip firm on her upper arms, Tyler grinned at her. She was laughing, her glasses were askew, her chest heaving. And he had the insane, almost overwhelming urge to kiss her.

What the hell? he thought, and leaned closer, his eyes on her soft, slightly parted lips. He was filled with an anticipation that even surpassed what he'd felt at the pool house with the masked lady, and that had been shocking in its intensity.

What he felt now was so alien to his jaded senses, he actually jerked when she spoke.

Her voice wasn't breathless. It was low and menacing. "Back off."

He did. Slowly regaining his wits, mortified by what he had almost done—to *Carlie,* for Pete's sake—Tyler managed an unconcerned shrug. "I've never really...played with a woman before. I was only going to—"

"Oh, please. Spare me. I know what you were doing."

"Uh, what?" Maybe she could tell him, for he certainly hadn't a clue what had been in his mind. *Carlie?* Good grief.

Carlie fussed with her glasses. "You're playing games. I already told you, I won't have it."

That sounded plausible, though not entirely true. But it helped him to regain his aplomb. "Of course I was playing. And so were you. That's why you should date me. Ah-ah, just hear me out." He waited until she sat down again. "Now, don't storm out on me. I think we could enjoy each other's company, at least, as long as we keep it platonic. I hope you didn't think I meant—"

"Why?" she interrupted, her tone sharp, her look suspicious. "Why would you want to spend more time with me?"

"I like you. *Really* like you. You make me laugh." Then he added, "And you keep me humble."

She snorted, then ignored his chastising look at the rude noise.

"It would be good for us both. You would learn to relax a little, to concentrate on something other than your obligation to the school, and like I said, I enjoy your company."

"Surely there are other women whose company you would enjoy more?"

"Perhaps. But for different reasons." She opened her mouth,

and he raised a hand in surrender. "I know. Uncalled for. Acquit me. But I've been really bored lately and…"

He frowned at her bubble of laughter. "I'm perfectly serious, I'll have you know. Here I am, laying my heart out to you, and you're rudely stomping all over it."

"You know what, Tyler?"

He didn't trust her grin. "Probably not."

"It has been fun at odd and varying moments, which if you're being sincere, is surprising to us both."

He grabbed his chest, feigning a heart attack. "What? You admit to enjoying my company? I'm not totally without redemption? I'm not totally cast down? Carlie McDaniels likes my company! What more encouragement could a man ask for?"

"At odd and varying moments," she clarified. "Okay, so where would we go and what would we do on these experimental, platonic dates?"

"Then you'll do it?"

"Absolutely not. Not until you answer my question."

"I don't know." He hadn't really thought things through. "The usual stuff?"

"Such as?"

"Dinner? Dancing?" He grinned, ready to elaborate and add to his list. "Roller skating? Bungee jumping? Body surfing?"

"I could maybe handle a movie. It's dark there and nobody would have to know I was out with a maniac."

He beamed at her. "Excellent choice. Tomorrow?"

"Tomorrow is Saturday. Don't you have a real date?"

"Carlie, Carlie, Carlie. This *will* be a real date. Up to, but excluding, the good-night kiss."

Carlie twisted her mouth in apparent thought, chewed the corner of her bottom lip and studied her short, neat nails.

"You're not contemplating death, you know," he said dryly.

"I'll even let you choose the movie." He watched the fleeting expressions on her face, and saw her indecision, her...nervousness? Damned unaccountable female. He couldn't remember the last time he'd had to actually beg for a date. It was a rather disturbing experience.

"I can choose what we'll see?"

His heartbeat picked up speed. "Absolutely."

"A true concession. All right. I'll go."

Tyler felt his muscles ease, and only then realized how stiff he'd been. He felt as if he'd accomplished something major. Carlie was no easy nut to crack. But he was determined to help her loosen up. He could help her with the children, easing some of her obligation, and also show her how to have a good time.

He suddenly realized that things were starting to pick up. Boredom was a thing of the past. First there was that night with the mysterious, timid masked lady, whose identity Brenda refused to reveal, no matter how he cajoled. His curiosity over that little episode was still extreme; he'd never met a woman like her before. Sooner or later, he *would* find out who she was.

Of course, he'd never met a woman like Carlie, either. She was as unique as any woman could be. He smiled, thinking of her again. Prickly, independent, outspoken Carlie. He surely had enough excitement to keep boredom at bay for some time to come.

"I can't believe you chose this movie."

Carlie smiled in the dim theater, very aware of Tyler sitting beside her. He was dressed in jeans and a dark sweater. She could smell his after-shave, and his own natural, masculine scent. It was comforting, stimulating and very distracting. "I love Mel Gibson."

"Now, why does that surprise me? Oh, yeah. You've made

it clear to me on several occasions that macho, sexy men are low on your list."

"No. I made it clear that men who *thought* they were macho, sexy men were low on my list."

"Don't look at me like that! I never claimed to be macho."

"Are you claiming to be sensitive, instead?"

"Certainly. Especially in specific areas. Like low on my stomach, the top of my spine…"

Carlie's breath caught and her skin suffused with heat. He wasn't lying. She remembered all too well just how sensitive he was in those particular areas. Throughout that one special night, he'd shown her how to give as well as take, and she'd thoroughly enjoyed each lesson.

She elbowed him roughly to cover her reaction. "You're impossible."

"Naw." He waited a heartbeat. "Just *very* sensitive."

"Hush, the movie is starting." Carlie knew she sounded rude, but she didn't care. Tyler's flirting was just that, flirting. He did it with every woman he came into contact with, be she nine or ninety. It shouldn't mean anything, and likely wouldn't if she wasn't the mystery woman. But she was, and his words affected her in numerous ways. Her head knew he wasn't serious, but her heart jumped into a wild cadence of excitement every time he teased.

"Lesson number one, Carlie. You don't rudely tell your date to hush."

She shifted her gaze, peering at him in the growing darkness. "Not even when the movie is starting and he's yakking on about his sexuality and very personal preferences?"

"That's right. You should have told me where you're sensitive, too."

"Oh. Well, let's see. My feet?"

"You're not trying to get in the mood here, are you?"

She chuckled, feeling some of her tension ebb at his dry expression. Leaning slightly toward him, she nudged him affectionately with her shoulder. The action surprised them both, and Tyler whispered, "That's better," then boldly put his arm around her.

It felt good. Comforting and exciting at the same time. But she had to remind herself this was only a game to him. And she was only a distraction.

"You shouldn't stiffen up so, either," he added. "I'm not getting fresh. Just relax."

The words had been whispered gently in her ear. She could have added it as another sensitive spot, yes, indeed. He was being so careful with her, lightly teasing and so solicitous. She wanted to lean against him, to feel more of his heat against her side. Instead, she stared straight ahead. "Shh. Don't make me miss the movie."

It would be okay, Carlie thought, once she managed to relax a little. Tyler would never connect her with the pool house. And he wasn't attempting to fondle her; his hand wasn't moving from her shoulder and he wasn't drawing her nearer to his body. He was just...there. Firm. Nice. Male.

They shared a huge bucket of extra-buttery popcorn and a large cola. Carlie felt Tyler's eyes on her when she unconsciously licked the butter from her fingers, but when she turned to him, he didn't say a word. He looked perplexed, annoyed and exasperated. Carlie frowned at him, but he shook his head and looked away. She couldn't begin to decipher his thoughts, and a few seconds later he excused himself to go buy candy. He returned with a box of chocolates.

"After all that popcorn, you have room for candy?"

Her tone had been whisper-soft, and he answered in kind. "You're doing it again. You don't talk your date as if he's a glutton. You should say, 'Oh, candy!' and thank him for it."

She contrived a blank expression. "Oh, candy! Thank you."

He laughed out loud, prompting the people behind him to grumble a complaint.

Carlie whispered, "I gather by your display of humor, I didn't do it right?"

"You are amusing, Carlie. You really are. Thank you for coming with me tonight."

Her throat felt tight when she tried to smile. She dropped her gaze to her lap for a moment, then raised it to look at him. "I'm having a good time, too. Thank you for asking me."

He held her eyes a moment longer, tightened his arm around her in an affectionate squeeze, then turned his attention back to the screen. Carlie silently studied his profile. He wasn't the puffed-up, conceited egomaniac she'd accused him of being. At least, not now, not with her.

Probably because he was with her; he wasn't trying to impress or seduce her. He'd claimed boredom, but she wasn't at all certain that was possible, given his reputation. There was no doubt Tyler Ramsey could have a different date every night of the week, without resorting to asking her out.

But it was nice being with him, knowing he didn't really see her as a woman, but rather as a companion, someone to spend a few hours with. She thought of the party and trembled.

Tyler accepted that she was heavy, plain and greatly lacking in good taste. He'd made no bones about detesting her choice in clothing. But it had taken only a few small modifications— a wig, colored contacts—and he hadn't recognized her at all.

With each passing hour, she found herself growing more attracted to him. It had started out being strictly physical. After all, Tyler Ramsey was the kind of man girls dreamed about and women fantasized over. And Carlie had recently lived a few of those fantasies. But now, she realized how easily she could lose her heart.

Carlie thought about the woman she used to be, so frivolous, so anxious to attract her husband's attention, wanting and needing his approval. She'd failed dismally then, and eventually had learned a valuable lesson. Not that she blamed her husband entirely, for she had failed him in numerous ways. But he hadn't even tried to be patient with her. He'd thrown out accusations without remorse or consideration to her age and inexperience. At first, she'd been crushed that she wasn't a sexual person, that she'd failed in the most basic female concepts.

She was older now, wiser, no longer taken in by men and their obscure promises. Her husband hadn't wasted any time in finding someone who suited his sexual tastes better than she did. It didn't hurt anymore to remember, nor did it fill her with disappointment and self-reproach. She'd vowed never again to be that vulnerable. And she'd never been tempted to waver from that pledge.

Until Tyler. Now she had a night to herself, a special night to remember when she felt the loneliness that would surely come one day.

Gaining Tyler's friendship was fun, but knowing him as a man, for that one special night, was a memory she would repeatedly indulge in recalling. Without even trying, he'd made her feel things she'd never felt before, things she'd thought herself incapable of feeling. He'd proven her husband had been wrong about her. That would have to be enough.

She would have to be very careful that he never became suspicious. Any more friendly, casual dates would have to be forgotten. She couldn't risk it. The possibility of emotional hurt was too great. But the program? Could she distance herself, even while working with him for hours on end?

It wouldn't be easy, but she had no choice.

"Tell me about Carlie."

Brenda paused in her efforts to finish folding her laundry. "Carlie? What do you want to know about her?"

Tyler shrugged. "I don't know. How long have you known her? Why isn't she married?"

Brenda swallowed, then looked away. "She was married. When she was very young. But it didn't work out. And since then...she just hasn't found the right man. She's intelligent, bright and funny and caring. She's very special."

Tyler was frowning slightly, then waved away Brenda's defense of Carlie. "You don't need to convince me. I've been with her a lot lately, and I like her, too." He was silent a moment, then shook his head. "I didn't know she'd been married. It was rough, huh?"

"I...ah, Carlie is very private, Tyler. I don't feel comfortable talking about her."

"I didn't mean to pry. I just think it's a shame she doesn't have anyone special."

Brenda turned and looked at him. "She told me you two went to the movies."

"Yeah. It was really fun. I enjoyed it. It's nice to be out with someone without having to worry about how the night will end. It was actually better than being with the guys. I didn't have to listen to, and return, all the raunchy jokes about sex and who had enjoyed the latest conquest. It was comfortable. Do you know what I mean?"

Very gently, Brenda smiled at him. "Don't look so confused, Tyler. I know exactly what you mean. Jason says he felt the same way after he met me. With other women and with his male friends, there was always a certain face he had to wear, a certain way he was expected to act. Around me, he could just be himself."

"There's a major difference here, Bren. Jason couldn't keep his hands off you."

Her sudden burst of laughter was quickly cut off. "That's

true enough, thank heavens. I don't suppose you suffered the same thing with Carlie?"

"Carlie? That woman gives new meaning to *bad taste*. Her clothes alone are enough to keep my stomach churning. And there were several times I would have dearly loved to yank those damned glasses off her nose and stomp on them."

"I've had the same thought myself, Tyler. But Carlie won't ever change. She won't dress to suit other people. And she's comfortable with herself and the style she's chosen."

"What style? There is no style to her." He grinned suddenly and admitted, "I've wondered what she would look like buck-naked, without her hair being tortured behind her head in that braid."

Brenda's mouth dropped open, then she sputtered. "Tyler Ramsey! Don't you dare seduce my friend out of idle curiosity. I'd never forgive you!"

Tyler stood, glancing at his watch. He sighed philosophically. "You don't want me to have any fun, Bren."

"Have *fun* with some other woman. But you leave Carlie alone."

"Carlie is safe enough." Then he added, "You sure you won't tell me who the harem girl is?"

"I can't. I promised her I wouldn't."

"But why? What is she hiding?"

"She…she knows your reputation. And…and I guess she just doesn't want to get involved." Brenda shrugged. "I'm sorry."

Tyler worked his jaw in frustration. "She doesn't trust me?"

"Well…no."

He exploded. "What is it with you women? I am not some overcharged male bimbo! Doesn't anyone allot me the benefit of having scruples?"

"You women?" Brenda grinned at him. "This sounds like a Carlie lecture. Has she been rough on you?"

"One minute, yes. I get the feeling she doesn't think very highly of me. But then she'll laugh and be outrageously funny." He paced a few feet away. "She keeps me guessing."

Brenda walked him to the door. "I know you have scruples, Tyler. And I think you're a very nice man, despite everything." She skipped away when he turned, grabbing playfully for her. Laughing, she continued, "But Carlie's different. I don't want to see her hurt."

"Hurt? Carlie's about as vulnerable as a porcupine. But if you're worrying I'll make her promises I can't keep, don't. I've told her I like her friendship, that's all. I admire her, despite her atrocious clothing, but I doubt I'd be even tempted to go beyond platonic with her. She's safe enough."

Even as he said the words, Tyler thought what an adept liar he was. He was tempted, more than tempted. It was just that the temptation had come in a different package. As often as not, he wanted to simply touch her, on the hand, on her smooth cheek. Holding her would be nice.

"Thank you, Tyler. I'm glad you've befriended Carlie. She needs some fun and excitement with men other than those stuffed shirts on the school board."

Tyler had been in the process of walking out, but he halted abruptly. "I didn't get the impression she was dating anyone in particular."

"Carlie doesn't consider going anywhere with them a date, because she works with them. She thinks that their interest is purely work-related. But I don't think so. I think they're as curious as you are, but probably don't have the conscience you have." She looked up at him, frowning. "So far, Carlie hasn't allowed them the chance to appease their curiosity."

"What about Carlie? Doesn't she get curious?"

"Carlie?" Brenda fidgeted with her hair, looking away from Tyler. "Naw. She just isn't interested anymore. Like her clothes, she thinks spending a lot of time on a social life is a waste of perfectly good brain waves."

Tyler grinned. "I can hear her saying that." He glanced at his watch again, then asked quickly, "So you knew her in school?"

"Carlie and I have known each other for years. Without her help, I'd never have made it through college."

Tyler was silent a moment, acknowledging Brenda's words. "Carlie's like a mother hen, isn't she? She *likes* helping people."

"Yeah. That's Carlie, all right."

Nodding in satisfaction, Tyler left, late for his appointment. His trip to his sister-in-law's had been spontaneous. Carlie had refused to see him again except at practice, claiming she had too many papers to grade and a big test to prepare. He'd missed her.

Carlie seemed to have an innate rapport with children. When he was younger, he'd thought it was only his mother who didn't like and understand kids. Women, in general, were supposed to be maternal, he'd thought. But as he'd matured, he'd learned exactly how wrong he could be.

His mother hadn't wanted him or Jason because they hampered her life-style, which basically meant they curtailed her sexual freedom. At least she claimed they did. Tyler could never recall his presence slowing her down.

From a very young age, he'd known what women did with men. He'd *seen* what women did with men. His mother hadn't been circumspect. His mother hadn't been much of a mother.

And since then, he'd met too many women who seemed to share her sentiments. Life was for enjoying; as long as you had money and looks and prestige. It was a life-style most women sought, with no place for kids. Children interfered with careers or ruined otherwise perfect figures.

He would probably never have any children of his own.

His life wasn't conducive to raising kids. And he would never cheat a child of the warmth and love they deserved. Children should enrich life; they should be cherished and protected, not considered a burden to be tolerated.

An image of Carlie, married and cradling a baby of her own, flitted through his mind. It left behind conflicting emotions; tenderness, because he knew she would be an excellent mother. But also possessiveness, which made no sense at all. He refused to dwell on that sentiment, and put the image firmly from his mind.

It disturbed him, how much she occupied his thoughts. Especially when he had other things to think about. He wouldn't give up on the mystery woman—he wasn't a man to leave a puzzle unsolved. But time and again, he found his thoughts veering to Carlie and her unusual wit, the gentleness and patience she gave her students.

Anyone who took the time to really know Carlie, would realize there was nothing plain about her, despite the horrendous clothing she wore. She was about as complex and complicated as any female could be. He hadn't exaggerated when he said she intrigued him.

Though he knew she'd had a good time with him, she had refused any future dates. She didn't return his calls, either. He would almost swear she was avoiding him, but why?

He would take his time, and sooner or later he would figure her out.

He intended to enjoy every minute.

Chapter Six

CARLIE SAW TYLER'S car pull up to the curb in front of Brenda's. His arrival was unexpected, and she went perfectly still. He jerked the car into Park, then jumped out, appearing determined—more than determined, if the look on his face was any indication. He disappeared past the window, then came to the kitchen door.

He knocked sharply, once, then stepped inside without waiting for an answer. Brenda met him there, her hands on her hips, blocking his vision of the kitchen table where Carlie sat.

"Tyler! What are you doing here?"

"I insist you tell me who she is."

"Who?"

He gave her a look of impatience. "Enough, Brenda. You know who I mean. The harem girl. Who is she?"

Brenda rolled her eyes. "For the last time, Tyler. No!"

Carlie wanted to disappear. It was a miserable Sunday morning, aptly suiting her mood. She'd come to Brenda's for solace, her emotions in turmoil. Nothing was as it had been only days before. She didn't know what to think, what to do. She'd learned so much lately. Too much.

One thing was certain: she couldn't just look at her experience with Tyler as a sexual lesson. Her one "date" with him had proven that. Tyler had touched more than her body. He'd thrown away the misconceptions she'd had about herself, stolen her fears and her disappointments.

And now that she saw him nearly every day, she feared he might very well steal her heart.

She couldn't let that happen. She needed time to think, to reason out her reactions. But here was Tyler, wanting to know who she really was. It was too ironic to bear.

"Your friends are something else, Bren. They're driving me crazy." He ran his hands roughly through his hair, the gesture filled with frustration.

"Friends?"

"Don't sound so innocent. First the harem girl refuses to tell me who she is. Then Carlie refuses to return my calls. I ask her out, and all she can say is no. I swear, that woman is totally—"

Brenda interrupted him then, clearing her throat loudly and gesturing with her eyes to draw his attention to the kitchen table. He looked, and Carlie saw his beautiful eyes narrow slightly.

His annoyance seemed to disappear; he became almost cheerful. "What the hell's the matter with you? You look awful."

After shooting him a disgusted frown, she turned away. "I have a cold," Carlie said. She sincerely hoped he wouldn't question her further, because her swollen, sleepy eyes had little to do with illness.

"And that made your hair all frizzy?"

"No, that didn't make my hair all frizzy." She mimicked

him perfectly. "I jogged over here in the rain, and the rain makes my hair go frizzy."

Tyler scrutinized her. "You just said you had a cold! Why the hell were you out in the rain?"

"I jog every Sunday. Why should today be any different? A little rain never killed anyone." She knew she was being more waspish than usual, but she hadn't planned on having to face him this morning. Her heart ached, and her head followed suit.

"No. Rain doesn't kill, it just makes some people's hair go frizzy." Tyler grinned. "At least a few strands found the excuse to escape that infernal braid. It's probably a hair rebellion."

He laughed at his own jest, and Carlie stiffened at the sound. She pushed her glasses up, then lifted her chin. "Maybe I should go now, Bren. Tyler obviously has something he wants to discuss with you. And I'd hate to get stuck in the downpour, anyway."

Brenda smacked Tyler, then hurried to Carlie. "Don't go, yet. We haven't finished...talking."

"Yeah, Carlie." Tyler pulled out a chair and straddled it, facing Carlie with a huge grin. "I probably won't get any information out of Brenda, anyway. She's looking very stubborn, don't you think?" Then he turned to Brenda. "But you and I will talk later."

"It won't do you any good. I already told you I'm sworn to secrecy."

Exasperated, he looked at Carlie pointedly. "Do you really want to discuss my personal life in front of company?"

Brenda scoffed. "Carlie isn't company."

"Gee, thanks, Bren," Carlie said.

"You know what I mean, Carlie. Besides, I'm sure you couldn't care less about Tyler's love life. Right?"

Carlie tightened her mouth, feeling caught in a nightmare. Brenda was trying to tease; she still wanted Carlie to tell Tyler the truth. Only Brenda didn't know what the truth was, and Carlie had no doubt she'd be shocked if she did. For that matter, Tyler would be shocked, too. And probably disappointed. Carlie couldn't bear that. "You're right. I don't care to sit through any details. So—" she stood "—I'm off."

Tyler caught her wrist. "You can't walk home, now. It's raining."

"Believe me, it won't bother me a bit."

"Now, Carlie, don't be obstinate."

"Tyler, I'm dangerously close to laying you low." She had to get away from him. Now.

"Violence? My, my, your cold is making you surly."

She tugged, but he didn't release her. "Tyler, what did you intend to do today, before you came here and decided to harass me?"

"I was going to harass Brenda, but you'll do better."

She could feel the warmth of his hand on her arm, feel the probing intensity of his eyes. "Let go. I want to leave."

Tyler looked down at his hand, still wrapped around Carlie's wrist. She saw what he saw. His fingers entirely encircled her. She had slim, fine-boned wrists. He said, "You've been avoiding me."

Her breath caught somewhere in her diaphragm, causing her chest to ache. It took a great deal of effort to banter with him. "I've been busy. And why are you calling me on a weekend, anyway? Surely your social calendar is fully penciled in."

He flashed her a grin. "No, and there were numerous disappointed ladies, I can tell you."

She knew him well enough now to know he was only baiting her. He wasn't nearly the egomaniac he pretended to be. A reluctant smile curved her lips. "Tyler, quit fooling around. Let go."

"Not until you promise to help entertain me. Let's do something, go someplace. I'm bored and despondent. I need company."

"Despondent?" He was charm personified, and much too appealing. It was strange, but not only had she played the part of two different women, she *felt* like two different women. Tyler was managing to lighten her mood, even though he was the cause of her foul disposition in the first place.

"That's right. And with good reason." He grinned at Brenda. "I got shunned by someone at Bren's party the other night, and now she won't tell me who the woman is."

With a theatrical gasp meant to cover her uneasiness with the topic, Carlie stared. "No! It can't be true."

"Sadly, it is. I fell in love, and the wench dumped me."

The words had obviously been said as a jest, but still Carlie jerked. Brenda said quickly, "He…he met a friend of mine during the party. They seemed to hit it off, but…she doesn't want to see him again. Ever." She ended with a shrug.

"Just tell me who she is, Bren. I can handle the rest."

Wanting to play her part properly, Carlie asked with laudable suspicion, "You don't know who she is?"

"Absurd, isn't it? But she refused to remove her mask, just so I wouldn't know who she was."

Carlie struggled to relax her tense muscles. "Smart girl."

"Oh, she wasn't a girl." He gave her a taunting smile, obviously irritated with her snide comment. "She was very much a woman. A damned sexy woman." He turned to Brenda, a mocking plea in his eyes. "Please! Tell me who she is. I promise you, she'll thank you later."

Brenda grinned at his woeful expression. "I don't know. What do you think, Carlie?"

Carlie would certainly strangle Brenda later. She cleared her throat. "I think if a woman had enough sense to avoid getting involved with Tyler, you should respect her wishes."

Tyler lost his smile, then said, his words deliberately precise, "There you go again, casting aspersions on my character. What makes you think you know so much about me, Carlie?" She tried to tug free, but he tightened his hold. "I've never coerced a woman into a relationship—other than you, of course, but that's a different matter, isn't it? Usually, the women are trying to coerce me. And they're up-front about it. They say what *they* want, what *they* need out of a relationship, and undying devotion isn't on top of their list. Now, that would make me the used, not the user, wouldn't you say?"

"No, I wouldn't. I have no interest in commenting on your exploits one way or the other."

"But you do often enough."

"Then I apologize." She stared down at his hand, still grasping her wrist. Her heart was thundering so rapidly, she could barely breathe. She'd never seen Tyler so intense, so direct about his private life. Maybe she had been misjudging him. It was something she needed to think about in the quiet of her own home. "Now, if you'll turn me loose, I'll get out of your hair."

His mood seemed to switch mercury quick. "But I want you in my hair today. Haven't you been paying attention? Even though you're wearing the most disgusting outfit I've even seen on man, woman or beast, I still want your company." He hesitated, then asked reluctantly, "Where did you find that, anyway? Surely there isn't a store that actually sold you that thing?"

Carlie looked down at her khaki green nylon jogging suit. It was lined and very warm. She was wearing a gray sweatshirt underneath.

"I wasn't trying to be fashionable, Tyler. I was jogging. In the rain, not on a runway. What does it matter how I look?"

She gave one final yank and freed her arm, then headed for the kitchen door. "I'll call you later, Bren."

Carlie hurried out the door, then jogged away in a loose-limbed stride, feeling the rain immediately soak her hair and drip down her face. She was nearly a block away, when Tyler caught up with her.

He pulled his car up to the curb and rolled down his window. "Hello, Carlie."

Without looking his way, she said plainly, "Go away."

He drove slowly, keeping pace with her. She ignored him. "You know, Brenda said I hurt your feelings."

That effectively stopped her. "Not on your best day, with your best shot."

"Then why are you so ill-tempered today?"

"Me! What about you?"

"I asked first."

Carlie briefly considered her options, then decided on one truth she could share. "I'm concerned about one of the children at school. His father's in the hospital, and it doesn't look good. When I called yesterday, their phone had been shut off."

They had both stopped. Tyler lowered his head. "That's rough."

"Yes, it is. I wish I knew some way to help."

"Maybe I can help."

"How?"

"I don't know. Let me think about it, all right?"

Carlie started off again. "Fine. And while you're doing that, leave me alone."

He shook his head sadly. "Can't. I told you. I'm despondent." Then in a clear pleading tone, he added, "I need you, Carlie."

Water dripped down her nose. She blinked at him, feeling her heart jump several beats and her throat go dry. He was a cad, a beautiful cad, but still, she couldn't give herself away. So she laughed. Hard.

"You're a cold, cruel woman."

She laughed again for good measure.

"Come on, Carlie. Get in before you get too wet. I don't want you to ruin my seat covers."

"I'm already soaked to the bone, Tyler. And you have leather seats. I would surely ruin them."

"I'll forgive you. I promise."

She could feel herself weakening against his insistence. "You really want company so badly?"

"No. I really want *your* company. You're good for my ego."

"Then I must be slipping."

Tyler got out and went to the passenger door. He opened it with a flourish, bowing for her to enter.

Carlie gave in gracefully. She realized that she didn't have it in her to deny him. She wanted his company too much. Already, she felt more buoyant, more alive. He didn't treat her like any other man she knew. He was honest with her. She knew where he was coming from and what he was thinking. She could trust him.

Tyler hurried back around the car and slid in behind the wheel. He sighed, then turned to grin at Carlie. "I'll take you home to change before we go to a movie."

"When did I agree to see a movie?"

"You will, won't you?"

Carlie waited a moment, then asked with a degree of curiosity and disbelief, "You're really bothered that this woman walked out on you?"

He didn't answer right away, and she prompted, "Tyler?"

"I liked her. So, yeah, it bothers me. We...well, things just really clicked. It was like I knew her already, you know?"

"But you see a lot of women."

He didn't dispute that, but he didn't confirm it, either. Again, she wondered if she'd misjudged him.

"What about you, Carlie? Have you ever met anyone that really felt *right* from the very beginning?"

"Brenda and I were instant friends, even though we're so different."

"That's not exactly what I meant, and you know it."

No, she knew what he meant, but she couldn't very well confide in him about her lack of a love life, about a lack of love, period. Until that night in the pool house, she hadn't believed she would ever enjoy the sexual side of a relationship. "I was married once. But things didn't work out."

She jumped when Tyler reached across the seat and took her hand. "Tell me what happened."

"No. Let it suffice to say, I was young and foolish and made some dumb mistakes. End of story."

"You must have been hurt."

A nervous laugh escaped her, and she covered her mouth with her hand. He'd said similar words at the pool house. She was playing a dangerous game, and it was wearing on her.

Tyler frowned at her. "Was that funny? I think I missed the punch line."

She shook her head. "No, I'm sorry. It's just...yes, I felt bad about it at the time. But as you can see, I got over it. Don't worry about it, okay?"

His hand tightened on hers, and he appeared disgruntled. "You know, you should probably be really careful about hooking up with anyone again. I mean, guys can really take advantage. You deserve to be treated special."

Carlie looked at him questioningly, seeing that he was agitated, but not understanding why. He smiled.

"You want to go home first to change and get dried off?" he asked.

"Yes. But you should know right now, Tyler, you won't like my change of clothes any better than you like this outfit. I refuse to dress up on Sundays. It's my day off, a day for comfort." And besides, the sloppier she looked, the less likely Tyler was to recognize her. Not that he had the slightest suspicion now.

"Fair enough. But can I at least request you avoid shades of green? It makes my stomach churn."

Carlie flashed a crooked grin. "I'll see what I can do."

"Ah, just what I like. A submissive woman."

That comment earned him a playful smack.

After they reached Carlie's house, she disappeared into her bedroom to change and Tyler nosed around her living room. Carlie emerged minutes later, her hair only slightly damp and combed into place, her wet jogging suit replaced with a dry one. It was blue, and hopefully less objectionable, at least in color; the fit was still very loose and concealing.

A short while later, they were back in the car, on their way to Tyler's house. The storm intensified, covering the streets with debris and filling the car with a steady drone of raindrops hitting the roof, interspersed with rumbling thunder. Carlie was relaxed in her seat, unconcerned with the weather.

"The storm doesn't bother you?"

She lazily swiveled her head toward Tyler, not raising it from the back of the seat. She was exhausted from too little sleep, and mind-weary from fretting about things she had no control over. "I love storms."

He grinned. "I should have known better than to think they would frighten you."

She smiled, her eyes still on his profile. "When I was a little girl, I used to sit on the porch and listen. The rain would blow under the overhang, wetting my legs and sometimes my face. But the smells…so clean and fresh. I've always thought of storms as being peaceful, despite their noise."

Tyler glanced at her, his eyes drifting over her face. He grinned teasingly. "I've always thought storms were sexy."

Carlie's heart jerked, memories of the storm the night they'd spent at the pool house flooding into her memory. She cleared her throat, but still her words emerged as a dry croak. "Is that right?"

He laughed. "Hmm. They have one hell of an effect on me."

"Good grief." Carlie had to joke to cover the heat that surged through her. A vivid mental picture had surfaced with his words, and she had to rely on wit to hide her feelings. "You won't embarrass me by attacking some poor, unsuspecting female at the movies, will you?"

His grin was wicked. "You're not concerned for your own safety?"

She snorted.

"You do that really well, you know? I don't think I've ever heard another female snort with quite your flair. It's very descriptive."

"Thank you."

Tyler laughed at her dry tone, then shot her a narrow-eyed look. "Have you ever made love during a storm?"

Forcing herself to breathe normally, Carlie peeked at him, then quickly looked away. She felt hot from the inside out, her skin tingling, her stomach coiling tight. *She had to lie.* She shook her head, then realizing he was watching the road, she whispered, "No."

That should have ended it, but she couldn't stop herself from asking, still in a whisper, "Have you?"

Tyler glanced at her again, his look unreadable. His words were quiet and carefully measured. "I thought you didn't want any details on my exploits."

She felt disgruntled by his evasion after she'd summoned up the nerve to ask. "No details. Just a statement. Yes or no?"

He stared straight ahead. "Yeah." He sighed. "Yeah, I have."

Carlie turned away. His husky tone nearly melted her, and she said without thinking, "It would probably be nice."

Tyler's eyes skipped quickly to Carlie and then back to the road again. "Carlie?"

"Hmm?"

Her head was laid back against the seat, her eyes closed. She could never have another sexual interlude with Tyler, but just being with him was nice, too. Maybe she should let that be enough, she thought. Maybe she should try to relax and enjoy her time with him, even though it was risky.

She didn't see his incredulous expression, or the way he was watching her.

"Carlie, did you mean you thought it would be 'nice' to make love to *me* during a storm?"

Her eyes shot wide open, her relaxed position shot to hell. She felt tense from her toes to her eyebrows, her heart going into spasms. She peered at Tyler, totally speechless.

They stopped at a traffic light and he turned to face her, bracing one arm on the back of the seat. "Well?"

Her laugh sounded a bit forced. "I didn't mean you specifically. I meant...the storm in general. Someone who really enjoyed sex would like it in this kind of weather." She was babbling, but she couldn't seem to stop.

His gaze was disturbingly intent. "You don't enjoy lovemaking?"

"I never said that!" She was flustered and had to struggle to keep from looking away. "I just meant there are a lot of people who don't. But someone like you, someone who appears, by all accounts, to like it very much, probably would enjoy it during a storm. I...I think I would, just because I love storms, I mean."

Carlie ground to a painful halt, her rambling finally at an

end. Tyler stared at her, and Carlie didn't want to know what he was thinking.

He cleared his throat, but the words came out sounding husky. "You should definitely try it sometime."

Conversation, after that bit of advice, was nil. When they arrived at the video-rental store, Carlie gaped. "What are we doing?"

"Renting a movie."

Uh-oh. "Renting a movie, to watch...where?"

Tyler shot her a grin. "My place. You said you didn't want to dress up, so I thought you'd be more comfortable at home."

Her home, maybe. Not this. She didn't want to go to his...

"Wait here, and I'll run in and get it. No reason for both of us to get soaked."

Carlie sat in his car, stupefied. How could she refuse without looking ridiculous? How could she explain the difference between being in a crowded theater and being *alone* with Tyler?

She was still pondering that problem when he returned, the DVD tucked inside his jacket, his dark hair glistening from the rain. "All set." He took his seat and started the car. "You're gonna love this movie."

She had her doubts.

There was an underground garage at Tyler's building, so they didn't get wet going in. Carlie walked slowly, hesitant to enter his private domain. But, like his office, Tyler's home was fairly generic. It was large, with a fantastic view, and very tastefully decorated. But everything looked... cold and impersonal. He explained it was a furnished apartment, and a cleaning crew came in weekly.

Carlie thought that was a sad way to live.

Tyler must have picked up on her sentiments, because he said, "Not exactly 'home sweet home,' is it?"

"If you don't like it, why did you move here?"

He shrugged, looking around the apartment. "When I was a kid, we lived in a dirty little hellhole with ratty furniture and peeling paint. I decided that when I picked a place of my own, I'd make sure it was nice." He shook his head. "At the time, I suppose I thought this place was nice." He winked at Carlie. "But I like your house much better."

She grinned. "Thank you. I like my house, too. I picked it because it's small. Grandfather had a huge old farmhouse. It was always cold and empty. I hated it."

"You said your parents died when you were young. Your grandfather raised you?"

Carlie nodded, but looked away. "My brother was already old enough to be on his own, and I didn't see him much. It was just me and Granddad."

"Were you lonely?"

"I suppose." Then she changed the subject. Talk of her childhood always made her melancholy. "So, are we going to start this movie or not?"

Tyler took her hand, gave it a soft squeeze, then left the room. After fetching colas and pretzels from a sterile kitchen, he turned off most of the lights. "A scary movie has to be watched in the dark...for effect."

Carlie relaxed, settling herself into the soft leather sofa. "I know why you wanted to come here to watch the movie." She waved a finger at him. "You didn't want witnesses when you get scared and start screaming."

"Perceptive girl." After putting in the DVD, Tyler took his seat next to Carlie. He sat very close, his damp hair pushed back from his face, his long legs stretched out.

Unexpectedly, Carlie leaned toward him and nudged him with her shoulder. "You're all right, Tyler."

He stared at her, grinning crookedly and looking very pleased by her offhand compliment.

He gently touched her cheek. "I'm glad you think so."

It was such an easy and natural thing to do. She leaned into his hand, and his fingers found a stray wisp of hair escaped over her temple. He toyed with it, running it through his fingers, then giving her a gentle tug.

He could make her stomach flip with just a word or a look, but he also made her feel accepted, made her a part of things in a way she'd never been. Being raised by her grandfather had left her sheltered but alone. Brenda had been her first real friend.

Now she had Tyler, too.

"I like you, Tyler. I'm…really glad we're friends."

"I am, too. Though I'll admit, I've never been just friends with a woman before." He tucked her hair behind her ear. "And by the way, this is another date. Try to remember the rules."

She immediately put on her best vacant expression, removed her glasses and batted her eyelashes. "Tyler," she whined, looking pathetically vulnerable, "I'm scared of the dark. Hold me."

He grinned and reached for her. She promptly shoved him back into his seat. "You've got the basics down right, but you're supposed to be clinging to me right about now."

"You big coward." She shook her head at him. "You better control yourself during this movie, Tyler. I mean it. Date or no date, I don't want you crawling all over me just because you chose a movie you couldn't handle."

He smiled slyly, apparently enjoying himself. "Did I tell you, I've seen this movie before? I'd be willing to wager that about halfway through, *you'll* be crawling all over *me*."

"I'll take that bet." She grabbed his hand and pumped it. "What will you give me when you lose?"

"I won't lose. You will. Then you'll invite me over for another home-cooked meal. Agreed?"

"Fine. But when *I* win? What do I get?"

"A kiss?"

"Ha! Why play if the stakes aren't worth much?"

"You're saying my kisses aren't to be devoutly sought?"

"Not by Carlie McDaniels."

"Carlie, Carlie. You've already forgotten that this is a date. You should have been more determined to win, with a kiss as the prize."

Carlie twisted her lips into a wry smile. "How about you help me grade tests next Friday night when you lose? You're college-educated. You could probably handle third-grade math."

"I would, of course, endeavor to do my best—if I lost, which I won't. Now, hush, the movie is about to start."

The picture began with a bloodcurdling scream, then continued with screams for quite some time. Ten minutes into the movie, Carlie was glaring at Tyler. "This is awful!"

"I know. Don't you love it?"

"Oh, I don't believe this! They almost die at the hands of a monstrous alien, and now, while hiding in a dark, dank hole, they're getting aroused?"

Tyler put his arm around her, reacting with world-weary logic. "These things happen."

"Good grief!" Her eyes were glued to the picture. "From blood and guts to pornography! It's obscene."

Halfway through the movie, Carlie was watching through her fingers, her hands covering her face. She was leaning toward Tyler, or he was pulling her close, she wasn't sure which.

But she liked it. Tyler kept smoothing his hand over her shoulder, not paying the least attention to the movie. When she gasped and moved close to him again, his arm tightened, instinctively offering her comfort.

He was unbelievably hard and warm. And he smelled good, like the storm outside, fresh and alive and very male. She wanted to cuddle closer, to turn her nose into his chest and breathe deeply of his unique scent.

Instead, she forced herself to pull away slightly.

Tyler refused to let her move too far. He turned her chin toward him. "You about ready to give up and crawl into my lap?"

"Very nearly," she whispered back, seeing the glimmer of his dark eyes in the dim light. She could feel the firm, un-yielding muscles of his upper arm pressing into her breast, and there was a strange tension in the air. Carlie wondered if Tyler felt it, too. Probably not.

She was beginning to accept how easily he could make her react to him. She'd never had the problem with any other man, and in fact, had been repulsed when they'd tried to become romantic. But not so with Tyler. He could easily infuriate her one minute, make her laugh the next, then fill her with sensual heat with only his smile.

But he didn't want her. He wanted a masked harem girl.

Suddenly, there was a particularly grotesque scene, accompanied by a blast of startling noise. Carlie launched herself against Tyler in reflex, and he pressed her face into his throat. Just as she turned her gaze back to the screen, she felt Tyler's lips skim her temple.

She went perfectly still, unable to believe what had just happened, wondering if she'd imagined the fleeting touch. But then she felt his breath, warm and gentle on her cheek, and the feel of his lips on her skin again, tentative and soft. He sighed quietly into her ear, sending ripples of sensation over her skin.

Oblivious to the movie, Carlie shuddered with the shock

of the erotic kiss. He lightly circled the rim of her ear with the tip of his tongue, then delicately slipped his tongue inside, teasing her with a leisurely attentiveness to detail.

Softly, with consternation, she asked, "Tyler?"

"Hmm?" He was laving her ear, tracing the swirls, his breath warm and moist.

"What...exactly...are you doing?"

"Exactly?" He asked the question against her temple, his voice husky and low. "Putting my tongue in your ear."

Carlie pulled back, incredulous at the easy way he made that confession. "You're putting your tongue in *my* ear?"

Tyler stared at her, his dark eyes appearing almost black in the dim shadows. "Well...yes."

"Whatever for?"

"You, ah, didn't like it?"

Carlie searched his face, unable to tell if he was being serious or clowning around again. She thought it must surely be another of his jokes, like the lessons in dating. "I don't know. I suppose you took me by surprise. I thought this was to be strictly platonic."

He shrugged, totally unconcerned. "I love women's ears. Yours are very nice."

Carlie opened her mouth, but then closed it again. He was playing with her, and she didn't like it. "I'm not at all certain you should be doing this, Tyler."

He ignored her vague protest. "I want to know if you liked it, Carlie."

"Why?"

"Most women have sensitive ears. I just—"

"No. I mean, why me? Why should you care if I liked it?"

"Curiosity?"

She frowned at him a moment, struggling to hide her disappointment. She shouldn't have asked, and now she wished she hadn't. Turning back to the movie, she pushed on her glasses. "I think it would be best if we forgot the idle curiosity."

"Aren't you just a little curious, too, Carlie?"

His insistence annoyed her. "I'm curious about a lot of things, Tyler. But sometimes curiosity is better left unappeased." She refused to look at him again, overwhelmed with uncertainty.

"I didn't mean to upset you."

"You didn't."

"You provoked me, you know."

She slanted him a quick look of exasperation, pretending a great interest in the movie. "I did no such thing."

"Sure you did. You crawled, just as I said you would, into my lap. I'm only a man, Carlie."

She gave him her full attention. He was behaving exactly like the cad she'd accused him of being, flirting with her simply because she was female and available. What other reason could there be? "Were you this pushy with your lady friend from the party?"

Tyler rubbed a hand over his face, then stared at Carlie in chagrin. "You know, as incredible as it seems, I'd all but forgotten about that little incident. I don't think I'll thank you for reminding me." He looked away from her, then said, "I knew you'd help me forget the mystery woman's desertion, but I didn't think you'd deliberately bring it up again."

"This morning, you acted as if you had to know who she was. How could you forget about her so easily, anyway?" As soon as she'd asked the question, Carlie wondered if she was losing it. She was purposely treading on very dangerous ground.

"You don't want to hear about my conquests, remember?"

"Ah, so it was a conquest. Not that I'd ever doubted otherwise, given your reputation. But it is unfortunate the lady was masked, don't you think? Otherwise, it might have been her here now, and I'm sure she'd be more appreciative of your charms than I am."

Tyler caught Carlie's hand, demanding her attention. "It isn't like that, Carlie. I—"

His innocent look of confusion infuriated her. "Isn't like what? I like you, Tyler, I really do. But I don't appreciate being treated like a fool. Does it make you feel macho to come on to every woman you meet, even those you don't really want?"

Tyler looked startled by her anger. He visibly collected himself. "I like you as a friend, too. More than I've ever liked a woman. I feel completely at ease with you. And I'm not 'playing' with you, Carlie. You're a woman. That's an irrevocable fact. I can't help being—"

"Don't you dare tell me again that you're *curious!*"

His hand came up to cradle her cheek. Smiling slightly, he said simply, "Then you'll have to stop being so unique, so intelligent and witty and fun to be with."

"So." Carlie tightened her mouth, and moved out of his reach. "What about your masked lady? Have you given up on finding her?"

She could see the frustration that replaced his smile. "I don't know." He gave her another smile and shrugged. "You know, I'd never met a woman who could so easily confuse me, and now I've met two. Not really sporting, is it?"

"Tyler…"

"Shh. Stop fending me off and just relax, okay? I promise not to attack you again. I won't lose my head and have my wicked way with you."

He was back to normal, or what she accepted as normal. When he talked complete nonsense, she was comfortable with his attention. Carlie finally smiled, then playfully slugged

Tyler in the arm before giving her attention back to the movie. "You're impossible."

Carlie wanted to linger once the movie ended, but Tyler didn't invite her to stay, and she didn't know how to ask. It didn't feel as though he was tired of her company, but rather that he was tired of his apartment.

He said, "I'm not here all that often. I only come home to sleep." Then he laughed. "I've probably only used that television a handful of times. But it was fun today, with you."

She berated him all the way home for showing her such an outrageous movie. And then he reminded her she owed him dinner.

"All right, though I don't think you played fair. You'd already seen the movie and knew what to expect."

Tyler grinned. It was still storming, and the driving was slow. The inside of the car was warm and humid and Carlie's hair had once again rebelled. She tried to get the damp tendrils back into place, but gave up after Tyler shook his head at her. He reached across the seat and took her hand with easy familiarity. "I suppose I did have the advantage. So how about I help you grade your papers, anyway? I wouldn't mind."

Carlie smiled. It would probably be best to refuse, but he gave her fingers a gentle squeeze, and she found herself agreeing. "Very sporting of you, Tyler. Thank you."

"You're welcome. And I'll bring dinner. Pizza or something. Okay?"

"Why are you so conciliatory all of a sudden? You're making me very suspicious."

They pulled up in front of Carlie's house. Tyler put the car into Park and turned off the engine, then shifted in his seat to face her. The air, sealed by the heavy rain outside, smelled of damp flesh and wet hair and Tyler, masculine and seductive.

"I meant what I said today, Carlie. I can't recall ever enjoying another person's company as much as I enjoy yours. I like helping the kids and I like the exercise. But I think I like arguing with you most of all. You get riled so easily."

"Arguing with you is my pleasure. And as to the rest, the children and I should thank you. You're making a difference, and we appreciate it." Tyler looked embarrassed by her praise. She knew she shouldn't, even debated with herself for several moments, but she couldn't resist inviting him in. "I don't have anything pressing to do. We could play cards or something."

"I thought that if I sat here in the rain, looking forlorn long enough, you would finally ask."

Carlie indicated the rain lashing the windows. "Are you ready then? We'll have to make a run for it."

Tyler grinned at her. "I'll race you."

They each dashed from the car as the rain pounded them with stinging force. They huddled together, Tyler protectively putting his arm around Carlie, trying to cover her as best he could. Laughing, they nearly tripped each other in their race for the house.

Stumbling onto the front stoop and under the tiny roof, they collapsed against the door. Gasping and winded, with rain dripping from their bodies, they shivered from the chill October air and tried to stifle their laughter.

Carlie pulled off her glasses and swiped at her eyes. She looked at Tyler, then burst out laughing again, falling against his shoulder. "Oh, Tyler, you're soaked!" She reached up and pushed a wet strand of dark hair from his forehead.

Tyler didn't move. She was huddled under his arm, her hair plastered to her skull, her glasses in her hand. He raised a finger and brushed gently against her eyelashes, spiked from the rain. Carlie smiled up at him.

Then his eyes dropped to her lips, and she parted them,

without speaking, without even breathing. The tension was back, nearly choking her now. She ached so badly...

"Carlie?"

His voice was husky. Carlie tried to lean away, but he held her firm. His eyes drifted over her face and she blinked at the tenderness there.

And then he kissed her.

Chapter Seven

CARLIE GASPED AND squirmed against him. The sound of Tyler's breathing was even louder than the rain pelting the roof of the overhang. Carlie felt his tongue touch the seam of her lips, and without conscious decision, she parted them. He groaned low in his throat, held her face between his hands and slanted his mouth over hers, stroking deep inside, imitating the lovemaking she was only recently familiar with. It made her body tingle with remembered heat.

He released her mouth, his lips traveling over her cheek and temple and the bridge of her nose. "Carlie..." He murmured her name wonderingly, over and over again. His hands slid down her shoulders, and one palm ventured forward to cover her breast, rubbing over her nipple with tantalizing expertise.

It was that expertise that brought her to her senses.

Shoving him away, Carlie covered herself with her hands. Tyler stood staring at her, apparently dazed. "Carlie...?"

"You...you..." She couldn't believe what she had almost let happen. Her thoughts were in turmoil, her emotions sensitized, and it was all his fault. "How dare you!"

He frowned, his eyes black with a mixture of passion and frustration. He shook his head the tiniest bit, then growled, "I don't know. I...hell." He turned his back, his hands flexing, but when Carlie began struggling with her keys to unlock the door, he jerked around to face her.

She flinched from the hand he reached toward her. She felt so confused and angry at Tyler for complicating things further, for apparently wanting his mystery woman, but willing to toy with her, as well. She concentrated on the anger, unreasonable as it seemed. "Don't you touch me! You lied!"

"About what?" His shout matched the volume of her words.

"You said you wouldn't attack me!"

"I didn't attack you, dammit! I kissed you. There's a big difference."

"You...you pawed me."

He loomed over her. "I touched your breast. That's all. Your nipples were hard and I saw that and—"

She gasped loudly at his audacity, feeling her face pulse with heat. "It's cold out here, you ass! My...my..."

"Nipples," he supplied, smirking at her.

His attitude infuriated her. "It's because of the cold, certainly not because of you."

"I know that. I'm not stupid to women's bodies. But the sight made me lose my head a little." He suddenly looked solemn, and a little confused himself. "You have very nice breasts, Carlie."

Her heart raced in her chest. "My...my..."

"Breasts!" He stared at her irritably. "They're called breasts, dammit."

"Well, they're none of your business! Keep your opinions to yourself."

"You're repressed," he accused, sounding disgusted with her. "It was no big deal. Forget about it."

No big deal. The words crushed her. And to call her repressed…that was the same label her husband had applied, though she now knew it wasn't true. She had the same feelings as any other woman, but right now, she wished she didn't. Maybe it wouldn't hurt so bad if the accusation was true. She swallowed, staring at Tyler and his dark expression of irritation. "I'd sooner forget you, Tyler Ramsey." And she meant it. "Go home and leave me alone."

Carlie turned, finally unlocking her door. She tried to enter, but Tyler stopped her. "You invited me in."

"I changed my mind."

"We need to talk, Carlie. This isn't going to go away."

"Of course it is. Just as soon as you do."

"No, it's not." He took her arm and forced his way into her house.

Carlie refused to close the door. She was trembling inside and felt ready to snap. She was furious, with herself, with Tyler, with the circumstances. "Get out."

"No. I want to talk to you."

She snorted. "You have a funny way of talking."

"Look, Carlie…" He tried to sound reasonable, but his eyes dropped to her breasts again, almost unintentionally, it seemed. "Let's get dried off. Then we can sort this out."

"There's nothing to sort out. You crossed the line and I don't want you to ever do that again."

"Well, I'm damn well going to do it again, and real soon if you don't get your butt in the other room and find something dry to wear that isn't showing off your…"

She fled the room, and purposely slammed her bedroom door. Hard.

Odious man! Carlie yanked off her sodden clothing, repeatedly shoving her glasses up on the bridge of her nose. And all the while she rained silent curses on Tyler's head. Talk about fickle! First, he claims to be depressed because he's without a date; then, he wants to see the mystery woman again and can't; and then, he makes a move on her, Carlie. She stopped in the process of pulling a thick terry-cloth, floor-length shift over her head.

He'd actually done that—made a pass at her. And he couldn't have been completely toying with her. He'd been affected also, she could see that. Slowly, she sat on the edge of her bed.

Tyler Ramsey wanted Carlie McDaniels? Good grief.

But, her thinking continued, he also wanted her alter ego, the mystery woman, and had already slept with her. *She* knew they were one and the same, but Tyler didn't. Was he only biding his time with her until he could discover the identity of the masked harem girl?

It was equal parts ridiculous and unreasonable, but she was feeling jealous of herself.

She finished dressing, then left the bedroom. Tyler was pacing the living room, his shirt discarded, a towel in his hands as he tried to dry himself off. He'd removed his shoes and socks and had left them by the front door. His jeans were dark, soaked from rain and molded to his thighs and buttocks. Carlie cleared her throat.

Turning, Tyler stared at her. She was nervous, she couldn't help that. Everything had suddenly shifted again, so many changes converging on her all at once. She was at a loss as to how to deal with it all.

His eyes swept over her, from her still-wet hair to her naked feet. He didn't say a word, but held her eyes, his hands hanging from his sides.

"I apologize if I overreacted," she said. "You took me by surprise. I never once suspected you might…"

A reluctant smile curved his mouth. "You acted as if I'd defiled you in some way. Was it really so bad, honey?"

"No." She shook her head, her heavy braid swinging behind her. "But I really don't think getting physical is a good idea. I like being friends with you too much to complicate things. And it wouldn't have the same effect on you—our being... involved—I mean, as it would on me."

He approached her slowly, then stopped in front of her. She lowered her eyes, unable to meet his probing gaze. He crouched slightly to look her in the face. "Carlie. Don't sell yourself short. You can't know how I might react to you."

But she could, because she knew how he'd reacted to the mysterious and provocative harem girl. She was simply Carlie. Plain and boring. "You're used to beautiful women. Tons of them."

"Tons, huh? Well, that's not true." He wrapped the towel around his neck, holding the ends. "I haven't had an ounce of experience with any real relationships. In fact, the only relationship I've ever had that was worth a damn was with my brother. And now Brenda. But that's not what we're talking about, is it? So give me a break here, okay?"

She stared up at him helplessly, and then he cupped her cheek, his thumb stroking her temple. "I like the way we are together, Carlie. We could have a good relationship."

She needed some space. With Tyler standing so close, she could see the water drops still clinging to the dark swirls of hair on his chest. His body was moist from the rain, his muscles slick and smooth. Her nipples tightened again and she stepped away. Space. She definitely needed space.

"Why don't you tell me what you really want, Tyler." She walked into the kitchen as casually as possible and pulled two mugs from the cabinet.

She was filling the glass coffeepot with water, when she felt

Tyler behind her. His hands lifted to her upper arms and he pulled her back against his chest. He murmured against her temple, "I'm not sure. I know I like spending time with you. And I know I'm going to want to kiss you again."

Carlie closed her eyes. "What about other women?"

"What other women?"

"Your masked lady, for one. Are you only wanting to spend time with me until you can convince Bren to give you her name? And if your harem girl wants to see you again, what then?"

She could feel the added tension in the way Tyler's hands gripped her. "You're jumping the gun, Carlie. Hell, I didn't ask you to marry me. I'm not asking for a lifetime commitment."

She pulled away, embarrassment vying with the anger rising within her. He made her sound desperate! "That isn't what I meant, Tyler. I certainly don't aspire to tie you down. I don't aspire to do anything with you. It's just that I know how you are about commitments, and I'm trying to point out that you would only be using me until something better came along. Right now, I like you as a friend. I'm grateful for the time you donate to helping the children. But if you…that is…if we…"

Tyler rolled his eyes in exasperation. "If I made love to you. That *is* what you're trying to say, isn't it?"

"Yes. If we…did that. I'm honest enough to admit my heart might get involved, and then my pride would suffer when you decided to toss me aside. I don't think I could forgive you, and our friendship, which I count more important than a bit of hanky-panky, would be ruined."

She couldn't look at him after that little speech. Instead, she went about setting out cookies and preparing some coffee. She felt like a fraud.

Tyler narrowed his eyes in disbelief. "You're amazing, you

know that? I'm surprised you didn't carry your predictions through to the end of Time. And you forgot to cover a few scenarios. I mean, what if that jerk you told me you used to love suddenly reappeared? Or what if one of your teacher buddies caught your eye? You could ditch me!" He stormed around the kitchen, his hands on his hips, his dark eyebrows lowered in a fierce frown. "I wasn't talking about some time in the distant future, dammit. I was talking about now."

Carlie choked on the sip of coffee she'd just taken. Tyler grumbled and proceeded to pound on her back.

"All right, all right! Don't beat me to death." She sucked in several desperate breaths, then glowered at him incredulously. "You're wanting to...to..."

He rolled his eyes again, and sighed loud enough to rattle the windowpanes. "Make love. It's called making love, Carlie. People have been doing it since the beginning of Time. They'll continue doing it until the end of Time. It's a necessary and enjoyable part of life, you know."

She gave him her patented snort. "I'm not as cavalier as you, Tyler. *I* certainly haven't been doing it." She realized her slip immediately. Tyler was looking at her curiously, and she stammered an explanation. "It isn't necessary. Enjoyable, maybe. But not necessary."

"God save us from liberated women." He advanced on her, and Carlie held her coffee cup between them like an insubstantial shield. Tyler took it from her. "Do you care about me, Carlie?"

"I care about a lot of men. That doesn't mean I want to sleep with them."

He stiffened, and his eyes grew hard. "Who? Who do you care about?"

"Jason, for one."

"My brother?"

"Yes. And several teachers who I've been friends with since I started teaching here. I care about some of the parents I've gotten to know, and a few of my neighbors…"

"Carlie." Tyler laid his finger against her lips. "There's caring, and then there's *caring*."

She nodded. Tyler removed his hand from her mouth, then stroked her cheek. "Tell me you care about me."

"This sounds suspiciously like a seduction routine you've practiced to perfection."

Tyler stepped back, shoving his hands into his pockets. "Obviously, I haven't practiced it enough."

Carlie smiled, her first real smile since he'd kissed her. He looked every bit as confused as she felt. "Tyler, be reasonable. I'm not going to jump into bed with you, just because you suddenly find me strange and interesting."

"I never said—"

"I'm different from other women you know, and the main difference is that I'm *not* trying to wend my way into your bed. You're just stymied, not really aroused. Go home and take a warm bath and you'll feel better in the morning."

He shook his head, being very precise. "I won't."

Carlie chuckled. "Don't pout, Tyler. Surely some woman somewhere has told you no before."

"Not that I would admit to. And just because you're not interested right now, doesn't mean I'll stop being interested. When you get used to the idea and accept it as a fact, you'll see that I was right."

She looked at him suspiciously. "About what?"

Quickly, before she could move away, Tyler bent down and kissed her, hard and fast. "We'll be good together. I'm sure of it. Very good."

That was an already proven fact, but Tyler couldn't know it. She mustered a shaky smile. "Bragging, Mr. Ramsey?"

"No." He stared intently into her eyes. "Making a promise."

Carlie felt the heat building in her stomach. But then Tyler pulled out a seat at the table and sprawled in it. "In the meantime…" He raised his arms and clasped his hands behind his head. "No pressure. You're the best friend I ever recall having. I suppose I can be content with that. For a time."

Carlie felt relief, and quelling disappointment. "Good. Then we can stop all this nonsense and play some cards." She pulled a deck from a drawer and sat across from Tyler.

"What would you like to play?" She looked at Tyler.

"Strip poker?"

Carlie started to rise, her mouth drawn in annoyance, but Tyler stopped her. He was laughing. "Okay, okay. Bad jest. Sorry."

She nodded grudgingly. "So. What should we play?"

With a twinkle in his eyes, he asked innocently, "Old maid?"

She threw the cards at him, then sat there glaring.

"Well, I suppose that decides it." He grinned wryly, a card sitting on top of his head, the rest scattered in his lap and on the floor. "Fifty-two pickup it is."

Tyler tried to keep his mind on the basketball game they were playing, but he couldn't keep his eyes off Carlie. She was trying to treat him the same as always, but he wasn't going to let her get away with it. Everything was different now, the way he felt when he was around her, the effect her smile had on him. She was doing her best to ignore his attention, but there was only ten more minutes before practice was over. Then he'd be going home with her again. That fact had his stomach in knots.

When was the last time he'd so anticipated spending time with a woman?

But Carlie wasn't just any woman. She wasn't impressed by monetary things. In fact, she almost seemed disdainful of them. And she wanted nothing from him, other than companionship and help with a group of children who deserved someone better than him.

He'd thought about that, too, about ways he could help. He'd never given much of himself—money didn't count, because that wasn't him. But for Carlie, for the kids...for himself, he was going to try to make a difference. And he had a plan he hoped would work.

Practice ended, and Tyler found the little boy whose family's phone had been disconnected. He walked him out to his mother's car. After discreetly questioning the woman, Tyler discovered that she used to be a secretary. He casually mentioned that he always had papers that had to be transcribed, and would be glad to have her assistance. When he mentioned what he was willing to pay, and that she could do the work at home, she readily accepted. He arranged to start sending her documents next week.

And in the meantime, he explained a scholarship of sorts he was setting up that would enable her to enroll her children in the extracurricular activities that they'd been forced to drop out of due to lack of funds.

By the time Tyler finished convincing her to take advantage of his offer, he was feeling pretty good. It was a damned nice thing to know you'd been some small help. But when he came back into the gym, he realized instantly that Carlie was disgruntled with him for having excluded her.

Well, that was just too bad. He intended to surprise her when things were settled, and not a moment sooner.

She was ready to leave, her keys in her hand. He realized he hadn't even changed out of his sweaty shirt yet.

"I'll just be a minute," he said, and started toward the

change-room door. She didn't answer, just stood there, tapping her foot. He chuckled. "I know what you're thinking. Curiosity is written all over your face."

She gave him a haughty look, and he prepared himself, knowing he was going to get an earful. "Actually," she said, a slight blush on her cheeks, "I was thinking how...sexy you look right now."

That stopped him. "Is that so?" He advanced slowly, seeing her struggle to stand her ground. "Enough to warrant a kiss?"

She leaned toward him, her expression smug. "Nope."

Tyler reached for her, but she ducked away. "You're a terrible tease, McDaniels!" Then he grinned. "I think I like it."

She was waiting for him to tell her why he'd been outside so long. He knew, and deliberately kept silent. Her mouth pursed, then she asked, "Are you still coming over?"

"Only if you'll give me a kiss. You can't tell a man he's sexy, then just walk away."

She shrugged. "Sure I can."

He grabbed her arm, grinning. "*No.* You can't. Besides, you want to kiss me. You know you do. What are you afraid of?"

Her lips parted, then she drew in a shaky breath, her gaze going to his mouth. "I'm not afraid of anything."

Tyler leaned back, bending his knees so he was looking directly into her eyes. Carlie squirmed, and he knew she was feeling much the same thing he was, even if she denied it. Finally, satisfied by what he saw, Tyler held out his arms. "Okay, if you're not afraid, then give me one kiss. My hands won't move, I promise."

It was a challenge, and he was willing to bet she wouldn't be able to resist. When she placed her hands on his shoulders, he felt his breath catch. When her gaze dropped to his mouth, his muscles clenched.

Going up on tiptoe, she lightly, quickly, brushed her lips over his, then settled back for his reaction.

His mouth twitched with humor. He left his arms out-stretched. "Well? Are you going to kiss me or not, honey? Oh, you mean that little wisp of air that blew over my mouth was your kiss? How disappointing. I thought you could do better than that."

She blinked at him. "You didn't...like it?"

"I have no idea. It was over with before I could decide. Hell, Brenda kisses me better than that. In *front* of Jason."

Her eyebrows lowered and she shoved her glasses higher on the bridge of her nose. Tyler could practically see her mentally hitching up her pants, and he had to fight a smile.

She tightened her hands on his shoulders, and came up again, this time pressing her mouth more firmly to his. Tyler lightly licked her lips, moving his mouth against hers. She went still for a single heartbeat, then accepted his challenge, and returned the gesture. But once her tongue touched him, he drew her inside, and the kiss became ravenous.

He heard her soft moan and instantly grew hard. The game was over. He pressed against her, forcing her to step backward until they reached the wall, then he trapped her there with his body. His hips settled against her groin, rubbing insistently. His mouth now took over, eating at hers, his tongue plunging inside, feeling her own tongue move in a way that made him tremble.

He had to stop. He groaned and raised his mouth. "Damn." His head dropped onto her shoulder, his face turned inward so he could inhale her scent.

He could feel her shaking. His body was laid against the length of her own from shoulders to knees. Her legs were open, accommodating his hips.

His chuckle was wry and filled with wonder. "I asked for that, I suppose." He lifted away from her shoulder, but kept his body close to her. His voice dropped to a whisper. "I want you, Carlie."

She shook her head.

He pressed his hips closer, holding her gaze. "You can feel how much I want you, sweetheart."

She snorted, then pushed him away. "This isn't the eighth grade, Tyler. So you're aroused. So what? It's the same reaction you'd have to any woman you were kissing."

He propped his hands on his hips, feeling his lips twitch with amusement again, despite the ache in his body. "Not quite."

Carlie waved away his rebuttal. "Are you also going to tell me you're in pain? That's next, isn't it?"

"I am in pain." He started toward her. "Your screeching denials are giving me a headache."

"I wasn't screeching! I was only pointing out... Tyler, don't you touch me again!"

He took her by the shoulders, and pulled her body roughly against his. With his nose touching her own, he gently demanded, "Admit you want me, too, Carlie. Now."

She hesitated only a second. "*I do.* It's just that..."

He released her. "I'm willing to give you all the time you need, honey, but..."

She snorted, louder than usual.

Tyler grinned. "Okay, so I've been pushing. I'm having a hard time keeping my hands off you. But you know you can trust me, Carlie. I would never try to force you to do anything you didn't want to do."

He waited, all shreds of humor gone, and finally Carlie nodded. "I know that."

"Good. Then don't keep denying everything I feel. Believe it or not, I want you. You, Carlie, not some other woman, not because you're handy, not because I can't get somebody else."

He stroked her cheek. "You're special, sweetheart. And what I feel for you is special."

Her eyes searched his, and she asked, "And what is it you feel, Tyler?"

He should have known she'd ask. "I'm not sure, yet—and don't snort at me!" He grinned again. "I'm trying to be honest here, Carlie. Be patient with me."

Carlie swiped up her gym bag from the bleachers and headed for the door. Tyler trotted after her. "Am I still invited for dinner?"

She didn't slow her pace. "If that's all you want. Because dinner is all you'll get."

"I promise not to do anything...that you don't want me to do."

He felt smug when her step faltered. But he also felt determined not to rush her. Carlie was worth waiting for, and she evidently needed a lot of reassurance. He could give her time. He could behave himself. It wouldn't be easy, but... He'd never known women could be so different. He'd never known a woman could be like Carlie.

And he no longer cared if he found out who the mystery woman was. Carlie, with her bristly independence and concealing wardrobe, was mystery enough to keep his attention for a long, long time. Maybe even forever.

"Hello?"

"Tyler?"

There was a pause, then, "Who's this?"

"We...ah, *met* at the party..."

Another pause. Carlie waited breathlessly, her hand gripping the receiver so tightly her fingers ached. She had deliberately disguised her voice, but it was shaking so badly, it had probably been an unnecessary measure.

"I didn't expect to hear from you again. Brenda refused to tell me how to reach you."

"I know. I…it has to be that way."

"I'll admit I'm curious to know why."

Traitor, Carlie thought. She was huddled in the middle of her bed, her nightgown twisted around her updrawn knees. Her hair was loose, hanging down to shield her face, which, even though Tyler couldn't see, was burning. "I'm sorry."

"You have no reason to be afraid of me."

"I know. But…"

"You ran out on me."

"Yes." Carlie squeezed her eyes shut. This wasn't going the way she'd planned. She'd convinced herself to call him, hopefully to find out how determined he was to meet the mystery woman or if he even still cared. He claimed to want her… "her" meaning Carlie. But could that be true if he was still intent on meeting another woman? Even if the other woman was herself? But he didn't know that…so…. It was just too confusing. Her brain felt muddled, and she was willing to try anything that might give her some real insight as to how Tyler truly felt about her.

But Tyler wasn't giving her a chance to question him. He was too busy pressing her.

"Tell me who you are." He sounded more annoyed than ever.

"No! I just…wanted to talk to you. To ask…"

"Ask me what?"

Surprised, Carlie accused softly, "You're angry."

"No, I'm frustrated. I don't like games. You're a grown woman. I understand what happened between us was unexpected. You couldn't have been any more surprised than I was. But it's too late to change things now." Then, very persuasively, "Tell me who you are."

Carlie shook her head, as tears gathered in her eyes. If only she could. "No."

"Dammit!"

She squeezed her eyes shut. "Please. Don't be angry." There was a tremor in her voice, and Tyler reacted to it.

"I'm sorry." He sounded almost weary. "We can talk. That's why you called, isn't it?"

Carlie was afraid to speak again. This was a stupid idea. She should hang up now before he figured out who she was.

He said again, "Do you want to talk about it?"

"Maybe you should just forget…"

"Not without knowing."

Those words, said so sincerely, washed over her. Her heart ached. If he wouldn't forget, then she would have to stay away from him entirely. She drew a deep breath, calming herself. "Why?"

It was Tyler's turn to be thoughtfully silent. "It was different. You were different. More intense. It didn't seem like just sex."

"No." It had been more, at least for her.

"You felt it, too?" he asked.

"I did."

"I want to meet you. I want to know who you are. Stop playing games."

"It's…it's not a game," she said. "You would be angry…"

"I'm angry now! This isn't the eighth grade, dammit!"

Carlie jumped at his raised voice. He'd unconsciously repeated her defense. It seemed like a betrayal. "Aren't you seeing anyone else?"

She hadn't meant to ask that. This wasn't a test he had to pass. She'd only wanted to understand why he was so determined to find her. But it was too late to call back the words.

She could feel his frustration, it was so keen. His reply, when it came, was carefully modulated, the words exact. "I'm not intimate with anyone right now, if that's what you mean."

"I see."

"How could you, when I don't? I hate this!" He growled in frustration. "I don't want anything from you! But I hate knowing you might pass me on the street, and I wouldn't even know it. I hate that you have intimate knowledge of me, but I don't even know your name."

Carlie trembled. She hadn't thought of it that way, how it would be for him. She was very sorry. "Tyler, please..."

"You'll see me somewhere and remember. While I'm saying hello, how do you do, you'll be thinking of how it feels to climax with me deep inside you."

His words were harsh now, deliberately taunting, baiting her. He was being ugly, and even while she understood his frustration, she hated it. "*Stop*. Please."

"*Tell me who you are, dammit.*"

"I can't." The words were rushed, husky with need. Carlie had to get them out before she did or said something she'd later regret. "It's impossible. I'm so sorry." Then she added in a tiny whisper, "You were wonderful, Tyler."

"Don't hang up...!"

Very gently, Carlie laid the receiver in the cradle, then curled onto her side. It had been a mistake to call him. She had to stop torturing herself and Tyler. Her heart ached with her decision.

He was right. She was behaving like a teenager with a sorry crush on the captain of the football team. She was leaving him to wonder about a woman who didn't exist. On Friday, when he came over again, she'd tell him. She wouldn't take the coward's way out by sending him a letter or giving her explanation and then running. It would be face-to-face, and she would accept his anger, for he would surely be enraged.

Carlie found sleep impossible that night. She pondered a thousand different ways Tyler might react. But it all came down to one final, irrevocable conclusion.

She had lost him, when she'd never really had him in the first place. And until now, she hadn't fully realized how badly she wanted him.

Chapter Eight

TYLER SET THE pizza on the table, then turned to Carlie. She'd been quiet, too damned quiet, all day. He caught her as she walked by to set the table.

He pulled her into his arms. She was more rigid than usual. "I missed you, Carlie. How about a hug?"

Her arms remained at her sides, and she looked beyond him. He was stymied. "What is it? Are you mad at me about something?"

"No, I'm not mad."

"Then what is it?" He bent to look into her eyes. "You can at least give me a hug, can't you?"

She did as he asked, but it was a measly effort at best. Tyler let his hands drift down her back, and realized suddenly that it was the first time he'd ever done so. Her back was narrow, her flesh firm, and her waist tapered in. His hands started to explore there, but she pulled away. He touched her chin, seeking her eyes again. "What is it?"

"We need to talk." She peered up at him, her eyebrows

lowered in a nervous frown, and shook her head. "But later, after we eat."

"Ah, intrigue. You don't have to work at keeping my interest, you know. I'm already caught."

Carlie slapped a huge piece of pizza onto his plate, splattering tomato sauce over the table.

Tyler raised his eyebrows. "You are entertaining, Carlie. When we don't have practice, I have nothing to look forward to at the end of the day. I think of you, though."

Carlie stopped in the middle of pouring the wine. She turned to Tyler, her expression serious. "Why?"

"What do you mean, 'why?' I like you."

"But *why,* Tyler? What is it about me that you like?"

He considered her question with grave seriousness. She was being very sober. His answer obviously mattered a great deal to her. The first thing that came to his mind was her honesty. "I can trust you. You don't play games, and I don't think you would ever lie to me. You're straightforward and genuine, blunt to a fault. I've never known a woman like you before."

Carlie looked stricken, which wasn't the reaction he had expected. She crossed her arms over her chest and turned away. He walked up behind her and wrapped her in his arms, holding her close despite her stiffness. He still felt frustrated and angry over his mysterious phone call, and now, with Carlie seeming so intent on separating herself from him, he actually felt needy. It wasn't a feeling he enjoyed.

"Carlie, talk to me. I don't like this. I'm used to you giving me hell and making me laugh and then making me so hot I can't breathe. I'm not used to this silence, sweetheart."

She turned abruptly, throwing her arms tight around him and he groaned in relief. His arms were around her middle, and it registered, rather abruptly, that she was actually slim. She was wearing her usual basketball clothes that consisted of baggy sweats, and since the day was cooler, she was layered under several pieces. But his hands were stroking up and down her ribs, and it amazed him how tiny her waist was. He pulled back, shocked.

Carlie was watching him. "Don't even say it."

He was amused by her fierce expression. "What?"

"Whatever you were thinking. I'm not stupid."

"No, you're not stupid. But you are a big faker." His mouth tilted in a quizzical smile. "There's not an ounce of extra fat on you, is there?"

Carlie propped one hand on her hip in an arrogant stance. She glanced down meaningfully at her chest, the implied message very clear.

Tyler choked back his laugh. "That's not fat, sweetheart. That's a bonus from Mother Nature." Then his eyes slid over her, and his amusement slowly disappeared. "I want to see you."

"You're looking right at me."

"You know what I mean."

Warm color bloomed in her cheeks. "Oh? You want me to strip naked and dance on the table perhaps?"

"Damn! You're not as unreasonable as I thought." He pulled out a chair and made a big production of seating himself. "Go ahead. I think I'm ready. Wait! Do you have smelling salts available? I'm not sure my heart can take this."

Carlie stared back at him blandly. Then she pulled out her own chair and sat down. She shoved a glass of wine toward him. "Eat. You need something to occupy that mouth of yours."

"True. But I could think of other...mmm!"

Carlie had jammed the piece of pizza into his mouth without concern for his clean face. He ended up laughing, and wiping pizza sauce from his nose and cheeks.

They ate in near silence but for the music Carlie had playing in the background. Tyler watched her, simply enjoying her nearness. After a moment, the quiet began to bother him. "I meant what I said earlier. About your being different. Until I met you, I thought all women were the same."

"That's an asinine comment unworthy of recognition."

"I know it sounds cynical, but it's true. Most of the women I've known were users. They would lie or mislead, even jump into my bed, just to get what they wanted."

Carlie looked slightly dazed. "What did they want?"

"Marriage, usually. You may not believe this, but I'm considered a prime catch. I'm single, and Jason and I run a successful law practice. I'm financially secure, and I drive a flashy car. That's all the criteria most women require. It wouldn't matter *who* I really was."

"I can't believe that."

"That's because you're just a little naive, honey." He studied her affectionately. "Other than Brenda, no woman has taken the time to really get to know me. Except you."

She searched his face, her eyes bright with curiosity. "What about your mother? Or other relatives?"

"I don't have other relatives. And all my mother ever wanted was for me and Jason to get out of her hair. Most times we did. It didn't matter where we went, as long as we weren't around to interfere in her affairs." He didn't quite meet her gaze, feeling her empathy, and not entirely comfortable with it. Discussing his past was not something he was familiar with.

"Jason was the one who convinced me I could get a degree. And at the time, that was no easy feat. I was so busy indulging in my bad-boy popularity, I'll admit I was something of a punk."

Carlie touched the bridge of his nose. "Brenda told me you broke your nose in a fight."

He sent her a small, brief smile. "Yeah. I did a lot of fighting back then. Mom loved it when I kicked ass. It was the only time she ever gave me any recognition." Tyler was amazed the words were coming so easily. But then, it was always easy to talk to Carlie. "You see, it really didn't matter who I was. It was what I did that was important."

"It always matters, Tyler. If not to someone else, then to yourself."

He was filled with satisfaction. "There, you see? You know that, but no other woman I've ever met has thought so. When Mom took off, and that was some time ago, she couldn't have cared less who I was or what I might become."

Carlie looked down at the remains of her pizza, then tightened her fingers around his hand. "You can't categorize all women based on one, Tyler. That isn't fair."

Tyler laughed wryly. "Don't go getting psychological on me. My mother and her many faults didn't form any lasting impression on me. It's the dozens of women since who've done that. All but you." He lifted her fingers and kissed them. "You, I'm convinced, are incapable of guile."

Carlie jumped to her feet, picked up the plates and carried them to the sink. "I'm just your basic female, Tyler, subject to the same flaws as anyone else. I can make mistakes, I—"

Tyler stood, going to Carlie and taking her face between his hands. She stared up at him, her body taut with apprehension. "You would never hurt me, Carlie. I know you wouldn't."

"You sound so positive."

He smiled as his thumbs stroked her cheeks. "That's because I know you care about me. You grouse and grumble and complain, but you do care, don't you?"

Her gaze was direct and fiercely earnest. "Yes, I do."

He hesitated, his smile disappearing. "A little?"

"A lot, Tyler. A lot."

He ached. She made him feel important to her. And most of all, he believed her. She truly cared for him.

His kiss wasn't meant to seduce, but rather to show tenderness and understanding. "Thank you, Carlie. For caring."

He was still cradling her face, but their bodies weren't touching. Carlie bit her lower lip, then hugged herself to him. Tyler had the awful suspicion she could look into his soul and see his vulnerability. It shook him, and he sought casual conversation to break the mood.

"It was the same for Jason, until he met Brenda. You should have seen him in action. He had women throwing themselves at him, and he seldom ducked to get out of the way. After we opened the law practice, it only got worse. It seemed every client who came in knew someone or was related to someone, or *was* someone, who they thought Jason should get to know intimately. It grew old real quick. He started sending the younger female clients to me."

"And now look how incorrigible you are."

He chuckled. "That's right, honey. Put the blame where it's deserved. I'm just a product of circumstance."

"You're a product of indulgence." Carlie leaned back to smile up at him. "I remember when Brenda went to work for Jason. She said he was gorgeous, charming and entirely insufferable. He tried giving her a bracelet once, you know."

"I remember. She threw it at him. Damned thing was heavy, too. Left a bruise on his shoulder."

"It was at the Christmas party you two had, where she kissed him under the mistletoe. She seemed to float for two days."

"Yeah. I got the load of the cases because Jason was too busy wooing Brenda to bother with anything as trivial as work. She really ran him ragged." And, Tyler thought, he now had a much better understanding of what his brother had gone through. Carlie could tie him up in knots with just a look.

But there was one major difference. Jason loved Brenda, whereas Tyler had no idea exactly what he felt for Carlie.

"She made him chase her until she caught him. But they both enjoyed it, and look how everything turned out." Carlie said the words quietly, with a strange, wistful smile.

"Brenda isn't the type of woman I would have figured Jason to fall for. Don't get me wrong. There's not a better person than Brenda. She's good for Jason, and I love her. But Jason always had a preference for tall, busty sophisticated brunettes. Not short, perky, domesticated redheads."

Carlie darted him a quick look. "I guess you never can tell."

"No." Tyler tilted his head, studying her, and then he agreed. "You never can tell."

Tugging her closer, he watched as her thick lashes lowered behind the lenses of her glasses. She gave a feeble protest when he reached up and removed them from her nose, laying them carefully on the table. "Tyler..."

"You're very pretty, Carlie." He toyed with her braid, dragging his curled fingers over the length of it. He reached the end, felt the cloth-covered rubber band holding the braid secure, and pulled it free. Carlie's eyes widened, but he didn't give her time to stop him.

His fingers sifted through the strands, separating them, then pulling her hair over her shoulders. It rippled with waves, a dozen different colors highlighted by the overhead light. It was beautiful—she was beautiful—and Tyler never felt so needful of anyone in his life.

Bunching her hair into his fists on either side of her head, he pulled her face up to his. "I want you, Carlie."

The kiss was devastating in its intensity, powerfully erotic, and sensually sweet. Her body leaned into him. Tyler walked her backward to the counter, then pressed himself hard against her. He swallowed her gasp and gave his groan in return.

And still he kissed her. He was in no hurry to speed things along. No one had ever tasted so good, so right and so perfect.

His hands moved down her body languidly, exploring, excited by the feel of what he'd never expected, never imagined. She was all full, soft curves, lush. Fine-boned, her arms were slim, her wrists and elbows tiny. Her waist was slight, her soft belly only a marginal curve, very feminine, utterly seductive. His palm lingered there. He heard her shuddered breathing as he stroked her, feeling her muscles quiver.

He palmed her bottom, finding it exquisitely soft and equally firm. He pulled her against his aroused body, rubbing and stroking. Carlie clung to him, and he loved it. He couldn't get enough of her or her response.

"I want to see you, honey."

"No." Her face dipped down and she pressed her lips into his throat. "Please…"

He kissed her again, his tongue thrusting, his breath coming in harsh pants.

"Take me to your bedroom, Carlie." He held her face until she opened her eyes and looked at him. "I'm going to make love to you."

It was inevitable. "Yes."

He threw back his head and closed his eyes for an instant. Then he pulled her from the counter and turned her toward the hallway. "Your bedroom."

She slowed as she neared her bedroom door. "I haven't showered."

"It doesn't matter." Nothing mattered except making her his, completely.

"But we…the basketball…"

Tyler shoved her gently inside, closing the door behind him. The room was in shadows, dim and close and intimate.

It smelled of Carlie, her elusive, feminine scent. He reached for her in the dark. "Believe me, it doesn't matter."

He held her close, one hand caressing her full, lush breasts, finding a stiffened nipple and tugging on it lightly, hearing her groan and then palming her, crushing her soft flesh delicately in his large hand.

"Where's the light?" The question was tinged with his haste, his need.

"No." Carlie threw herself against him. "Not tonight, Tyler. Give me tonight."

He didn't understand her, but he relished her obvious urgency. He forgot the light—there was enough moonlight to illuminate the room with vague, slanted beams of opalescence. The shadows were thick and heavy, but he could see Carlie, could read her expression by the gleam in her beautiful hazel eyes, the wet sheen of her tongue as she flicked it over her lips. Her hands touched his chest tentatively, her fingers kneading the muscles, as inquisitive about his body as he was about hers. They explored each other leisurely, their excitement growing, the air thick with sexual tension. Tyler kept trying to calm himself, to call on his control, but it was nonexistent. He throbbed with need, and he was with Carlie. It was unbelievable.

Carlie kicked out of her sneakers and pulled off her socks as Tyler simultaneously whisked off her sweatshirt. They nearly toppled each other to the floor, but Tyler caught her by the waist and they landed on her bed. The covers billowed around them, soft and fragrant as Tyler's weight pressed Carlie deep into the mattress.

"You feel so good, Carlie." He rubbed against her, but she protested, tugging at his sweatshirt. Going up on his knees, Tyler jerked off the shirt.

An instant later, they were together again, each frantic to

touch the other. Carlie raked her nails gently through the dark, curling hair on his chest.

Tyler reared back, unable to control himself with her innocent, curious touch. He stared down at her partial nudity—a stray beam of moonlight slashed across her breasts, showing them to be milky white and smooth, full and firm. His hands covered her, and she arched into him.

"God, Carlie. I can't believe how you hid yourself. Never again, sweetheart, do you hear me? You're mine now. I won't let you hide from me again."

He lowered his head, unable to wait a moment longer, and caught a nipple, nibbling with his lips, lightly flicking with his tongue.

"Tyler, please..."

"Yes, honey. Soon, soon." His sharp teeth closed on her, carefully tugging, and when she groaned, throwing her head back and turning her face away as she gripped the blankets in fierce pleasure, he tugged again, pulling sweetly, taunting her. Her hands settled in his hair, urging him closer toward her. He drew her in, suckling gently, then hard, until her hips were writhing against him.

He hadn't planned his seduction, didn't have premeditated intentions of devastating her with his finesse. It just didn't occur to him to end the pleasure anytime soon. He'd waited so long, a lifetime, it seemed, for Carlie to be like this with him, and his senses were rioting, his body moving of its own volition.

He was mindless to everything but taking and giving pleasure. And at the moment, hearing Carlie's gasps and soft feminine moans gave him more pleasure than he thought he could endure.

Tyler slid to the side of her, his hand coasting languidly over her midriff and beneath the waistband of her pants to caress her soft belly. Carlie turned to face him. "Tyler, I think I'm going to die."

"No. You won't die, sweetheart." He sat up. "Let me get these other clothes off you."

She was trembling all over, her body taut and aching, and as Tyler slid the pants down her long legs, his fingers touched her, skimming over her soft flesh, teasing the insides of her thighs. He pulled the pants free of her ankles, then sat there at her side, simply looking at her. Restless, her long legs moved in subtle, impatient turns. She looked at him, seeing his gaze so intent on her body, then turned away, her eyes closing, only to look at him again.

"I can see all of you, Carlie, despite the dark." His hand slid down her thigh, stopping at her knees, slowly easing her legs farther apart. She gasped, and he smiled in the moonlight. "I love looking at you, a woman with a woman's body. You have nothing to hide, nothing to be ashamed of."

"I'm...I'm..." Carlie gasped again, not able to get the words out.

His finger sifted through her curls, finding her flesh hot and swollen, wet with need. He wanted to shout with excitement. "You're perfect. Just the way nature intended a woman to be." As he talked, he stroked her, slowly, one finger dipping just inside her, withdrawing when her hips rose sharply.

"Feel how wet you are for me, Carlie." He pressed his finger inside her again, this time deeper, and she groaned, her legs spreading wider without his instruction. Her every move inflamed him, she was so special...yet somehow, it all seemed familiar.

His body rocked with his pounding heartbeat and he bent to press his face into her belly. He could smell her, the spicy scent of her desire filling him, shaking him profoundly.

Sliding off the bed, he went to his knees between her legs.

Before she could voice a protest, before he could even think about what he was doing, he'd caught her thighs and tugged her to the very edge of the mattress. Her legs hung over the side, Tyler between them. She raised herself on an elbow, peering down at him in confusion, and he quickly lifted her knees over his shoulders, then pressed his face into her heat.

Her gasp was immediate, her protest loud. He ignored her, locking his arms around her hips, holding her still. "You taste so good, Carlie. So damn good." She fell back with a low cry, lifting herself to his seeking tongue.

Her trembling increased, her body arching from the mattress. He caught her sensitized flesh carefully between his teeth, holding her captive for his hot tongue, intent on her climax now, devastating her, enjoying her, driving her closer with each and every movement he made. She called his name, softly, over and over. He slid his hands against her, abruptly pushing two fingers deep inside her.

Wild, shattering sensations swept through her body, and Tyler could feel her contractions against his mouth and tongue, pressing closer, relishing every second of her pleasure. It seemed to go on and on, and he pushed her for more.

When Carlie finally went limp, Tyler raised himself, scooting up to lie upon her. "You're beautiful." Her hair was tangled about her head and a fine sheen of moisture glistened on her skin. He kissed her slack mouth, then stood, quickly removing his pants.

Carlie opened her eyes, but she didn't smile. She seemed dazed, her gaze intent on his body. Tyler leaned forward, naked, to brush his fingers through the curls between her thighs. She sucked in a startled breath, her hips pressing into the mattress.

His touch eased, barely skimming her, and she trembled.

"Too sensitive?" He watched her nod, seeing the confusion in her bright eyes. He palmed her, his hand still and warm.

Sitting on the bed beside her, he looked over her body. Her legs were still sprawled, her knees bent so her calves hung over the bed. Her arms were limp, lying palm up beside her head. She was watching him closely.

He looked at her breasts, still heaving slightly, and leaned down to gently take a nipple between his teeth. She groaned, her body clenching once again. "Tyler, *please.*"

"Just a minute, sweetheart. I have to protect you."

It took him only a moment, but she was frantic with need, and Tyler closed his eyes in anticipation. He felt her thighs open wider, accommodating him, and with only the subtlest of movement, he was ready to enter her.

Poised on his forearms, he watched every nuance of her expression as he slowly, inexorably, sank into her, giving her his length, stretching her with his hardness.

She moved anxiously against him, and forced him past his control. Thrusting smoothly and deeply, he wound his hands in Carlie's hair, anchoring her head so he could kiss her, swallowing her gasping breaths and soft, broken moans.

When he felt her tightening again, this time around his arousal, squeezing him, giving him unbelievable pleasure, he found his own explosive orgasm. Closing his arms around her, he held her tight until the spasms had faded.

It was several minutes before Tyler found the strength to move away from her warm body. He rolled to his side, but immediately pulled her close. He felt oddly disturbed, and frankly disloyal. He'd never known anything like what he'd just experienced with Carlie—except for that one night in the pool house. He hadn't wanted those memories to interfere. They no longer mattered; he no longer cared.

But thoughts of that night, images and heated memories,

had danced through his mind even as his senses filled with Carlie. *His Carlie.* He squeezed her closer, trying to chase away the images, but they didn't budge. Carlie leaned up to look at him.

"Tyler? What's wrong?"

She sounded anxious, and he rushed to reassure her. "What could possibly be wrong? Other than the fact I think you may have killed me with pleasure. I'm certain I no longer have legs. At least, if I do, they're totally useless right now." He cupped her cheek. "You're incredible, do you know that?"

She cuddled back down to his chest, her hands stroking through the dark curls there. "No. It was you. You were wonderful, Tyler."

He froze. The masked lady had said virtually the same thing on the phone. It unnerved him. Especially since the two women were so different. The woman at the party had been reserved, nearly frightened and so timid about each move he made, but Carlie had participated wholeheartedly. She was everything a man could want or hope to have in a mate.

He felt as though he'd somehow tainted the otherwise exquisite experience by envisioning another woman. No matter that the thought had come out of the blue. *How* could another woman, any woman, have intruded when he was with his Carlie? And she *was* his now. Savage possessiveness gripped him; he would never let her go.

Thinking that, he lowered his head to press a kiss to her temple. "You can't ever close me out again, Carlie. I won't let you."

Her reaction was immediate, and again, unexpected. She went perfectly still, almost stunned. He ran his hand over her shoulder. "You're mine, Carlie. I need you."

She looked at him from beneath her lashes. "Tyler, there's something you need to know."

He didn't like the sound of that. She was already trying to escape him, but he wouldn't let her. He kissed her again, then rose from the bed. "*Now,* we need that shower."

Her eyes widened. "I can't…!"

"Of course you can. Come on, I'll wash your back. And anything else that needs my attention."

He could sense her thinking, plotting. She twisted her hands in the sheets. "I'm too tired. You've exhausted me. Please, just come back to bed."

It hit him like a lightning bolt. She didn't want him to see her, really see her, without her clothing hiding her figure, making her look frumpy. He frowned thoughtfully, uncertain how to proceed. If she had a scar or some other reason to be embarrassed…but he'd touched every inch of her; certainly he would have noticed if anything was wrong. Still, her anxiety was very real, almost tangible, and he couldn't push her. Not after all she'd already given him, not after sharing herself so completely.

He touched her cheek. "I'll be right back."

He walked out of the room unconcerned with his own nudity, returning only moments later with a damp cloth. He left the lights off and seated himself beside her, content with the way she followed his progress. "Your eyes are so wide, you must think I'm intending some kind of mayhem."

Carlie shifted fretfully. "What are you intending?"

"Only to wash you. Now lie still and behave."

With a rapid peddling motion of her long legs, she scooted backward until she was pressed against the headboard. "Tyler, no! Good grief, I'm perfectly capable of tending myself."

He caught her foot, stroking the damp cloth up her calf and behind her knee. "But I want to do it. Now relax and stop fighting me."

She remained stiff, but she didn't struggle against him. "You're outrageous, Tyler."

"Don't sound so sulky. Before long, you'll learn to enjoy my outrageousness, I promise."

Tyler was thorough, using the cool cloth to stroke slowly over her body, removing all traces of their lovemaking. Carlie finally gave up her inhibitions, relaxing and enjoying his ministrations. Tyler chuckled when she moaned softly, then he bent to kiss a soft pink nipple.

"Sleep, Carlie. We need sleep." She frowned at him, and he stroked her one last time. "I'll be right back."

Tyler showered in a hurry, not wanting to take the chance Carlie would recover and send him home. He wanted to hold her in his arms all night.

He wanted to wake in the morning and look at her in the full light of day. And make love to her again.

She was an enigma, but he was slowly coming to understand her, completely and without doubts. She was trustworthy, the only trustworthy woman he'd ever known.

With his hair still damp, a towel wrapped loosely around his hips, he reentered the bedroom. He could see Carlie's huge golden eyes shining at him in the darkness. He hesitated, waiting only a heartbeat, and she leaned forward, throwing back the blankets, silently inviting him into her bed.

He dropped the towel over a chair and slid in beside her. She immediately curled against him, settling her hand on his chest. In the smallest voice he'd ever heard from Carlie, she whispered, "Thank you, Tyler."

"Thank you? That's an unusual sentiment from a woman who just gave herself to a man."

"I didn't. Give myself to you, that is. You gave yourself to me. And you did it perfectly. It was wonderful, you were wonderful, and I thank you."

His chuckle nearly jarred her from her position against his shoulder. "You're very welcome…and by far the most appreciative woman I've ever made love to."

Her hand moved slowly over his chest, kneading the swell of muscle, teasing her fingers through the fine, dark hair. "We'll talk in the morning, okay?"

She sounded wary, unsure of herself. Tyler kissed the top of her head, then yawned hugely. "We'll talk, but only after I've gotten a chance to enjoy waking up with you."

Carlie was silent, her face turned into his skin, and he felt the sweet, very brief touch of her lips. He wasn't certain what to make of this new mood of hers, but then, it didn't matter. She was his, and nothing was going to change that. He wouldn't let it.

It was the sunlight streaming in that first stirred Tyler. His eyes opened slowly. Remembrance came in a rush of contentment, and he looked down to see Carlie still close to him, but now turned so that her bottom was nestled securely against his groin. His palm rested on her breast. Her skin was warm and silky and smooth.

She was peaceful in her sleep, her body lax, one hand curled beneath her cheek giving the illusion of childlike innocence. But she was no child.

Very quietly, Tyler raised himself onto one elbow, gazing down at her, a strange, stirring mix of emotions swamping him. He wanted to wake her and make love to her; he wanted to lie down and hold her forever.

He forced himself to be considerate and do neither. She was exhausted, and she needed her sleep. She didn't move so much as an eyelash when he carefully slid out of the bed.

The first order of business was a shave. His morning beard was harsh, and he didn't want to scratch her tender skin. And he didn't want to have to avoid kissing her in all the most delectable places because of beard stubble. He smiled at the thought.

Carlie wasn't the straitlaced, narrow-minded prude he'd expected. All her talk of reputations and gossip had been misleading. She was magnificent. Wild and open and honest with her feelings. She'd told him he was wonderful.

The mysterious masked woman had told him the same thing.

That wayward thought had him scowling at himself in the mirror. It was traitorous. Carlie deserved much better. He was a cad to still concern himself with another woman's identity. If he never discovered the truth, it wouldn't matter.

Deliberately, he shoved those disturbing thoughts from his mind. The mystery woman may have been a fantasy come to life, but Carlie was a living fantasy. Her effect on him was unbelievable, and he couldn't seem to get enough of her.

Naked, he stood in the bathroom and looked around. Surely Carlie had a razor somewhere. He checked in the vanity drawers, then the medicine cabinet. He didn't find a a razor, but a small contact case caught his attention.

Smiling, he envisioned Carlie wearing contacts, relegating the ugly glasses to the desk drawer forever. She had beautiful eyes, the hazel clear and unique and pure.

It was idle curiosity that prompted him to open the case. For a moment, he stared stupidly at the colored lenses. They were a very bright, familiar blue. Then his face reddened.

He'd seen that color before. The night of the party.

Reality beat a swift path into his brain.

His guileless, forthright, *honest* Carlie had played him for a fool. He remembered the recent phone call, and his face burned, the heat of humiliation spreading rapidly down his neck. He was filled with fierce blinding anger, and the most devastating disappointment he'd ever known.

He'd thought of Carlie as near-perfect; dedicated to the children and to loftier causes for the common good. He'd thought her stubborn, headstrong and thoroughly independent. But not a liar.

She was still sleeping when he entered the bedroom. He was intent on his course, not about to be swayed by the alluring picture she made. Deliberately, he sat on the side of the bed, promptly waking her.

Her long lashes fluttered and her eyes opened slowly. She looked up into his unsmiling face, and reached for him.

"Tyler." Her hand landed on his naked thigh, and she stroked him. He dropped forward on one elbow so they were nose to nose. "Good morning, sweetheart. I trust you slept well?"

Her hand came up to his cheek, and she nodded. She felt his stubbly chin, then smiled slowly. "You're so very dark."

His look was grim. Pushing away the covers, he surveyed her body. "You're certainly not." His eyes fell to the tight curls between her thighs. "Light brown. Close to the color of your beautiful head. Maybe not as golden. Certainly not black."

She gasped.

"Who are we today, Carlie? Maybe you'd like me to run home and fetch my pirate costume? I could pretend you were a virgin maiden, and 'pillage' you to my heart's content."

He saw her pale throat move as she swallowed, but otherwise she remained still, not even blinking. The hurt in her golden eyes enraged him all the more. He couldn't stop himself from taunting her. "No? You don't like that idea? Then how about I rent a sheikh costume? That role you would surely approve of. After all, you wear the veils so well. Maybe I could convince you to dance for me. I'd like that, I'm sure."

She pulled away without touching him. Her look was distant and wary. "You don't understand, Tyler."

"Now, there's where you're wrong." He reached out to wrap a lock of long hair around his finger, tugging her face closer to his own. "I understand perfectly. You wanted to experiment, and were too much the coward to come out from behind your spinster disguise. But now there's no reason to pretend. Hell, I enjoyed myself last night. What red-blooded male wouldn't have?"

"Tyler…"

"Don't look so concerned, sweetheart. I'm still willing to play. I only wish you'd told me the way of it sooner. Just think of all the time we've wasted. We could have been enjoying ourselves quite a bit." He gazed mockingly down the length of her exposed body. He ignored the way her pulse beat frantically in her slim throat, just as he ignored the horrified expression on her face, the tears starting to glisten in her eyes. He wouldn't be a fool again. Once was more than enough. It was more than he could bear.

He hurt so badly. He had never felt so betrayed in his life, not even when he'd finally realized how little he meant to his mother. He'd expected deception and manipulation from her. But he'd trusted Carlie. *Fool.*

Not for the world would he let her know that. He forced a wicked grin, hiding his hurt. Then he bent to press a hard, possessive kiss to her parted lips. He hadn't completely lost, he thought. He was still with her, and they were both in bed.

He could prove to her it didn't matter, that she meant little to him.

And then maybe he could prove it to himself.

Chapter Nine

"NO, DAMN YOU!" Carlie gave Tyler a shove that nearly knocked him from the bed. She scrambled away from him, quickly rising.

He lounged back, surveying her with a look of arrogant annoyance, his arms behind his head. "Calm down, Carlie."

"Get out! Get out now." She was trembling from head to foot, still completely naked, her hands squeezed together so tight her knuckles ached. Did he actually think he could make love to her while he was angry?

His eyes coasted over her slowly, with deliberate insult. But his words were a contrast, and terribly hurtful. "You're magnificent."

Carlie was speechless for just a moment. Then she narrowed her eyes. "I want you to leave now, Tyler." Her words quavered, but she couldn't help it. Everything had fallen apart. Tyler was acting like a stranger, treating her with the same callous insolence her husband had always employed whenever he'd been angry with her. She couldn't bear it.

Realizing that she was standing there, completely naked,

waiting to see what else he would do or say made her throat go dry. She wasn't helpless and she was no longer young and naive. She angled her chin toward him, then forced a semblance of calm into her voice. "I won't let you do this, Tyler."

"Let me do what? You're the one who lied and made a fool of me, Carlie." His gaze pierced her, hot and hard and filled with contempt. She briefly closed her eyes against the pain of it.

"I'm sorry. I never intended it to be this way. I should never have done any of it. You're right to be angry. I knew you would be. That's why I decided to put off telling you until this morning."

"You want me to believe you would have actually confessed? I'm not stupid, Carlie. Look at you. You're shocked that I know. You wouldn't have said a word if I hadn't stumbled across your contacts and found out on my own."

She couldn't deny she was shocked, but it was because of Tyler's reaction, his disdain. She expected anger, but not disgust.

She watched Tyler rise from the bed, unmindful of his nudity as he stalked toward her. She couldn't bear his touch, not now, not with the way he felt about her. She pressed back against the wall.

Tyler glared at her retreat, then roughly ran his hands through his hair. Carlie realized, rather stupidly, that he was even gorgeous in the morning, beard stubble and all. His voice, when he spoke, was practically a sneer. "What's with the timid act, Carlie? I thought that little charade ended at the pool house."

Of course, it hadn't been an act, but she wasn't going to remind him of that. She understood his anger completely; she simply couldn't deal with it at the moment. She scooped up his pants and threw them at him. "Get dressed and go, Tyler."

She pulled a robe from her closet and quickly slipped it on.

Tyler watched her, his eyes taking in every minute movement of her body. She hated his scrutiny.

His sweatshirt hit him in the chest when she threw it. He caught the garment, but made no move to put it on. He clutched the clothing in his big hands and started toward her again.

Carlie steeled herself, pushing away her guilt and nervousness, calling on her anger. No man would ever intimidate her again. She held up her hand, and Tyler halted. "I'm sorry for what happened, Tyler. Sorrier than you can know. I take full blame and I understand your anger. But it's over now. I won't bother you again. I promise."

His eyes looked dangerously bright. "Is that right?"

"Yes." She swallowed heavily. "I understand how you feel…"

Tyler threw back his head and laughed harshly. "Lady, you haven't got a clue. How could you understand my feelings when you don't have any of your own? Hell, you're not even real. You're make-believe—and there's too damn many of you for me to keep track of."

"I don't know what you're talking about." She hated feeling defensive, and she hated lying. Deep down, she knew exactly what he was talking about.

"Who are you now, Carlie? I haven't met this woman before. The harem girl I know intimately, I met that timid little kitten at the pool house. She blew my socks off, wanting my body and very little conversation. A good woman if ever there was one. And then I met the schoolteacher. Prickly woman, with the worst taste in clothing I have ever seen. Of course, she made up for it with her show of honesty and compassion and concern. A born actress. And now you. A woman who offers abject apologies left and right. A woman who lied and manipulated without a single qualm, and now, apparently, is sorry for it. It's a good act, I admit, but somehow I can't quite believe you're all that repentant. You played your little game too damn convincingly."

Carlie's mind went blank. All her barely contained emotions settled into one dull ache that she suppressed deep inside herself. The more emotion she gave him, the more he would mock her. And she couldn't bear it. "You're right. But each of those women had something in common, Tyler. Something you obviously missed. They were each a fool and an idiot. And you can believe me this time—liar that I am—they're gone. You won't see them again. Well, perhaps you'll see the schoolteacher, but that's entirely up to you. If you wish to quit the program at school, I'll understand. I even encourage you to do so. I'll find someone else. It would be for the best if we didn't expose the children to any animosity."

She turned and began pulling clothes from her closet, all but dismissing Tyler. She wasn't going to continue to apologize. He obviously didn't want to hear it, and just as certainly, he didn't believe her regret. She'd learned long ago, if one apology wasn't sufficient, a hundred wouldn't do, either.

Tyler caught her arm, turning her to face him. "You're trying to make me out to be the villain here, Carlie." His eyes were clouded with confusion. "I'm the one who was used, the one who was made to look like a fool."

Carlie jerked her arm free. His touch was still disturbing, regardless of all that had happened. "I've thought you many things, Tyler, but never a fool. And as I recall, you didn't object overly to being used. *You* initiated the…intimacies. And as far as the other…well, you should remember I tried to keep our relationship platonic. You're the one who pushed, not me."

"You called me one night," he accused softly, ignoring her words. "Why would you do that except to taunt me?"

Carlie managed a casual shrug, but it was difficult. Her humiliation was gone, buried with her regret. But he was so large and imposing, she couldn't help being very aware of him, of his maleness in contrast to her femininity. He was naked, he was angry and there was no avoiding a confrontation.

She refused to cower, to lower her eyes from his perceptive stare. "I already admitted to being a fool. Just think of that call as another example of my foolishness." She wasn't about to tell him she'd been searching for some truth behind his attentiveness, some sign that he wasn't just playing with her. She'd already given enough of herself away.

"But why, Carlie? Why the damned charade in the first place?" He was back to shouting, his face dark with renewed anger.

And he still hadn't put a stitch of clothing on.

Carlie stepped quickly away from him, and headed for the bathroom. She had to get away, had to find a moment's privacy to collect herself and call up her reserve. She had the choking need to break down and cry like a baby. She would never feel a loss as greatly as she felt it now. She had lost Tyler.

Who was she kidding? She'd never had Tyler in the first place. She'd reminded herself of that often enough. But somehow, because they had shared sex—she would no longer consider it lovemaking—she had allowed herself to indulge in a whimsical dream. She was such a fraud.

She turned back to Tyler, and caught him watching her intently, a look closely resembling concern shining in his eyes. She disregarded that possibility. He hated her now. She could feel it. "The charade was unintentional, if you'll remember correctly. I had left the party. *You* followed *me*. But I suppose some part of me was pathetic enough to appreciate the attention you gave me. It surprised me. It…" She swallowed. "I was flattered. But I learn from my mistakes, Tyler. Believe me."

She laughed, then, a bubbling, nervous sound. She lowered her head with the force of it.

She felt Tyler move toward her and reach out a hand. "Carlie?"

The single word was sharp, edged with a vague emotion Carlie couldn't begin to fathom. She stepped away from him, still chuckling. "Oh, it's too funny. Tyler Ramsey, the stud of the community, feeling used by Carlie McDaniels! It's too absurd to be real. But don't worry, Tyler. I won't tell a single soul. After all, who would ever believe me?"

He flexed his jaw, his stance deceptively mild. "You think it's funny?"

Her smile twisted into a sneer and her eyes narrowed. "I think it's hilarious. One of those too-strange-to-be-true scenarios better shoved to the back of the closet, never to be thought of again."

Tyler caught her chin, and her grin vanished instantly. "You won't be able to forget, Carlie. At least be honest with yourself now." His thumb teased over her bottom lip, and there was genuine regret in the words he muttered. "You won't ever be able to forget." Then he straightened, all signs of disappointment magically disappearing. "I'd actually thought you were different. And in a way you are. You were able to fool me completely. No other woman has done that. You're to be congratulated."

Carlie nearly cried out at those words. Instead, she bit her lip, whirled and slammed into the bathroom, locking the door behind her. The pain nearly suffocated her, making her knees weak and stealing her resolve. She sank, defeated, to the edge of the tub, her fist in her mouth to stifle her low sobs.

She stayed there, hearing Tyler dress quietly, hearing the sounds of him preparing to leave. And then the closing of the door, so soft, so final, so very, very real.

And she broke, crying with all the energy of someone who knows she's lost something invaluable. Something she's never had but always desperately wanted.

"Tyler! My goodness, you're a sight!"

"Why the hell didn't you tell me, Brenda!" He stuck his face close to hers. "I'm your brother-in-law! I'm family! I can't believe you would stab me in the back like this!"

Brenda covered her chest with one hand, her eyes wide. "Whatever are you shouting about? What's happened?"

Jason entered the room, took one look at his brother and put himself in front of his wife. "Calm down, Tyler."

"Calm down! Do you know...?"

"Yes." Jason's voice was very quiet in comparison to Tyler's. "I know. But I can't let you yell at my wife. Now settle down."

Tyler was thunderstruck. "You knew, too?"

"Don't look so shocked. No one told me, but I figured it out quickly enough. I have to admit, I was surprised you didn't."

Brenda gasped then, shoving her husband aside. She faced Tyler with the most alarmed expression he'd ever seen on her face. "This is about Carlie? You've found out?"

"Yes, dammit! Your little game is over. Did you two sit down to tea and laugh over watching me make a fool of myself? Did she give you all the juicy details?"

Jason opened his mouth, but Brenda didn't give him time to interject. "Oh, Tyler, it wasn't like that!" Then she bit her lip. "You're angry. You...you didn't hurt her, did you?"

Tyler threw up his hands in a gesture of despair. "I don't believe you asked me that! Since when have I been such a bastard that I'd hurt a woman? I may have felt like strangling you both, but I would never—"

"I don't mean physically. I know you would never lay a hand on a woman." Then she reached up to touch his cheek.

"But she's so fragile, Tyler. She's been hurt so much. Please, tell me you didn't do or say anything to hurt her feelings."

She was looking so anxious, Tyler frowned at her. Reluctantly, he admitted, "I was damned angry."

Brenda searched his face, then turned to Jason, her eyes huge. "I'm going to go check on her."

Jason nodded, then bent to kiss her cheek. "Be careful driving. Don't hurry. I doubt she's going anywhere." He handed Brenda the car keys from a hook by the phone, catching her just before she started out. "Everything will work out."

Brenda glanced quickly at Tyler, who only looked back in exasperation. She sighed. "Don't be so sure of that, Jason. I'm not."

Tyler watched her rush out, then turned to his brother. "Aren't you the least bit irate on my behalf? Do you even know the whole story? I was *lied* to."

Jason sat, crossing his arms on the kitchen table. "No, you weren't. Unfortunately, Carlie's been honest with you from the start. She's been herself, and that's as honest as it gets. Now, I sincerely hope you're going to sit down here and tell me you didn't just manage to ruin the best thing that's ever happened to you."

Tyler sat, but it wasn't a concession as much as he suddenly needed the stability of a chair. He could hardly credit his brother's defection. "A woman who lies to me and plays juvenile games is the best thing that's ever happened to me? What the hell would be the worst?"

Jason gave him a long look, then sighed. "The worst, the way I see it, is if you just did so much damage, Carlie crawls back into her shell and never gives you a second chance. And that's a very real possibility." Jason looked his brother over, taking in Tyler's still-disheveled hair and unshaven face. "Why don't you tell me what happened?"

Tyler realized how foolish his part sounded in the charade, but he needed to talk. He could barely absorb the reality of what he'd discovered. "I just realized that Carlie and my mystery woman are one and the same." He laughed in self-derision. "Do you know, I was actually feeling guilty because I thought I cared so much for Carlie, and yet I was still curious to know who the other woman was. What a joke."

"What did you do?"

Tyler winced at the suspicion in his brother's words. "I kicked up a fuss, of course. I mean, Carlie knew it was her I had—" Tyler halted. He hadn't told anyone he'd made love to his harem girl—and he was pretty certain Carlie hadn't said anything either. Regardless of what had happened now, that night was special, and he wouldn't ruin it. He stared at his brother, then looked away. "Hell, Bren probably told Carlie I'd been asking about her. It's all so humiliating."

"Yeah. Imagine how Carlie feels."

Tyler's jaw dropped open, but he shut it with a snap. "What about me?"

Jason snorted in disgust. It was a good simulation of Carlie's snort, but without her flair.

"You're a big boy. You've been around. So you were a bit embarrassed? You two could have talked about it, about why Carlie felt so unsure of herself as a woman that she'd have to hide behind a disguise in the first place. Who knows, you may have even been able to laugh about it."

"Fat chance!"

There was silence, and Jason got up to pour Tyler a cup of coffee. After setting the cup on the table, he clasped Tyler's shoulder, giving him a brotherly squeeze.

Tyler shook his head. Jason always did that. He could give Tyler hell about something, but he always let him know he cared, either by a pat on the back, a squeeze to the shoulder or an occasional bear hug. They were closer than most brothers, and Tyler never doubted his loyalty.

He waited another second or two until Jason had reseated himself, then he took the bait. "So why is Carlie so insecure?"

Jason idly traced the edge of his coffee cup with his fingertip. "Don't you think that's a question you ought to ask Carlie?"

Swamped with emotions he couldn't sort out, Tyler chose to go on the defensive. "I shouldn't have to ask. If she has a good reason for doing what she did, she ought to come to me and tell me."

"And if she doesn't do that?"

Tyler stubbornly shook his head. "I don't know."

"I think you better make up your mind fast."

That was impossible to do. God, things could get so tangled. He'd only just decided he loved Carlie.... Tyler felt his chest squeeze tight. *Love?* That word had the ability to scare him spitless, but that was probably what it was. Because now that things had soured, he was hurting worse than he'd ever hurt in his life. Surely only love could do that to a man. And what if Carlie did have good reason for doing what she'd done? He hadn't even asked her. He'd let his injured pride guide him, when in his heart, he knew Carlie was incapable of simply using anyone. If she felt she had to resort to deception, she must have had a very good reason.

And he'd probably just ruined whatever trust she'd previously had in him.

Tyler dropped his head onto the table, and it landed with a solid thud.

Jason went on, apparently unmoved by his brother's dejection. "This is going to be really hard for Carlie to take. It's not enough that you know, but now both Bren and I do, as well. I would imagine she's feeling utterly alone right now. She doesn't have anyone, you know. No family, no—"

Tyler raised his head, and pounded it back down on the table. Twice.

"Tyler, quit trying to shake your brains loose and tell me what you're going to do."

He sat back up, his eyes bloodshot and burning, his head aching abominably, feeling totally defeated. "I think I might have blown it, Jason. Some of the things I said..."

"So you're going to try to work it out?"

Tyler covered his face with his hands. "I don't know. Hell, she'll probably never speak to me again."

"Give her a few days. She'll calm down."

"Yeah, maybe." But he didn't believe it. He thought of the look on Carlie's face as he'd hurled accusations...the way she'd backed away from him. Her nearly hysterical laugh.

Tyler closed his eyes, and pinched the bridge of his nose. He was afraid he'd thrown away something precious. All because of his injured pride. "She's incredible, you know. Absolutely incredible."

Jason raised an eyebrow. "Are we talking about in bed?"

Tyler looked up, a frown solidly in place. "No! I mean..." He narrowed his eyes at his brother, then shook his head. "I was talking about other things."

Jason watched him, a slight smile on his face. Tyler didn't even notice. "She's terrific with the kids. So patient and gentle, but boy, do they ever listen to her. They go out of their way to please her. And the parents! They hang on to her every word, as if she speaks the gospel. And she's so intelligent. Loads of common sense—except when it comes to her own worth. She hides behind those damned ugly clothes. I hate that."

Tipping his head back, Tyler stared at the ceiling, feeling hopeless and lost. "We had fun, Jason. Real, genuine fun. I would have sooner spent time with Carlie than anyone I know."

"You love her."

Still staring at the ceiling, Tyler said, "Yeah. I think I do. But love is a damn strange thing. I can't decide if I like it or not."

"I know I hated it when I fell for Brenda. I went through major denial. But then I'd see some clown talking to her, and I'd want to kill him. And I couldn't keep my hands off her. She'd yawn and I'd want her. She'd smile and I'd get hard as a rock."

Tyler scoffed, even though he was suffering the same thing. "I remember. You were warped."

Jason merely grinned. "I still am. It's terrific."

Tyler made a quick decision, and immediately felt better. "I have to go see her."

Jason gave him a cautious look. "Do you think that's wise? Carlie needs time to—"

"I don't mean right this minute. We both need time to think and I'm not sure I can think straight at all when I'm around her." Then he grinned. "Hell, I can hardly think when I'm not around her. At least, not about anything other than her."

Jason clasped Tyler's shoulder, walking with him to the door. "It's love, all right." Then he grew serious. "But you have to be sure, Tyler. You have to be certain of what you want. Get your own thoughts straight before you make matters worse. The way you look now, you'd only go there and end up fighting with her again."

Tyler smiled ruefully. "Don't worry. It's not fighting I have in mind."

Jason slapped him on the back. "Remember that."

What a waste of time crying was.

It never solved anything and it was embarrassing. Brenda was sympathetic, but Carlie didn't want sympathy. She wanted solitude, she wanted time to think, and luckily, Brenda was a good enough friend to realize it.

It had been almost two days since she'd last seen Tyler, since the morning he'd walked out her door with the obvious intent of never coming back. Luckily, there hadn't been any basketball practices scheduled, so she didn't have to worry about seeing him at school.

At least, not yet. She had no idea how Tyler intended to handle that. *She* certainly wouldn't quit. That would smack of cowardice, and she had too much pride to be the first to give up. But the thought of seeing him, of trying to be sociable under the circumstances, was nearly too much. She had to get her act together, and she had to do it now.

A warm shower helped to revive her somewhat, and she tried to concentrate her thoughts on the children, on figuring out some way to help the more financially unfortunate families. She also needed some exercise to rid her of her tension.

She had a plan. It was foolproof, which was necessary, since she'd proven herself several times a fool. Part of the secret of recovering from shame and heartache was to make everyone else believe it didn't matter one whit, and pretty soon, after convincing them, you automatically convinced yourself.

Carlie dressed in several layers of sweats, tied her sneakers neatly, and went out the door. The November air was very brisk, and the sky was overcast and gray. The wind was playful, blowing hard one minute, sending stray wisps of hair slashing across her eyes, and then dying, leaving the air strangely still and silent.

Carlie breathed deeply of the scents of approaching winter. It would snow soon, and before long the holidays would be here. That fact meant nothing to Carlie. She hadn't celebrated a holiday since she'd finally escaped her husband over two years ago. Holidays brought memories, and memories only served to destroy her carefully erected peace of mind.

She ran hard for the first few blocks, and then, winded, her lungs aching, she switched to a slow-paced jog. She usually ran for about three miles. It was what she had always done for peace and contentment. Hopefully, it would work again.

But the hurdles seemed insurmountable today. Every step she took brought back thoughts of Tyler. And each thought ended with the angry flash of his dark eyes. What he must be thinking of her now....

It was as if she'd conjured him with her worries. She rounded the corner, laboring for breath, her cheeks stinging from the cold, and there he was. He was watching her, sitting on her front step, his hands shoved deep into the pockets of his leather jacket.

Her heart lurched, her throat went dry and her skin felt tight—much too tight. But she smiled, a serene, undisturbed smile. "Hello, Tyler."

He blinked. Obviously that wasn't what he'd expected to hear. Especially not in such a cordial tone. Carlie was very pleased with herself.

He stood slowly, his eyes drifting over her jogging suit in obvious distaste. "You were out jogging."

"Very astute of you. What gave me away? The suit itself or the fact that I just returned, still huffing?" She was trembling inside and her stomach was tied in knots, but she hid it well, knowing she'd rather die than have him know how badly he'd hurt her.

Tyler tilted his head, studying her warily. "I thought we should talk."

Carlie bent over, placing her hands on her thighs. It looked as though she was trying to catch her breath, but in truth she needed a moment to regain her emotional balance. She hadn't expected to see him again this soon. She wasn't ready. The fact that Tyler was here, so near and looking so handsome made the chore of feigning nonchalance that much more difficult. She drew one last deep breath and straightened.

"I'm sorry, I really can't right now. It's a bad time for me. Papers to grade, lessons to plan. And I have a few phone calls to make." She smiled politely.

"Carlie…"

"Yes?"

He rubbed the bridge of his nose. "Things didn't go exactly as I planned the other day. It took me by surprise—"

"That's putting a pretty face on it, Tyler. It shocked the hell out of you. And enraged you. And I understand completely. I probably would have felt the same. But I've already apologized. There's nothing more I can do. I can't change what's already been done. Believe me, I wish I could."

"What would you change, honey?"

Oh, that tone, so sweet and gentle. Carlie forced herself to stand just a little straighter. "All of it, of course. From the day Brenda invited me to that stupid party, to yesterday. I'd erase it all." She smiled at him serenely, hoping to put him at ease with her declaration. But it cost her. Her stomach felt so tight now, she feared she might throw up.

Tyler had probably come over with some vague notion that she might pursue him. She'd die first.

He touched her cheek briefly. "Then I'll be eternally grateful you don't possess magic powers. Because I wouldn't trade the time I've spent with you for anything." He waited a moment, then added softly, "I don't really believe you would, either, Carlie."

Chapter Ten

OH, GOD, OH, GOD. He couldn't know that. Carlie summoned a smile, but her serenity had about run out. "You're wrong."

"I've been wrong about a lot of things."

Her eyes widened behind the lenses of her glasses, and she pressed a hand dramatically to her heart. "No! Not you, Tyler! Say it isn't so, or all my grand delusions will blow away in the wind."

"Dammit, Carlie..."

She chuckled. The sound was just a bit rusty, but convincing, all the same. "Go home, Tyler. It's cold out here, too cold to stand around trading recriminations." She went up the steps, fishing her key out of her pocket.

Carlie went inside and then turned to tell Tyler goodbye. He didn't give her the chance. Pushing his way through, he was over the threshold before Carlie could voice a complaint.

He didn't smile. He closed the door and leaned against it, watching her.

Warily, she faced him. "What are you doing?"

Tyler hesitated, then shrugged. "I can help you grade your papers. I still owe you, don't I?"

"I don't remember. But I'd rather you didn't. I don't have time to be distracted."

He came away from the door. "Do I distract you, Carlie?"

She blinked at him, then laughed. "Turn your hormones off, Tyler. I was referring to your inane chatter."

"You can't be that indifferent to me, Carlie. I was there that night, too, you know. I recall perfectly everything that happened between us."

Carlie moved away from the heat of his gaze. It was almost tangible, covering her in waves, penetrating her flesh. She sauntered as casually as possible to the kitchen, Tyler following.

She pulled out a chair and lowered herself into it, while all the time her mind was working furiously. This time, it wasn't as easy to affect a carefree air. Her feelings were even more deeply involved now than when she'd first got divorced. She wasn't a kid who had been disillusioned. And her feelings for Tyler surpassed infatuation.

When Tyler automatically sat opposite her, she regarded him seriously. "Maybe we should talk."

He seemed relieved. "Yes. I want to explain—"

"Let me go first, Tyler." Her heart was racing, her breath was shallow, but she knew she had to have her say and get it over with as cleanly as possible. Even though it cost her, she leaned forward and placed her hand over his. He couldn't know how hurt she was. Pride was all she had left.

Tyler turned his palm upward, clasping her fingers. "Tyler," she started uncertainly, "what happened between us was nice. I'll grant you that." His eyes narrowed, and she released his hand. "Don't interrupt, please. I want you to understand. It was nice, and I believe I already thanked you. But it won't happen again. Ever."

"I don't believe you."

"Then once again, I'm sorry. But it's true. If you're determined for us to remain friends, that's fine with me. I like you. You're a good person and you're a lot of fun. But I won't sleep with you again. Sex isn't on my agenda. It was an aberration that we got together at all. Call it temporary insanity, and the key word there is 'temporary.'"

"People can't just turn off their emotions, Carlie. You were with me every step of the way that night, and it was a damned sight more than 'nice.' Hell, it was more than sex, more than anything I've ever known before. It won't go away."

"There's where you're wrong, Tyler. I can make it go away. I can turn off my feelings with a snap of my fingers. I can do anything I put my mind to. And right now, I'm sending you home." She stood, but Tyler didn't budge. Carlie couldn't believe he'd thought she would abide a casual affair. Without mutual caring between them, it was impossible. But obviously, Tyler didn't realize that. It was just as obvious he didn't know her at all.

He eyed her speculatively. "Is that what you're trying to do now? Turn off your feelings, close off your heart? That's no way to live, honey."

Carlie definitely didn't want Tyler Ramsey rummaging around in her head, trying to decipher what made her click. She gave him a sardonic smile, reminiscent of the Carlie he met so long ago. "Wait, I think I can unearth some violin music around here somewhere to go with all this melodrama." She shook her head. "It's the only way to live, Tyler. At least, for me."

Tyler looked down at his clasped hands resting on the tabletop. "I don't think you can do it, Carlie. I think we shared something very special. It may not have been what either of us is used to, but it was still wonderful, almost explosive. And erotic." He slowly raised his gaze, locking it with hers. "Someday, I'd like to see you in that harem costume again. I swear, I get aroused just thinking about it."

Carlie's head snapped back as if he'd slapped her. She tried to compose herself, but vivid, humiliating images were suddenly whirling through her mind. Her voice was a croak as she tried to regain control. "I want you to leave now, Tyler. I mean it."

He came slowly to his feet, his eyes on her pale face. "Before I screwed things up, I think you would have laughed if I suggested that. I'll get you to laugh again, Carlie. I'm not going to let you run away from me like this."

Carlie snorted, recovering slightly with his calm, arrogant statement. "I don't run from anyone. Not anymore. But I'll be up-front with you. If you persist in making sexual innuendos, I won't associate with you. I mean it."

Tyler tried that word out on his tongue. "Associate? Hmm. Sounds suspiciously like a business relationship."

"Or a casual friendship. The choice is yours." It took all Carlie's resolve to maintain eye contact. His eyes appeared almost black with emotion. He looked very tired.

Tyler gave her a gentle, sincere smile. "If the choice was mine, we'd be back in bed right now, everything else forgotten."

Carlie went rigid. "You were wrong, Tyler. I detest your outrageousness. Now please leave."

He scrutinized her. "Talk to me about your divorce."

He was changing subjects as she'd wanted, but she didn't like this new direction at all. She stared at him, annoyed. "Why?"

"I want to understand. And despite all your dictums, I care about you. I'm beginning to realize I always will."

Her heart took a giant leap, but she repressed the feeling his statement incited. She looked at him with indifference, hoping she was masking her reaction. She couldn't be that big a fool. Not again.

"Will you tell me about him, Carlie?" Then Tyler shook his head, his look almost apologetic. "Let me put that another way. I'm not leaving until you do."

Hiding her exasperation was no mean feat. But she did, because to try to deny him would only cause him to dig deeper, she knew. Tyler could be very stubborn on occasion. She shrugged and went to the refrigerator to pull out a soda, without offering him one. It was a deliberate act of rudeness, but to her chagrin, Tyler merely fetched his own, then sat, watching her expectantly.

Carlie crossed her legs and propped one elbow on the table. "I met him in college. He was one of the 'popular ones,' if you know what I mean. I was a nobody. I worked my way through college, and there was very little time for a social life. It took most of my time just keeping my grades up and working enough hours to make ends meet. I was flattered that he paid attention to me. We spent my last year there dating off and on.

"In spite of the time I'd been seeing him, I guess I didn't really know him. Things between us were pretty casual, and he dated other women, too, not just me. But when I graduated, he asked me to marry him, and I agreed. You see, my grandfather had already told me not to come home. And my brother...he never kept in touch. I was pretty much...alone." She smiled, feeling somewhat foolish for pointing out so many details in her defense. It didn't matter what Tyler thought. At least it shouldn't. "I wanted a family. I wanted someone to want me. I thought he did. Pretty dumb reason to get married, isn't it?"

"It's a hell of a lot more reasonable than some I've heard. So go on. When did things start to go wrong?"

"About ten minutes after I said, 'I do.' We'd gotten married at a justice of the peace. It was a package deal, one of those that included a night at a honeymoon cabin. We went there directly."

Tyler was starting to get an idea where the story was going, Carlie surmised, when he began to scowl at her. "You were a virgin?"

She gazed down at her soda can, running her finger around the rim. It was tough to get the words out, remembering how naive she'd been. "Yes. So I didn't understand that it wasn't supposed to hurt so much. His lovemaking was...crude. And rough." Her eyes found his. "It wasn't at all like what you showed me. I hated it. But he said it was normal. I was totally ignorant of men and I wanted to be reasonable, so I accepted his explanations. Only it didn't get any better."

Tyler lunged from his chair, nearly overturning it. He paced across the room, keeping his back to Carlie.

She spoke mildly, as if it didn't matter one way or the other. "If you'd rather not hear this now, I'll understand." The truth was, she couldn't believe she was actually telling him. She hadn't shared intimate details of her past with anyone, not even Brenda. But in a way, it felt good to talk about it, to say things out loud. She drew a deep breath, then looked at Tyler again.

He was watching her closely. After a few seconds, he resumed his seat. "Go on."

His expression was rigid and his eyes blazed despite his obvious effort at control. Carlie couldn't help herself. She felt a genuine smile pull at her lips. "So outraged on my behalf?"

"I'd dearly love to get my hands on him."

He said it so levelly, with so much gravity, Carlie believed him. She was shocked. Without thinking, she patted his arm. "Relax. It wasn't all that bad."

Tyler growled at her. "Don't lie to me, Carlie, ever."

"You mean 'ever again,' don't you?"

"I don't consider your little masquerade at the pool house lying."

Her eyes widened, he seemed so sincere. "You don't?"

"No. You would have told me the whole of it soon enough, if I hadn't jumped the gun and been such a jerk. Now quit dodging the topic and finish your story."

"All right. The first time I really complained, he said it was my fault. He blamed me completely, excusing himself by saying I didn't respond the way I should. He said I should act more like a woman, and dress up a little more. I tried. I always tried to do what he told me to do. It...just didn't work. I couldn't be...ready as quickly as he wanted, and he would get angry, and...it was a fiasco."

"It wasn't your fault."

He was so vehement, so sure, Carlie felt comforted, despite herself. She nodded. "I know that. Now. But I believed him when he said I was frigid. And I couldn't see making him abstain just because something was wrong with me. I...tolerated him, which only made matters worse. After a while, we grew so distant, I decided it wasn't worth having a home or family or husband if I had to put up with the sex."

She didn't say another word until Tyler prompted her. "So you asked for a divorce?" He sounded impatient, and she swallowed the hurt that always swamped her whenever she thought of those times.

She shook her head. "I felt so guilty. But then I came home early one day, and I caught him in bed with another woman. *She* didn't appear to be having any difficulty enjoying him. He wasn't overly concerned that I found them, either. In fact, he seemed almost proud. I think he needed to prove to me that it wasn't him. That it was me, and only me, that caused the problem."

"And you believed him."

It was a statement, and Tyler sounded somehow disappointed with her deduction. She sighed. "What was I supposed to think? I certainly didn't have anything to compare with. But I was more than ready for the divorce. The only problem was, he didn't want it. He was very possessive of me, and he fought the divorce for a long time. He hounded me for so long, I had to move to get away from him. Looking back, I think it would have been impossible for him to accept any part of the blame. It would have been a mark against his masculinity. I can almost understand him, now. But then...I just wanted out."

"And when you finally got out, you decided you never wanted in again, is that it?"

Carlie tried to draw forth some of the energy she'd been feeling earlier. She needed it now to get her through the next few minutes. It was emotionally debilitating discussing her past, but even more so discussing it with Tyler. She didn't want him to look at her with pity, to feel sorry for the naive, foolish, young woman she'd been.

She angled her head proudly, refusing to turn away from his probing gaze. Surprisingly, she didn't see pity in his eyes. Just determination. "I'm strong, Tyler. I don't need a man. I'm perfectly capable of taking care of myself. I dress to please myself, and I work at a job I enjoy. What I can't get on my own, I don't really need."

"I understand what you're saying, Carlie. But everyone needs other people. You can't just close yourself off."

She stood again. "I can. I did. I finally got that divorce, finally got my freedom, and I don't intend to ever put myself in that position again. It was difficult and stupid, relying on someone else for my happiness. But I'm intelligent enough to remember the lesson, even if I occasionally have a memory lapse."

Tyler stood also, looking very intent. He took a small step

toward her. "What we have is more than a memory lapse, sweetheart. And I'm going to prove it to you."

Carlie stiffened. "You're going to go home." Her words were firm and unrelenting.

"Yes. But I'll be back." She relaxed slightly at his easy compliance. Then he continued. "You have to accept that I'm not like him, Carlie."

A rush of soft laughter escaped her. "Don't you think I know that? You're nothing like him. But I'm still myself. And I can't change."

A smile twitched on his lips. "You change so often, I can't keep up with you. I'm only beginning to discover who Carlie McDaniels is."

"Don't be ridiculous. I've told you who I am."

He shook his head. "You don't know yourself, honey, so how could you tell me?" Then he cupped her cheeks in his palms, holding her gently captive. Against her lips, he breathed, "We'll find her together, Carlie. I promise."

His kiss was light and filled with tenderness, a mere brushing of his lips. Then he turned to go. Carlie didn't say a word. What was there to say? He'd find out soon enough she was exactly who she seemed to be. And then he'd leave her alone. She was strong enough to wait him out.

At least, she hoped she was.

Tyler would be showing up any minute. She'd spent her morning girding herself for the impact of seeing him again. He hadn't canceled on the school project, so she would have to continue working with him. But she was ready.

He sauntered onto the gym floor with his usual air of confidence, and several of the children ran to greet him. Lucy had taken a particular liking to him, and when she threw her arms around him, he tugged on one of her braids.

Tyler took a few minutes to address the other kids, talking with each one, asking about school, joking and teasing and being teased in return.

Carlie felt herself softening. Whoever would have thought Tyler would show so much understanding with children? And it was innate, she was sure, not something that could be summoned forth at will. Children knew if an adult really liked them. And Tyler truly cared about the children.

It hit Carlie then. Tyler, too, had an alter ego, just as she did. In fact, more than one.

There was Tyler the businessman, the astute lawyer who handled cases with flair and savvy. And there was also Tyler, the ladies' man, with a reputation well known by the female population. In fact, Carlie now realized that reputation had been encouraged more by the ladies than by Tyler himself. The things he valued in a woman, as far as she could tell, were intelligence and laughter, not her measurements and unfailing willingness.

And he was also a very perceptive man, considerate and indulgent, with a gentleness toward all things weaker or smaller. That was why he dealt so well with children.

Tyler looked up and caught her scrutinizing him. He strolled over, dribbling the ball. With a slight smile, he stopped directly in front of her. "I know what I'm thinking. Are your thoughts the same?"

Carlie shrugged, stealing the ball away from him. "I was thinking you should get married and have children of your own. You're very good with them." She glanced at him, saw his shock and smiled with satisfaction. "That's all."

"That's all! Hey, wait a minute."

He was too late. She blew the whistle and the children lined up. For the next two hours, Carlie made certain she kept her distance from Tyler, always making sure she had at least one of the kids close to her. It was an ingenious plan—and it was obviously frustrating Tyler. He scowled at her throughout the last fifteen minutes of the practice.

Tyler walked two of the children out to their parents' cars, talking with the moms and dads a few minutes before coming back to the gym. She wasn't going to bother asking him what the discussions were about this time. He'd never confided in her last time. When he noticed she was still in the gym, he headed toward her, falling into step beside her as she started for the locker room.

"I want to talk to you, Carlie."

"Can't right now. I'm running late as it is." That was an easy truth to give, though Tyler didn't accept it.

"Late for what, dammit?"

She didn't look at him. "Don't curse at me, Tyler."

"Then stop avoiding me!"

"In other words, if I don't, you're going to continue to blast me with your foul language?"

He grabbed her arm, halting her. "Talk to me. Please."

It unnerved her, seeing him so abjectly sincere. "I'm sorry. Really. But I'm starting some night courses and I'm running late. I should have left ten minutes ago."

He searched her face. "What time will you get home?"

"Late."

"Too late to see me?"

"There's no reason for me to see you. I told you that."

"And I didn't accept it. I guess we're at an impasse."

"*We* aren't anywhere. I'm late and you should be getting home. Goodbye."

"No. I'm not leaving until you tell me what you meant by that crack about children."

"It wasn't a crack." She glanced at her watch, a deliberate show of impatience. "You'd make an excellent father. You should find yourself a woman like Bren, and settle down. It would relieve the boredom you're forever complaining about."

"I haven't complained about being bored since I met you. And I don't want a woman like Bren. I want a woman like you."

It took great willpower not to react to that statement. Her stomach had lurched and her pulse had skipped a beat. But he was only being Tyler, flirting and teasing. She couldn't take him seriously. "You want a woman who doesn't want you back? I don't know, Tyler. That might be kind of hard. Didn't you tell me that all the women want you?"

"No. I don't recall saying that. But I know you do, Carlie. Shall I prove it?"

Carlie flushed, silently cursing him for challenging her, especially when she knew she couldn't win. "I can't deny I enjoyed sex with you, Tyler. That isn't what I meant, and you know it. Why don't you take up a hobby? Collect stamps or something so you can entertain yourself without annoying me."

"I wasn't trying to annoy you! I'm trying to talk to you. I want you to forgive me, I want—"

"You're forgiven."

"That was a little precipitous, wasn't it?" He eyed her suspiciously. "What are you forgiving me for?"

"I have no idea. You're the one who wanted forgiveness." She raised her eyebrows politely. "You tell me."

He took a deep breath. "I'm sorry for yelling at you, for jumping to conclusions and saying hateful, uncalled-for things."

"They were called for. And you were justified." She looked down at her clasped hands and made the necessary effort to relax. "Will you forgive me, also? For deceiving you and using you and causing you embarrassment?"

"Carlie." He pulled her against his chest, despite her stiff, unyielding posture. "There's nothing to forgive, honey. I understand why you didn't tell me."

Carlie slowly stepped away, then started toward the gym door. "It's in the past, Tyler," she called over her shoulder. "Forget about it. We're both obviously very sorry and determined not to make the same mistakes again. That's good enough for me. Now, I have to go. I'll see you Wednesday."

"Carlie…"

She didn't stop, didn't turn to him, didn't slow her pace at all. But she could feel his eyes boring into her and just before the heavy back door swung shut behind her, she heard a bang that sounded suspiciously like a fist hitting a locker.

"You're going to have to help out here, Bren!" Tyler said as he paced the kitchen, his hands shoved deep into his pockets. Carlie was being entirely unreasonable. She wouldn't see him beyond practices and wouldn't take the time to talk to him when it wasn't absolutely necessary. He'd about run out of ideas. And he was getting desperate.

Brenda and Jason stared at him as he paced. Brenda shook her head. "Carlie would never forgive me if I got in the middle of this."

"Just try talking to her for me. She'll listen to you."

"Not a chance. Carlie won't listen to anything I have to say. Not with things so fouled up."

Tyler glowered at her. "Things are not fouled up! Carlie and I being together is not a mistake."

"Hah! Carlie's more determined than ever to stay away from men. She won't even go out with that old school-board guy, and he's certainly no threat."

Tyler halted, then looked at Brenda. "What are you talking about?"

"There's some old stuffed shirt on the school board—"

"He's only thirty-six, Bren," Jason interrupted.

"Well, he seems old, he's so uppity." She gave her attention back to Tyler. "Anyway, she's gone out with him a couple of times. Mostly to talk over school stuff, or so he says. Personally, I think he's trying to ingratiate himself. Now he wants her to help him head up a new fund-raiser at the school. Carlie said she needs to get together with him this weekend to discuss the particulars."

"Where?"

Jason stood. "Now, Tyler..."

He ignored his brother. The thought of Carlie with another man made him see red. He repeated, "Where?"

Jason cleared his throat to hide his smile. "At her house, I believe."

"The time?"

Jason glanced at Brenda, who was doing her best to look innocent. "I think she said around noon, but I can't be sure," she said.

Tyler turned on his heel and headed out, not bothering to say goodbye. He didn't see the smug grin on his sister-in-law's face.

Jason pursed his lips. "I thought you weren't going to interfere."

"Of course I wouldn't!" Brenda gasped. "I gave Carlie my word."

"Then what was this little scene you just enacted?"

"A slip of the tongue?"

"Clever. Just what I love in a wife!"

On his drive home, Tyler formulated his plan. It was Friday evening—he'd gone to his brother's house, frustrated after another unsatisfying attempt to gain Carlie's attention during the practice. She was getting very good at ignoring him. And after practice, she had to hurry off for her classes. He had no doubt they'd been planned just to thwart him. It annoyed the hell out of him.

But he could be just as devious as Carlie. Since he had no intention of giving up on Carlie, he had to overcome her obstacles.

And he had a secret weapon—his own project he'd been working on for some time. He'd planned to surprise Carlie with it. Now it would prove invaluable. But first he needed to get her alone for a bit. He hadn't missed her response the day he'd held her only briefly. But he had been stymied by the fact that she seemed to find it so easy to walk away. She hadn't even looked back as he'd willed her to do. Stubborn wench.

At least she was never boring. He remembered the way she had held him so tight when he'd entered her, how she told him she cared. Not a little, but a lot. He had to believe that. She still cared, and she would get over her anger. He'd help her. Hell, he'd insist upon it.

Tyler planned his arrival perfectly, even to the point of driving around the block twice, waiting for the strange car to show up in front of Carlie's house. He parked and got out, whistling, a sheath of papers in his hand.

He knocked on the door, then waited, doing his best to hide his smile. Carlie answered, dressed in her usual distasteful clothes. This time, it was a long skirt, hanging below her knees. Her slim calves and ankles were hidden by boots, the skirt topped by a large sweater which had no waist or any other defining lines. It was ugly as sin.

"You look beautiful today, Carlie." He spoke loudly enough for her company to hear. She glared at him, but he knew he had her. She was forced to be polite when a member of the school board was in earshot.

"Hello, Tyler. What brings you here today?"

He quickly shouldered his way inside before she could tell him she was busy. "I have some things to discuss with you about your project."

"The team?"

"That's right. I had some ideas to go over with you."

A man entered, dressed in a business suit and looking every bit as stuffy as Brenda had claimed he was. He didn't so much as glance at Tyler. "Is something wrong, Carlie?"

She looked harassed. "Ah, no." Then she grudgingly made the introductions. "Tyler, this is Brad Shaw. Brad, meet Tyler Ramsey, the man I told you about. He's proving to be a big help with the after-school basketball program."

The men shook hands. Tyler smiled with devious innocence. "I'm sorry, Carlie. I didn't realize you had a date tonight."

She didn't disappoint him with her reaction. He grinned as she turned beet-red. Tyler had the feeling it was mostly due to anger. "Brad is a member of the school board. We were going to discuss a new fund-raiser."

"Is that right? Maybe I could help. I'm always willing to help support the schools."

It was obvious he'd gotten Brad's interest. He may have wanted to be alone with Carlie, but apparently he also wanted financial aid. He opted for the money. "Won't you join us, Mr. Ramsey?"

He grinned. "Tyler, please. I'd be delighted." Then he turned to Carlie. "But I do need to discuss a few things with you, also."

"Of course. We have the afternoon free." Brad was being very charming. "Isn't that right, Carlie?"

With a strained, slightly malicious smile, Carlie nodded. "Certainly. Tyler knows how interested I am in doing what I can for the school."

Tyler watched her, satisfied. He made certain she was aware of his intent in visiting. He wasn't planning to be devious—yet. That would come later. Maybe after he'd lulled her with false confidence.

"Would anyone like anything to drink?" Carlie headed for the kitchen. Tyler watched her, knowing she was only using the excuse to fume in private. He gave her thirty seconds, then left Brad looking around an empty living room so he could "give Carlie some help."

She had her back to him, setting glasses on the counter and filling them with iced tea. Silently, he moved up behind her, then bent and kissed her exposed neck.

Carlie jerked, nearly knocking over one of the glasses. Tyler caught it, set it back on the counter, then met her outraged gaze. "I've missed you so much, sweetheart."

"Don't you *ever* do that—"

Tyler quickly covered her mouth with his own. Her startled gasp was held suspended somewhere between them.

Her lips were soft and moist, and she tasted delicious. Using all his experience, he seduced her mouth, nibbling at her soft lips, licking gently, reclaiming her, urging her closer.

"Carlie." He forgot his purpose. It seemed so long since he'd kissed her. Without really intending to, his hand came up to cup her breast.

Instinct alone saved him. Ducking and catching her open palm just inches from his cheek, Tyler chided her. "Sweetheart, if you hit me, how will you explain it to your date?"

Through set teeth, she growled, "He's not my date, you ass!"

"Shh. Do you want him to know what we're doing?"

"I'm not doing anything! You're the one…!"

He watched with interest as her chest heaved angrily. Then he smiled. "You don't have to *do* anything. I read the morning paper and I want you. My secretary, who must be going on eighty, brings me coffee and I want you. I see you standing at the counter pouring tea and I positively throb."

Carlie closed her eyes in exasperation. "What are you doing here, Tyler?"

"I had to see you."

She turned away, picking up the tray. "Now you've seen me. Will you please go home?"

"And leave you here alone with Casanova? No way."

Carlie started out of the kitchen. Tyler took the tray from her. "He's only an associate," she said.

Tyler sent her a doubtful look. "With higher aspirations."

She snorted.

The sound was beautiful to his ears, so much like his old Carlie. He grinned at her, and to his besotted happiness, she actually grinned back. Then she shook her head and whispered for him to behave. He made no promises.

It quickly became a business meeting, just as Carlie had said. And surprisingly, Tyler enjoyed himself. He offered a lot of helpful input concerning the fund-raiser, legal advice Carlie or Brad wouldn't have thought of, and some suggestions of his own which proved very sound.

Brad was clearly impressed with Tyler, and before they called it quits, he was behaving as if they were old friends. "Could I call on you at your office sometime to discuss any problems that might arise?"

Tyler felt smug, but he hid it behind a facade of graciousness. "Of course. Just tell my secretary I said it was fine. She's a real stickler about keeping out people without appointments."

Brad shook his hand. "I appreciate that. Well, I better be

off. I'm sorry I can't stay and help with your project, but I'm running a little late."

"Think nothing of it." Tyler simply wanted him gone. "Carlie and I can muddle through."

"If you're sure, then?"

Carlie stood abruptly and went to the door, obviously tired of playing cat and mouse. "Thank you for coming by, Brad. Let me know if there's anything else I can do to help."

She stood at the door, waiting until Brad had gotten into his car and driven away before closing it and facing Tyler.

He saw immediately that she was incensed. He forestalled her tirade by tossing out his own stack of papers. "I want to start a scholarship fund at your school."

Her mouth, already open to blast him, snapped shut.

"You could use it as you see fit. To pay for sports equipment, to help with school fees or lunches, or even to start special classes. Whatever. I've been giving this some thought for a while now." He gave her a slightly sheepish look. "After our practices, I offered to help out a few of the parents who were having difficulties. It's a tough thing, trying to give assistance without making it look like charity. I sent papers to be typed up at one house, and then gave some plumbing business from our offices to another. But it wasn't enough. I didn't want to offend anyone, so I came up with the idea of a scholarship.

"Jason has agreed to pitch in, too, and I think some of the other businesses in the area will follow suit. It would be great publicity for their services. 'Caring for the community' and all that." He drew to a halt. "What do you think?"

Her expression blank, Carlie walked to the table where Tyler had tossed the documents. She picked up the top sheet and scanned it. She looked staggered by the amount of his donation.

Raising her eyes to his, she whispered, "You're serious?"

"Of course. I have a contract ready. I hope you don't mind,

but I left the distribution of my donation in your capable hands. As others come in, you could put them before a board of advisers if you want. But you already know the kids and their families so well, what they need and so forth, I thought you'd be perfect for the job."

Carlie was speechless. She stared at him.

"I think the contributing businesses would also agree to hire a few of the parents on a part-time basis. I know I always need papers transcribed and letters sent out. What do you—" He stopped midsentence. "Carlie? Is everything all right?"

She sat on the edge of the couch, his papers clutched in her hand, looking dumbfounded. "You're amazing, Tyler."

He actually felt himself blush. Gruffly, he said, "I'm just trying to help out. I have the money." He shrugged, dismissing her praise. "I wanted to surprise you."

Carlie laid her hand over his. "Thank you, Tyler. This means so much. I can already think of three families who will really benefit from this."

He grinned in satisfaction, retaining his hold on her hand. "There you go! Use it as you see fit. I'll see what I can do about getting some of the other businesses in on it. But in the meantime, if you need more money, let me know."

That did it. She looked near tears, overwhelmed with his generosity and goodness of spirit. And he felt not a single moment's guilt.

After all, he reasoned, he had donated the money. If the timing of his surprise seemed just a bit suspicious, it didn't matter. He needed all the help he could get.

Seeing her so obviously softened toward him, Tyler eased her into his arms. "You're not going to cry, are you? I can't abide watery women."

Pulling away as far as his arms would allow, Carlie gazed at him with a small smile. "I promise not to cry." But no sooner had she made that promise than she broke it, choking on a low sob.

Tyler shook his head. "So you really think I'm amazing?"

"I do."

The words were whispered with such sincerity, Tyler caught his breath. And then he smiled. "Excellent." His thoughts slowed to concentrate on one fact: he was with Carlie, and she still cared. But as he leaned toward her, she protested.

"Ah, Tyler, I didn't mean..."

"Shh. Kiss me again, Carlie."

"You kissed me! I didn't..."

"Don't argue semantics. I can think of better things to do." His tone was deep and suggestive as his arms slowly tightened around her.

With slightly narrowed eyes and a dangerously soft voice, she inquired, "Are you suggesting we have sex?"

"I, ah, well, I suppose the thought had entered my mind." About a million times in the past hour, he silently added. But Carlie was suddenly looking so furious, he kept that little tidbit to himself.

"Because you donated money to needy children," she clarified, "you think I should sleep with you? That's despicable! How could you propose such a thing?"

Anger and frustration rushed through him, and he jumped to his feet. "All right, dammit! You don't like that proposition? Well, here's another one." He sucked in a deep breath. "Marry me."

Chapter Eleven

CARLIE STARED AT Tyler blankly. "Don't you think humor is a little misplaced at this point?"

"I..." He shut his mouth. Truth be told, he'd surprised himself as much as he had Carlie with that sudden command. *Marry me.* Damn, but it did seem the right thing to say at the right time.

He grinned. "I'm not joking. I want to marry you."

She eyed him warily. "Why?"

He gave her a mock frown of disapproval over her rude questioning. "You don't seem to know any more about accepting proposals than you did about dates. Let me instruct you. This is the part where you fall into my arms, tearfully showing your gratitude and devotion, and shout a resounding, 'Yes!' You got all that?"

"Provided, of course, the answer would be yes?"

Tyler felt a moment's misgiving. "Don't toy with me, Carlie. I've never proposed to anyone in my life. I could have a major attack of insecurity here, if you're not careful." He hoped his teasing tone belied the truth behind his words. He felt almost sick with dread.

Carlie chewed her bottom lip and her eyes were dark with shadows. "Tyler, I don't want to get married. It's not just you. I don't want to marry anyone. Ever. I followed that route once, and as you know, it didn't go all that well."

Tyler sat beside her and took her hands in his. He needed to touch her, to make her understand. "It wouldn't be that way with me, Carlie. I'm not like him."

She went on, all brisk and businesslike. "Of course you're not. I told you, you're amazing. Kind and compassionate, and too attractive to be turned loose on polite society. But I value my independence. I don't intend to give it up."

It took him a minute to recover from her compliments. He was still beaming when the rest of what she'd said sank in. "I'm not asking you to give up anything."

She gave him a sardonic look. "Be honest, Tyler. Don't you think you'd start hounding me right away over how I dress? Or how I wear my hair?"

"Well," he hedged. She had a point. But a poor one. "You can't go on hiding the rest of your life, Carlie. You're a beautiful woman. That's something to be proud of. It's a part of you. And once we're married, there won't be any reason to look so shabby. I wouldn't let other men ogle you."

She tossed up her hands in exasperation. "There, you see? Not only are you changing me, but you'll be playing barbarian protector as well. I don't need a protector, Tyler."

"Not dressed like that you won't."

Carlie sighed, ignoring his provocation. "Please try to understand."

"I understand. You said you cared for me, but it wasn't exactly the truth." He stood, towering over her. He felt dejected, rejected and unbearably weary. He tweaked her chin, giving her a crooked smile. "You know something, honey? You're just a bit selfish."

Carlie raised an eyebrow at the criticism, but he continued.

"I've bent over backward, made all the concessions I can make, humiliated myself several times now trying to win you over. But you have a hard heart. I don't hold that against you. Considering your past, I suppose it's even expected. But damned if I know what else to do.

"It hurts, Carlie. It hurts to care so much about someone, and then have them turn you away again and again. I've been closer to you than I have to any other soul on earth, Jason included. And I was determined not to give up on you."

Carlie was staring down at her lap, and Tyler couldn't see her face. He decided it was just as well. He was spilling his guts, laying his heart on the table, and if she looked at him with pity, he might very well lose it. His tone was indifferent now, his expression impassive. "I can't do it anymore. You must be stronger than I am, because I can't take the rejections again. If you want to go on living in a cocoon, there's no way I can stop you. But I won't hang around indefinitely waiting for you to emerge, either."

She remained silent, and Tyler sighed in disgust. She wasn't making it any easier for him. "I won't be at the practice on Monday. I'll get Jason to fill in until you can find someone more permanent. Explain to the kids for me, if you will. And if you need any more money, let me know. You can leave a message with my secretary." He walked to the door and waited, but she didn't move. He nearly choked on his rage and frustration. Damn her, she had pulled him in, made him love her and now she didn't care.

He walked out, closing the door softly behind him.

Carlie waited on Monday, her stomach roiling, her head aching, her eyes burning. And true to his word, Tyler didn't come. She felt awful, even though she hadn't wanted to marry him, *couldn't* marry him. The idea was absurd.

So why had her heart threatened to burst when he'd proposed? And when he'd left, after such a touching speech, she'd felt like she was coming apart.

Oh God, she hurt.

Jason entered, dressed in an old college sweatshirt and gym shorts that showed his hairy legs. He spared her a glance, then picked up a ball and began bouncing it. Carlie approached him.

"Hello, Jason."

He inclined his head. "Carlie."

"I appreciate your filling in like this. On such short notice, I mean."

He looked at her. "Tyler needed me. I love him. He's my brother."

"I...I know." She hesitated, swallowing hard. Jason's mood was apparently not conducive to small talk. But she needed to know. "How is Tyler?"

Very casually, still bouncing the ball, Jason said, "Miserable. Thanks for asking."

Carlie flinched at his tone. "Jason, I never meant to—"

"Of course, you didn't. In your book, all men are jerks, right? Tyler certainly can't be any different."

She shook her head, then started to turn away. Jason held the ball. "Carlie? I'm sorry. It's not my place to..."

She didn't look at him. "It's okay, Jason. I understand."

"No. I don't think you do. But it's my opinion you never will, so I'm glad you broke things off with Tyler now, before he got even more involved. I'm the only person he's ever had care for him. His life hasn't exactly encouraged him to trust women. So when he does marry, I damned well want it to be to a woman who's capable of loving him. He deserves that much."

She was crushed by the hard words, but acknowledged the truth in them. Tyler did deserve the best. If only...

Oh, God. She really had done it this time. No matter how deep she buried the past, it always seemed to come back and torment her.

Or was she only tormenting herself?

After two weeks had passed, Carlie knew it was time to face facts. She loved Tyler and always would. She missed him terribly, and with each day that went by, the feeling grew worse. When she was with him, she felt alive. Without him, she felt dull and drained.

She needed him, and even though she'd sworn never to need anyone again, she felt comforted by the admission. She no longer had to deny herself or her emotions. It wasn't a bad thing to need Tyler. He wouldn't take advantage of her feelings, wouldn't try to dominate her or weaken her to suit his own needs. She believed that. She trusted him.

But she had hurt him badly, and he might not forgive her.

Carlie knew she was too much the coward to call Tyler outright. She needed a reason for calling, and when more donations to the scholarship fund came in from various businesses, she decided that excuse would work well enough. She'd start out by thanking him, and work into telling him she loved him madly.

It was a bold plan, she thought, and would have worked, except that Tyler didn't answer the phone. She got a message saying he was out of the office for some time and all calls could be forwarded to Jason. When she tried him at home, his answering machine picked up. Concerned, she called Brenda.

What she discovered wasn't encouraging.

Tyler planned to take an extended vacation to Chicago, where he was considering joining a new firm. Jason, of course, was livid and blaming Carlie. Brenda was apologetic, but very upset by it all.

Carlie had a hard time breathing. She knew exactly what was happening. She'd done the same after her divorce. She'd tried to leave the pain behind.

She could have told Tyler it didn't work. Because right now, the pain was unbearable. Everything had gone wrong, and it was all her own fault. She was a miserable coward, and it was time she stopped hiding, just as Tyler had suggested.

She had to do something, and she had to do it now.

It was Jason who answered the door. Just the fact that Carlie was knocking at the front entrance, rather than entering through the kitchen, as usual, was indicative of her uneasiness. She had no idea if she'd be welcome, given the present situation. But Jason was polite. Painfully so.

"Hello, Carlie. Come in."

"Thanks. Ah, Tyler isn't here, is he?"

Jason eyed her. "No. He's been avoiding us as much as you have."

Carlie flushed, but she refused to back down. "I'm sorry about that." She came in and Jason shut the door behind her. With her hands in her pockets, she looked around the room. "Is Bren around?"

"I'll get her for you. Make yourself at home."

It felt exceedingly odd for Jason to say such a thing. It had never been necessary before.

Brenda flew into the room, her eyes alight with expectation. "Carlie! I'm so glad to see you!"

Carlie ducked out of reach. "No hugging, Bren. I'm dangerously close to coming unglued here, and any excess of kind consideration will definitely put me over the edge."

Brenda blinked. "What are you talking about?"

Carlie had been calm enough until that moment. The simple truth was, she still suffered a few qualms over her own appeal. She was unbelievably apprehensive about confronting Tyler, no matter how she tried to deny it. Her lips started to quiver. She felt like a fool, but she couldn't stop it. She clasped her hands, opened her mouth to calmly and intelligently explain, then broke into tears. "I love him!"

Brenda smiled. "Oh, Carlie."

Despite Carlie's objections, Brenda pulled her into a fierce hug. "I think that's wonderful."

"I don't know, Bren." She sniffed, then swiped the tears from her cheeks. "I hurt him. I've never hurt anyone in my life. I can't stand it."

"Have you told him?"

Carlie shook her head. "I can't just go up to him and say, 'Well, guess what? I do love you, after all.' I've been so terrible."

"No, you haven't. And Tyler will understand."

Carlie raised her chin. Enough was enough. She'd had her little show of vulnerability. "I sincerely hope you're right. Because I do love him. In fact, I'm crazy about him. But he's never actually said he loved me. He asked me to marry him, and he makes no bones about wanting me…that way. But he's never actually mentioned the word *love*."

Jason stepped into the room. "Gossiping about my brother again?"

Brenda turned and nearly snapped his head off. "We weren't gossiping! I was going to convince Carlie that Tyler loves her."

Jason rolled his eyes. "Of course he does. Why do you think he's been so impossible lately?"

"Don't tell me," Brenda demanded. "Tell Carlie."

Jason walked over to Carlie. "Tyler loves you. Now, what are you going to do about it?"

Carlie bit her bottom lip. Tyler had tried to tell her the depth of his feelings right before he left her house the last time. But she hadn't responded. At all. It made her ache to imagine how he must have felt. How could she tell him how scared she had been, that she'd been petrified at the idea of accepting too much happiness because it left her vulnerable?

Just as vulnerable as he must have felt when she'd failed to accept his proposal.

Suddenly, she realized what she had to do. "I have to make it up to him. I need to show him how much I care."

"Just tell him," Jason suggested.

But Carlie shook her head. "I have a plan. But I'll need your help."

"Oh, no." Jason put a hand to his head, looking ready to expire. "You're starting to sound just like my wife."

Brenda laughed. "Go ahead, Carlie, I'm listening. You know I dearly love a good plan."

Jason sat, and the women looked at him pointedly. "I'm not budging. You two are plotting something against my poor brother, and I need to be here to look after his interests."

"Well, all right." Carlie leaned forward, and Jason and Brenda followed suit. "Here's want I want to do."

Tyler stared at Jason, dressed in an elegant suit and obviously preparing to leave the house. "I thought you wanted me to help you with some work around here today."

Jason smacked his palm to his forehead theatrically. "Oh, boy. I forgot, Tyler. Bren made plans for us to go out tonight. Do you mind?"

"Well, no." Actually, Tyler had been looking forward to working with his brother. He needed some physical labor to drain him, to weary his mind enough to drive out thoughts of other things. He only hoped his disappointment didn't show.

Shoving his hands into his jeans pockets, Tyler stepped around Jason. He didn't want to return to his apartment. The mere thought was enough to make him shudder. Lately, all he could do was think of Carlie. Oh, how the mighty did fall. Flat on their faces.

And it still hurt, dammit.

Moving away was a desperate decision. He couldn't be so close to Carlie, knowing she was only minutes away, and constantly be reminded of how he had failed, both her and himself. He needed to get on with his life, but no one had ever told him how to do that.

Jason interrupted his thoughts, slapping him on the shoulder. "I have a favor to ask. If you don't have anything else pressing to do, could you go ahead and get started on a few things for me? You know how I'm already rushed for time, especially now that I've started helping with the after-school basketball program."

Tyler winced. "How are they? The kids, I mean. Little Lucy is doing all right?"

"They're all the same." Jason's answer was deliberately vague. "A few of the parents asked me to extend their thanks for your help. It was great of you to figure out a way for them to earn extra money. I hadn't realized you were doing so much."

Tyler frowned, uncomfortable with the praise, but Jason didn't give him time to argue. "I made a list of a few jobs that had to be done."

Tyler forced a smile. "I wouldn't mind helping out. I don't have anything else to do today, anyway."

Jason almost grinned. "You're sure? I'd really appreciate it."

"No problem. What's first on the list?"

Jason produced a folded piece of paper and stuck it into the front breast pocket of Tyler's flannel shirt. "I gotta run. Do me a favor first, though, will you? Carlie called the other day and said she left something in the pool house. I don't remember what. Go down and check it out, will you? Look around and see if you find anything."

Tyler didn't move a single muscle. "She's not stopping by here, is she?" He knew he sounded panicked, but to be alone with Carlie would nearly kill him. He couldn't trust himself not to act like an ass again.

Jason waved away his concern. "You don't have to worry about her dropping in." He turned away quickly. "I really do appreciate this, Tyler. Bren and I won't be home till late, so help yourself to anything you need, and..." Jason grinned suddenly. "Relax, will you? Things are never as bad as they seem."

Tyler had no answer for that. Things seemed pretty damned bad to him.

Despite himself, he was anxious to see what Carlie had left in the pool house. Her mask? Some small part of that alluring harem costume? Maybe he'd find it and keep it. As a memento. What could she say? Not a thing.

He waited till he heard Jason's car drive away, then went out the back, heading for the pool house. It seemed so achingly familiar, each step he took on the flagstone walk brought the memories closer. But instead of soft party lights to guide his way, the sun was shining brightly. The breeze chilled him, and he hunkered his shoulders forward, his head down.

The pool house door was slightly ajar, but Tyler paid no attention to that small detail. He was too overcome with memories. Odd, but knowing now that it had been Carlie, not another woman, only enhanced the memory, made it more erotic and more tantalizing.

Heat washed over him in waves as he closed the door behind him, but it wasn't from the warmth of the room. Just looking around caused his body to react, and when he spotted the couch, his thighs clenched and his stomach tightened.

"Tyler?"

He froze. He couldn't possibly be dreaming, not so vividly, not with such stark reality. He turned slowly, and felt his breath catch in his throat.

She was almost exactly as he remembered, hovering in the corner, her back to the wall. But there was no wig, and somehow he knew the mask was for effect, not concealment.

Tyler stared, his eyes so hot he could barely see. There were no shadows today. Each and every lamp had been turned on. Carlie's hair, appearing more blond than brown in the bright light, hung loose about her shoulders. It was in gentle waves, sexy and shimmering and tempting him to touch it. Her hazel eyes, brightly lit with anticipation and anxiety, stared at him, direct and unblinking.

Very slowly, not daring to breathe, he walked toward her. Reaching out, his fingers touched the mask. "May I remove it?"

Her smile quavered, dimpling her cheeks, but then vanished quickly. It was a nervous reaction, he knew, and his love for her doubled.

"If you like." Carlie held his eyes, her breathing suspended, her heart pounding erratically. She loved him so much. "Whatever you like, Tyler."

"I like you." He slipped the mask from her face, gently laying it aside. Cupping her cheeks, he smiled at her. "Do you realize how rare and special that is, Carlie? I like everything about you. I like being with you, I like looking at you, I like talking with you."

He kissed her lightly, fleetingly, on her trembling lips. "I'll never grow bored of you or try to change you."

Carlie rubbed her cheek against his palm. "Except my clothes?"

It was an attempt at humor, but Tyler didn't laugh. "You can wear any damned thing you like. I don't care."

Her eyes welled with tears, and she had to fight to keep from pressing herself against him. But they had to talk. She had to make him understand. Drawing a deep breath, she looked up at him. "I want to make you happy, Tyler. I…I love you."

He closed his eyes, then hugged her tight. "I love you, too, Carlie. So damned much."

Her smile was tremulous. "It's a little scary, isn't it?"

"No!" He held her away from him, his expression fierce. "Losing you is scary. Loving you is easy, and unbelievably exciting." Then he smiled, his hand dropping to finger the edge of her skimpy bodice. "Much like this costume of yours."

Very seriously, without any hesitation, Carlie whispered, "I want to be whatever you want me to be."

"I want you to be yourself." He pressed his face into her shoulder, inhaling her soft, feminine scent. "You're a beautiful woman, Carlie. And so special. Just be yourself for me, honey. Stop hiding."

She almost laughed out loud, she felt so relieved. Teasing Tyler with a smile, she asked, "Did Jason tell you what I lost here?"

He looked struck, having all but forgotten about his brother. He grinned. "No. What did you lose?"

She ducked her head. "I lost my heart."

"No." He tipped her chin up. "It's not lost. I have it, and I'm not giving it back."

Carlie started to say something more, but Tyler touched his fingers to her lips. "Did you wear this costume only to torment me, or do you plan on making my fantasies come true?"

"A little of both." She almost made it out of reach before Tyler grabbed her and held her close.

A long kiss followed, and Carlie was finally able to hug herself to him. It felt so right, so perfect. Paper rattled when she leaned into his chest, and Tyler pulled away. With a suspicious look, he tugged out the note Jason had given him. Keeping Carlie close, he read the message aloud. "Women have fantasies, too, or so Bren insists. There's a large paper bag behind the couch. Have fun, kids."

Carlie laughed, then squirmed from his grasp to retrieve the bag. She looked inside, then grinning, she tossed the bag to Tyler. "Here you go."

He caught it automatically. "What is it?"

"Your pirate costume." She bobbed her eyebrows comically. "Remind me to thank your brother."

Tyler grinned wickedly as he began unbuttoning his shirt. "I'm not a man you can trifle with, sweetheart. If you want to play games, you're going to have to promise to marry me."

Carlie watched him remove his shirt, her gaze rapt. "I'll marry you, I'll choose a whole new wardrobe, I'll even get rid of my glasses. But you have to promise me something, too."

He unsnapped his jeans, then slowly shoved them down his hips. "What's that?"

"You can never stop being outrageous."

He laughed, sounding smug. "Told you you'd like it."

Carlie walked into his arms, feeling loved and in love. Happy. She didn't stop until Tyler was holding her close again. "Indeed I do, Tyler. Indeed I do."

★ ★ ★ ★ ★

Outrageous

Chapter One

SHE HAD THE biggest brown eyes Judd had ever seen.

She also looked innocent as hell, despite the ridiculous clothes she wore and the huge, frayed canvas tote bag she carried. Did she actually think she blended in, just because her coat was tattered and her hat was a little ratty? Did she think anyone would ever believe her to be homeless? Not likely.

So what was she doing here at this time of night? The lower east side of Springfield was no place for a lady like her. She strolled past him again, this time more slowly, and her eyes were so wide it looked as if they could take in her surroundings in a single glance. They took in Judd.

He felt a thrill of awareness, sharper than anything he'd ever felt before. She looked away, but not before he detected the faint pink blush that washed over her fine features. That blush had been obvious even in the dim evening light, with only the moon and corner street lamp for illumination. She had flawless skin.

Dammit. He had enough to worry about without some damn Miss Priss with manicured nails and salon-styled hair trying to fob herself off as a local. Judd had only stepped outside the bar to get a breath of fresh air. The smell of perfume inside was overwhelming, and enough to turn his stomach.

He could hear the music in the bar grow louder and knew the dancers were coming onstage. In less than ten minutes, he'd have to go back in there, baring himself in the line of duty.

Damn. He hated this cover. What decent, hardworking cop should have to peel off his clothes for a bunch of sex-starved, groping women? For nearly two weeks now he'd been entertaining the female masses with the sight of his body, hoping to uncover enough evidence to make a bust. He was now, at thirty-two, in his prime, more fit than ever and completely alone. Not only did he meet the necessary requirements to pull off such a ludicrous cover, he had a vested, very personal interest this time. He knew for a fact the room above the bar was the site for shady business meetings, yet he hadn't seen hide nor hair of a gun deal. Clayton Donner was lying low.

It was discouraging, but he wasn't giving up.

He was definitely going to get Donner, but that didn't mean he enjoyed displaying himself nightly.

Each of the strippers had a gimmick. He thought his was rather ironic. He played out the tough street cop, complete with black pants held together with strategically placed Velcro. They came off with only the smallest tug. He even had Max's original leather jacket—a prized possession, to be sure—to add to his authenticity. The women loved it.

He wondered if old Max had known how sexy the cop persona was to females. Or if he would have cared.

God, he couldn't think about Max and still do his job, which was to appear unscrupulous enough that Donner would think him available. Clayton always needed new pigeons to run his scams. Judd intended to be the next. It was the only way he could get close enough to make a clean bust.

And the last thing he needed now was a distraction with big brown eyes. Despite his resolve, his gaze wandered back to the woman. She was loitering on the corner beneath the street lamp, holding that large, lumpy bag to her chest and trying to fit in. Judd snorted. That old coat was buttoned so high she was damn near strangling herself. What the hell was she doing here?

He'd just about convinced himself not to care, not to get involved, when three young men seemed to notice her. Judd watched as they approached her. She started to back away, then evidently changed her mind. She nodded a greeting, but it was a wimpy effort. Hell, the men looked determined to get to know her, without any encouragement on her part. She, on the other hand, looked ready to faint.

Walk away, he thought, willing the woman to move. But she stood her ground. He sensed, then he knew for certain, she was getting in over her head. His body was already tensing, his eyes narrowed, waiting for the trouble to start. They seemed to be talking, or, more to the point, she was trying to speak to them. She gestured with her hands, her expression earnest. Then one of the men grabbed her and she let loose a startled screech. In the next instant, those huge brown eyes of hers turned his way, demanding that he help her.

The little twit thought he was a regular street cop. At this rate she'd blow his cover.

Well, hell, he couldn't allow her to be manhandled. He pushed himself away from the doorway and started forward. The men were obviously drunk. One of them was doing his best to pull her close, but she kept sidestepping him. Judd approached them all with a casual air.

"Here now, boys." He kept his tone low and deep, deliberately commanding. "Why don't you leave the lady alone."

Judd could see her trembling, could see the paleness of her

face in the yellow light of the street lamp. The man didn't release her; if anything, he tightened his grip. "Go to hell."

The words were slurred, and Judd wondered just how drunk they were. They might believe him to be a cop, but in this neighborhood, being a law enforcement officer carried very little clout and regularly drew vicious disdain. Damn.

He couldn't get into a brawl—he might literally lose his pants. Not that he wouldn't enjoy knocking some heads together, but still.... Where was a real uniformed cop when you needed one?

He turned his gaze on the woman. "Do you want their company?"

She swallowed, her throat working convulsively. "No."

One of the men shook his fist in Judd's face, stumbling drunkenly as he did so. "She's already made a deal with us." The man grinned stupidly at the woman, then added, "You can't expect a little thing like her to run around here without a weapon to protect herself..."

One of the other men slugged the speaker. "Shut up, you fool."

Judd went very still, scrutinizing the woman's face. "Well?"

Again, she swallowed. "Well...what?"

"Why do you need a weapon? You planning to kill someone?" Whisper-soft, his question still demanded an immediate answer.

Shaking her head, then looking around as if desperately seeking a means of escape, she managed to pique his interest. He couldn't walk away now. Whatever she was up to, she didn't want him to know. Because she thought he was a cop?

Disgusted, Judd propped his hands on his hips, his eyebrows drawn together in a frown. "Do you want the company of these men or not?"

She peered cautiously at the drunken, leering face so close to her own. Her lips tightened in disapproval and disdain. "Ah...no. Not particularly."

A genuine smile tipped his mouth before he caught himself. She had gumption, he'd give her that. She was no bigger than a ten-year-old sickly kid. The coat she wore practically swallowed her up. She was fine-boned, petite, and everything about her seemed fragile. "There you go, fellas. The lady doesn't find you to her liking. Turn her loose and go find something else to do."

"I got somethin' to do already." Her captor's hold seemed to loosen just a bit as he spoke, and taking advantage, she suddenly jerked free. Then she did the dumbest thing Judd had ever seen. She sent her knee into the man's groin.

Unbelievable. Judd shook his head, even as he yanked her behind him, trying to protect her from the ensuing chaos. He couldn't do any real damage to the men without attracting more spectators, which would threaten his cover. And the woman was gasping behind him, scared out of her wits from the sound of it. But damn it all, he definitely *did not* want to lose his pants out here scuffling in the middle of the sidewalk with common drunks. One of the men started to throw a punch.

Judd cursed loudly as the woman ran around him, evidently not as frightened as he'd thought, and leaped onto his attacker's back. She couldn't weigh over a hundred pounds, but she wound her fingers in the man's hair and pulled with all her might.

Enough was enough. A glimpse at his watch told him it was time for his performance. Judd grabbed the man away from her and sent him reeling with a firm kick to the rear end, then stalked the other two, every muscle in his body tensed. Too drunk to persist in their efforts, the men scurried away.

Judd turned to face the woman, and she was...tidying her hair? Good God, was she nuts? He saw her look toward her canvas bag, which now lay in a puddle on the sidewalk, but she made no move to retrieve it.

"You don't want your bag?" he asked with all the sarcasm he could muster.

"Oh." She glanced at him. "Well, of course..." She made a move in its direction, but he shook his head. He could see more raggedy clothing falling out the opening, and if there was one thing this woman didn't need, it was hand-me-downs.

He took her arm in a firm but gentle hold, ignoring her resistance, and started her toward the bar. He automatically moved her to his right side, bringing her between his body and the building, protecting her from passersby. He held his temper for all of about three seconds, then gave up the effort.

"Of all the stupid, *harebrained*...lady, what the hell did you think you were doing back there?" He wondered if she could be a journalist, or a TV newswoman? She damn well wasn't used to living in alleys, or going without. Everything about her screamed money. Even now, with him hustling her down the sidewalk, she had a certain grace, a definite poise, that didn't come from being underprivileged.

She glanced up at him, and he noticed she smelled nice, too. Not heavily perfumed like the women in the bar, just... very feminine. Her wavy shoulder-length hair, a light brown that looked as baby soft as her eyes, bounced as he hurried her along. She was practically running, but he couldn't help that. He was going to be late. He could hear the music for his number starting. Taking off his clothes in public was bad enough. He didn't intend to make a grand entrance by jumping in late.

She cleared her throat. "I appreciate your assistance, Officer."

Without slowing his pace, he glared at her. "Answer my question. Who are you? What the hell are you up to?"

"That's two questions."

He growled, his patience at an end. *"Answer me, dammit!"*

She stumbled, then glared up at him defiantly. "That's really none of your business."

Everything inside his body clenched. "I'm making it my business."

Digging in her heels as he tried to haul her through the front door, she forced him to slow down. She was wide-eyed again and he noticed her mouth was hanging open as he dragged her into the bar. "What are you doing?"

There was a note of shrill panic in her voice as she took in her surroundings. Judd had no time to explain, and no time to consider her delicate sensibilities. Everyone in this part of town thought of him as a money-hungry, oversexed, willing exhibitionist—Clayton Donner included. It was a necessary cover and one he wasn't ready to forfeit. Donner would show up again soon, and once he decided Judd was a familiar face in the area, the gun dealer would make his move. It would happen. He'd make it happen.

Still gripping her arm, Judd trotted her toward the nearest bar stool. *"Stay right here."* He stared down at her, trying to intimidate her with his blackest scowl. The music was picking up tempo, signaling his cue.

She popped right back off the seat, those eyes of hers accurately portraying her shock. "Now see here! I have no intention of waiting—"

He picked her up, dropped her onto the stool again, then called to the bartender. "Keep her here, Freddie. Make certain she doesn't budge."

Freddie, a huge, jovial sort with two front teeth missing, grinned and nodded. "What'd she do?"

"She owes me. Big. Keep your eye on her."

"And if she tries to pike it?"

Judd gave Freddie a conspiratorial wink. "Make her sorry if she so much as flinches."

Freddie looked ferocious, but Judd knew he wouldn't hurt a fly. That was the reason they had not one, but two bouncers on the premises. But the little lady didn't know that, and Judd wanted to find out exactly what she was up to. Gut instinct told him he wouldn't like what he found.

Suddenly the spotlight swirled around the floor. Cursing, then forcing a grin to his mouth, Judd sauntered forward into the light. Women screamed.

In the short time he'd been performing here, he'd discovered a wealth of information about his gun dealer...and become a favorite of the bar. The owner had promised to double his pay, but that was nothing compared to the bills that always ended up stuffed in his skimpy briefs. He refused, absolutely *refused,* to wear a G-string. His naked butt was not something he showed to more than one woman at a time, and even *those* exhibitions were few and far between. But his modesty worked to his advantage. The women customers thought he was a tease, and appreciated his show all the more.

As he moved, he glanced over his shoulder to make certain the lady was still there. She hadn't moved. She didn't look as though she could. Her eyes were even larger now, huge and luminous and filled with shock and disbelief. He held her gaze, and slowly, backing into the center of the floor, slid the zipper down on the leather jacket. He saw her gasp.

Her intent expression, of innocence mixed with curious wonder, annoyed him, making him feel more exposed than he ever had while performing. That he could feel his face heat angered him. He was too old, and too cynical now, to actually blush. *Damn her.*

Purposefully holding her gaze, determined to make her look away, he let his fingers move to the top of his pants. As he slowly unhooked the fly, one snap at a time, teasing his audience, teasing her more, she reeled back and one dainty hand touched her chest. She looked distressed. She looked shocked.

But she didn't look away.

Oh, Lord. Oh, Lord. This can't be happening, Emily! It's too outrageous. There can't possibly be a large, gorgeous man peeling his clothes off in front of you.

Even as she told herself she was delirious, that the scene in front of her was a figment of her fantastical imagination, Emily watched him kick off his boots, then with one smooth jerk, toss his pants aside. She wouldn't have missed a single instant of his disrobing. She couldn't. She was spellbound.

Vaguely, in the back of her mind, she heard the crowd yelling, urging him on. He looked away from her finally, releasing her from his dark gaze. But still she watched him.

He was the most beautiful man she'd ever seen. Raw, sexual, but also…gentle. She could feel his gentleness, had felt it outside when she'd first walked past him. It was as if she recognized he didn't belong here, in this seedy neighborhood, any more than she did.

But they *were* both here. Her reason was plain; she needed to find out who had sold her younger brother the gun that backfired, nearly causing him to lose an eye. He would recover, but that wouldn't remove the fact that he'd bought the gun illegally, that he was involved in something he had no business being involved in and that he would probably be scarred for life. Emily had to find the man who'd almost ruined her brother's life. She couldn't imagine what kind of monster would sell a sixteen-year-old a gun—a defective gun, at that.

Her parents refused to take the matter to the police. Luckily, John had only been using the gun for target practice, so no one even knew he had the thing. And more important, no one else had been hurt. When she thought about what could have happened, the consequences...

But that was history. Now all she could do was make certain that the same man didn't continue selling guns to kids. She had no compunction about going to the police once she had solid evidence, enough that she didn't have to involve her brother.

Her parents would never forgive her if she sullied the family name. Again.

Her heart raced, climbing into her throat to choke her when the officer—obviously *not* an officer—started toward her. She couldn't take her eyes off his bare, hair-brushed chest, his long, naked thighs. The way the shiny black briefs cupped him... Oh God, it was getting warm in here...

Well-bred ladies most definitely did not react this way!

There were social standards to uphold, a certain degree of expected poise... The litany she'd been reciting to herself came to a screeching halt as the man stopped in front of her.

His eyes, a fierce green, reflected the spotlight. He stared directly at her, then moved so close she could smell the clean male fragrance of him, could feel his body heat. And God, he was hot.

Panting, Emily realized he was waiting for her to give him money. Of all the insane notions...but there were numerous dollars sticking out of those small briefs, and she knew, with unwavering instinct, he wouldn't budge until she'd done as he silently demanded.

Blindly, unable to pull her gaze away, she fumbled in the huge pockets of her worn coat until her fist closed on a bill. She stuck out her hand, offering the money to him.

Wicked was the only way to describe his smile. With a small, barely discernible motion, he shook his head. She dropped her gaze for an instant to where his briefs held all the cash. She'd watched the women put the money there, trying to touch him, but he'd eluded their grasping hands. He'd played up to the audience, getting only close enough to collect a few dollars, then dancing away.

She didn't want to touch him.

Oh, what a lie! She wanted to touch him, all right, but she wouldn't, not here in front of an audience, not ever. She was a respectable lady, she was... She squeaked, leaning back on her seat as he put one hand on the light frame over the bar, the other beside her on the bar stool. She was caged in, unable to breathe. She could see the light sheen of sweat caught in his chest hair, see the small, dark tuft of fine hair under his arm. It seemed almost indecent, and somehow very personal, to see his armpit.

Her body throbbed with heat, and she couldn't swallow. He stood there, demanding, insistent, so very carefully, using only her fingertips, she tucked the bill into his shorts. She registered warm, taut skin, and a sprinkling of crisp hair.

Still holding her gaze, he smiled, his eyes narrowing only the slightest bit. He leaned down next to her face, then placed a small, chaste kiss on her cheek. It had been whisper-light, almost not there, but so potent she felt herself close to fainting.

The audience screamed, loving it, loving him. He laughed, his expression filled with satisfaction, then went back to his dancing. Women begged for the same attention he'd given her, but he didn't comply. Emily figured one pawn in the audience was enough.

Though his focus was now directed elsewhere, it still took Emily several minutes to calm her galloping heartbeat. She continued to watch him, and that kept her tense, because despite everything she'd been brought up to believe, the man excited her.

His dark hair, long in the back, was damp with sweat and beginning to curl. With each movement he made, his shoulders flexed, displaying well-defined muscles and sinew. His backside, held tight in the black briefs, was trim and taut. And his thighs, so long and well-sculpted, looked like the legs of an athlete.

His face was beautiful, almost too beautiful. It was the kind of face that should make innocent women wary of losing their virtue. Green eyes, framed by deliciously long dark lashes and thick eyebrows, held cynical humor and were painfully direct and probing when he chose to use them that way. His nose was straight and narrow, his jaw firm.

Emily realized she was being fanciful, and silently gathered her thoughts. She needed to concentrate on what she'd come to do—finding the gun dealer. According to her brother, who at sixteen had no business hanging out in this part of town, he'd bought the gun on this street. It had been a shady trade-off from the start, cash for the illegal weapon. But John was in a rebellious stage, and his companions of late had ranged from minor gang members to very experienced young ladies. Emily prayed she could help him get back on the straight and narrow, that he could find his peace on an easier road than she'd taken. When she thought of the scars he'd have to live with, the regrets, she knew, deep in her heart, the only way to give him that peace was to find enough evidence to put the gun dealer away.

Though Emily planned to change his mind, John thought his life was over. What attractive, popular teenager could handle the idea of going through life with his face scarred? Then she thought of other kids—kids who might buy a duplicate of the same gun; kids who might be blinded rather than scarred. Or worse. The way the gun had exploded, it could easily have killed someone. And despite her parents' wishes, Emily couldn't stand back and allow that to happen. Her conscience wouldn't allow it.

The show finally ended, the music fading with the lighting until the floor was in darkness. The applause was deafening. And seconds later, the officer was back, his leather jacket slung over his shoulder, his pants and boots in his hand. He thanked the bartender, then took Emily's arm without any explanation, and rapidly pulled her toward an inside door. They narrowly missed the mob of advancing women.

Emily wanted to run, but she'd never in her life resorted to such a display. Besides, now that she knew he wasn't really a policeman, a plan was forming in her mind.

He pulled her into a back room, shut the door, then flipped on a light switch. Emily found herself in a storage closet of sorts, lined with shelves where cleaning supplies sat and a smelly mop tainted the air. A leather satchel rested in the corner. He didn't bother dressing. Instead, he tossed his clothes to the side and moved to stand a hairbreadth away from her.

"You gave me a fifty."

Emily blinked. His words were nowhere near what she'd expected to hear. She tucked in her chin. "I beg your pardon?"

He pulled the cash from his briefs, stacking the bills together neatly in his large hands. "You gave me a fifty-dollar bill. I hadn't realized my show was quite that good."

A fifty! Oh, Lord, Emily. She had no intention of telling him it hadn't been deliberate, that she'd been unable to pull her gaze away from him long enough to find the proper bills. What she'd given him was part of the money earmarked for buying information.

Maybe she could still do that.

Shrugging, she forced her eyes away from his body and stared at the dingy mop. "Since you're not a law enforcement officer, I was hoping the money would…entice you to help me."

He snorted, not buying her line for a second. Emily was relieved he was gentleman enough not to say so. He gave her a look that curled her toes, then asked, "What kind of *help* do you need, lady?"

It was unbelievably difficult to talk with him so near, and so nearly naked. He smelled delicious, of warm, damp male flesh, though she tried her best not to notice. But his body was too fine to ignore for long, despite her resolve not to give in to un-ladylike tendencies—such as overwhelming lust—ever again.

She licked her dry lips, then met his eyes. His gaze lingered on her mouth, then slowly coasted over the rest of her body. She knew she wasn't particularly attractive. She had pondered many disguises for this night, disguises ranging anywhere from that of a frumpy homeless lady, to a streetwalker. Somehow, she couldn't imagine herself making a convincing hooker. She was slight of build and her body had never quite…bloomed, as she'd always hoped for. She did, however, think she made an adequate transient.

She cleared her throat. Stiffening her spine, which already felt close to snapping, she said, "I need information."

"Your little trio of drunks didn't tell you enough?"

Since he appeared to have guessed her mission, she didn't bother denying it. "No. They didn't really know anything. And I had to be careful. They didn't seem all that trustworthy. But it's imperative I find out some facts. You…you seem well acquainted with the area?"

She'd said it as a question, and he answered with a nod.

"Good. I want to know of anyone who's selling guns."

He closed his eyes, his mouth twisting in an ironic smirk. "Guns? Just like that, you want to know who's dealing in guns? God, lady, you look like you could go to the nearest reputable dealer and buy any damn thing you wanted." He took a step closer, reaching out his hand to flip a piece of her hair. "I don't know who you thought you'd fool, but you walk like money, talk like money…hell, you even smell like money. What is it? The thrill of going slumming that has you traipsing around here dressed in that getup?"

Emily sucked in her breath at his vulgar question and felt her temper rise. "You have fifty dollars of my money. The least you can do is behave in a civilized, polite manner."

"Wrong." He stepped even closer, the dark, sweat-damp hair on his chest nearly brushing against the tip of her nose. He had to bend low to look her in the eyes, but he managed. "The least I can do is steer your fancy little tail back where you belong. Go home, little girl. Get your thrills somewhere else, somewhere where it's safe."

Suffused with heat at both his nearness and his derisive attitude, it was all Emily could do to keep from cowering. She clicked her teeth together, then swallowed hard. "You don't want to help me. Fine. I'm certain I'll find someone else who will. After all, I'm willing to pay a thousand dollars." Then, turning to make a grand exit, certain she'd made him sorry over losing out on so much money, she said over her shoulder, "I imagine I'll find someone much more agreeable than you within the hour. Goodbye."

There was a split second of stunned silence, then an explosive curse, and Emily decided good breeding could take second place to caution. She reached for the door and almost had it open, when his large hand landed on the wood with a loud crack, slamming it shut again. His warm, hard chest pressed to her back, pinning her to the door. She could barely move; she could barely breathe.

Then his lips touched her ear, whisper-soft, and he said, "You're not going anywhere, sweetheart."

Chapter Two

SHE FELT LIGHT-HEADED, but she summoned a cool smile. He was deliberately trying to frighten her—she didn't know how she knew that, but she was certain of it. Slowly turning in what little space he allowed her, Emily faced him, her chin held high. "Would you mind giving me a little breathing room, please?"

"I might."

Might mind, or might move? Emily shook her head. "You have a rather nasty habit of looming over me, Mr....?"

For a moment, he remained still and silent, then thankfully, he took two steps back. He looked at her as if she might not be entirely sane. Emily stuck out her hand. "I'm Emily Cooper."

His gaze dropped to her hand, then with a resigned look of disgust, he enfolded her small hand in his much larger one, pumping it twice before abruptly releasing her. He stared at the ceiling. "Judd Sanders."

"It's very nice to meet you, Mr. San—"

"Judd will do." He shook his head, and his gaze came back to her face. "Look, lady, you can't just come to this part of town and start waving money around. You'll get yourself dragged into a dark alley and mugged, possibly raped. Or worse."

Emily wondered what exactly could be worse than being mugged and raped in a dark alley, but she didn't bother asking him. She felt certain he'd come up with some dire consequence to frighten her.

He was watching her closely, and she tried to decide if it was actual concern she saw on his face. She liked to think so. Things still didn't fit. He didn't seem any more suited to this part of town than she did, regardless of his crude manners and bossy disposition.

But now that he'd backed up and given her some room, she was able to think again. "I made certain to stay in front of the stores and in plain sight at all times. If mischief had started, someone surely would have offered assistance." Her eyebrows lifted and she smiled. "You did."

He muttered under his breath, and pointed an accusing finger at her. "You're a menace."

Glaring at him wouldn't get her anywhere, she decided. She needed help, that much was obvious. And who better to help her than a man who evidently knew his way around this part of town, and was well acquainted with its inhabitants. She cleared her throat. "I realize I don't entirely understand how things should be done. Although I'm familiar with the neighborhood, since I work in the soup kitchen twice a week…" She hesitated, then added, "I bought this coat from one of the ladies who comes in regularly. On her, it looked authentic enough. That was even her bag I carried—"

"Miss Cooper."

He said her name in a long, drawn-out sigh. Emily cleared her throat again, then laced her fingers together. "Anyway, while I know the area, at least during the day, I'm not at all acquainted with the workings of the criminal mind. That's why, as I said, I'd like to hire you."

"Because you think *I* do understand the criminal mind?"

"I meant no insult." She felt a little uncertain with him glaring at her like that. "I did get the impression you could handle yourself in almost any situation. Look at how well you took care of those drunkards? You didn't even get bruised, and there were three of them."

"Yeah. But you'd already laid one of them low."

She could feel the blush starting at her hairline and traveling down to cover her entire face. "Yes, well…"

He seemed to give up. One minute he was rigid, his posture so imposing she had to use all her willpower not to cower. Then suddenly, he was idly rubbing his forehead. "Let's get out of here and you can tell me exactly what you want."

Oh, no. She wouldn't tell him that, because what she wanted from him and what was proper were two very different things. But she forgave herself the mental transgression. No woman could possibly be in the same room with this man without having a few fantasies wing through her mind.

Trying for some vagrant humor to lighten his sour mood, she asked, "Wouldn't you like to change first?"

Staring at her, his jaw worked as if he was grinding his teeth. Then he gave one brisk nod. "Turn your head."

Emily blinked. "Turn my… Now wait just a minute! I'll go out to the bar and—"

"No way. I can't trust you not to disappear. Just turn around and stare at the door. I'll only be a minute."

"But I'll know what you're doing!"

He smirked, that was the only word for it. "What's the matter, honey? You afraid you won't be able to resist peeking, knowing I'll be buck naked?"

That was a pretty accurate guess. Emily shook her head. "Don't be ridiculous. It just isn't right, that's all."

"Afraid one of your society friends might meander along and catch you doing something naughty?" He snorted. "Trust me. Not too many upper-crust types visit this part of town. You won't catch yourself in the middle of a scandal."

But she had been caught once, and it had been the most humiliating experience of her life. She'd been alienated from her family ever since.

She thought of that horrid man and nearly cringed. She'd thought herself so above her parents, so understanding of the underprivileged. And she still believed that way. A gentleman was a gentleman, no matter his circumstances. Decency wasn't something that could be bought. But the man who had swept her off her feet, shown her passion and excitement, had proven himself to be anything but decent.

She'd nearly married him before she'd realized he only wanted her money. Not her. Never her. He'd used her, used her family, made a newsworthy pest of himself, and her parents had never forgiven her for it.

She could still hear herself trying to explain her actions. But her mother believed a lady didn't involve herself in such situations, under any circumstances.

A lady never lost her head to something as primal as lust.

Lifting her chin, Emily gave Judd the frostiest stare she could devise. "I can most certainly control myself." Then she turned her back on him. "Go right ahead, Mr. Sanders. But please make it quick. It is getting rather late."

Emily heard him chuckling, heard the rustle of clothing, and she held her breath. It was only a matter of a minute and a half before he told her she could turn around.

Very slowly, just in case he was toying with her, Emily peered at him. He was dressed in jeans, and had pulled on a flannel shirt. He was sitting on a crate, tugging on low boots. When he stood to fasten his shirt, Emily noticed he hadn't yet done up his jeans. She tried not to blush, but it was a futile effort.

He ignored her embarrassment. "So, Emily. Where exactly are you from?"

Her gaze was on his hands as he shoved his shirttails into his pants. "The Crystal Lakes area," she said. "And you?"

He gave a low, soft whistle. "The Crystal Lakes? Damn. No kidding?"

Annoyed, she finally forced her attention to his face. "I certainly wouldn't lie about it."

He took her arm and led her out of the storeroom. He had stuffed his dance props into the leather satchel he carried in his other hand. "I'll bet you live in a big old place with plenty of rooms, don't you?"

Emily eyed him with a wary frown. She wasn't certain how much she should tell him about herself. "I have enough space, I suppose."

He asked abruptly, "How did you get here?"

"Actually, I took the bus. I didn't think parking my car here would be such a good idea."

"No doubt. What do you drive, anyway? A Rolls?"

"Of course not."

"So?" He pulled her out the door and into the brisk night. "What do you tool around in?"

"Tool around? I drive a Saab."

"Ah."

"What does that mean? Ah?" He was moving her along again, treating her like a dog on a leash. And with his long-legged stride, it was all she could do to keep up. He stopped near a back alley, and Emily realized they were at the rear of the bar. "Why didn't we just go out the back door instead of walking all the way around?"

"'Ah' means your choice of transportation shouldn't surprise me. And we came this way so I could spare you from being harassed. Believe me, the men working in the back would have a field day with an innocent like you."

Don't ask. Don't ask. "What makes you believe I'm an innocent?"

Judd opened the door to a rusty, disreputable pickup truck and motioned for her to get inside. She hesitated, suddenly not certain she should trust him.

But he only stood there, watching her with that intense, probing green gaze. Finally, Emily grabbed the door frame to hoist herself inside.

Judd shook his head. "And you ask how I know you're an innocent?"

Before Emily could reply, he slammed the door and walked around to get in behind the wheel. "Buckle up."

She watched his profile as he steered the truck out of the alley and onto the main road. The lights from well-spaced street lamps flashed across his features. Trying to avoid staring at him, she looked around the truck and she saw a strip of delicate black lace draped over the rearview mirror.

Judd noticed her fascination with the sheer lace and grinned. "A memento of my youth."

Trying for disinterest, Emily muttered, "Really."

"I was sixteen, she was eighteen."

Sixteen. The same age as her brother—and obviously into as much mischief as John.

Judd ran his fingers down the lace as if in fond memory. "We were in such a hurry, we ripped her panties getting them off." He flashed her a grin. "Black lace still makes me crazy."

Emily went perfectly quiet, then tightly crossed her legs.

There's no way he can know what your panties look like, Emily, she told herself. But still, she made an effort to bring the conversation back to her purpose. She had to find a way to help John.

Reminded of the reason she was with Judd in the first place, Emily turned to him. Taking a deep breath, she said, "I need to find out who's selling semiautomatic weapons to kids. I...I know a boy who had one blow up in his face. He was badly injured. Luckily, no one else was around."

The truck swerved, and Judd shot her a look that could have cut ice. *"Blew up?"*

His tone was harsh, and Emily couldn't help huddling closer against her door. "Yes. He very nearly lost an eye."

Judd muttered a curse, but when he glanced at her again, his expression was carefully controlled. "Did you go to the police?"

"I can't." She tightened her lips, feeling frustrated all over again. "The boy's parents won't allow him to be implicated. They refuse to realize just how serious this situation is. They have money, so they took him out of the country to be treated. They won't return until they're certain he's safe."

"Yeah. A lot of parents believe bad things will go away if you ignore them. Unfortunately, that's not true. But Emily, you have to know, there's nothing you can do to stop the crime on these streets. The drugs, the gangs and the selling of illegal arms, it'll go on forever."

"I refuse to believe that!" She turned in her seat, taking her frustration out on him. "I have to do something. Maybe I can figure out a way to stop this guy who sold that gun. If everyone would get involved—"

Judd laughed, cutting her off. "Like the folks who whisked their baby boy out of the country? How old was this kid, anyway? Old enough to know better, I'll bet." He shook his head, giving her a look that blatantly called her a fool. "Don't waste your time. Go back to your rich neighborhood, your fancy car and your fancier friends. Let the cops take care of things."

She was so angry, she nearly cried. It had always been that way. She never shed a tear over pain or hurt feelings, but let her get really mad, and she bawled like an infant. His attitude toward her brother infuriated her.

Judd stopped at a traffic light, and she jerked her door open, trying to step out. His long hard fingers immediately wrapped around her upper arm, preventing her from leaving.

"What the hell do you think you're doing?"

"Let me go." She was proud of her feral tone. "Did you hear me? Get your hands off me." She struggled, pulling against his hold.

"Dammit! Get back in this truck!"

The light had changed and the driver of the car behind them blasted his horn. "I've changed my mind, Mr. Sanders," she told him. "I no longer require your help. I'll find someone else, someone who won't choose to ridicule me every other second."

He peered at her closely, then sighed. "Aw, hell. Don't tell me you're going to cry."

"No, I am not going to cry!" But she could feel the tears stinging her eyes, which angered her all the more. How could she have been so wrong about him—and he so wrong about her? She didn't have fancy friends; she didn't have any friends. Most of the time, she didn't have anybody—except her brother. She loved him dearly, and John trusted her. When the rest of her family had turned their backs on her, her brother had been there for her, making her laugh, giving her the support she needed to get through it all.

She couldn't let him down now, even if he didn't realize he needed her help. He was the only loving family she could claim, the only one who still cared about her, despite her numerous faults. And she knew, regardless of the gun incident, John was a good person.

Several cars were blaring their horns now, and Judd yanked her back inside, retaining his hold as he moved out of the stream of traffic and over to the curb. He didn't release her. "Look, I'm sorry. Don't go and get weepy on me, okay?"

"You, Mr. Sanders, are an obnoxious ass!" Emily jerked against him, but he held firm. "I always cry when I'm angry."

"Well...don't be angry then."

Unbelievable. The man had been derisive, insulting and arrogant from the moment she'd met him, but now his tone had changed to a soft, gentle rebuke. He had a problem with female tears? She almost considered giving in to a real tantrum just to make him suffer, but that had never been her way. The last thing she wanted from Judd was pity.

"Ignore me," she muttered, feeling like a fool. "It's been a trying week. But I am determined to see this thing through. I'll find the man who sold that gun. I have a plan, a very solid plan. I could certainly use your help, but if you're only going to be nasty, I believe I'd rather just find someone else."

Judd was amazed by her speech. Then his eyes narrowed. No way in hell was he going to let her run loose. She was a menace. She was a pain.

She was unbelievably innocent and naive.

Judd shook his head, then steered the truck back into the street. "Believe me, lady. I'm about as nice as you're going to find in these parts. Besides, I think I might be interested in your little plan, after all. I mean, what the hell? A thousand bucks is a thousand bucks. That was the agreed amount, right?"

Emily nodded.

Lifting one shoulder, Judd said, "Can't very well turn down money like that."

"No. No, I wouldn't think so." She watched him warily, and Judd thought, what the hell? It would be easier to work with her, than around her. If he turned her down, she'd only manage to get in his way, or get herself hurt. That was such a repugnant thought, he actually groaned.

He'd have to keep his cool, maintain his cover, and while he was at it, he could keep an eye on her. Maybe he could pretend to help her, but actually steer her far enough away from the trouble that she wouldn't be any problem at all.

Yeah, right.

It would probably be better to try to convince her to give up her ridiculous plan first. He glanced at her, saw the rigid way she held herself, and knew exactly how to dissuade her. "There are a few conditions we should discuss."

Emily heaved a deep breath. "Conditions?"

"Yeah. The money's great. But I'll still have to work nights at the bar. Actually, only Tuesdays and Thursdays. *Ladies' nights.*"

Emily hastened to reassure him. "I don't have a problem with that. I wouldn't want to interfere with your...career."

His laugh was quick and sharp, then he shook his head. "Right. My career." He glanced at her again, grinning, wondering if she could possibly realize how uncomfortable he was with that particular career. "That's not the only thing, though."

"There's something else?"

"Yeah. You see, we'll need a place to meet. Neutral ground and all that. Someplace away from prying eyes."

Emily stared.

"You stand out like a sore thumb, honey. We can't just have

you traipsing around in that neighborhood. People will wonder what you're up to. It could blow the whole thing."

"I see."

"My apartment is close to here. No one would pay any attention to you coming in or out. It wouldn't even matter what time we met. We'll need to work closely together, finesse these plans of yours. What d'ya say?"

Her mouth opened, but all that came out was, "Oh God."

Lifting one dark eyebrow, Judd felt triumphant. She was already realizing the implications of spending so much time alone with him. He hid his relief and said, "Come again?"

Emily shook her head, then at the same time said, "Yes, that is...I suppose..." She heaved a sigh, straightened her back, and then nodded. "Okay."

Judd stared at her, trying not to show his disbelief. "What do you mean, okay?" He'd thought for certain, since everything else had failed, that this would send her running. But no. She seemed to like the damn idea. She was actually smiling now.

"I mean, if you think we could successfully operate from your apartment, I'll agree to meet you there."

Contrary female. "Emily..." He faltered. He liked saying her name, liked how it sounded, all fresh and pure. She looked at him, with those huge, doe eyes steady on his face. She was too trusting. She was a danger to herself. If he didn't keep close tabs on her, she'd end up in trouble. He was sure of it.

"You were going to say something, Mr. Sanders?"

Nothing she would like hearing. He shook his head. "Just be quiet and let me think."

Obediently, she turned away and stared out her window. He wasn't buying her compliance for a minute. He had a gut feeling there wasn't an obedient bone in her slim body. He also suspected she was as stubborn as all hell, once she'd set her mind on something. And she was set to find a gun dealer.

The truck was heating up. It was late spring and even though the nights were still a little chilly, the days were warming up into the seventies. Without any fanfare, and apparently trying not to draw undue attention to herself, Emily began unbuttoning the oversize coat. Judd watched from the corner of his eye.

Just to razz her, because she took the bait so easily, he asked, "Would you like me to give you a drumroll?"

She turned to face him. "I beg your pardon?"

She looked honestly confused. He tried to hide his grin. "Every good striptease needs music."

"I'm not stripping!"

He shrugged, amused by the blush on her cheeks that was visible even in the dark interior of the truck. She was apparently unused to masculine teasing, maybe even to men in general.

He snorted at his own foolishness. It was men like himself, coarse and inelegant, that she wasn't used to. He imagined she had plenty of sophisticated guys clamoring for her attention. And that fact nettled him, even though it shouldn't. Grumbling, he said, "You should try it. Everyone should experience stripping just once. It's a rush."

She held her coat together with clenched fingers, her look incredulous. If she knew him better, she'd know what a lie he'd just told. He hated taking off his clothes in front of so many voracious women. But she didn't know him, and most likely never would. He should keep that fact in mind before he did something stupid. *Like what, you idiot? Like promising you'd take care of her gun dealer for her, so she could take her cute little backside and big brown eyes back home where it's safe?* No, he most definitely couldn't do that, no matter how much he'd like to.

They came to the entrance to Crystal Lakes. "Which way?"

He'd startled her. She'd practically jumped out of her seat, and he was left wondering exactly where her mind had been. "Which way to your place? You didn't think I'd take you to my apartment tonight, did you? In case you haven't noticed, lady, it's after midnight. And I've put in a full day. Tomorrow will be soon enough."

The truck was left to idle while they stared at each other. Finally in a small voice filled with suspicion, Emily said, "You're not just getting rid of me, are you? You'll really help me?"

Those eyes of hers could be lethal. He wanted nothing more than to tug her close and promise her he wouldn't leave her, that he'd take care of everything, that he'd... She looked so damn vulnerable. It didn't make a bit of sense. Usually people with big money went around feeling confident that money would get them anything. They didn't bother with doubts.

Irritated now, he rubbed the bridge of his nose, then said in a low tone, "Since I haven't gotten my thousand bucks yet, you can be sure I'll be sticking around."

After heaving a small sigh, she said, "Of course."

Now, why did she have to sound so disappointed? And why did he feel like such a jerk?

"Left, up the hill, then the first street on the right."

Judd knew he had no business forming fantasies over a woman who blushed every time she spoke. Especially since he'd have to keep her close, more to protect her than anything else. She didn't understand the magnitude of what she was tampering with, the lethal hold gun dealers had on the city.

An idea had been forming in his mind ever since he'd realized he couldn't discourage her from trying to save the world. He'd thought, if he became aggressive enough, she'd run back home to safety.

Instead, she'd only threatened to find someone else to help

her. And he couldn't let that happen. She might get herself killed, or maybe she'd actually find out something and inadvertently get in the way. He'd worked too hard for that to happen. He wouldn't allow anything—or anyone—to interfere. He *would* get the bastard who'd shot Max. But damn, he'd never expected Emily to openly accept his plans.

Crystal Lakes, as exclusive and ritzy as it was, sat only about twenty-five minutes from the lower east side. It was one of those areas where you could feel the gradual change as you left hell and entered heaven. The grass started looking greener, the business district slipped away, and eventually everything was clean and untainted.

Emily pointed out her house, a large white Colonial, with a huge front porch. It looked as if it had been standing there for more than a hundred years, and was surprisingly different from the newer, immense homes recently built in the area.

There were golden lights in every window, providing a sense of warmth. A profusion of freshly planted spring flowers surrounded the perimeter, and blooming dogwoods randomly filled the yard. All in all, the place was very impressive, but not quite what he'd expected. Somehow, he'd envisioned her stationed in real money. Any truly successful businessperson could afford this house.

Judd stared around the isolated grounds. "Do you live here by yourself?"

She nodded, not quite looking at him, her hands clasped nervously in her lap.

"No husband or little ones to help fill up the space?"

"No. No husband. No children."

"Why not? I thought all debutantes were married off at an early age."

He didn't think she'd answer at first, but then she licked her lips and her skittish gaze settled on his face. "I was...engaged once. But things didn't work out." She rushed through her words, seemingly unable to stop herself. "I bought this house about a year ago. My parents don't particularly like it—it's one of the smaller homes in the community. But it was an original estate, not one built when the Lakes was developed. It's been renovated, and I think it's charming."

She said the words defensively, as if she expected some scathing comment from him. Judd didn't like being affected this way, but there was something about Emily that touched him. He could *feel* her emotions, had been feeling them since first making eye contact with her. And right now, she seemed almost wounded.

Very gently, he asked, "Did you see to the renovations yourself?"

"Yes."

He looked around the dark, secluded yard and shook his head. "Your parents approve of your living here alone?"

"No, but it doesn't matter what they think. When my grandmother died, she left me a large inheritance. My parents expected me to buy a condo near them and then invest the rest using their suggestions." Her hands tightened in her lap and she swallowed. "But I loved this house on sight. I'd already planned to buy it, and receiving the inheritance let me do so sooner than I'd planned. I don't regret a single penny I spent on the place. Everything is just as I want it."

"What if you hadn't gotten the inheritance?"

"I would have found a job. I'm educated. I'm not helpless." She gave him a narrow-eyed look. "But this way, I don't have to. I'm financially independent."

And alone. "How old are you, Emily?"

She raised her chin, a curious habit he'd noticed she used whenever she felt threatened. "Thirty."

He couldn't hide his surprise. "You don't look more than

twenty." Without thinking, he reached out and touched her cheek, his fingertips drifting over her fine, porcelain skin. "Twenty and untouched."

She jerked away. "Are we going to sit in the driveway all night? Go around the back, to the kitchen door."

He shouldn't let her give him orders, but what the hell. He put the truck in gear and did as directed.

The darkness of the hour had hidden quite a few things. There was a small lake behind her property, pretty with the moon reflecting off its surface. Of course, there were some twenty such lakes in the Crystal Lakes community, so he shouldn't have been surprised.

"Is the lake stocked?"

"Yes. But it's seldom used. Occasionally, one or two of the neighborhood children come here to fish. My lake is the most shallow, so it's the safest. And it's the only one on this side of the community. Most of the lakes are farther up."

"You don't mind the kids trampling around your yard?"

"Of course not. They're good kids. They usually feed the ducks and catch a frog or two. I enjoy watching them."

Judd stared back at the house. There was a large window that faced the backyard and the lake. He could picture her sitting there, content to watch the children play. Maybe longing for things she didn't have. Things money couldn't buy.

Hell, he was becoming fanciful.

Disgusted with himself, knowing he'd been away from normal society too long and that was probably the reason she seemed so appealing, he parked the truck and got out. The fresh air cleared his head.

He opened Emily's door to help her out, but she held back, watching him nervously. "I'll make sure you get inside okay, then I'll take off. We can hook up again tomorrow morning."

"Oh. Yes. That will be fine."

She sounded relieved that he didn't intend to come inside tonight, and perversely, he changed his mind. He'd come in, all right, but with his imagination so active, he couldn't trust himself to be alone with her any length of time. Anyway, he told himself, she wasn't his type—not even close. She was much too small and frail. He liked his women big, with bountiful breasts and lush hips.

As far as he could tell, Emily didn't have a figure.

But those eyes... She walked up a small, tidy patio fronted by three shallow steps, then unlocked the back door and flipped a switch. Bright fluorescent light cascaded through a spotless kitchen and spilled outside onto the patio. Judd saw flowerpots everywhere, filled with spring flowers, and a small outdoor seating group arranged to his right. Everything seemed cheery and colorful...like a real home, and not at all what he'd expected.

Damn, he'd have to find some way to dissuade her from her plan before he got in over his head.

She turned and gave him a small, uncertain smile. "About tomorrow..."

He interrupted her, coming up the three steps and catching her gaze. "Let's make sure we understand each other, Emily, so there won't be any mistakes."

She nodded, and he deliberately stepped closer, watching with satisfaction as she tried to pull back, even though there was no place to go. Good, he thought. At least she had some sense of self-preservation.

He braced his hands on the door frame, deliberately looming over her. "From this second on, I call the shots, with no arguments from you. If you really want my help, you'll do as I tell you, whatever I tell you." He waited until she'd backed all the way into the kitchen, then he added, "You understand all that?"

Chapter Three

EMILY'S MOUTH OPENED twice, but nothing came out. She was too stunned to think rationally, too appalled to react with any real thought. Judd dropped his arms and stepped completely into the kitchen, watching her, and by reflex alone, she started sidling toward the hall door. She had made a terrible mistake. Her instincts had been off by a long shot.

Judd's smile was pure wickedness. "Where ya' goin', Emily?"

"I, ah, I just thought of something..."

Like a loud blast, his laugh erupted, filling the silence of the kitchen.

She halted, a spark of suspicion beginning to form. "*What is so funny?*"

"The look on your face. Did you think I had visions of taking you instead of the money?" He shook his head, and Emily felt her cheeks flame. He was still chuckling when he said, "It only makes sense that I'd be in charge—after all, that's what you'll be paying me for. Like I told you, a rich little lady like yourself would only draw a lot of unnecessary attention hanging around that area. You'll have to follow my lead, and do as I tell you if you want to stay safe. And another thing, we need to figure out some reason for you being there at all. I think we'll have to do a little acting. Your part will be easy, since you'll just be the rich lady. That leaves me as the kept man." He spread his arms wide. "As far as everyone will be concerned, I'm yours. There's no other reason why a woman like you would be around a man like me, unless she was slumming. So that's the reason we'll use."

She was so mortified, she wanted to die. Stiff-backed, she turned away from him and walked over to lean against the tiled counter near the sink. She heard Judd close the door, and seconds later, his hands landed on her shoulders, holding her firm.

"Don't get all huffy now. We have things to discuss. Serious things."

"You mean, you don't intend to taunt me anymore? My goodness, how gracious."

"You've got a real smart mouth, don't you? No, don't answer that. I'm sorry I teased you, but I couldn't resist. You're just too damn easy to fluster." He turned her to face him, then tipped up her chin.

"Here, now, don't go blushing again. Not that you don't look cute when you do, but I really think we should talk."

Emily stepped carefully away, not wanting him to know how his nearness, his touch, affected her. Even after all his taunting, she still went breathless and too warm inside when he was close. And ridiculously, it angered her when he belittled himself, claiming she could have no interest in him other than as a sex partner. The physical appeal was there, but it was more than that. Much more. He had helped her. He'd actually taken on three inebriated men to protect her, even though he wasn't a real cop. And he was willing to help her again. She discounted the money; what she was asking could put his life at risk. He must be motivated by more than money to get involved.

But for now, she couldn't sort it all out. Especially not with her senses still rioting at his nearness. She drew a deep breath, then let it out again. "I thought we were going to wait until morning to make any plans. It is getting rather late."

"No, I've decided it can't wait. But I won't keep you long. Pull up a chair and get comfortable."

Emily didn't particularly want to get comfortable, but she also didn't want to risk driving Judd away. For the moment, he was the best hope she had of ever finding the man who'd sold her brother the gun. She knew her limitations, and fitting in around the lower east side of Springfield was probably the biggest of them. She needed him.

As she headed for a chair, Judd caught the back of her coat, drawing her up short. "It's warm in here. Why don't you take this off?"

He was watching her closely again, and she couldn't fathom his thoughts. She shrugged, then started to slip the shabby wool coat from her shoulders. Judd's eyes went immediately to the tiny camera she wore on a strap around her neck.

"What the hell is that?"

She jumped, then lost her temper with his barking tone. "Will you please quit cursing at me!"

He seemed stunned by her outburst, but he did nod. "Answer me."

"It's rather obviously a camera."

Closing his eyes and looking as though he were involved in deep prayer, Judd said, "Please tell me you weren't taking pictures tonight."

"No. I didn't take any." She lifted her chin, knowing what his reaction would be, then added, "Tonight."

"You just had to clarify that, didn't you, before I could really relax." His sigh was long and drawn out, then he led her to the polished pine table sitting in the middle of her quarry-stone kitchen floor. He pulled out a chair for her, silently insisting that she sit. "So when did you take pictures?"

"I've been checking that area for three nights now." She ignored his wide-eyed amazement, and his muttered cursing. "The first night, I took some shots of things that didn't look quite right. You know, groups of men who were huddled together talking. Cars that were parked where they probably shouldn't be. Things like that. Not that I really suspected them of anything. But I didn't want to come home empty-handed.

"I was hoping to find something concrete tonight, so I brought the camera again. Let's face it. If I did find out anything, I doubt the police would simply take my word for it. I mean, if they were at all concerned with that awful man who's selling defective guns, well...they'd be doing something right now." Judd cringed, but Emily rushed on. "If I had something on film, I'd have solid evidence. The police would have to get involved. But there wasn't anything incriminating."

Judd's mouth was tight and his eyes grew more narrow with each word she spoke. "You've been hanging out in the lower east side for three days...rather, nights?"

"Yes."

His palm slapped the table and he leaned forward to loom over her again, caging her in her chair. Emily slid back in her seat, stunned by his fury. And he *was* furious, she had no doubt of that.

"Never again, you got that!" He was so close, his breath hit her face in hot gusts. "From this day on, you don't even think about going anywhere, especially to the lower east side, without me. Ever. You got that?"

Emily bolted upright, forcing him to move away so they wouldn't smack noses. "You don't give me orders, Mr. Sanders!"

"Judd, dammit," he said, now sounding merely disgruntled. "I told you to call me Judd."

"I hired you, *Judd,* not the other way around."

He grabbed her shoulders and pushed her into her seat. His tone was lower, but no less firm. "I'm serious, Emily. You obviously don't have the sense God gave a goose, and if you want my help on this, I insist you stay in one piece. That won't happen if you go wandering around in areas where you shouldn't be. It's too dangerous. Hell, it's a wonder you've survived as long as you have."

Emily tried to calm herself, but he was so close, she couldn't think straight. She recognized his real concern, something money couldn't possibly buy. Satisfied that her instincts hadn't failed her after all, she tried to reassure him. Her voice emerged as a whisper. "I have been careful, Judd. I promise. No one saw me take the pictures. But just in case, I took shots of inconsequential things, too. Like the children who were playing in the street, and the vagrant standing on the corner. If anyone saw me, they'd just think I was doing an exposé. They'd be flattered, not concerned."

"You can't know that."

He, too, was easing back, as if suddenly aware of their positions. Slipping the camera off over her head, he said, "I'll take this, in case there is anything important on the film."

Emily started to object, even though she truly didn't believe she had photographed anything relevant. Then she noticed where his gaze had wandered. Very briefly, his eyes lit on her mouth, then her throat. Emily could feel her pulse racing there.

Still frowning, but also looking a little confused, Judd laid the camera on the table, then caught the lapels of her coat and eased them wide. He just stood there, holding her coat open, looking at her. He didn't move, but his look was so hot, and he was still so near she grew breathless.

She felt choked by the neck of her dress, a high-collared affair that buttoned up the front and was long enough to hang to midcalf. It was sprinkled with small, dainty blue flowers, a little outdated maybe, but she liked it. She'd long ago accepted she had no fashion sense, so she bought what pleased her, not what the designers dictated.

Judd lifted a finger, almost reluctantly, and touched the small blue bow that tied her collar at her throat. She could hear his breathing, could see his intense concentration as he watched the movement of his hand. With a slow, gentle tug, he released the bow, and the pad of his finger touched her warm skin.

Emily parted her lips to breathe. She wasn't thinking about what he was doing or why. She was only feeling, the sensations overwhelming, swamping her senses. She surrendered to them—to Judd—without a whimper, good sense and caution lost in the need to be wanted, to share herself with another person.

Judd lifted his gaze to her face. He searched her expression for a timeless moment, his eyes hard and bright. Then abruptly, he moved away. He stalked to the door, his head down, his hands fisted on his hips.

He inhaled deeply, and Emily watched the play of muscles across his back. "I want your promise, Emily. I don't want you to make a single move without me."

Gruff and low, it took a second for his words to filter into her mind. They were so different from her own thoughts, so distant from the mood he'd created. She cleared her throat and tried to clear her mind. Judd still had his back to her, his arms now crossed over his chest. He sounded almost angry, and she didn't understand him. Could he, who barely knew her, truly be so concerned for her well-being? "You'll help me? You're not just putting me off?"

"I'll help. But we move when I say, and not before."

She wished he'd look at her so she could see his face, but he didn't. "Since I assume you know the best time to find information, I'll wait."

Finally, he turned to her. "This house is secure?"

"Very."

He picked up the camera, then opened the door. "I've got to go. I have a few things to do yet. But I want you to promise me you'll stay inside—no more investigating tonight."

Nervously, Emily fingered the loose ties to her bow. She considered retying it, but decided against drawing any further attention to the silly thing. Judd glanced down at her fingers, and his expression hardened. "Promise me you'll stay in your castle, princess. We can talk more in the morning."

"Yes. I won't go anywhere else tonight." She tried to make her tone firm, but some of her fear came through in her next question. "How will I reach you tomorrow?"

Judd stood silently watching her a minute longer. "You got a pen and paper anywhere around here?"

Emily opened a drawer and pulled out a pad and pencil. Judd quickly scrawled several lines. "This is my number at the apartment, and this is the one at the bar. And just in case, here's my address. Now, I mean it, Emily. Don't make a move without me."

She tried not to look too greedy when she snatched the paper out of his hand. "I promise."

He hesitated another moment, then stepped outside, pulling the door shut behind him. Emily watched through the window as his truck drove away, wondering where he was going, but knowing she didn't have the right to ask. Perhaps he had a lady friend waiting on him.

Of course he does, Emily, she told herself. *A man like him prob-*

ably has dozens of women. But they're not ladies. He wouldn't want a lady.

And for some reason, that thought sent a small, forbidden thrill curling through her insides.

Anger and frustration were not a good combination. Judd didn't understand himself. Or more to the point, he didn't understand his reaction to Emily.

He'd been a hairbreadth away from kissing her. Not a sweet little peck. No, he'd wanted his tongue in her mouth, his lips covering hers, feeling her urgency. He'd wanted, dammit, to devour her completely.

And she would have loved it, he could tell that much from her racing pulse and her soft, inviting eyes. She may play the proper little Miss Priss to perfection, but she had fire. Enough to burn him if he let her.

It wasn't the time and she wasn't the person for him to be getting ideas about. But he'd taunted her without mercy, wanting to conquer her, to show her he was male to her female. To prove...what? That he could and would protect her? That he'd solve her problems so she could smile more? He didn't know.

He'd had women, of course, but none that meant anything beyond physical pleasure. None that he'd wanted to claim, to brand in the most primal, basic way. He didn't know what it was, but Emily was simply different. And she affected him differently.

That dress of hers...so feminine, so deceiving. He'd always heard other men joke about having a lady in the parlor and a wanton in the bedroom. The dress had looked innocent enough, but her eyes...

He knew, even though he wasn't happy knowing, that Emily fit the descriptive mix of lady and wanton to a tee. It was an explosive fantasy, the thought of having a woman who would unleash her passion for just one man, that no one would ever guess unless they were with her, covering her, inside her.

Beneath her dress, he could make out the faint, delicate curve of her breasts, her narrow rib cage. She was so slight of build, but so feminine. She had the finest skin he'd ever seen, warm and smooth and pale. And loyalty. She must be damn loyal to this kid—whoever he was—to take such risks for him.

Judd's thighs clenched and his heart raced. He hadn't been able to resist touching her, and she hadn't protested when he did.

She was too trusting for her own good. And he was too intuitive to be fooled by her prissy demeanor. Emily Cooper had more than her fair share of backbone, and that was almost as sexy as her eyes.

Stopping at a corner drugstore and leaving the truck at the curb, Judd got out to use the lighted pay phone. He never used the phone in his apartment to contact headquarters, in case there were prying ears. To his disgust, his hands shook as he fished a quarter out of his jeans pocket. He made the call, and then waited.

Lieutenant Howell picked up on the first ring. "Yeah?"

"Sanders here."

"It's about time. Where the hell have you been?"

Judd closed his eyes, not relishing the chore ahead of him. This wasn't going to be easy. He took a deep breath, then told his boss, "We have a little problem."

"I'm waiting."

"I met a lady tonight."

"Is that supposed to surprise me, Judd? Hell, you're working as a male stripper. I imagine you meet a lot of broads every damn night."

"Not a broad," Judd said, the edge in his tone evident. "A lady. And she was actively looking for Donner, though she hasn't put a name to him yet. Seems she knows a kid who had a faulty automatic blow up in his face, and she's pegged Donner as the seller."

There was a low whistle, then, "No kidding?"

"The kid's alive, but from what I understand, he's in pretty bad shape. His parents have taken him out of the country." Then, in a drier tone, Judd added, "They're upper-league."

Judd expected the cursing, then the inevitable demand for details. The telling took all of three minutes, and during that time, Howell didn't make a single sound. Judd tried to down-play his initial meeting with Emily and the fact she'd seen him perform, but there was no way to get around it completely. When Judd finished, he heard a rough rumble from Howell that could have been either a chuckle or a curse. "She could throw a wrench into the works."

Judd chose his words very carefully. "Maybe not. I've been thinking about it, and it might actually strengthen my case. Being a stripper in such a sleazy joint makes me look pretty unethical. And I've made it known I'd do just about anything, including stripping, to make a fast buck."

"But Donner hasn't taken the bait yet."

"He will." Judd was certain of that. Donner always used available locals. That was how he worked. "It will happen. But maybe, with a classy woman hanging around to make me look all the more unscrupulous, Donner will buy in a little quicker."

"You think he'll figure the little lady is keeping you?"

"What else would he think? We're hardly the perfect cou-ple. As long as she's informed and close enough for me to keep an eye on her, she'll be safe. And Donner will definitely get curious. Besides, I don't have much choice. She made it real plain she'd investigate on her own if I didn't see fit to help her. It's a sure bet she'd tip Donner off and send him running."

Howell chuckled. "Sounds like you got everything nicely under control."

No. He didn't have his libido under control, or his protective male instincts that had him wanting to look after her despite his obligations to the job and his loyalty to Max. "I can handle things, I think. It would have been better not to have a civilian involved, but my options are limited now."

"I could have her picked up for some trumped-up violation. That might buy you a little time to settle things without her around."

The thought of Emily being humiliated that way, being harassed—by anyone other than himself, was unthinkable. "No. I'll keep an eye on her. Besides, she's so clean, she squeaks. I doubt you'd find anything. And I already tried scaring her off, but she's sticking to her guns."

"Determined, huh?"

Judd snorted. "I almost think she wants Donner as bad as I do. She was taking pictures. Can you imagine? I took the film. I don't think there's anything important on it, but I don't want to take any chances. Not with this case." *And not with her.* "So I'll let her hang around a while, and use the situation to our advantage. In any case, she'll probably be with me when I perform at the bar on Tuesday."

"Keep me posted as soon as you know about the film. And in the meantime, watch your backside. Don't go getting romantic ideas and blow this whole thing."

"Fat chance." He hoped he sounded convincing. "I just wanted you to know what was going on."

"You need any backup on hand, just in case?"

"No." Everything had gone better than he could have hoped. His performance was convincing, even superior to the other dancers'. But he didn't intend to share all that over the phone. It was humiliating. "I don't want to take a chance on blowing it now. I'm accepted. No one suspects me of being anything but a stripper."

"Yeah, you fit the bill real good."

Judd ignored that taunting comment. They'd checked the place over in minute detail before setting up the stakeout. Donner definitely used the room above the bar to make his deals and meet contacts. So it was imperative that Judd be on hand. Unfortunately, the bar was such a damn landmark, having been there for generations, the only transient positions available were the dancers'. The bartenders had been there for years and the bar's ownership hadn't changed hands except within the same family. If Judd wanted Donner he was stuck stripping. And he wanted Donner real bad.

"As I said, it's a believable cover, but I hope like hell we can wrap it up soon. I don't want to take any unnecessary chances."

And he didn't want Emily to get caught in the middle of his own personal war.

"Judd? Is there something you're not telling me? Has something happened? Is it time?"

His instincts told him things would come to a head soon, but he kept that thought to himself. "Hell, it's past time, but who knows? Something's bound to break soon. Either a deal or my back. Those ladies can be real demanding when you're peeling off your clothes."

As he'd intended, his cryptic complaints lightened the mood. "You're the perfect guy for the job. Just don't start enjoying yourself and decide to leave us for bigger and better things." Howell laughed, then cleared his throat. "Stay in touch, and for God's sake, stay alert. Get the hell out if things go sour."

"I'll keep my eyes open."

Judd felt a certain finality settle over him as he replaced the receiver. His superior hadn't nixed his plans with Emily, and it was too late to call off the cover, regardless of his personal feelings. He'd be spending a lot of time in Emily's company. And that filled him with both dread and sizzling anticipation.

He hadn't slept a wink. The combination of worry and excitement from his vivid dreams of Emily worked to keep him tossing all night. But the knock on the apartment door sounded insistent, so he reluctantly forced himself out from under the sheet, then wrapped it around himself to cover his nudity.

"Just a damn minute!" On his way out of the room, he picked up his watch and saw it was only eight-thirty. Just dandy.

Carrying his pistol, he looked out the peephole, then cursed. He stuck the gun in a drawer, just before jerking the door open. He managed to startle Emily, who nearly dropped a large basket she was holding in both hands. "Are you one of those perverse people who rises with the sun?"

Emily didn't look at his face. She was too busy staring at his body. Judd sighed in disgust. "I'm showing less now than I did last night, and you didn't faint then, so please, pull it together, will ya?"

That moony-eyed look of hers was going to be the death of him. A man could take only so much.

And she was looking especially fetching this morning in some kind of light, spring dress. It was just as concealing as the one she'd worn last night, but there was no tie at her throat, only a pearl brooch that looked as if it cost a small fortune. This dress nipped in at the waist, and showed how tiny she was. He could easily span her waist with his hands. His palms tingled at the thought.

"What the hell are you doing here, Emily? It's still early."

"I...actually, I thought we might have breakfast. You did say we would talk this morning."

"Eager to get started, are you?" Turning away, Judd stared

toward the kitchen, then back to Emily. "I wasn't up yet. If you want coffee, you'll have to make it."

Emily seemed to shake herself. "Ah, no. Actually, I thought… you know, to thank you for everything you did for me last night…taking me home and all that, well…I cooked for you."

She ended in a shrug, and Judd realized how embarrassed she was. Or maybe she thought he'd mock her again, ridicule her for her consideration.

He raked a hand through his hair, still holding the sheet with a fist. "What have you got in there?"

He indicated the basket with a toss of his head. Emily's smile was fleeting, and very relieved. She glanced around the room, taking in the apartment's minimal furnishings: a couch, a small table with two chairs, a few lamps, a stereo, but no television. His bedroom sat off to the right, where the open door allowed her to see a small night table and a rumpled bed. The kitchen was merely a room divided by a small, three-foot bar.

He liked the place, even though the neighborhood was rough and the tenants noisy. It wasn't home, but then he'd never really had a home, at least not one of his own. He'd lived with Max Henley a while, and that had seemed as close as he'd ever get to having a family. But that was before Max died. Ever since, his life had been centered on nailing Donner. Where he lived was a trivial matter.

He waited to see Emily's reactions to the apartment, but she didn't so much as blink. After a brief smile, she set the basket on the wobbly table, then opened it with a flourish. "Blueberry muffins, sausage links and fresh fruit." She flashed him a quick, sweet smile. "And coffee."

He was touched, he couldn't help it. "I can't believe you made me breakfast."

"It's not fancy, but you didn't strike me as a man who would want escargots so early in the morning."

He grimaced, then ended with a smile. "And you didn't strike me as the type who would cook for a man."

"I like to cook. My mother thinks it's some faulty gene inherited from my ancestors. But since I'm not married, I don't get to indulge very often."

"What about dates? You could do some real nice entertaining in your house."

She busied herself with setting out the food. "I don't go out much."

He wasn't immune to her vulnerability. He reached out and touched her hand. "No woman has ever cooked for me before."

She stared at him, shocked. "You're kidding."

Feeling a little stupid now for mentioning it, Judd shook his head. "Nope."

"What about your mother?"

"Left when I was real little. My father raised me."

"Oh." Then she tilted her head. "The two of you are close?"

He laughed. "Hardly. Dad stayed drunk most of the time, and I tried to stay out of his hair, 'cause Dad could get real mean when he drank."

"That's awful!" She looked so outraged on his behalf, he grinned.

"It wasn't as bad as all that, Em."

"Of course it was. I think it sounds horrid. Did you have any brothers or sisters?"

"Nope."

"So you were all alone?"

That was the softest, saddest voice he'd ever heard, and for some fool reason, he liked hearing it from her. "Naw. I had Max."

"Max?"

"Yeah. See, I wasn't all that respectable when I was younger, and Max Henley busted me trying to steal the tip he'd left for a waitress. With Max being a cop and all, I thought I'd end up in jail. But instead, he bought me lunch, chewed me out real good, then made me listen to about two hours' worth of lectures on right and wrong and being a good man. I was only fourteen, so I can't say I paid that much attention. When I finally got out of that restaurant, I didn't think I'd ever go back. But I did. See, I knew Max ate his lunch there every day, so the next day, when he saw me hanging around, he invited me to join him. It became a routine, and that summer, he gave me a job keeping up his yard. After a while, Max kind of became like family to me."

Emily was grinning now, too. "He was a father figure?"

"Father, mother, and sometimes as grumpy as an old schoolmarm. But he took good care of me. I guess you could say he was a complete 'family figure.'" *And Donner had robbed Judd of that family.*

"He sounds like a wonderful man."

"Yeah." Judd looked away, wishing he'd never brought up the subject. "Max was the best. He's dead now."

"I'm sorry."

Judd bit his upper lip, barely controlling the urge to hug her close. She had spoken so softly, with so much sincerity, her words felt like a caress. Somehow, she managed to lessen the pain he always felt whenever he thought of Max. God, he still missed him, though it had been nearly six months since Donner had killed him.

Judd nodded, then waited through an awkward silence while Emily looked around for something to do.

She went back to unloading her basket. As she opened the dishes, Judd inhaled the aromas. "Mmm. Smells good. Why don't you get things ready while I put on some pants. Okay?"

"I'll have the table set in a snap." Then she grinned again. "I hope you're hungry. I made plenty."

Judd shook his head. She was wooing him with breakfast, a ploy as old as mankind, and he was succumbing without a struggle. If he was ever going to keep her safe, he'd have to keep his head and maintain the control. The only way to do that was to make certain some distance existed between them. He couldn't be moved by every small gesture she made.

When he emerged from the bedroom two minutes later, Emily had everything on plates. He noticed there were two settings, so obviously she planned to eat with him. He also saw that, other than coffee mugs, she'd found only paper plates and plastic cutlery in his kitchen. But she didn't seem put off by that fact. A tall thermos of coffee sat in the middle of the table. It smelled strong, just the way he liked it.

"This is terrific, Emily. I appreciate it." Normally, he didn't eat breakfast, but his stomach growled as he approached the table, and he couldn't deny how hungry he was.

Emily poured his coffee, still smiling. "I thought we could talk while we eat. Maybe get to know each other a little better. I mean, we will be working together, and we're practically strangers."

He glanced up at her. "I wouldn't say that."

She blinked, then looked away. "How long have you been... ah..."

"Stripping?"

"Yes." There was another bright blush on her cheeks. Judd wondered how she kept from catching fire.

"A while," he said, keeping his answer vague.

"You...you like it?"

Good Lord. He laid down his fork and stared at her. She was the most unpredictable woman he'd ever met. Watching her eyes, he said, "Everyone should experience stripping at least once. It's a fantasy, but most people don't have the guts to try it."

She sucked in her breath. The fork she had in front of her held a piece of sausage, ready to fall off. She looked guilty.

Ah. He smiled, reading her thoughts. "Admit it, Emily. You've thought of it, haven't you? Imagine the men, or even one man, getting hotter with every piece of clothing you remove. Imagine his eyes staring at you, imagine him wanting you so bad he can't stand it. But you make him wait, until you're ready, until you're completely...naked."

She trembled, then put down her fork, folding her hands in her lap. Judd didn't feel like smiling now; he felt like laying her across the table, tossing the skirt of her dress up around her shoulders and viewing all of her, naked. For him. He wanted to drive into her slim body and hear her scream his name. It angered him, the unaccountable way she could provoke his emotions, leaving him raw.

"You want to strip for me, Emily? I'll be a willing audience, I can promise you that."

"Why are you doing this?"

Her tone was breathless, faint. With arousal or humiliation? He slashed his hand in the air, disgusted with himself. "Eat your breakfast."

"Judd..."

"I'm sorry, Emily. I'm not usually such a bastard. Just forget it, all right?"

She didn't look as though she wanted to. Instead, she looked ready to launch into another round of questions and he couldn't take it. He began eating, ignoring her, giving all his attention to his food.

He waited until she'd taken a bite of her muffin, then said, "I've decided if I'm going to help you, I'll need more information."

Emily swallowed quickly and looked at him, her eyes wide. "I told you everything."

"No. I need the whole truth now, Emily. How you're in-volved, and why. What really happened." He took a sip of cof-fee, watching her over the rim of his mug. "Who's the kid? But most of all, what does he have to do with you?"

Chapter Four

EMILY KNEW HER luck had just run out. And though it surprised her he'd figured her out so soon, she had expected it. Judd wasn't an idiot, far from it. And she supposed it was his obvious intelligence and insight that made her feel so sure he would help her.

How much to tell him was her quandary.

Judd evidently grew impatient with her silence. "Stop trying to think up some elaborate lie. You're no good at it, anyway. Hell, if I can tell you're planning to lie, you'll never be able to carry it off. So just the truth, if you please. Now."

Emily frowned at him. He didn't have to sound so surly. And he didn't have to look so...sexy. He'd shocked her but good, answering the door near-naked. Even now, with his pants on, he still looked sleep-rumpled and much too appealing. She cleared her throat and stared down at her plate.

"All I can tell you is that someone I hold dear was injured when that gun misfired. Since I know no one else is going to do anything about it, I have to. And the only thing I can think of is to make sure that the man who sold the gun is brought to justice."

"Is the guy a lover?"

Emily blinked. "Who?"

"The man who is *dear to you.*"

His sneering tone had her leaning back in surprise. "Don't be ridiculous. He's just a boy. Only sixteen."

Judd shrugged. "So who is he? A relative?"

Why wouldn't he just let it rest? Why wouldn't he—

"Dammit, Emily, who is he?"

He shocked her so badly with his sudden shout, she blurted out, "My brother!"

"Ah. I suppose that could motivate a person. Never having had a brother myself, I wouldn't know for certain, of course. But I can see where you'd want to protect a little brother." Judd rubbed his whiskered jaw, then added, "Why don't your parents just go to the police?"

Emily stood up and walked away from the table. How had he gotten her to reveal so much, so easily? She knew she had no talent for subterfuge, but she hadn't thought she'd crack so quickly. When she turned to face Judd again, she caught him staring at her ankles. Her silence drew his attention, and when his gaze lifted to her face, he didn't apologize, but merely lifted a dark eyebrow.

Trying to ignore the heat in her face, Emily folded her hands over her waist and said, "My parents hate scandal more than anything. They'd rather move to another country than have their name sullied with damaging speculation."

"Don't they love their son?"

"Well, of course they do." Appalled that she'd given him the wrong impression, Emily took her seat again, leaning forward to get his attention. "It's just that they've got some pretty stringent notions about propriety. Their reputations, and the family name, mean a lot to them."

"More than their son, evidently." Then Judd shook his head. "No, Emily, don't start defending them again. I really don't give a damn what kind of parents you have. But it seems to me, if they're willing to sweep the incident under the carpet, you should be, too. What can you hope to prove, anyway?"

This was the tricky part, trying to make him understand how important it was for John to see now, before it was too late, exactly what road he was choosing. She didn't want to see the same disdain in Judd's eyes when she mentioned her brother as he apparently felt for her parents. Why his opinion mattered to her, she didn't know. But it did.

Keeping her voice low, she said, "John bought the gun, I think, because he wanted my parents' attention. You'd have to understand how hard he tried to find his…niche. I remember last Christmas, John was crushed when my parents sent him a gift from Europe." Her lips tilted in a vague smile. "It was a check, a substantial check, but still, it was only money. John sat in front of the stupid Christmas tree, seven feet high and professionally decorated, and he cried. I didn't let him know I was there because I knew it would embarrass him."

Judd looked down at his feet. "I never had a Christmas tree until Max took me in. It was only a spindly little thing, but I liked it. It beat the hell out of seeing my father passed out drunk in the front room where the Christmas tree should have been but wasn't."

"Oh, Judd."

"Now, don't start, Em. We're talking about John, remember? I only mentioned that memory because I guess I always assumed people with money had a better holiday. I mean, more gifts, better food, a lot of cheer and all that." He shook his head. "Shoots that theory all to hell, doesn't it?"

"People usually think having money is wonderful, but that's not always true. Sometimes…money spoils things. It can make people self-centered, maybe even neglectful. Because it's so easy to do what you want, when you want, it's easy to forget about the others who…might depend on you. It's easy to forget that everyone can't be bought, and money doesn't solve every problem."

Judd didn't say a word, but his hand, so large and warm and rough, curled around her fingers and held on. Emily started, surprised at the gentleness of his touch, at how comforting it felt to make physical contact with him. She glanced up, and his eyes held hers. There was no more derision, and certainly no pity. Only understanding.

It was nearly her undoing.

"My…my brother, he's a good kid, Judd, just a bit misguided. And though he's trying to play it tough right now, he's scared. He doesn't know if he'll ever look the same as he did before the accident. My parents keep assuring him they'll find a good plastic surgeon to take care of everything, but he's hurting. Not physically, but inside. He wanted my parents' attention, but all he's gained is their annoyance. They never once asked him why he bought the gun or how. They only complained about him doing something so stupid. And they made it clear, had he wanted a gun, they could have bought the finest hunting rifle available, and supplied him with lessons on how to handle it."

"They missed the point entirely."

Emily felt his deep voice wash over her, and she smiled. "Yes, they did."

"Okay. So what will nailing the guy who sold him the gun prove to your brother?"

"That I love him. That I know what's right and wrong, and that he knows it, too, if he'll only open his eyes and realize that he is a good person, that he doesn't need affirmation from anyone but himself."

"Is that what you learned, honey? Do you understand your brother so well, because you've gone through the same thing?"

Emily forced a laugh and tried to pull her hand free, but Judd wouldn't let her go. He wouldn't let her look away, either. His gaze held her as securely as his fingers held her hand. "I've never felt the need to purchase a gun, Judd."

"No, but you must have wanted approval from your family as much as your brother does. What did you do, Emily, to get them to notice you?"

She cleared her throat and tried to change the subject. "This is ridiculous. It doesn't have anything to do with our deal."

"To hell with the deal. What did you do, Em?"

Panic began to edge through her. Not for anything would she lay the humiliation she'd suffered out for him to see. Besides, she'd buried the memory deep. It was no longer a part of her. At least, she hoped it wasn't.

"I've made my fair share of mistakes," she told him. "But I've forgiven myself and gotten on with my life. That's all any of us can do." Once she said that, she came to her feet, knowing she had to do something, occupy herself somehow, or she'd become maudlin. A display of emotions wouldn't serve her purpose.

But as she stood, so did Judd, and before she could move away, he had her tugged close. The morning whiskers on his jaw felt slightly abrasive, and arousing, as he brushed against her cheek. The warmth of his palms seeped through her dress to her back where he carefully stroked her in a comforting, soothing manner. She could smell his musky, male scent, and breathed deeply, filling herself with him, uncaring what had brought on this show of concern. It simply felt too good to have him hold her.

"You should always remember, Em, what a good person you are. Don't let anyone convince you otherwise."

His raspy tone sounded close to her ear, sending gooseflesh up her arms. And her emotions must have been closer to the surface than she'd wanted to admit, because she could feel the sting of tears behind her lids.

Not wanting Judd to know how he affected her, she hid her face in his shoulder and tried a laugh. It sounded a little wobbly, but it was the best she could produce. "You hardly know me, Judd. What makes you think I'm such a fine specimen of humanity?"

He rocked her from side to side, and she could hear the smile in his voice when he spoke. "Are you kidding me? You're obviously damn loyal since you're willing to risk your pretty little neck for your brother, just to keep him on the right track. You've opened your property to the neighborhood kids, not caring that they might trample your flowers or muddy up your yard. And you told me you volunteer at the soup kitchen. I'll bet you've got a whole group of charity organizations you donate to, don't you?"

Emily squeezed herself closer, loving the solid feel of his chest against her cheek, the strength of his arms around her. She couldn't recall ever feeling so safe. "I'm the one who benefits from the organizations. I've met so many really good, caring people, who just need a little help to get their lives straightened out. We talk, we laugh. Sometimes...I don't know what I'd do without them."

Judd groaned, and then his hand was beneath her chin, tilting her face up. Emily smiled, thinking he had a few more questions for her, when his mouth closed over hers and she couldn't think at all.

Heat was her first impression. The added warmth seemed to be everything, touching her everywhere. She felt it in her toes as he lifted her to meet him better, to fit her more fully against him. She felt it in her breasts, pressed tight against his chest. And in her stomach, as the heat curled and expanded.

His mouth was firm, his tongue wet as he licked over her

lips, insisting she open. When she did, he tasted her deeply, his hands coming up to hold her face still as he slanted his mouth over hers again and again.

Emily had never known such a kiss. She'd thought she'd experienced lust while she was engaged, but it had been nothing like this. She made a small sound of surprise, wanting the contact to go on forever—and suddenly Judd pulled away.

Emily grabbed the back of the chair to keep herself grounded. Judd stared at her, looking appalled and fascinated and...hungry. *Oh, Lord, Emily, now you've really done it.*

She should have felt guilty for behaving so improperly, but all her mind kept repeating was, *Let's do it again.* She shook her head at herself, dismissing that errant notion and trying to remember her purpose. Judd must have misunderstood, because he turned away.

"I'm sorry," he said.

Emily blinked several times. "I beg your pardon?"

Judd whirled to face her, once again furious. "I said, I'm sorry, dammit. I shouldn't have done that. It won't happen again."

Oh, darn. "No, of course not. It was my fault. I shouldn't have been telling you all my problems and—"

"Shut up, Emily."

She did, and stared at him, waiting to see what he would do, what he wanted her to do.

"Damn." He snatched her close again, pressed another hard, entirely too quick kiss to her lips, then set her away. "I take it back. It probably will happen again. Hopefully, not for a while, but...I'm not making any promises. If you don't want me ever to touch you, just say so, all right?"

Emily remained perfectly still, unwilling to take a chance that he might misunderstand her response if she moved. She prided herself on the fact she wasn't a hypocrite. No, she wanted Judd, and she was thrilled beyond reason that he apparently wanted her, too. And since he held rather obvious scorn for her background—that of money and privilege—he wouldn't expect her to play the part of the proper lady. No, Judd had already made it clear where his preferences lay. Any man who could strip for a living was obviously on the earthy side, primal and lusty and...her heart skipped two beats while she waited to see what he'd do next.

He laughed. It wasn't a humorous laugh, but one of wonder and disbelief. "You're something else, Emily, you know that? Here, sit down." He loosened her death grip on the chair back and nudged her toward the seat. "Don't go away. I'm going to shower and finish getting dressed, then we'll make some plans, okay?"

She sat. She nodded. She felt ready to explode with anticipation.

Judd ruffled her hair, still shaking his head, and left the room.

He made certain it was a cold shower, but the temperature of the water didn't help to cool the heat of his body. Never could he remember being hit so hard. Holding her felt right, talking to her felt right. Hell, kissing her had been as right as it could get—bordering on blissful death.

He could only imagine how it would feel to...no. He'd better not imagine or he'd find himself right back in the shower.

How could one woman be so damn sweet? He'd have thought all that money and her parents' attitudes would have soured her, but it hadn't. Emily loved. She loved her brother, she loved the children in her neighborhood. She even loved the homeless who visited the kitchen where she volunteered. He'd heard it in her tone, seen it in her eyes.

God, she was killing him.

He had to stay objective, and that meant getting back to

business. He finished dragging a comb through his damp hair and left the bathroom.

Emily hadn't moved a single inch. And if he hadn't already had a little taste of her, he'd believe her prissy pose, with her knees pressed tightly together, and her slim hands folded in her lap. Ha! What a facade. He dragged his eyes away from her wary gaze and began stuffing her thermos and empty dishes back into the basket. "You ready to go?"

"Ah...go where?"

He flicked an impatient glance her way. "To find your gun dealer. I thought we'd hit some of the local establishments. The pool hall, first. Then maybe the diner. And tonight, the bar."

"Are you...dancing tonight?"

"No. I've got all weekend free. I only dance on Tuesdays and Thursdays, remember?" He noticed her sigh of relief and frowned at her. "But you will be there when I dance, Em. To pull this off, you're going to have to be my biggest fan. Everyone will have to believe I'm yours. You can be as territorial as you like. Besides, I can use you as a smoke screen. If the ladies all believe I'm already spoken for, they might not be so persistent."

Emily pursed her lips, her shoulders going a little straighter. "Are you certain that's what you want? I don't wish to interfere in your social life."

"You know, Em, you don't sound the least bit sincere."

She looked totally flustered now, and it was all he could do not to laugh. "Come on, let's get going."

Holding her arm, a manner that felt as right as everything else he did with her, Judd hustled her down to the street and into his truck. He waited until she'd settled herself, then asked, "Did your brother mention what the guy who sold him the gun looked like?"

Emily shook her head. "He wasn't in much condition to

talk when I saw him last. I did get him to tell me where he'd bought it, though. But all he said about the man was that he'd grinned when he sold him the gun."

Judd noticed she'd tucked her hands into fists again, and he reached over to entwine her fingers with his. "When was your brother hurt?"

"Not quite a month ago. I saw him right afterward and then my parents took him away as soon as the hospital allowed it. I didn't even get to say goodbye."

"So you have no idea how he's doing?"

Emily turned away to stare out the side window. Her voice dropped to a low pitch, indicating her worry. "I've talked to him on the phone. He...he's very depressed. Though my parents evidently refuse to believe it, the plastic surgeons have already done all they can. The worst of the scars have been minimized. But the burns from the backfire did some extensive damage to the underlying tissue around his upper cheek and temple. He claims his face still looks horrid, but I don't believe it's as bad as he thinks. He's...he's always been popular in school, especially with the girls. I guess he thinks his life is over. I tried to make him look on the positive side, that his eyesight wasn't permanently damaged, but I don't suppose he can see a bright side right now."

Her voice broke, but Judd pretended he hadn't heard. He instinctively knew she wouldn't appreciate her loss of control. For such a small woman, she had an overabundance of pride and gumption, and he had no intention of denting it.

He squeezed her fingers again and kept his eyes focused on the road. "When will he be home again?"

"I don't know. I haven't spoken with my parents." She sent him a tilted smile. "They're blaming me for this. They say I'm a bad influence on him."

"You?" Judd couldn't hide his surprise.

"I work with the underprivileged. I don't own a single fur coat. And I live in an old house that constantly needs repair."

"Your house? I thought your house was terrific."

She seemed genuinely pleased by his praise. "Thank you. But the plumbing is dreadful. I've had almost everything replaced, but now the hot-water heater is about to go. Either the water is ice-cold, or so hot it could scald you. I thought my father would disown me when he burned his hand on the kitchen faucet. But even more than my house, my parents hate that I refuse to marry a man they approve of. They want me to 'settle into my station in life.'" Emily laughed. "Doesn't that sound ridiculous?"

"Settling down? Not really. I think you'd make a fantastic wife and mother." Dead silence followed his claim, and Judd could have bitten his tongue in two. It was bad enough that he still yearned for a real family. But to say as much to Emily? She was probably worried, especially after that kiss he'd given her, that he might have designs on her.

He slanted a look her way, and noticed a bright blush on her cheeks. Trying to put her at ease, he said, "You look like a domestic little creature, Em. That's all I meant."

Those wide brown eyes of hers blinked, and then she started mumbling to herself. He couldn't quite catch what she was saying. Judging from the tone, though, he probably wouldn't want to hear it, anyway. He had the suspicion she was giving him a proper set-down—in her own, polite way.

Judd was contemplating her reaction, and the reason for it, when they pulled up in front of the pool hall. It was still early, well before noon, so he didn't expect the place to be overly crowded. Only the regulars would be there, the men who made shooting pool an active part of their livelihood.

Clayton Donner was one of those men.

Judd didn't expect to see him here today, but he never knew

when he might get lucky. And in the meantime, he'd find out a little more about Donner.

Emily was silent as he led her into the smoky interior. Unlike the lighting at the bar, it was bright here, and country music twanged from a jukebox in the far corner. Some of the men looked as if they'd been there all night and the low-hanging fluorescent lights added a gray cast to their skin. Others looked merely bored, and still others were intent on their game. But they all looked up at Emily. Judd could feel her uneasiness, but for the moment, he played his role and, other than put his arm around her shoulders to mark his claim, he paid her little attention.

Leaning down to whisper in her ear, he said, "Play along with me now. And remember, no matter what happens, don't lose your cool." Then he gave her a kiss on the cheek and a swat on the behind. "Get me a drink, will ya, honey?"

He gave a silent prayer she'd do as she was told, then sauntered over to the nearest table. "Hey, Frog. You been here all night?"

Frog, as his friends called him, had a croak for a voice, due to a chop to the larynx that had damaged his throat during a street fight. Frog didn't croak now, though. He was too busy watching Emily as she made her way cautiously to the bar, careful not to touch anyone or anything.

Judd gave a feral grin. "That's mine, Frog, so put your eyes back in your head."

Frog grunted. "What the hell are you doing with her? She ain't your type."

Judd shrugged. "She's rich. She's my type."

Frog thought that was hilarious, and was still laughing when Emily carried a glass of cola to Judd. He took a sip, then choked. Glaring in mock anger, Judd demanded, "What the hell is that?"

Emily raised her eyebrows, but didn't look particularly intimidated by his tone. "A drink?"

"Damn, I don't want soda. I meant a real drink." Actually, Judd never touched liquor. He knew alcoholism tended to run in families, and after living with his father, he wouldn't ever take the chance of becoming like him. Still, he handed the glass back to Emily, then said with disgust, "You drink it. And stay out of my way. I'm going to shoot some pool here with Frog."

Emily huffed. She started to walk away, but Judd caught her arm and she landed against his chest. Before she could draw a breath, he kissed her. It wasn't a killer kiss like the one he'd given her earlier, but it was enough to show everyone they were definitely an item. He drew away, but couldn't resist giving her a quick, soft peck before adding, "Behave yourself, honey. I won't be long."

Emily nodded, apparently appeased, and went to perch on a stool. Judd looked at her a moment longer, appreciating the pretty picture she made, waiting there for him. She dutifully smiled, and looked as if she'd wait all day if that was what he wanted.

It was the kind of fantasy he could really get into, having a woman like Emily for his own. But he couldn't spare the time or the energy to get involved with her or anyone else. He needed, and wanted, to focus all his attention on taking Donner off the streets. The man had stolen a huge hunk of his life when he'd killed Max. Judd wasn't ever going to forget that.

So instead of indulging in the pleasure he got by simply watching Emily, he turned away. He knew she didn't realize what he'd done, making her look like a woman he could control with just a little physical contact, but every man in the room understood.

And even though that had been his intent, Judd hated every damn one of them for thinking that about Emily. It was bad enough that he'd sold himself to trap Donner, but now he was selling Emily, too. It didn't sit right with him, but at the moment, his choices were limited, and the only alternative was to postpone his plans. Which was really no alternative at all.

Emily had no idea investigating could be so exhausting, though Judd did the actual work. All she did was pretend to be his ornament. It rankled, but until she could get him alone and set him straight about how this little partnership was going to work, she didn't want to take the chance of messing things up.

Judd had been shooting pool for quite some time when the door opened and three men walked in. One was a heavy-set man, dirty and dressed all in black, with the name Jonesie written across his T-shirt. Another was a relatively young man, looking somewhat awed by his own presence.

It was the third man, though, that caught and held Emily's attention. There was something about him, a sense of self-confidence, that set him apart. He didn't look like a criminal, but something about him made Emily uncomfortable. He wore only a pair of pleated slacks and a polo shirt. His blond ponytail was interesting, but not actually unusual. In truth, Emily supposed he could be called handsome, but he held no appeal for her. He simply seemed too…pompous.

When his gaze landed on her, she quickly looked away and kept her eyes focused on Judd. And because she was watching Judd so intently, she saw the almost imperceptible stiffening of his body. He'd only glanced up once to see who had walked in, then he'd continued with his shot, smoothly pocketing the nine ball. But Emily felt she was coming to know him well enough to see the tension in his body.

She was still pondering the meaning of that tension when the men approached where she sat.

"Hey, Clay, you want something to drink?"

The blonde smiled toward Emily and took the stool next to her before answering Jonesie. "No. I'm fine. I think I'll just watch the...scenery, for a while."

Emily wanted to move away, but she didn't. Not even on the threat of death would she turn and meet that smile, though she felt it as the man, Clay, continued to watch her. When he touched her arm, she jumped.

"Well, now, honey. No need to be nervous. I was only going to get acquainted."

Emily shook her head and tried to shrug his hand away. Instead of complying with her obvious wish, his well-manicured fingers curled around her arm. His touch repulsed her. She jumped off the stool and stepped back...right into the younger of the three men. She was caught.

This was nothing like talking to the drunks the other night. She'd felt some sense of control then. But now, as Clay chuckled at her reaction and reached out to stroke her cheek, she felt a scream catch in her throat. His fingers almost touched her skin—and then Judd was there, gripping the man's arm by the wrist and looking as impenetrable as a stone wall.

"The lady is mine. And no one touches her but me."

Judd narrowed his eyes, hoping, without the benefit of common sense, that Clayton would take him up on his challenge. He knew he wasn't thinking straight. He could destroy his entire case if he unleashed his temper now, but at the moment, none of that mattered.

He'd kept Donner in his sights from the moment he'd walked in, and he'd thought he'd be able to keep his cool even after Donner noticed Emily. But he hadn't counted on Emily's reaction.

When he'd seen her face and realized she was frightened, all he'd cared about was getting to her, staking his claim and making certain she knew there was nothing to fear. The fact that she was afraid should have angered him, and probably would once he had time to think about it. Didn't she know he wouldn't let anyone hurt her? Hell, he'd take the whole place apart before he'd see her hair get mussed.

But he supposed she couldn't know that, because even now, with him beside her, she still looked horrified. And then she got a hold of herself and smiled, a false smile, to be sure, and stepped to his side. "It's okay, Judd. Really."

Clayton looked down at his wrist where Judd still held him. The gesture was a silent command to be released, but Judd wasn't exactly in an accommodating mood. He tightened his hold for the briefest of seconds, gaining a raised eyebrow from Donner, then he let go. The younger man took a step forward, and Judd bared his teeth in a parody of a grin, encouraging him.

Emily seemed nearly frantic now, saying, "Come on, Judd. Let's go."

But he had no intention of going anywhere. Emily didn't know, couldn't know, the riot of emotions he was suffering right now. His desire to avenge Max mixed with his need to protect Emily, and he felt ready to explode with repressed energy. This was what he'd been waiting for. He could feel Donner's interest, his curiosity, and he knew he'd finally succeeded. If Donner's crony wanted to take him on, he was ready. More than ready. At this point, Donner would only be impressed with his ruthlessness. His muscles twitched in anticipation.

Then Donner laughed. "Don't be a fool, Mick. Our friend here is only trying to protect his interests. I can understand that."

The young man, Mick, moved away, but he did so reluctantly. Judd flexed his hands and tried to get himself under control. He stared at Clayton, then nodded and turned away, making certain he blocked Emily with his body. He knew

Donner wouldn't like being dismissed, but he also didn't want to appear too eager.

Frog was standing at the pool table with his mouth hanging open, and Judd had to remind him it was his shot.

"No more for me," Frog said. "I'm done."

And in the next instant, Clayton was there, slapping Frog on the back and smiling. "So, what do you have for me, Frog?"

Frog pulled money out of his pocket, looking decidedly uncomfortable, and handed the bills to Clayton. As he counted, Clayton continued to smile, and then he asked, "That's it?"

Frog shifted his feet, glancing up at Judd and then away again. "I lost some of it."

"Is that so?"

Judd carefully laid his pool cue on the table then faced Clayton with a smile. He couldn't have asked for a better setup. "It seems I was having a lucky morning." His smile turned deliberately mocking, and he flicked his own stack of bills.

Again, Mick started forward, clearly unwilling to overlook such an insult to Clayton, and this time Jonesie was with him. But again, Clayton raised a hand. "Let's not be hasty." And to Judd, he said, "I'd like to meet the man who just took two hundred dollars of my money."

Judd heard Emily gasp, but he ignored her surprise. "Your money? Now, how can that be, when Frog told me he'd won that money last night shooting pool? And now that I've won it, I'd say it's my money."

Clayton lost his smile. "Do I know you from somewhere?"

Mick blurted out, "He's one of them strippers. I seen him at the bar the other night."

"Ah, that's right. I remember now. You've been something of a sensation, haven't you?"

Judd shrugged. "Hey, I make a buck wherever I can. A man can't be overly choosy."

"Obviously." Clayton looked down a moment, then his smile reappeared. "Maybe we can do business together sometime. I have several different ventures that might interest you. Especially since you're not choosy."

Again, Judd shrugged, careful not to show his savage satisfaction. Then he took Emily by the arm. "Maybe." He deliberately dismissed Clayton once more, knowing it would infuriate him, but probably intrigue him, as well. As he started out the door, he said, "You can look me up if anything really...interesting comes along."

They were barely out the door, when Emily started to speak. Judd squeezed her arm. "Not a word, Em. Not one single word."

The tension was still rushing through him, and he knew Clayton was watching them through the large front glass of the pool hall. Playing it cool had never been so difficult; no other assignment had been so personal. Playing up to Donner turned his stomach and filled him with rage. He wanted to hit something. He wanted to shout.

He wanted to make love to Emily.

But, he couldn't do any of those things, so he had to content himself with the knowledge he'd set Clayton up good. Not only had he more or less managed to steal two hundred dollars Clayton had earmarked as his own, but he knew damn well Clayton didn't consider their business finished. Not by a long shot. He'd hear from Donner again, and soon.

He only hoped he could manage to keep Emily out of the way.

Chapter Five

EMILY THOUGHT SHE'D shown great restraint and a good deal of patience. But her patience was now at an end.

Judd had refused to talk to her while he aimlessly drove around the lower east side, burning off his sour mood and occasionally grunting at the questions she asked. Twice they had stopped while he got out of the truck and talked to different people loitering on the sidewalk. Emily had been instructed to wait in the pickup.

When she asked him what he was doing, he'd said only, "Investigating." When she asked what he'd found out, he'd said, "Quiet. Let me think."

It had been nearly two hours since they'd left the pool hall, and her frustration had grown with each passing minute. She tried to maintain her decorum, tried to keep her temper in check and behave in a civilized manner, but he was making that impossible. *You're the boss here, Emily. You hired him. Demand a few answers.* She decided she would do exactly that, when Judd pulled up in front of the diner.

Apparently, he expected her to get out and follow him like

a well-trained puppy, because he stepped out and started to walk away without a single word to her. She refused to budge.

Of course, Judd was halfway through the diner door before he realized she was still in the truck. Then he did an about-face, and stomped back to her side, looking very put out. "What's the holdup?"

Emily gave him a serene smile. "I want to talk to you."

"So? Let's get a seat inside and you can talk. God knows, that's all you've done for the past hour, anyway."

She stiffened with the insult, but refused to lower herself to his irritating level. "You're not going to make me angry, Judd. I know you're just trying to get me off the track. But I want to know what that was all about in the pool hall. And don't you dare shake your head at me again!"

He looked undecided for a long moment, then let out a disgusted sigh. "All right, all right. Come in, sit, and we'll…talk."

Emily wasn't certain she believed him, he still looked as stubborn as a mule, but she left the truck and allowed Judd to lead her inside. They sat at a back booth, and a waitress immediately came to take their order. The woman seemed a little hostile to Emily, then she all but melted over Judd.

Judd treated her to a full smile and a wink. "You got anything for me, Suze?"

You got anything for me, Suze, Emily silently repeated, thinking Suze had just received a much warmer greeting from Judd than she herself had managed to garner all day.

The waitress looked over at Emily, one slim eyebrow lifted, and Judd grinned. "She's fine. Just tell me what you've got."

"Well…"

Emily rolled her eyes. Suze obviously had a flair for the dramatic, given the way she glanced around the diner in a covert manner, as if she were preparing to part with government secrets. She also patted her platinum blond hair and primped for a good ten seconds before finally exalting them with her supposed wisdom. *What a waste of time.*

Emily no sooner had that thought than she regretted it. Suze turned out to be a fount of information.

"He's been in twice since we spoke and something is definitely going down. He met with the same guy both times, that punk kid who distributes for him. I'd say something will happen within a week or two. That's usually the routine, you know."

"You couldn't catch an actual date?"

"Hell, no, sugar. If Donner caught me snooping, he'd have my fanny."

Judd reached out to smack the fanny-in-peril. "We wouldn't want that to happen. But Suze? If anything more concrete comes up, you know where to find me."

She knew where to find him? Emily knew she had no right to be jealous. After all, her relationship with Judd was strictly business. But still, she didn't like the idea of him...consorting with this woman. Of course, Suze seemed to know a great deal about the gun dealer. In fact, she seemed to know almost too much. Emily narrowed her eyes, wondering exactly when Judd had contacted this woman, and what their relationship might be. Judd seemed to be on awfully familiar terms with her.

But Suze did appear to be helping, and Emily certainly had no claims on Judd. She decided to concentrate on that fact, but she couldn't keep herself from glaring at the waitress. Suze didn't seem to notice.

She was back to primping. "Of course I know where you'll be. I wouldn't miss an act. Do something special for me Tuesday night, all right?"

Judd laughed and shook his head.

Suddenly, Suze was all business. "You two want anything

to drink or something? It don't look right me standing here gabbing without you orderin' anything."

"Two coffees, Suze. That's it."

Emily barely waited for the waitress to go swaying away before she leaned across the table and demanded Judd's attention. "Was she talking about who I think she was talking about?"

"Who did you think she was—"

"That's not funny, Judd!"

"No, I guess it isn't. And yes, she was talking about our friendly, neighborhood gun trafficker."

Emily was aghast. "She *knows* him?" She couldn't believe the waitress had called him by name. Why, if he was that well known...

"Everyone knows who commits the crimes, Em. It's just coming up with proof that's so damn difficult."

Her breath caught in her throat and she choked. "You know who he is, too?"

Judd shrugged, his eyes dropping to the top of the table. Then he quirked a sardonic smile. "You met him yourself, honey."

"I did..." Suddenly it fit, and Emily fell back against the seat. "The guy at the pool hall?"

"Yep. That was him. Clayton Donner."

It took her a minute, and then she felt the steam. It had to be coming out her ears, she was so enraged. Judd had let her get close to the man who'd hurt her brother, and he hadn't even told her.

He was speaking to her now, but she couldn't hear him over the ringing in her ears. Her entire body felt taut, and her stomach felt queasy. No wonder she had reacted so strongly to that man. He'd been that close and...

Emily didn't make a conscious decision on what to do. She just suddenly found herself standing then walking toward the door. She somehow knew Judd was following, though she didn't turn to look. When she stepped outside, and started past his truck, he grabbed her arm and pulled her around to face him.

"Dammit, Emily! What the hell is the matter with you?"

"Let me go." She felt proud of the strength in her voice, though she knew she might fall apart at any moment.

"Are you kidding? I've tried every damn intimidation tactic I could think of—"

"Ha! So you admit to bullying me?"

"—to send you running, but you clung like flypaper. And now, with one little scare, you want me to turn you loose?"

Flypaper! How dare he compare her to... No, Emily, don't get sidetracked by a measly insult. The man deceived you. She lifted her chin and met his gaze. "I wish to leave now. Alone."

"No way, baby. You wanted in, and now you're in."

Her heartbeat shook her, it pounded so hard, and her fingers ached from being held in such tight fists. If she wasn't a lady, she'd smack him one, but good. "When were you going to tell me, Judd? When?"

Judd stiffened, and his jaw went hard. "Get in the truck, Em."

"I will not. I..."

"Get in the damn truck!"

Well. Put that way... Emily became aware of people watching, and also that Judd was every bit as angry as she was. But why? What possible reason did he have for being so mad? She was the one who'd been misled, kept in the dark, lied to... well, not really. But lies of omission definitely counted, and Judd had omitted telling her a great deal.

And after he'd insisted she bare her soul.

When he continued to glare at her, she realized how foolish they both must appear, and she opened the truck door to get in. It wouldn't do to make a public spectacle of herself.

"Put your seat belt on."

Emily stared out her window, determined not to answer him, to ignore him as completely as he'd ignored her all day. But then she muttered, *"Flypaper."*

She heard Judd make a small sound that could have been a chuckle but she didn't look to see. If the man dared to smile, she'd probably forget all about avoiding a scene. But then, thoughts of attacking that gorgeous body left her a little breathless, and she decided ignoring him was better, by far.

Judd reached over and strapped her in. He stayed leaning close for a second or two, then flicked his finger over her bottom lip. "Stop pouting, Em, and act like an adult."

It took a major effort, but she didn't bite that finger. She could just imagine how appalled her parents would have been by that thought.

Judd's sigh was long and drawn-out. "Fine. Have it your way, honey. But if you decide you want to talk, just speak up."

Fifteen minutes later, Emily was wishing she could do just that. Judd pulled into her driveway with the obvious intent of being well rid of her, and she desperately didn't want him to go. She felt confused and still angry and…hurt. If he could explain, then maybe she could forgive him and… *And what, Emily? Maybe he'd let you have one of those killer smiles like the one he gave Suze?* She'd been taken in by one man, and though she honestly believed Judd was different, she wouldn't, couldn't, put all her trust in him. Not on blind faith. Not without some explanations.

When all was said and done, he worked for her, and she deserved to know what was going on. She had to find evidence against Donner, and she needed Judd to do that. But only if he didn't shut her out.

He stopped the truck, and she sat there, trying to think of

some way, without losing every ounce of pride, to talk things out with him.

But Judd saved her the trouble. He got out of the pickup, slamming his door then stomping over to the passenger side. She stared at him, her eyes wide with surprise, when he opened the door and hauled her out.

"What do you think you're doing?" His hold was gentle on her arm as he led her up the steps to her back door. She practically had to run to keep up with his long-legged, impatient stride.

"We're going to talk, Em. I don't like you treating me as if I've just kicked your puppy."

Uh-oh. He sounded even angrier than she'd first assumed. "I don't even have a dog—"

Judd snatched her key from her hand, unlocked the door and ushered her inside. "Do you need to punch in your code for the alarm system?"

It took her a second to comprehend his words since her mind still wrestled with why he was in her house, and what he planned to do there. "Oh, ah, no. I only turn it on when I'm in the house. The rest of the time, I just lock up."

Judd stared. "Why the hell would you get a fancy alarm system, and not use it?"

"Because twice I forgot to turn it off when I came in, and the outside alarms went off, and then several neighbors showed up at my door and the central office called, and it was embarrassing." Judd rolled his eyes in exasperation, and Emily felt her cheeks heat. She hadn't meant to tell him all that. "Judd? I don't want to talk about my alarm system."

Looking restless and still a bit angry, Judd paced across the kitchen. Then he stalked back to her. "Tell me this, Emily. What would you have done if I'd spoken up and introduced you to Donner?"

She watched as he propped his hands on his hips and glared

at her. "I don't know what I would have done. But I know I would have done…something."

"Something like accuse him? Or something like demand he give himself up? I thought you needed proof. I thought that was what we were doing, trying to nail him."

His scowl was much more fierce than her own, and her anger diminished to mere exasperation. The man could be so remarkably impossible. "We?" she asked, lacing her tone with sarcasm. "There was certainly no 'we' today. You've refused to tell me anything." When he crossed his arms, looking determined, she added in a gentler tone, "Judd, I can't very well find evidence against this Donner person if I don't know who he is."

Judd came to stand in front of her and gripped her shoulders. "I was working on finding evidence. Or did you think I just enjoyed toying with that bastard? Besides, you were scared out of your wits, Em. And that was without knowing who he was. He had a damn strange effect on you, which now that I think of it again, isn't very complimentary for me. I thought you knew I wouldn't let anyone hurt you."

Emily swallowed, feeling a tinge of guilt. "I'm sorry. Of course I assume you'll protect me, but—"

"Don't assume, Emily. Know. As long as you do as I tell you and follow my lead, you won't get hurt."

"Just like that? You tell me what to do, and I do it, no questions asked? I'm not a child, Judd—"

"So I noticed."

"And… You noticed?" Emily quickly shook her head so she wouldn't get sidetracked. "If you want me to trust you, you have to be totally honest with me, not just expect me to sit around and watch you work, without telling me what you're working on."

"You're making too much of this. I was only shooting pool."

"But you had a goal in mind. And you kept that from me. I despise dishonesty, Judd. I won't tolerate it." He winced, but she didn't give him time to interrupt. "I had no idea today that you were deliberately taking money from one of Donner's men. If I had known, maybe I wouldn't have been so surprised…"

"Exactly. Do you think I want Donner or any other punk to look at you and think you know the score?"

That silenced Emily for a moment. Why would Judd care what other men thought of her? "I quit worrying about others' opinions long ago."

"Why?"

"What do you mean, 'why'?"

"Everyone cares what other people think, even when they know it shouldn't matter."

Busying her fingers by pleating and unpleating her skirt, Emily felt her exasperation grow. "Certain things…happened in my past, that assured me public opinion meant very little, but that honesty meant a great deal."

"Like what?"

When she didn't answer, he said, "Okay, we'll come back to that later."

"No, we won't."

"Dammit, Em. I'd much rather you come off looking like an innocent out for a few kicks, than to have some jerk assume you've been around."

Emily swallowed hard. Judd had evidently made some incorrect assumptions about her character, and it was up to her to explain the truth. "Judd, I don't know why you persist in thinking I'm…I'm innocent. I believe I told you once that I'd been engaged. Well…"

She couldn't look at him, her eyes were locked on her busy fingers. And then she heard him chuckle. Her gaze shot to his face, and she was treated to the most tender smile she'd ever seen.

"Honey, it wouldn't matter if you'd been engaged twenty times. You're still so damn innocent, you terrify me."

Emily didn't understand that statement, or the way he reached out and touched her cheek, then smoothed her hair behind her ear.

She felt disoriented, and much too warm. She wanted to lean into Judd, but she knew she had to settle things before she forgot what it was that she wanted settled. Once before she'd let her passionate nature guide her. That had been a huge error, and this was too important to be sidetracked by anything—including Judd's heated effect on her.

"The thing is, Em, this whole deal will work out better if your reactions to Donner and his men are real. You can't lie worth a damn, and I don't think, if Donner got close again, you'd be able to hide your feelings from him. You could blow everything."

She cleared her throat and spoke with more conviction than she actually felt. "You don't know that for sure."

His expression hardened, turning grim. "And I'm not willing to take the risk. Things could backfire real easy, and someone could get hurt."

She understood his reasoning, but she couldn't accept it. "This isn't going to work, Judd. Not unless you're willing to tell me everything."

He stared at her, hard, then muttered a curse and looked away. "No, you're right. It won't work. Which is why I've come up with an alternate plan. I decided I'd just find this guy for you, but on my own. You can stay in your little palace and play it safe."

"*What?*"

"You heard me. From here on, you're out of it."

Emily sputtered, then stiffened her spine. "You said I was 'in,' remember?"

"I've changed my mind."

"Well, you can just unchange it, because I'm not going to be left out."

"I refuse to risk your getting hurt, and your reaction today was proof positive you aren't ready to mingle with the meaner side of life. Let's face it, Em, you're just a baby."

"Oh, no, you don't." She propped her hands on her hips and glared at him. "You're not going to pull me into an argument by slinging horrid insults at me. We had a deal and you're the one who isn't following the rules. Well, you can just stop it right now."

He blinked at her in amazement. "I wasn't insulting you, dammit!"

Emily could tell by his expression he hadn't seen anything insulting in his attitude. But that only made the insult worse. She pursed her lips and tilted her head back so she could look down her nose at him. "I'm not entirely helpless, Judd. I can take care of myself."

There was a minute curving of his lips before he shook his head and spoke in a gentle, but firm, tone. "I'm sorry, Em. My mind's made up."

He acted as if he hadn't just dumped her, as if he hadn't just let her down and destroyed all her plans. But it was even more than her plans now. It was Judd, and she cared about him. She took one step closer and poked him in the chest with her finger. "Okay, fine. You don't want to help me, then I'll find another way."

Startled, he grabbed her finger and held on. "You already have a way. Me. I can do this, you know. I'm more than capable, and I damn sure don't need you looking after me. It'll be easier without you."

That hurt, but she didn't show it. She lifted her chin and

met his intent gaze. "No. I won't let you risk yourself for me, not while I sit around and do nothing."

Judd bit his upper lip and his eyes narrowed. He suddenly looked...dangerous, and Emily shivered in expectation of what he might say. She knew it would be something outrageous, but she was prepared for the worst.

"So you'll pay me a five-hundred-dollar bonus. No big deal."

He had a very credible sneer. Emily frowned. She couldn't believe he'd just said that. And she couldn't believe he was really doing this only for the money. She couldn't have been that wrong.

A deep breath didn't help to relieve the sudden pain in her chest, or the tightness in her throat. She still sounded strained as she whispered, "Fine, if money's the issue, I'll pay you to forget you ever met me." She waited for his reaction, and though Judd remained rigid, she noticed his hands were now curled into tight fists.

There's a reaction for you, Emily. He doesn't seem at all pleased by being bought off. She decided to push him, just to see what it would take to force him to drop his charade. "Five thousand dollars, Judd. But I don't want you risking yourself. Take it or leave it." Then she opened the door and waited to see if he would actually leave.

"Damn you, Emily." The door slammed shut and she found herself pinned to the wall by his hard chest, his arms caging her in, his lips pressed to her hair. She could hear him panting, struggling for control of his temper.

Relief washed over her—and hot excitement. "Judd?"

He didn't answer. He kissed her instead, and if the first kiss had been hungry, this one was ravenous. Emily moaned and wrapped her arms around him, holding him tight as his tongue pushed deep into her mouth. How she'd come to care so much about him so quickly, she didn't know. Perhaps it was because she sensed the same emptiness in him that she'd often felt. When he'd told of his past, as different as it was from hers, she still saw a lot of similarities.

Emily knew she was being fanciful, but she couldn't deny the way she felt. It seemed to her sometimes there were no real heroes left in the world, people willing to do what was right—just because it was the right thing to do.

But Judd was a hero, despite his chosen profession, despite his lack of manners and sometimes overbearing arrogance. A hero was a man who could do what needed to be done, when it was needed. And Judd was as capable as they came.

"Oh, Em." His mouth touched her throat, her chin, then her lips again. "I have to stop."

She tried to shake her head, since stopping was the last thing she wanted, but she couldn't. His hands cupped her cheeks and he had her pressed flush against the wall, pinned from chest to knees, his erection hard and throbbing against her belly. It was glorious. She was well and truly trapped, and she loved it. "Judd..."

"No, honey." He was still breathing hard, his mouth touching soft and warm against her flesh, planting small biting kisses that tingled and tickled and stole her breath. "Neither one of us is ready for this. Hell, you've got me so crazy, I don't know what I'm doing. I need time to think. And so do you."

Don't beg, Emily. Don't beg. "Judd...I—"

He touched her lips with his thumb, then his eyes dropped to where she knew her nipples puckered tight against the front of her dress. His voice, when he spoke, was a low, raspy growl. "You're killing me, Em. Please understand."

"I've never felt like this before, Judd."

He groaned, then kissed her again, this time so soft and sweet, she trembled. He pressed his hips hard against her once, then forcibly pulled away. When he touched her cheek, his hand shook. "I'll call you later tonight, okay?"

She swallowed hard, not wanting him to leave, but knowing he was right. It *was* too soon to make a commitment.

It was difficult, but she managed to pull herself together. He was leaving; she knew that was for the best. But she had to recall what had started this whole argument and make certain he understood her position. "I was serious about what I said, Judd. I don't want you doing anything on your own. I don't want the…responsibility of your safety."

He pressed his forehead to hers and gave a loud sigh. "I know. I promise not to do anything until we've figured it all out." Then he chuckled, and it sounded so nice to her ears, she laughed, too. "I must be crazy." He gave her one more quick, hard kiss, then moved her away from the door. "I have to go before I forget my good intentions and ravish you right here. Any red-blooded male can only take so much provocation, you know. And honey, you're damn provoking."

She smiled again, and as he stepped out, Judd said, "Emily? Thanks again for breakfast."

Emily contained herself until she saw Judd drive away. Then she whirled and laughed. Her emotions had been on a roller coaster all day. Whether it had been good or bad, it had definitely been exciting. In fact, her time spent with Judd was easily the most exciting time she'd ever known.

He thought her provocative, and because of that, she felt provocative. That, too, was new, but decidedly delicious. She should feel guilty, since she hadn't done anything to help her brother yet. But she couldn't manage a single dollop of guilt. She simply felt too exhilarated.

Hours later, Emily stood looking out her kitchen window, impatiently waiting for Judd's call. The house was dark and dim, just like her yard. She hadn't bothered to turn on the lights as she'd watched the sunset. The kitchen was her favorite room in the house. The pine cabinets had a warm golden hue, and the antique Tiffany lamp that hung over her table provided a touch of bright color. She thought of Judd sitting at that table with her, of the kiss he'd given her against the wall, and she wondered what he was up to, if he was safe...if he was with Suze.

That vagrant thought had her scowling, and she decided a soothing cup of chamomile tea was just what she needed. Without turning on the lights, she retrieved a cup from the cabinet and turned on the hot water. She knew her kitchen well and didn't need the light intruding on her warm, intimate mood.

It wasn't until she heard a sound and looked up that she realized she'd never reset the alarm. Her heart lodged in her throat as she saw a large body looming outside her kitchen door. Frozen in fear, she stood there as the hot water grew hotter and steam wafted upward around her face. A soft click sounded, and then another. When the door swung silently open and a man entered, his body a shadowed silhouette, she finally reacted. Emily let out the loudest ear-piercing scream she could manage. And after a stunned second and a low curse, the man pounced on her.

Emily didn't have time to run.

Chapter Six

JUDD WHISTLED AS he kicked off his shoes and dropped back onto the lumpy couch. God, it felt good to get off his feet. And to finally get home. He wanted to talk to Emily. He needed to make certain she'd understood his motives this afternoon. He'd seen the shock on her face, then the determination when she'd thought he was dumping her.

It had felt as if she'd snatched his heart right out of his chest. But what the hell else was he supposed to do? Watch her get involved? He hadn't counted on every guy around, including Donner, wanting to cozy up to her. He supposed that elusive sensuality he'd noticed in her right away was as visible to every other guy around as it was to him.

But he didn't like it. He didn't like other men looking at her and seeing tangled sheets and mussed hair and warm silky skin. He didn't like other guys thinking the thoughts he had.

He also couldn't hurt her. He'd just have to find a way to keep her close, and himself detached. That was going to be the real trick, especially when she did crazy things like offering him money just to keep him safe. He sure wasn't used to anyone trying to protect him, not since Max had been killed.

But he could get used to it, if he let himself.

His eyes narrowed at the thought. He couldn't get distracted from his purpose now, not when he was so close. Emily was a danger, and she didn't even realize it. She had the power to help him forget, and he didn't want that. Donner had hurt her brother, but he'd taken the only family Judd had ever known. Whenever he remembered Max's face, usually smiling, sometimes solemn, occasionally stern, his stomach tightened into a knot. Max was the finest, most honest person Judd had ever known, the only one who'd really cared about him.

Except for Emily.

Judd squeezed his eyes shut to block the thought. What Emily felt or didn't feel for him couldn't matter. Not now. Probably not ever. Judd wouldn't give up until Donner was put away. And after that, he'd have no more reason to be with her.

He was just reaching for the phone to call Emily, when the damn thing rang, causing him to jump. He snatched the receiver. "Yeah?"

"Judd, I'm glad I could reach you. Are you sitting down?"

Startled, it took Judd a second to answer. The lieutenant knew better than to call him at his apartment. It was a real breach of security. Something big must have happened. Trying to sound casual, he said, "As a matter of fact, I'd just propped my feet up. I've had a hell of a long—"

Howell interrupted. "Well, your day's about to get a whole lot longer." He hesitated, then added, "You remember that little lady you mentioned to me the other day? The rich one. She still hanging around with you?"

"Emily?" Judd didn't say that he couldn't forget her even if he tried. He cleared his throat. Even though he was as sure as he could be that no bugs existed in the apartment, he wouldn't take any chances. "Sure. In fact, I was just thinking about her. I guess we've got a regular thing going, at least for a while."

"I see." Judd could hear the restrained frustration in Howell's tone. "That being the case and all, I thought you ought to know, I just heard the little lady had her house broken into."

Judd felt his stomach lurch. "What?"

There was an expectant silence, then, "I recognize that tone, Judd. Just calm down and let me tell you what I know."

"Is Emily all right?"

"She's fine, just a little shaken up, I gather. It only happened a few minutes ago, but I thought... Judd?"

Judd cursed and pushed his feet back into his shoes, "I'm on my way."

He vaguely heard Howell protesting, and knew he'd catch hell later for hanging up on the lieutenant, but the only thought that mattered was seeing Emily. He raced out the front door, only stopping long enough to grab his jacket and his Beretta.

Ten minutes and three red lights later—which he ran—Judd decided he was too old to take this kind of stress. His palms were sweating and his head was pounding. He hadn't felt this kind of nauseating fear since the call telling him Max had been shot in the line of duty. But Judd hadn't made it then. He'd gotten to the hospital too late. Max had died only minutes before he arrived.

He stepped more firmly on the accelerator, pushing the old truck and thanking the powers that be for the near-empty roads that lessened the danger of his recklessness. His hands tightened on the wheel as his urgency increased. He could literally taste his fear.

When he sped into the curving driveway and saw the two black and whites parked there, he didn't stop to think about an excuse for his timely arrival. He simply busted through the door, his eyes searching until he found Emily.

She sat at the kitchen table holding an ice pack to her cheek. That alone was enough to make his blood freeze. She looked up, and the moment she saw him, her eyes widened, and then she smiled. "Judd."

He stalked toward her, sank to the floor beside her seat and took her hand in his. With his other hand, he lifted the ice pack so he could survey the damage. "Are you all right?"

She blinked away tears then glanced nervously at the hovering officers. "I'm fine, Judd. But how—"

Already her cheek was bruising and her eye was a bit puffy. Still holding her hand, Judd came to his feet and glared at the officers. "Who did this?"

"We don't know, Detective. We're still trying to find out all the details."

"Did you check the house? Has anyone searched the yard?" He didn't wait for an answer, but bent back to Emily. "Tell me what happened, honey."

She gave a nervous laugh, then quickly sobered. "Really, Judd, there's no reason to yell at the nice officers. They came almost as soon as I called."

"Why didn't you call me?"

He realized what a ridiculous question that was almost as soon as he made the demand. Emily thought he was a male stripper. Why would she call him? That fact had his temper rising again.

She leaned toward him and patted his shoulder. "Shh. It's all right, Judd. Just calm down."

She was trying to soothe him? Judd gave her a blank stare, then shook his head. "Emily..."

"I was waiting for your call. I guess after you left...I forgot to reset the alarm, because I was making tea when suddenly someone started opening the door."

"Oh, honey." Judd wrapped her in his arms, lifting her from the seat at the same time. "You must have been scared half to death."

Emily had to speak against his chest, since he was still holding her tight. He couldn't let her go just yet. He was still suffering from all the terrible thoughts that had raced through his head after Lieutenant Howell's call.

"I suppose I was scared at first," she said. "I know I screamed loud enough to startle the ducks on the lake. Then the man sort of just jumped toward me. And without really thinking about it, I turned the faucet sprayer on him." She leaned back to see Judd's face. "Do you remember me telling you the water heater was in need of repair? Well, I had the water running hot for my tea, and when he came at me, I just grabbed the hose and aimed at his face. At least, I think I hit his face. It was dark in here and everything happened so fast. I do know he yelled really loud, so I think the hot water must have hurt him."

Judd touched his fingers to her bruised cheek. "How did this happen?"

Emily looked very sheepish now, and her cheeks turned a bright pink. "It's really rather silly. You see, after the man yelled, I jerked away and ran for the library so I could use the phone. But, uh…" It was obvious to Judd she was embarrassed as her eyes again went to the two cops. "I tripped just inside the door. I hit my cheek on the leg of a chair."

Bemused, Judd asked, "The guy who broke in didn't do this to you?"

"No. I did it to myself. I think he left right after I shot him with the water. I locked the library door and called the police. When they got here, he was gone."

One of the cops cleared his throat. "We checked the water

in her faucet. It's scalding hot. It's a wonder she hasn't burned herself before." Then he grinned. "You might want to get that checked."

Judd stared.

Emily pulled on his sleeve, regaining his attention. "Do you remember me telling you about my father burning his hand on the faucet? It really does get hot, hot enough to make tea without boiling the water. I wouldn't be at all surprised if the fellow has a serious burn on his face."

Feeling as though he'd walked into bedlam, Judd shook his head then turned his attention to the two officers. "Call Howell and tell him I'm spending the night here. And go check the area. With any luck, the bastard might still be out there if he's burned all that bad."

Both men nodded and started away. Judd turned to Emily, ready to lecture her on the importance of keeping her alarm set, when he felt her stiffen. She looked paper-white and her bottom lip trembled. He grabbed her arm and gently forced her back into her chair.

"Emily, I thought you said you were all right."

Her lips moved, but she didn't make a sound.

"Are you going to faint? Are you hurt somewhere?" He very carefully shook her. "Tell me what's wrong."

His urgency must have gotten through to her, for she suddenly cleared her throat, and her expression slowly changed to a suspicious frown. "One of the officers called you detective. And you're ordering them around as if you have the right. And even more ridiculous than that, they're letting you."

"Oh, hell." Judd wondered if there was any way for him to get out of this one. How could he have been so careless? Howell would surely have his head. His mind whirled with possible lies, but he couldn't see Emily believing any of them. She wasn't stupid, after all, just a bit naive.

He watched her face as he tried to come up with a logical, believable explanation, and he saw the confusion in her eyes, then the growing anger. One of the uniforms came around the corner and said, "Detective, I have Lieutenant Howell on the phone. He said he needed to talk to you, sir, uh...now." And Judd knew Emily had finally guessed the truth.

Before she could move, he cupped her cheeks, being especially gentle with her injury. "I can explain, honey. I swear. Just sit tight a second, okay? Right now, I have to pacify an enraged superior."

"Oh, I'll wait right here, Detective. You can count on it."

Judd didn't like the sound of that one little bit. But it was her look, one of mean anticipation, that had him frowning. This whole damn day had been screwy, starting with Emily cooking him breakfast. He should have known right then he wouldn't end it with his safe little world intact.

No, Emily had turned him upside down.

The hell of it was, he liked it.

Emily listened as Judd went through a long series of explanations over the phone. Yes, he could handle everything... No, his cover wasn't blown as long as Howell set things right with the two officers. Ha! His cover was most definitely *blown*. Emily wanted to interject at that point, but Judd watched her as he spoke, and so she kept herself still, her expression masked, she hoped.

Her cheek was still stinging, but not as much as her pride. *Lord, Emily, you've been a fool.* Hadn't she known from the start that Judd didn't belong in the east side of Springfield? He talked the talk, and dressed the code, but something about him had been completely out of sync. He could be every bit as hard and cynical as the other roughnecks, but his behavior was forced. It wasn't something that came to him naturally.

She closed her eyes as she remembered offering him money to drop the case. If he reminded her of that, she just might... no. She would not lower herself to his level of deceit.

That decision did her little good when Judd hung up the phone and came back to kneel by her chair. He lifted the ice pack again and surveyed her bruised cheek with a worried frown. "I wonder if you should go to the hospital and have this checked."

"No."

Her curt response didn't put him off. "Does it hurt?"

"No."

His fingertips touched her, coasting over her abraded skin and causing goose bumps to rise on her arms. He ended by cupping her cheek and slowly rubbing his thumb over her lips. Then he sighed. "Just sit tight and I'll make you that tea. After everyone's cleared out, we'll talk."

Emily watched him bustle around the kitchen, thinking he looked curiously *right* there. It was almost as if the room had been built for his masculine presence.

The quarry-stone floor seemed every bit as sturdy and hard as Judd, the thick, polished pine cabinets just as comforting. There were no frilly curtains, no pastel colors to clash with his no-nonsense demeanor.

Emily made a disgusted face at herself. Comparing Judd to a kitchen? Maybe she had hit her head harder than she thought.

When he sat the tea in front of her, she accepted it with a mumbled thanks. Moments later, the officer who'd been outside came in and shook his head. "Not a sign of anything. It doesn't even look as if the door was tampered with."

Judd turned to Emily with a stern expression. "It was locked, wasn't it?"

Since she was already mortified over the evening's events,

she didn't bother to try to hide her blush. "I really have no idea. I can't recall locking it, but sometimes I just do it by rote."

"Emily…"

She knew that tone. "Don't lecture me now, *Detective*. I'm really not in the mood."

She was saved from his annoyance by the remaining officer coming downstairs. "I checked out the other rooms. They're clean. I don't believe he ever left the kitchen. Probably took off right after she splashed him, going out the way he came in."

Judd worked his jaw. "I suppose you're right. You guys can take off now. I'll stay with Miss Cooper."

Since Emily had a lot of questions she wanted answered, she didn't refute him. It took the officers another five minutes to actually go, and then finally, she and Judd were alone. Sitting opposite him at the table, Emily prepared to launch into her diatribe on the importance of honesty and to vent her feelings of abuse, when Judd spoke in a low, nearly inaudible tone.

"Clayton Donner shot Max about six months ago. I was out on assignment, and by the time I got to the hospital, Max was dead. I've made it my personal business to get Donner, and I'll damn well do whatever I have to until he's locked up."

Emily didn't move. She heard the unspoken words, telling her he wouldn't let her—or her feelings for him—get in his way. She'd thought she had a good personal reason to want Donner, but her motivation was nothing compared to Judd's. Without thinking, she reached out and took his hand. She didn't say a word, and after a few seconds, Judd continued.

"I told you Max had taken me in. He was everything to me, the only family I'd ever had. He was a regular street cop, and his run-in with Donner was pure coincidence. Max had only been doing a routine check on a disturbance, but he inadvertently got too close to the place where Donner was making a deal." Suddenly Judd's fist slammed down on the table and he squeezed his eyes shut.

"Judd?"

"Max got shot in the back." Judd drew a deep breath and squeezed Emily's hand. She squeezed back. He wouldn't look at her, but she could see his jaw was rigid, his eyes red. Her heart felt as though it were crumbling.

"We all knew it was Donner, but we couldn't get anything concrete on him. And to try him without enough evidence, and take the chance of letting him go free...I don't think I could stand it. I have to see him put away. Regardless of anything, or anyone, I'll get him."

Wishing he'd told her all this because he wanted to, not because he'd been forced, wouldn't get Emily anywhere. And she couldn't, in good conscience, interfere. Not when she could see how much getting Donner meant to him. "I understand."

"Do you?" For the first time, Judd looked up at her, and that look held so many different emotions, Emily couldn't begin to name them all. But the determination, the obsession, was clear, and it scared her. "I left everything behind when I followed Donner here," he said. "Springfield is just like my own home ground. Every city has an area with run-down housing and poverty, a place where kids are forgotten or ignored, where crime is commonplace and accepted. I fit in there, Em. I'm right at home. Sooner or later, I will get Donner. But not if you blow my cover. What happened tonight can't happen again."

Emily knew he wasn't talking about the break-in. "What—exactly—did happen, Judd?"

"I lost my head, and that's bad. I can't be sidetracked from this assignment."

"You know I want Donner, too."

"Not like I do."

She would have liked to probe that a little more, but she held her tongue. She was afraid he was trying to find a way to say goodbye, to explain why he couldn't see her anymore. "What do you want me to do?"

Judd shot from his chair with an excess of energy. He shoved his hands into his back pockets and stalked the perimeter of the room as if seeking an escape. Finally, he stopped in front of the window, keeping his back to Emily. "I want you to understand that I can't let you get in my way. I can't...can't care about you. But when I think about what might have happened tonight..."

"You need me to stay out of your way?" Emily heard the trembling in her tone, but hoped Judd hadn't.

He whirled to face her. "No. Just the opposite, in fact."

She blinked twice and tried to still the frantic pounding of her pulse.

Again, Judd took his seat. "I work as a stripper in the bar because Donner does a lot of his business in the office upstairs. I've set myself up to get hired by him."

"That's what you were doing in the pool hall," Emily said with sudden insight. "You were impressing him, by being like him."

Judd nodded. "Everyone around there believes I'm out for a fast buck, a little fun, and not much else. That makes me Donner's ideal man. Making contact with him today was important. He'll be coming to me soon, I'm sure of it. He's intrigued, because he doesn't like people to refuse him, the way I refused him at the pool hall. I'd like to steer clear of you, to keep you uninvolved." He cast her a frustrated glance. "But it's too late for that."

Her stomach curled. "It is?"

One brisk nod was her answer. "I need you, Em. My superior thinks it's risky to make any changes now. He's already furious that you know my cover, but that can't be helped, short of calling everything off. And I don't want that. He'll pull the officers who were here tonight, because by rights, they screwed up, too. They shouldn't have acknowledged me as a detective, but they're rookies and…" He trailed off, then frowned at her. "If you suddenly stopped hanging around, after the scene we played out today at the pool hall, Donner might get suspicious. The whole deal could be blown. And it's too late for that."

Emily tried to look understanding, but she was still reacting to Judd's casual words. *He needs you, Emily.* She knew she would do whatever she could for him. "Has…has something come up? Something definite?"

"I think so. I visited Frog again after I left here. Next Wednesday night, Donner will be making a pickup."

"What kind of pickup?"

"He gets the guns dirt cheap since they're usually stolen. Then he sells them on the street for a much higher price. The man he buys from has a shipment ready. That would be the best time to bust him. In fact, it's probably the only way to make sure we nail him."

Seeing the determination in his eyes, Emily knew Judd would find a way to get Clayton Donner, with or without her help. But she wanted to be near him any way she could. "Since I still have my own reasons for wanting him caught, I'll be glad to help however I can." She hesitated, then asked, "You're certain Donner is the one who sold my brother the gun?"

"As certain as I can be. We traced him to Springfield by the weapons he sold. One whole shipment was faulty guns. I don't know yet how Donner got hold of them, but from what you told me, it's safe to say your brother got one of them."

A resurgence of anger flooded through her. So Donner had known the guns were faulty before he sold them? He had deliberately risked her brother's life, and that fact made her determination almost equal to Judd's. "I look forward to doing whatever I can to help."

Judd let out a long breath. Then he leaned across the table and took both her hands. "I don't want to have to worry about you. I want your word that you won't try anything on your own. I don't even want you in that part of town without me. Promise me."

"I work there at the soup kitchen..."

"Not until this is over, Em. I mean it. It's just too risky. Promise me."

"Judd—"

"I lost Max, dammit! Isn't that enough?"

His sudden loss of control shook her. She stared at his eyes, hard now with determination and an emotion that closely resembled fear. Reluctantly, she nodded. The last thing she wanted to do was distract him. Already, it seemed to her, he was too emotionally involved, and that weakened his objectivity, putting him in danger. It was obvious that Max Henley had been, and still was, the most important person in the world to Judd. Emily decided she might very well be able to keep an eye on Judd as long as he let her stay close. And evidently, the only way to do that, was to agree to his rules.

"All right. I promise. But I want a promise from you, too, Judd."

It took him a moment to regain his calm demeanor. Then he lifted an eyebrow in question.

"From now on, you have to be honest with me," she said. "There are few things I really abhor, but lying is one of them. You've lied to me from the start."

Judd turned his head. "I was on assignment, Em. And you just came tripping into my case, nearly messing everything up. I did what I thought was best."

"And of course telling me the truth never entered your mind?" When he gave her a severe frown, she quickly added, "Okay, not at first. But since then? Surely you had to realize I wasn't a threat?"

His stare was hard. "You're a bigger threat than you know."

Emily had no idea what that was supposed to mean. And while she did understand Judd's position, she couldn't help feeling like a fool. First she thought he was a cop, then she believed he was a stripper. Now she finds out he actually is a cop. A small, humorless laugh escaped her. "I suppose it really is funny. Did you laugh at the irony of it, Judd?"

"Not once."

"Oh, come on. I must have looked like an idiot. And here you were, trying to keep the poor naive little fool out of trouble."

"It wasn't like that, Em."

She stood, suddenly wanting to be alone. "I should have learned my lesson long ago." She knew Judd had no idea what she was talking about, that she was remembering her sad lack of judgment so many years ago. She shook her head, not at all certain she'd ever tell him. Lord, she probably wouldn't have the chance to tell him. Once this ordeal with Donner was over—and, according to Judd, it would be over soon—Judd would go on about his business, and she would have to forget about him.

"I wonder if my parents were right."

Judd hadn't moved. He sat in the chair watching her. "About what?"

"About me being such a bad judge of character. They always claim I have a very unrealistic perception of mankind, they say that I should accept the world, and my place in it, and stop trying to change things. I suppose I ought to give up and let them have their way."

Judd stiffened, and his expression looked dangerous. "You don't mean that."

With a shake of her head and another small smile, Emily turned to leave. Just before she reached the hallway entrance, she stopped. "One more thing, Judd."

She turned to face him and her gaze locked with his. "The man who came in here? He mumbled something, just before I ran, about only wanting the film."

Judd shot to his feet. *"What?"*

Her smile turned a bit crooked. "I didn't want to tell the police, because I thought it might be important. I was going to wait and tell you so we could figure out what the man meant. But now, since you are the police..." She shrugged.

Judd was busy cursing.

"What are you going to do?" she asked him.

"First, I'm going to get someone over here to check your door for fingerprints."

"It won't do any good. He wore gloves. I felt them when he grabbed me."

"Another tidbit you were saving only for me?"

"Uh-huh. I honestly don't know anything else, though." She stifled a forced yawn. "I think I'll get ready for bed now."

Judd moved to stand directly in front of her. "I'm staying the night, Em."

"That's not necessary." *But, oh, it would be so nice.* She sincerely hoped he would insist. For some reason, the thought of being all alone was very unsettling. And even more unsettling was the thought of letting Judd out of her sight.

"I think it is. I won't bother you, if that's what you're worried about."

"I wasn't worried."

He accepted that statement with a smile of his own. "Good.

Why don't you show me where you want me to sleep? Then I've got a few more calls to make."

Since Emily wouldn't show him where she really wanted him to sleep, which was with her, she led him to the room down the hall from her bedroom. Decorated in muted shades of blue, it had only a twin bed and was considered her guest room. There were two other bedrooms, one was John's room, since he dropped in often whenever there were problems with her parents, and the other room served as a small upstairs sitting room.

Judd nodded his approval, then took Emily's shoulders. "Try to sleep. But honey, if you need anything, don't hesitate to let me know."

He doesn't mean what you're thinking, Em. Didn't he just tell you earlier tonight it was too soon? "Thank you, Judd. Good night." Emily forced her feet to move down the hall, then she forced herself inside her room and closed the door. Her forehead made a soft *thwack* when she dropped it against the wood, and her cheek started throbbing again.

But none of it was as apparent as the drumming of her heart. It was all just beginning to sink in, from the slapstick beginning to the frightening end. Judd was an officer, who chose to take his clothes off in an undercover case, using a police uniform as a costume. It was too ironic. And Lord help her, so was her situation.

She was falling in love with a thoroughly outrageous man.

Judd lay in the narrow bed, stripped down to his underwear, with only the sheet covering him. His arms were propped behind his head and he listened to the strange sounds of the house as it settled. He'd left the door open in case Emily needed him.

God, what a mess.

Howell had raised holy hell with him, and for good reason. He'd behaved like a rookie with no experience at all. He knew better, hell, he was damn good at his job. But he just kept thinking of what could have happened. The thought of Emily being hurt was untenable. He had to find some way to wrap this operation up, and quickly. He didn't want to be involved with her, didn't want to care about her. But he knew it was too late.

Did two people ever come from more different backgrounds? Emily was cultured, refined, elegant. She had a poise that never seemed to leave her, and a way of talking that implied gentleness and kindness and...all the things he wasn't. That refined speech of hers turned him on. Everything about her turned him on.

He had to quell those thoughts. Emily wasn't for him. From what he knew of her parents, they would balk at the mere mention of her getting involved with someone like him. And he didn't want to add to her problems there. She evidently had some very real differences with her parents, but at least she had parents. And probably aunts and uncles and grandparents, all of them educated and smelling of old money.

The only smells Judd had been familiar with around his house were stale beer and unwashed dishes. Max had tried to teach him a better way, but Max had been a simple man with simple manners. He hadn't owned a speck of real silver, yet that was exactly what Emily stirred her tea with. And he couldn't be certain, but he thought the teacup she'd used earlier was authentic china. It had seemed delicate and fragile—just like Emily.

He squeezed his eyes shut, trying to close out the image of her lying soft and warm in her own bed, her dark hair fanned out on the pillow, those big brown eyes sleepy, her skin flushed. He wanted her, more than he'd ever wanted anything in his life. He hadn't known a man could want this much and live through it. She was right down the hall, and he suspected if he went to her, she wouldn't send him away.

But as bad as he wanted her, he also knew he had no right to her. So he continued to stare at the ceiling.

Somewhere downstairs he heard a clock chime eleven. Then he heard a different noise, one he hadn't heard yet, and he turned his head on the pillow to look toward the door.

Emily stood there, a slight form silhouetted by the vague light of the moon coming through the window. He couldn't quite draw a breath deep enough to chase away the tightness in his chest. When she didn't move, he leaned up on one elbow. His voice sounded low and rough when he spoke. "Are you all right, babe?"

She made another small, helpless sound, then took a tiny step into the room. Every muscle in his body tensed.

He couldn't make out her face, but he could tell her gown was long and pale and he could feel her nervousness. He didn't know why she was here, but his body had a few ideas and was reacting accordingly. He was instantly and painfully aroused. "Em?"

She took another step, then whispered in a trembling tone, "I know you said it was too soon. And you're right, of course. I told myself this wasn't proper, that I should behave with some decorum." Her hands twisted together and she drew a deep, shaky breath. "But you see, the thing is..."

Judd knew his heart was going to slam right through his ribs. He couldn't wait another second for her to finish her sketchy explanation. She was here, she wanted him, and despite all the reasons he'd just given himself for why he shouldn't, he knew he wanted her too badly to send her away.

He stared at her in the darkness, and then lifted the sheet. "Come here, Emily."

Chapter Seven

SHE MOVED SO FAST, Judd barely had time to brace himself for her weight. Not that she weighed anything at all. She was soft and sweet and she smelled so incredibly inviting—like a woman aroused. Like feminine heat and excitement. Her brushed-cotton gown tangled around his legs when he turned and pinned her beneath him. He felt her body sigh into his, her slim legs parting, her pelvis arching up. In the next instant, her hands cupped his face and she kissed him. It wasn't a gentle kiss. She ate at his mouth, hungry and anxious and needy.

So many feelings swamped him. Lust, of course, since Emily always inspired that base craving, even when she wasn't intent on seducing him. And need, a need he didn't like acknowledging, but one that was so powerful, so all-consuming, he couldn't minimize it as anything less than what it was.

But first and foremost was tenderness, laced with a touch of relief that he wouldn't have to pull back this time; she would finally be his. She had come to him, and she was kissing him as if she wanted him every bit as badly as he wanted her. That wasn't possible, but if her need was anywhere close to his, they both might damn well explode.

"Emily…"

Her kisses, hot and urgent, landed against his jaw, his chin, the side of his mouth. Her nipples were taut against his chest, her breath hot and fast. He wanted to touch her everywhere, all at once, and he wanted to simply hold her, to let her know how precious she was. He slid one hand down her side, felt her shiver, heard her moan, and he nearly lost his mind. He gripped her small backside with both hands and urged her higher against his throbbing erection, rubbing sinuously, slow and deep, again and again. He wanted to drown in the hot friction, the sensual feel of her warm body giving way to him. Her legs parted wide and she bent her knees, cradling him, offering herself.

Judd groaned low in his throat and went still, aware of the soft heat between her thighs now touching him. He knew she was excited, and the fact was making him crazy. "Too fast, honey. Way too fast."

Emily wasn't listening. Her hands frantically stroked his naked back and her legs shifted restlessly, rubbing against his, holding him. She continued to lift her hips into him, exciting herself, exciting him more. Judd dropped his full weight on her to keep her still, then carefully caged her face. She whimpered, trying to move.

"Shh. It's all right, Em. We've got all night." Then he kissed her. She tasted hot and sweet, and when he slipped his tongue between her lips, she sucked on him with greedy excitement.

Judd had never known kissing to be such a deeply sensual experience. To him, it had always been pleasant, sometimes a prelude to sex, sometimes not. But he'd never felt such a keen desire just from kissing. Emily was driving him over the edge, and he hadn't even touched her yet.

He caught her slim wrists in one hand and trapped them over her head. He had to take control or he'd never last. She muttered a low protest and her hips moved, rubbing and seeking beneath his, finding his erection and grinding against it. Her nightgown was in his way and he knotted one fist in the material and lifted, urgently. He needed to touch all of her, to explore her body, to brand her as his own. Emily squirmed to accommodate him, allowing the material to be jerked above her waist. When Judd felt her bare, slender thighs against his own, he growled and pushed against her.

It almost struck him as funny, the effect she had on him. Prim, polite, proper little Emily. He dipped his head and nuzzled her breasts at the same time he slid his hand over her silky mound, letting his fingers tangle in her damp curls. Emily stopped moving; she even stopped breathing. Judd felt her suspended anticipation.

He released her wrists long enough to jerk the buttons open on the bodice of her nightgown so he could taste her nipples, feel the heat of her flesh, and then he wedged his hand back between her thighs. He pressed his face to her breast and kissed her soft skin, his mouth open and wet. Emily shifted so her puckered nipple brushed against his cheek and Judd smiled, then began to suckle, drawing her in deep, stroking with his tongue, nipping with his teeth.

Her ragged moan was low and so damn sexy he moaned with her. His fingers slid over the tight curls, felt her slick and wet, hot and swollen with wanting him, and then he slid a finger deep inside her. She was incredibly tight and he added another finger, hearing her groan, feeling her body clasp his fingers as he forced them a bit deeper, stretching her.

He began a smooth rhythm, and with a breathless moan, her body moved with him. His thumb lifted to glide over the apex of her mound, finding her most sensitive flesh and stroking it, while his mouth still drew greedily on her nipple, and Emily suddenly stiffened, then screamed out her climax. Judd went still with shock.

Her slim body shuddered and lifted beneath his, her face pulled tight in her pleasure. He watched her every movement, her intense delight expressed in her narrowed eyes, her parted lips, the sweet sounds she made. Judd knew he had never seen anything so beautiful, so right. It seemed to go on and on, and as her cries turned to low breathless moans, he kissed her, taking her pleasure into himself.

When she stilled, he continued to cuddle her close, his own need now put on hold. A tenderness he'd never experienced before swirled through him, and he couldn't help smiling. Miss Cooper was a red-hot firecracker, and he must be the luckiest man alive. "You okay, Em?"

She didn't answer. Her breasts were still heaving and her heartbeat thundered against his chest. Judd placed one last gentle kiss on her open mouth, then lifted himself away to reach for his pants. He fumbled in the pockets until he found his wallet and located a condom. When he turned back to Emily, he saw her watching him, her dark eyes so wide they filled her face. Her bottom lip trembled as she slowly drew in uneven breaths. Damp curls framed her face and her expression was wary.

She was probably a bit embarrassed by her unrestrained display. He didn't have time to soothe her, though. He needed to be inside her, right now, feeling her body clasped tight around his erection just as it had clasped his fingers. With the help of the moonlight, he could see her pale belly and still-open thighs. He bent and pressed his mouth to her moist female flesh, breathing in her scent and his need for her overwhelmed him. His tongue flicked out, stroking her, rasping over her delicate tissues and he gained one small taste of her excitement before Emily gasped and began struggling away.

He caught the hem of her gown and wrestled it over her head, chuckling at the way she tried to stop him. She slapped at his hands, and when she realized he had won the tug-of-war, she covered her face with her hands. Once the gown was free, Judd tossed it aside and then immediately pulled her hands away from her face. The feel of her naked body, so warm and soft and ready, made him shudder. He covered her completely and said in the same breath, "You are so beautiful, Em. I've never known a woman like you."

She peeked one eye open and studied him. "Really?"

"Oh, yes," he answered in his most fervent tone.

She said a small, "Oh," and then he lifted her knees with his hands, spread her legs wide and pushed inside her. She was tight and hot and so wet… Slowly, her body accepted his length, taking him in by inches, her softness giving way to his hardness. Judd had to clench his teeth and strain for control. She made small sounds of distress, and he knew he was stretching her, but she didn't fight him, didn't push him away. Her small hands clenched on his shoulders and held him close.

It didn't take her long to forget her embarrassment once he was fully inside her. He ground against her, his gaze holding her own, seeing her eyes go hot and dark and intent. She pulled her bottom lip between her teeth and arched her neck.

"That's it, sweetheart." He drew a deep breath and began moving. Emily rocked against him, meeting his rhythm, holding him tight. He pressed his lips to her neck, breathing in her scent. He slid his hands down her back and cupped her soft bottom, lifting her higher. He felt her nipples rasp against his chest. Every touch, every breath, seemed to heighten his arousal. When she tightened her thighs and sobbed, her internal muscles milking his erection until he wanted to die, he gave up any effort at control and climaxed with a low, rough endless growl.

It took him a few minutes to realize he was probably squashing Emily. She didn't complain, but then, she wouldn't.

He lifted up and stared at her face. His eyes had adjusted to the darkness, and he could see her fine, dark hair lying in disheveled curls on the pillow. Her eyes were closed, her lashes weaving long thick shadows across her cheeks. The whiteness of her breasts reflected the moonlight, and Judd couldn't resist leaning down to softly lathe a smooth, pink nipple. It immediately puckered.

He smiled and blew against her skin.

Emily squirmed. "You're still inside me."

"Mmm. I'm still hard, too."

"I noticed."

Her shy, quiet voice touched him and he smoothed her hair away from her forehead. "I've wanted you a long time, Emily."

"We haven't known each other a long time."

She still hadn't opened her eyes. He kissed the tip of her nose. "I've wanted you for as long as I can remember. It doesn't matter that we hadn't met yet." She shivered and Judd touched his tongue to her shoulder. "Your skin is so damn soft and smooth. I love touching you. And tasting you."

He licked a path up her throat, then over to her earlobe. "I could stay like this forever."

Emily drew in a shuddering breath. "No, you couldn't."

He laughed, knowing she'd felt the involuntary flex of his erection deep inside her. He wanted her again. "If I get another condom, do you promise to stay exactly like this?"

"Will you let me touch you a little this time, too?"

His stomach tightened at the thought. And he hurriedly searched through the wallet he'd tossed on the floor only minutes earlier.

But once he was ready, he still couldn't let Emily have her way. Watching her react, touching her and seeing his effect on her, was stimulant enough. He'd thought to go slowly this time, to savor his time with her. But every little sound she made drove him closer to the edge. And when he entered her, the friction felt so unbearably good, he knew he wouldn't be able to slow down.

He'd told her the truth. He'd been waiting for her forever. But now he had her, and he didn't want to let her go.

Emily woke the next day feeling fuzzy and warm and remarkably content. Then she realized Judd was beside her, one arm thrown over her hips, his face pressed into her breasts. His chest hair tickled her belly and their legs were entwined. They were both buck naked.

She should have been appalled, but seeing Judd looking so vulnerable, his hair mussed, his face relaxed, made her heart swell with emotion. Very carefully, so she wouldn't awaken him, she sifted her fingers through his hair. It felt cool and silky soft. Emily wouldn't have guessed there was anything soft about Judd. She placed a very careful kiss on his crown.

He shifted slightly, nuzzling closer to her breasts and she held her breath. But he continued sleeping. She was used to seeing the shadow of a beard on his face, but feeling it against her tender skin added something to the experience. She looked down the length of their bodies, and the vivid contrast excited her. He was so dark, so hard and muscled, while she was smooth and pale and seemed nearly fragile beside him.

She almost wished he would wake up, but he appeared totally exhausted. His breathing was deep and even, and when she slipped away from him, he merely grumbled a complaint and rolled over onto his back.

Lord help him. The man did have a fine body. It was certainly shameful of her to stand there leering at him, but she couldn't quite pull her eyes away. Dark hair covered his body in very strategic places, sometimes concealing, sometimes enhancing his masculinity. And Judd Sanders was most definitely masculine. He took her breath away.

Emily might have stood there gawking until he did wake up, if she hadn't heard a knock on her front door. She gave a guilty start, her hand going to her throat, before she realized Judd had slept through the sound, and the person at the door had no notion she was presently entertaining herself with the sight of a naked man.

She snatched her gown, then ran to her own bedroom to retrieve the matching robe. By the time she got downstairs, the knocking had become much louder. "Just a minute," she mumbled.

When she peeked out the small window in the door, she couldn't have been more surprised. For the longest moment, she simply stood there, crying and laughing. When her brother shook his head and laughed back, she remembered to open the door and let him in.

She grabbed him into her arms, even though he stood much taller than herself, and squeezed him as tight as she could. She couldn't stem the tide of tears, and didn't bother trying. "Oh, John, it's so good to see you."

"You, too, Emmie. What took you so long to let me in?"

Emily froze. Uh-oh.

"Emmie? Hey, what's up?"

She shook her head. "What are you doing here, John? I thought you were still out of the country. Did Mother and Father come with you?"

He set two suitcases just inside the door then walked past her, heading for the kitchen. Ever since she'd bought the house, the kitchen had become a kind of informal meeting place. Whenever John visited, they sat at the kitchen table and talked until late into the night.

"John?"

"Could I have something to drink first, Em? It's been a long trip."

Emily stared at John, trying to be objective. He looked better, so much better. The scars on his right temple and upper cheek had diminished, and now only a thin, jagged line cut through his eyebrow. He'd healed nicely, but his eyes still worried her. They seemed tired and sad and...hopeless.

"You look wonderful, John. The plastic surgeons did a great job."

He scoffed. "You call this a great job? This is as good as it gets, Em, though Mom keeps insisting she'll find a better surgeon who'll make me look as 'good as new.' She refuses to believe nothing more can be done."

Emily closed her eyes, wondering why her mother couldn't see the hurt she caused with such careless comments. "John, I never thought the scars were that bad. I was more concerned about your eyesight, and once we realized there wouldn't be any permanent damage there, I was grateful. You should be, too."

"Oh, yeah. I'm real grateful to look like a freak."

For one of the few times in her life, Emily lost her temper with her baby brother. It was so rare for her to be angry with John, she almost didn't recognize the feeling. And then she slammed her hand onto the counter and whirled to face him. "Don't you ever say something so horrible again! You're my brother, dammit, and I love you. You are not a freak."

John seemed stunned by her display. He sat there, silently watching her, his dark eyes round, his body still. Emily covered her mouth with her hand and tried to collect her emotions. Then she cleared her throat. "Are you hungry?"

A small, relieved smile quirked on his lips. "Yeah, a little."

"I'll start breakfast. The coffee should be ready in just a minute. There's also juice in the refrigerator."

John tilted his head. "Since when do you drink coffee? The last time I asked, you said it was bad for me and gave me tea instead."

"Uh…" She'd bought the coffee for Judd, but it didn't seem prudent to tell John that. "You're older now. I see no reason why you can't drink coffee if you like."

"Okay." John still seemed a little bemused, but then he squared his shoulders. "I ran away, Emmie. Mom and Dad refused to bring me home, and I couldn't take another minute of sitting around waiting to see which doctor they'd produce next."

Suddenly, Emily felt so tired she wanted to collapse. "They'll be worried sick, John."

"Ha! I left them a note. You watch. When they can't reach me at home, they'll call here, probably blame you somehow, then carry on as if they're on vacation. We both know they'll be glad to be rid of me. Lately, I've been an *embarrassment*."

Since Emily had suffered similarly at the hands of her parents, she knew she couldn't truthfully deny what he said. She decided to stick to the facts, and to try to figure out what to do. "You came straight here from the airport?"

"Yeah. Mom and Dad probably don't even realize I'm gone yet. They had a couple of parties to attend."

The disdain, and the hurt, were obvious in his tone. She wished she could make it all better for John, but she didn't have any answers. "You know you're welcome here as long as you like."

John stared at his feet. "Thanks."

"You also know you'll have to face them again sooner or later."

"I don't see why," he said. "They're disgusted with me now, but they won't say so. They never really say anything. You know how they are. I won't hang around and let them treat me the way they treat you. Do you remember how they acted when that fiancé of yours tried to scam them for money? Did they offer you support or comfort? No, they wouldn't even come right out and yell at you. They just made you feel like dirt. And they never forget. I don't think you've been to the house since, that Mom didn't manage to bring it up, always in some polite way, that she'd been right all along about him, that you'd been used by that jerk, just so he could get his hands on your money." John shook his head. "No thanks, I don't want to put up with that. I can just imagine…how…I'd…"

Emily looked up from pouring the coffee when John's voice trailed off. She'd heard it all before, his anger on her behalf, his indignation that she let her parents indulge in their little barbs.

She didn't understand what had silenced him now until she followed his gaze and saw Judd leaning against the doorjamb. He had his jeans on—just barely. The top button was undone and they rode low on his hips. His feet were bare, he wore no shirt and his hair fell over his forehead in disarray. He looked incredibly sexy, and the way he watched her, with so much heat, instantly had her blushing.

Then John stood. "Who the hell are you, and what are you doing in my sister's house?"

Judd wished Emily's little brother had waited just a bit longer before noticing him. The conversation had taken a rather interesting turn, and he wouldn't have minded gaining a little more insight into Emily. But he supposed he could question her later on this fiancé of hers and find out exactly what had happened.

He was careful not to look overlong at the boy's scars, not that they were really all that noticeable, anyway. But just from the little he'd heard, he knew John was very sensitive about them. He was actually a good-looking kid, with the all-American look of wealth. Now, however, he appeared mightily provoked and ready to attack.

Judd ignored him.

His gaze locked on Emily, and suddenly he was cursing. "Damn, Em, are you okay?"

Emily faltered. "What?"

He strode forward until he could gently touch the side of her face. "You've got a black eye."

"I do?" Her hand went instantly to her cheek.

"It's not bad, babe. But it looks like it might hurt like hell."

She cleared her throat and cast a nervous glance at her brother. "No, it feels fine."

Judd smiled, then deliberately leaned down to press a gentle kiss to the bruise. Before Emily could step away, he caught her hands and lifted them out to her sides. In a low, husky tone, he said, "Look at you." His eyes skimmed over the white cotton eyelet robe. The hem of her gown was visible beneath and showed a row of lace and ice-blue satin trim. It was feminine and romantic and had him hard in a heartbeat.

Leaning down by her ear, Judd whispered in a low tone so her brother wouldn't hear, "I woke up and missed you. You shouldn't have left me."

He could feel the heat of her blush and smiled to himself, then turned to greet her brother. The kid looked about to self-destruct. Judd stuck out his hand. "Hi. Judd Sanders."

John glared. "What are you doing in my sister's house?" he repeated.

"That's none of your damn business." Then in the next breath, Judd asked, "Didn't you notice Emily's black eye?"

John stiffened, a guilty flush staining his lean cheeks. "It's not that noticeable. And besides, Emily was asking about me, so I didn't have time—"

"Yeah, right." Judd turned to Emily. "Why don't you sit down and rest? I'll fix breakfast. What do you feel like eating?"

"Hey, wait a minute!" John's neck had turned red now, too. He apparently didn't like being ignored.

Judd sighed. "What?"

For a moment, John seemed to forget what he wanted. He opened his mouth twice, and his hand went self-consciously to his scar. Then he asked, with a good dose of suspicion, "How did Emmie get a black eye?"

Judd smiled to himself. He folded his arms over his chest and braced his bare feet apart. "Some guy broke in here—"

"It was nothing, John." Emily frowned at Judd and then rushed toward her brother. "Would you like to go freshen up, John, before breakfast?"

"Women freshen up, Em. Not men."

She glared at Judd for that observation.

Judd lifted his eyebrow. "He has every right to know what happened to you. He's your brother and you care about him, so it only stands to reason that he cares for you, too." Judd looked toward John. "Am I right?"

"Yeah." John stepped forward. "What did happen?"

Emily looked so harassed, Judd took pity on her. "Why don't you go upstairs and…freshen up, Em, or change or whatever. I'll entertain your brother for you and start breakfast." Then he leaned down close to her ear. "Not that I don't like what you're wearing. You look damn sexy. But little brother looks ready to attack."

Her eyes widened and she cast a quick glance at John. "Yes, well, I suppose I ought to get dressed…" She rushed from the room. Judd watched her go, admiring the way her delectable rear swayed in the soft gown.

"What did you say to her?"

Little brothers were apparently a pain in the butt, and Judd wasn't known for his patience. But he supposed, for Emily, he ought to make the effort. "I told her how attractive she is. I get the feeling she isn't used to hearing compliments very often." The way he said it placed part of the blame for that condition directly on John. Judd didn't think it would hurt him to know Emily needed comforting every bit as much as anyone else. "Emily's a woman. They like to know when they look nice."

As he spoke, Judd opened the cabinets and rummaged around for pancake mix and syrup. It was one of the few breakfast things he knew how to make. He wanted to pamper Emily, to make her realize how special she was.

Last night had been unexpected, something he hadn't dared dream about, something he supposed shouldn't have happened. But it had happened, and even though he didn't know what he was going to do about it yet, how to balance his feelings for Emily with his need to get Donner, he knew he didn't want her to be uncomfortable around him.

He thought breakfast might be a good start. Besides, he owed her one from yesterday.

John interrupted his thoughts with a lot of grousing and grumbling. "I'm good to Emily."

"Are you?" He pulled out a couple of eggs to put in the mix, his mind whirling on possible ways to proceed against Donner, while keeping Emily uninvolved. Perhaps having her brother here would distract her from capturing the gun dealer.

"She's been worried about me."

Judd glanced at John as he pulled down a large glass mixing bowl. "I don't see why. You seem healthy and strong. Hell, you're twice her size." He took the milk from the refrigerator and added it to the mix.

"I nearly lost my eyesight not too long ago. And now I've got these damn scars."

Judd gave up for a moment on the pancakes. He turned to give John his full attention. "That little scar on the side of your face?"

John nearly choked. "Little?"

"It's not that big a deal. So you've got a scar? You're a man. Men are expected to get banged up a little. Happens all the time. It's not like you're disabled or anything. You'll still be able to work and support yourself, won't you?"

"I'm only sixteen."

Judd shrugged. "I was thinking long term."

"My face is ruined."

"Naw. You're still a good-lookin' kid. And in a few more years, that scar will most likely fade until you can barely see it. Besides, you'll probably get all kinds of sympathy from the females once you hit college. So what's the problem?"

John collapsed back in his chair. "You really don't think the scars are all that bad?"

Judd went back to mixing the batter. "I didn't even notice them at first. Of course, with Emily around that's not saying much. I wouldn't notice an elephant at the table when she looks at me with those big brown eyes. Your sister is a real charmer."

There was a stretch of silence. "You and Emily got something going?"

"Yeah. Something. I'm not sure what. Hey, how many pancakes can you eat? About ten?"

"I suppose. I didn't know Emily was dating anyone."

"We aren't actually dating."

"Oh." Another silence. "Should I be worried about this?"

That brought Judd around. "Well, hallelujah. I didn't think anyone ever worried about Em."

John frowned. "She's my sister. Of course I worry about her."

"Good. But no, you don't have to worry right now. I'll take care of her."

"And I'm just supposed to believe you because you say so?"

He almost smiled again. John sounded just like his sister. "Why not? Emily does."

That brought a laugh. "My parents would have a field day with that analogy. They don't think Emily has very good judgment."

"And what do you think?"

"I think she's too naive, too trusting and a very good person."

Judd grinned. "Me, too."

"So tell me how she got the black eye."

Suddenly, John looked much older, and very serious. Judd gave one sharp nod. "You can set the table while I talk."

Fifteen minutes later, Judd had three plates full of pancakes, and he'd finished a rather convoluted explanation of Emily's exploits. It was an abridged version, because even though Judd admitted to helping Emily, he didn't say anything about going undercover as a male stripper, or his overwhelming attraction to Emily, or their newly discovered sexual chemistry. In fact, he wasn't certain yet just what that chemistry was, so he sure as hell wasn't about to discuss it with anyone, let alone Emily's little brother.

John was appalled to learn what steps Emily had taken to try to help him.

And he hadn't even noticed her black eye.

Judd knew he was feeling guilty, which hopefully would help bring him out of his self-pity. "So you can see how serious Emily is about this."

"Damn." John rubbed one hand over his scar, then across his neck. "What can I do to help?"

Ah. Just the reaction he'd hoped for. From what Emily had told him about John, Judd hadn't known for sure what to expect. By all accounts, John could have been a very spoiled, selfish punk. But then, he had Emily for a sister, so that scenario didn't seem entirely feasible. "You want to help? Stay out of the east end. And stay out of trouble."

"But there must be something—"

"No." When John started to object, Judd cursed. "I'm having enough trouble keeping an eye on Emily. And she has enough to do without worrying about you more than she already does. Give her a rest, John. Get your act together and keep it together."

"That's easy for you to say. You don't know my parents."

"No. But I do know your sister. If she turned out so great, I suppose you can, too."

John laughed. "That's one way of looking at it."

Emily walked into the room just then, and Judd immediately went to her. He tried to keep his eyes on her face as he talked to her, but she was wearing another one of those soft, ladylike dresses. But what really drove him insane was the white lace tie that circled her throat and ended in a bow. Without meaning to, his fingers began toying with it. "I told your brother what happened."

The frown she gave him showed both irritation and concern. "Judd."

"Hey, it's okay," John said as he took a plate of pancakes and smothered them in warm syrup. "I'm glad he told me. And I'm glad he's looking after you."

"Judd is not looking after me. He's a…well, a partner of sorts."

Judd lowered his eyebrows as if in deep thought, then gave a slow, very serious nod. "Of sorts."

The look she sent him insisted he behave himself. He wasn't going to, though. A slight tug on the bow brought her an inch or two closer. His eyes drifted from her neatly brushed hair, her slender stockinged legs and her flat, black shoes. Her attire was casual, but also very elegant. "You look real pretty in that dress, Em. Do you always wear such...feminine stuff?"

Trying to act as though she wasn't flushed a bright pink, Emily stepped out of his reach and picked up her own plate. She stared at the huge stack of pancakes. "Most of my wardrobe is similar, yes. This is one of my older dresses because I have some work to do today."

"I like it."

John suddenly laughed. "I think you've caught a live one, Emmie. I don't remember what's-his-name ever acting this outrageous. He always tried to suck up to Mom and Dad by being as stuffy and proper as they are."

After frowning at her brother and giving a quick shake of her head, she said, "I can't truly imagine Judd ever 'sucking up' to anyone. Can you?"

"It'll be interesting to see what the folks think of him."

An expression of horror passed over her face. "For heaven's sake, John. I doubt Judd has any interest in meeting our parents."

Judd narrowed his eyes at the way she'd said that. So she didn't want him to meet them? It was no skin off his nose. He wasn't into doing the family thing, anyway. He couldn't remember one single woman he'd ever dated who wanted to rush him home to meet her mama.

But somehow, coming from Emily, the implicit rejection smarted. "There wouldn't be any reason for me to meet them. Especially since they're out of the country, right?"

Emily stared at her fork. "Yes. And we should have everything resolved before they return if we're as close to finishing this business as you say."

And once everything was resolved, there would be no reason to keep him around? Judd wanted to ask, but he couldn't. It was annoying to admit, but he felt vulnerable. He couldn't quite credit Emily with using him; she simply wasn't that mercenary. But that didn't mean she wouldn't gladly take advantage of a situation when it presented itself. He'd known from the start that she wanted him. They'd met, and sparks had shot off all around them. And if she wanted to have a fling on what she considered "the wild side of life," Judd was more than willing to oblige. For a time.

He would get a great deal of satisfaction when Donner was taken care of, and he'd be able to return to his normal routine: life without a driving purpose. He'd be alone again, without Max and without the overwhelming need to avenge him. Actually, he'd have no commitments, no obligations at all, unless Emily...

Judd shook his head. With any luck, he'd be wrong in what he was feeling, and he wouldn't miss her. The time he had with Emily right now would be enough.

Hell, he'd make it enough.

With that thought in mind, he urged Emily to eat, and he dug into his own pancakes. When she was almost finished, curiosity got the better of him and he asked, "So who was this bozo who tried to schmooze your parents?"

Emily choked. He took the time to whack her on the back a few times, then caught her chin and turned her face his way. "Emily?"

When she didn't answer right away, John spoke up. "Emmie was engaged to a guy for a while. She loved him, but he only wanted to use her to get in good with my parents. Luckily, everyone found out in time, before the wedding."

"Thank you very much, John."

"Oh, come on, sis. It wasn't your fault. The guy was a con artist."

"Yes, he was. And that is all in the past. I'd appreciate it if we found something else to talk about."

Judd transferred his gaze to John. "Your folks are pretty hard on her about it still?"

"God, yes. And she lets them. I don't think I've ever heard her really defend herself, though I'd like to see her tell them where to go. They even try to bully her into giving up her work with the homeless. They keep reminding her how she got burned once. It was a real embarrassing event. The papers got wind of it and all of society knew." John made a face, then added, "My parents really hate being publicly embarrassed."

With a disgusted sound of protest, Emily stood and took her plate to the sink. Judd glanced toward her, then back to John. "She's still a little touchy about it."

"Yeah. It was pretty hard on her. But Emmie is tough, and she doesn't let anything really get her down. Including Mom and Dad. That's why she moved here, away from my folks. She won't argue with them, but she will walk away. Of course, they hate this house, too. I don't know why she puts up with them."

Swiveling in his chair, Judd saw the stiff set to Emily's shoulders, the way she clenched her hands on the sink counter. He wanted to hold her, to comfort her, but the time wasn't right. Later, though... "Did you love him, Em?"

It took her so long to answer, Judd thought she'd decided to ignore him. It wasn't any of his business, but he wanted to know. The thought of her still pining over some guy didn't sit right with him.

Then she finally shook her head. "I suppose I thought I did...maybe I did. But now, it doesn't seem like I could have. I was so wrong about him. He was out of work and needed me, and I thought he cared about me, too. But he turned out to be a really horrible man."

Judd was out of his seat and standing behind her in a heartbeat. "That was one incident."

She turned and smiled at him. "Are you thinking I might decide I was wrong about you, too, Detective?"

"Since I don't know what you think about me, how am I supposed to answer that?"

When it came, her smile was sweet enough and warm enough to make his muscles clench. He caged her waist between his hands and waited.

"I think you're probably a real-life hero, Judd, and unlike any man I've ever known."

The words hit him like a blow. He stared into her dark eyes, dumbfounded. He saw her acceptance, her giving. He was a man with no family, no ties, a cop out to do a job, and willing to use her to do it. He was certainly no hero. But if that was what Emily wanted...

John cleared his throat. "Maybe I should make myself scarce."

Remembering where they were and who was with them, Judd forced himself to release Emily and take two steps back—away from temptation. "No. You can help me do the dishes while Emily calls to see if she can get someone here to repair the hot-water heater."

"Do the dishes? But I don't know how..."

Judd smirked. "It's easy. I'll show you what to do."

"But—"

"Do you want to be able to take care of yourself or not?"

Emily laughed. "Well put. I'll leave you two to tend to your chores." But she stopped at the doorway. "By the way, Judd. What if there was something on that film?"

"I'm picking it up today. Then we'll know."

"I'll go with you."

"No, you won't."

"But..."

His sigh was exaggerated. "You're as bad as your brother, Em. I thought we had an agreement."

When she turned around and practically stomped away without a word, Judd decided she was mad. "Well, hell."

John only laughed. "Gee, I'm really tired. Too much traveling, I guess. I think I might need to spend a lot of time in my room, resting up."

"What's that supposed to mean?"

With a buddy-type punch in the shoulder, John said, "I think you're going to have your hands full with Emmie. She can be as stubborn as a mule, and it's no telling who will win. I don't want to get caught in the cross fire."

And I don't want Emily caught in the cross fire, he thought. *Which is why I'm leaving her here.* There was really no other choice. He would get Donner, one way or another. The past, and Max, couldn't be forgotten. And he couldn't pretend it had never happened, not without finding some justice.

It would be only too easy to get wrapped up in Emily's problems. *It would be much too easy to get wrapped up in Emily.* But he wouldn't. Judd was afraid Emily could easily make him reevaluate himself and his purpose. Arresting Donner and seeing him prosecuted had to remain a priority. But he was beginning to feel like a juggler in a circus, wanting his time with Emily, and still needing to seek vengeance on Donner.

He'd have all weekend to spend with Emily before anything more could be done on the case. His body tightened in anticipation with just the thought. Somehow he'd have to manage—without letting her get hurt.

He only hoped Emily understood his motivations.

Chapter Eight

"I WANT YOU, EM."

Emily jumped, her heart lodging in her throat. "Good heavens, Judd. You startled me."

His hands slid from her waist to her hips, then pulled her back against him. She could feel the heat of his body on her back, her bottom... "Judd, stop that before John sees."

His growl reverberated along her spine, his mouth nipping on her nape. "John's taking a nap. He's still suffering jet lag."

With shaking hands, Emily carefully laid aside the picture she'd been looking at. She already knew Judd wanted her. He'd made that clear with every look he sent her way. But her brother was here now, and she wasn't comfortable being intimate with John in the house. She cleared her throat and tried to come up with a distraction.

"I don't see anything in these pictures that would prompt anyone to steal them."

Judd pressed closer and his hands came around her waist to rest on her belly. She sucked in a quick breath. His deep voice, so close to her ear, added to her growing excitement. "You have innocent eyes, honey."

"What do you mean?"

"Innocent, sexy eyes." He leaned over to see her face, his gaze dark and searching. "You really don't know what sexy eyes you have, do you?"

It took her a second to remember what she'd been talking about. "No, I... The pictures, Judd?"

His gaze dropped to her mouth and he gave her a soft, warm kiss, then picked up one of the photos. His expression changed as he looked at it, turning dark and threatening. "The guy in the doorway of the deli is an associate of Donner's. My guess is, he only visits this part of town when making a deal. Since the deal surely concerns guns, I'd say he's the one who instigated your break-in."

Emily gave the photo another look. "Really?"

Judd cursed, then tossed the picture back on the kitchen counter. "Unfortunately, I can't do anything about it yet without taking the risk of tipping off Donner and blowing my cover. If we grab this guy, we put a halt to the deal, and lose our advantage." He tightened his mouth. "That's not something I'm willing to do."

"I see." But she didn't, not really. Why was Judd so upset?

"Do you? Do you have any idea how I'd love to get my hands on that guy—*now*—for scaring you like he did?"

His possessive tone made her heart flutter, and she had to force herself to think about the case. "Then you think he was the one who broke in here?"

"Probably not. Like Donner, he has flunkies to do that kind of thing for him. But your taking this picture has obviously annoyed him. Hopefully, it'll help strengthen our case against Donner, too, and we'll be able to make another connection there once we prosecute."

Emily licked her lips and tried for a casual tone. "Do you think the picture alone will be enough to incriminate Donner?"

Judd shrugged. "Possibly. But I don't want to incriminate him. I want to nail the bastard red-handed."

Emily had known that would be his answer, but still… "Judd, maybe it's time to rethink all this. I mean, is it really worth risking your life—"

He laid his finger across her lips before she could finish. "I'm not giving up, Em. I've already gone too far, and I have no intention of letting Donner win. But in the meantime, until he's put away and everything's settled, I don't want you staying here alone."

So. There it was. Emily knew he was up to something the minute he came back in with the developed pictures. She'd been surveying the pictures, not seeing anything out of the ordinary, when Judd started acting amorous.

Acting, Emily? Can't you feel the man's body behind you? He's not acting. No, and as much as that tempted her, she had to remember he only wanted to stay at her house to protect her. It had nothing to do with actually wanting her. Well, maybe it had a little to do with that, but wanting her wasn't his primary motive. She had to remember that.

Smiling slightly, she said over her shoulder, "My brother will be here with me."

He opened his thighs and pulled her bottom closer to him, his hand still firm on her belly, now caressing. "Not good enough. I want to be certain you're safe."

"I…I'll remember to turn on the alarm system." *Lord, Emily. You sound as if you've run five miles.*

Apparently done with talking, Judd dipped his hand lower and his fingers stroked between her thighs, urging her legs apart and moving in a slow, deep rhythm. The material of her dress slid over her as his fingers probed. Heat rushed through her, flushing her face, making her legs tremble, her nipples tighten. She slumped back against him and her head fell to his shoulder. How could she let this happen again when she still felt embarrassed over her wild display the night before? It was as if she had no control of her reactions.

Judd lifted his other hand to her breast, his fingertips finding a taut nipple then gently plucking.

"Judd—"

"Let me." He nuzzled her throat, his warm breath wafting over her skin. "I love how you feel, Em. I love how you come apart for me."

But you don't love me. She almost cried out at the realization that she wanted his love. She wanted it so bad. All the old insecurities returned, the memories of how she'd tried, just as her brother was trying, to gain a modicum of real emotion, real affection from someone. They all swamped her and suddenly she couldn't breathe. She jerked away, hitting her hip on the counter and hanging her head so Judd couldn't see her face. She felt breathless and frightened and so damn foolish.

His hand touched her shoulder, then tightened when she flinched. "Shh. I'm sorry, babe. I didn't mean to push you."

He turned her to hold her in his arms, no longer seducing, but comforting. And that seemed even worse. The tears started and she couldn't stop them.

His palm cradled the back of her head, his fingers kneading her scalp, tangling in her hair. "Tell me what's wrong, Em. I'll fix it if I can."

Through her tears, she managed a laugh. He was the most wondrous man. She pulled away to retrieve a tissue, then cleaned up her tear-stained face before turning back to him. He looked so concerned, so caring, she almost blurted out, *I love you.* But she managed to keep the words inside. She had no idea how Judd would feel about such a declaration, but she couldn't imagine him welcoming it, not now, not while he had to concentrate on getting Donner.

"I guess I'm just a little overwrought," she said lamely. She quickly added, "I mean, with my brother being here, and worrying over him and the break-in."

Judd still looked concerned, but he nodded. "I understand. Would you like to take a nap, too?"

She'd never be able to sleep. "No. I have housework to do, and the yard needs some work. And I thought I'd put on a roast to cook for dinner."

Looking sheepish, and somewhat anxious, Judd asked, "You mind if I hang around and help?"

He could be so adorable... *Lord, Emily, are you crazy? The man is devastating, not adorable.* "Of course you're welcome to stay. But you don't have to help out. And I'm still not certain that it's a good idea for you to stay overnight."

"I think it's a hell of an idea. And I insist." When she frowned, he added, "It'll only be for a few days. I have to be back at the bar Tuesday. I have the feeling Donner will approach me then. He's getting restless, and he's made it clear he thinks we'll work well together. Since he doesn't like losing, he'll probably make me an offer that no normal stripper could refuse."

It was a small grab for humor, so Emily dutifully smiled. But inside, she felt like crying. The thought of Judd getting more involved with Donner made her skin crawl. They both knew how dangerous he could be.

"Stop frowning, Em. I should be able to set something up with him, find out when and where his next shipment will be, and then I'll bust him. It'll be over with before you know it."

And he'd go out of her life as quickly as he'd entered it. Emily bit her lip. "I'm worried, Judd."

"Don't be. I can take care of myself."

She supposed that was true, since he'd been doing just that

since he'd been a child. But for once, she'd like to see him taken care of.

Just that quick, she had a change of heart. Judd might never love her, but he deserved to be loved. And she could easily smother him with affection. She'd enjoy taking care of him, and maybe, just maybe, he'd enjoy it, too.

They spent the day together, and though she tried, Judd didn't let her do any actual work around the house. She couldn't convince him that she enjoyed getting her hands dirty once in a while, and since he seemed so determined to have his way, she allowed it. Judd followed her direction, and she simply enjoyed her time with him.

He was a pleasure to watch, to talk to. He moved with easy grace, his muscles flexing and bunching. It was almost a shame he wasn't a real stripper, for he was certainly suited for the job.

When Judd suddenly stripped off his shirt, Emily thought he might have read her mind. He didn't look at her, though, merely went back to work. She heard herself say, "Are you performing for me, Judd?"

She'd meant only to tease him, but he slowly turned to face her, and his eyes were intent, almost hot as he caught and held her gaze. "I could be convinced to…in a private performance."

Not a single answer came to mind. She sat there, staring stupidly. Judd walked to her, pulled her close then kissed her. It was such a devouring kiss, Emily had to hold on to him. His tongue pushed into her mouth, hot and wet and insistent. Judd slanted his head and continued to kiss her until they were both breathless.

When he pulled away, she stared up at him, dazed. He drew a deep breath and tipped up her chin. "Anytime, Emily. You just let me know."

After that, she refrained from provoking comments. Judd might handle them very well, but she didn't think she'd live through another one. Instead, she asked about Max, Judd's past, and about his work. She wanted to know everything about him.

Emily went out of her way to show Judd, again and again, how important he was to her. At times he looked bemused, and at times wary. But more often than not, he looked frustrated.

She understood that frustration since she felt a measure of her own. But having her brother there did inhibit her a bit. Of course, so did her unaccountable response to Judd. It was scandalous, the way he could make her feel. But she suspected he didn't mind, even if it did embarrass her, so she decided she'd try to see to his frustration—and her own—once John had gone to bed for the evening.

That thought kept her flushed and filled with forbidden anticipation the entire time they worked.

Midafternoon, John joined them, and Emily was amazed to see how John reacted to Judd. It had startled her that morning when John had spoken so openly to Judd. Usually, her brother was stubbornly quiet, refusing to give up his thoughts, brooding in his silence. But with Judd, he seemed almost anxious to talk. And Judd listened.

Emily was so proud of Judd, she could have cried again. No one had ever reached her brother so easily. In a way, she was jealous, because she'd tried so hard to help John. But she supposed it took a male to understand, and Judd not only listened, he gave glimpses into his own past, allowing John to make a connection of sorts. They found a lot of things in common, though their upbringings had been worlds apart.

Emily decided she was seeing male bonding at its best, and went inside to give them more privacy.

She was starting dinner when they both walked in, looking windblown and handsome. Judd winked at Emily when he caught her eye, and John laughed.

"A man's coming tomorrow to replace my water heater." She more or less blurted that out from sheer nervousness when Judd started her way. He had that glint in his eyes again, and she truly felt embarrassed carrying on in front of her brother.

But Judd only placed a kiss on her cheek, and flicked a finger over the tip of her nose. "Good." Then he turned to John. "Make sure you're here when he comes. I don't think Emily should be alone in this big house with a strange man."

"I'll be here."

Emily might have objected to their protective attitudes, except that she heard a new strength in John's tone, that of confidence and maturity. She gave both men a tender smile. They stared back in obvious confusion.

Backing out of the room, John said, "I think I'll go watch some TV." But he glanced at Judd, then back to Emily. "Uh... that is, unless you need me to do anything else?"

"No. You can go do whatever you like."

Once he'd left the room, Emily turned a wondering look on Judd. "How did you do that?"

His grin was smug. "Do what?"

"Turn my little brother into a helpful stranger."

He laughed outright. "First of all, you could stop calling him your little brother. He's a head taller than you, Em. Respect his maturity."

"I hadn't realized he possessed any maturity."

"No, I guess you haven't seen that side of him. But I know Max had to work hard at getting me turned around. And the first thing he did was explain that I was old enough to know better. Put that way, I felt too embarrassed to act like a kid. And little by little, Max pointed out ways to distinguish what it takes to be an adult. Your brother's no different. He just needed some new choices."

Emily stood there feeling dumbfounded by his logic. She

had enough sense to know it wasn't that simple, to realize what John needed was someone to identify with, someone who cared. That Judd was that man only made her love him more. "Thank you."

Judd stared at her, his gaze traveling from her eyes to her mouth, then slowly moving down her body. He muttered a quiet curse, and started toward her. Emily felt her heart trip. But the phone gave a sudden loud peal, and Judd halted.

Hoping she looked apologetic rather than relieved, Emily asked, "Could you get that, please?"

It rang two more times before Judd turned and picked up the receiver.

She knew right away that asking him to answer the phone had been a mistake. The look on Judd's face as he tried to explain who he was would have been comical if Emily hadn't already suspected who her caller was.

When Judd held a palm over the mouthpiece and turned to her, she braced herself.

"It's your father, and he wants to talk to John. By the way, he also wants to know who I am and what I'm doing here answering your phone." Judd tilted his head. "What do you want me to tell him, babe?"

Lord, Emily. You're in for it now.

"It's over and done with, Em. You might as well forget it."

Ha! That was easy for Judd to say. Emily had no doubt her parents were headed home right this minute. Of course, it would take them time to get here, but still, she was already dreading that confrontation.

"Come on, Emily. You know John didn't mean to upset you."

"Of course he didn't. It's just that my parents could rattle anyone." But why did John have to tell them Judd was her boyfriend. Lord, if they showed up before everything was settled, she'd either have to admit Judd was a detective, and accept their unending annoyance for involving herself in something they'd expressly forbidden, or she'd have to tell them he was a...a stripper. She could just imagine their reactions to that.

"I wish I'd talked to them, instead of John."

Judd turned his face away from her. "I offered you the phone, honey. But you just gave me a blank look. I didn't think you wanted to talk to them. And even if you had, what could you have told them? That I was a traveling salesman who just picks up other people's phones?"

She shook her head. "No. But I might have thought of something. And John's been so solemn since he talked with Father. I have no idea what they talked about—other than their conversation about me—but I know it couldn't have been pleasant. John's been sullen and sulky ever since, barely eating his dinner and running off to bed early. I wish he'd talk to me about it."

"He's all right, Em. He just needs a little time to himself."

Emily barely heard him. She stood up and started to pace the room, her mind whirling. Then she threw up her hands in frustration. "Oh, this is just awful. What am I going to do?" She didn't really expect Judd to answer, since he'd only been watching her with a strange look on his face. "You can't possibly realize what a trial my father can be. He's so judgmental, so rigid. Once he takes a stand, he never backs down."

Judd put his hand at the small of her back and nudged her toward the stairs. "Come on. It won't do you any good sitting down here and worrying about it. I'd say you probably have a couple of days before your folks get here, and by then, I'll be gone. So you're probably worrying about nothing."

They were halfway up the stairs, when Emily realized what

he'd said. She turned to him and gripped his arm. "What are you talking about?"

He wouldn't look at her, but continued up the steps. "I don't want to cause you any problems. So I'll make certain I'm out of the way before they get here. Maybe John can say he misunderstood the situation, or something."

Judd started to go to the room Emily had given him the night before. She rushed up the remaining steps to catch him. "Wait a minute."

Judd lifted one dark eyebrow in question. "What?"

What are you going to do now, Emily? Just blurt out that you want him? He doesn't really seem all that interested anymore. She swallowed and tried to find a way to phrase her request without sounding too outrageous. "I...um."

Judd frowned and walked closer to her. "What is it?"

She glanced toward her brother's room, then took Judd's hand and urged him away from the door. When they were outside her bedroom, she stopped. Judd made a quick glance at the door, and this time both his eyebrows lifted.

Emily drew a calming breath. "I don't want to disturb John. And I don't want you to misunderstand."

Judd waited.

"It's about what I said before. I didn't mean that I wanted you to leave. I was worrying about John, not myself. My parents might not approve of my having you here, but then, they approve of very little when it comes to me. I'm almost immune to their criticism. But John isn't."

"So you're worried about him, not yourself?"

She didn't want to lie to him, that wouldn't be fair. "I can't say I'm looking forward to explaining you. After all, if I tell them the truth, they might interfere, and then your case could be jeopardized."

"What will you tell them?"

Judd had slowly moved closer to her until he stood only a few inches away. Already she was responding to him, and he hadn't even touched her yet. "I don't know. But I don't want you to—"

He laid one finger against her lips. "You've told me all kinds of things you don't want, Emily. Now tell me what you *do* want."

"You."

The way his eyes blazed after she said it reassured her. Her fingers trembled when she reached up to touch his chest. "I want you, Judd. It's a little overwhelming, what you make me feel. I've never felt anything like it before. But last night, you gave a part of yourself to me. Now, I want to do the same for you."

His eyes closed and he drew a deep breath.

Emily took his hand and placed it against her heart. "Do you see what you do to me? It's probably wrong of me to like it so much—" She had to stop to clear her throat as Judd's fingers curled around her breast. The heat in her face told her she was blushing, both with excitement and with her audacity, but she was determined to tell him all of it. "When I was engaged, I thought I knew what excitement was, and it was wonderful because it was forbidden. I felt wild, and just a little bit sinful. But that was nothing compared to how I feel with you."

"How do you feel?"

"Alive. Carnal." She felt the heat in her cheeks intensify with her outrageous admission, but she continued, "Not the least bit refined."

"God, Emily, you're the most refined, the most graceful woman I've ever seen." His tone dropped and his thumb rubbed over her nipple. "You're also remarkably feminine and sexy. Just thinking about how wild you get makes me so hard I hurt."

She licked her lips, then stepped closer still so she could hide her face against his chest. "There are...things, I've wanted to do to you, Judd."

His body seemed to clench, and his voice, when he spoke, was hoarse, "What...things?"

Smiling, Emily whispered, "Don't you think we ought to get out of the hall before we...ah, discuss it?"

She'd barely finished speaking before Judd had opened her bedroom door and ushered her inside. The light was out, but Judd quickly flipped the wall switch. Now that they were out of the dim hall and she had his undivided attention, Emily felt very uncertain about what she had to say. But Judd was staring intently, and waiting, so she forged ahead.

"The last time...well, I know I took you by surprise."

He traced her mouth with a finger. "You can surprise me anytime you like."

"That's not what I mean. You see, even though I try very hard to be proper..." She glanced at his face, saw his fascination, then carefully pulled his teasing fingertip between her lips. Her tongue curled around him as she gently sucked and she heard him gasp. She licked at his flesh, lightly biting him.

"Oh, Emily."

She forgot he watched her with intense scrutiny. She forgot that such displays could be embarrassing. She could only think of the many things she wanted...

She released his finger and he dropped his hand to her buttocks, cuddling her. With a deep breath and a nervous smile, she blurted out, "I'm afraid I'm a fraud. I'm not at all proper. At least, you see, not when I'm..."

"Turned on?" His words were a breathless rasp.

She gave a painful nod of agreement.

There was no smile now, but his eyes showed wicked anticipation, and a touch of something more, something she couldn't recognize. "Are you turned on now, Em?"

The rapid beating of her heart shook her. Heat pulsed beneath her skin, making her warm all over, making her nipples taut, her belly tingle. It was so debilitating, wanting him like this. "Very."

"And you want to do...things? To me?"

Again, she nodded, feeling the husky timbre of his voice deep inside herself. "If you wouldn't mind."

His long fingers curved over her bottom and began a rhythmic caressing. "Tell me what things, Em."

Pressed so close to his body, it was impossible to ignore the length of his erection against her belly, or the warmth of his breath fanning her cheek. She went on tiptoe and nuzzled her mouth against his throat. "I want to taste you...everywhere."

His hands stilled, then clenched tight on her flesh. Against her ear, he whispered, "Oh, yeah."

She pulled his shirt open, and rubbed her cheek over the soft, curling hair there. "I'd like to have you...beneath me, so I could watch your face. You are such an incredibly handsome man, Judd. When you stripped for me...at least, it felt like it was just for me..."

"It was. It made me crazy, the way you ate me up with your eyes. I had to fight damn hard to keep from embarrassing myself that day."

Not quite understanding what he meant, she tilted her head back and stared up at him. "How so?"

His lips twitched into a smile. "You make me hard, Em, without even trying. But watching you watch me... It was the first time I thought stripping was a turn-on. Before that, it was only damn embarrassing."

"I'm looking forward to watching you again."

He groaned, then kissed her, sucking her tongue into his

mouth. Emily almost forgot that she wanted to control things this time, but with a soft moan, she pushed Judd away.

"Emily..."

"No, wait." She had to pant for breath, but she was determined. "Will you take your clothes off for me, Judd?"

He blinked. "Will I... How about we take them off together?"

Reaching for his shirt, she said, "Of course," but Judd stopped her hands.

"I meant, we should take *our* clothes off, Em. I want you naked, too. All those things you want to do to me, well, I want to do them to you."

Her mouth went dry. Just the thought of Judd kissing her... She shook her head. "No. Not a good idea. This is my turn..."

"Let's not argue about it, okay?"

She could see the humor in his gaze, and his crooked smile. He was so endearing, so charming, so... "I've never undressed for anyone before."

There. She'd made that admission. She knew her face was scarlet, but she simply hadn't considered that he might want her to display herself. He was the stripper, not her.

Even as his fingers went to the waistband of his jeans, Judd murmured, "Fair's fair, Em." His eyes challenged her, and while her fascinated gaze stayed glued to his busily working fingers, Emily nodded.

She started to untie the bow to her dress, but Judd caught her hands. "No. This one is mine. I thought about doing this—so many times—since we first met." He took the very tip of the lace tie between his finger and thumb, then gently tugged. It pulled open and the ends landed, curling around her breasts. Judd carefully separated the looped strips, while the backs of his fingers brushed over her nipples again and again. Then he slid the tie—so very slowly—out of her collar. Through it all, Emily didn't move.

It was the most erotic thing she'd ever had done to her.

She barely noticed when Judd tucked the lace tie into the back pocket of his jeans. And then he began stripping again, prompting her with a look to do the same. She felt horribly awkward, and very self-conscious. Her body wasn't perfect like his, but rather too slim, too slight. Where Judd looked like every woman's vision of masculine perfection, she was a far sight from the women's bodies displayed in men's magazines.

After unbuttoning her dress, she stepped out of her shoes, trying to concentrate on what Judd was doing, rather than on her own actions. Next, she took off her nylons, tossing them onto the chair by her bed. She saw Judd go still for a moment, then saw his nostrils flare. It hit her that her disrobing excited him. He'd already removed his shirt, and now his jeans, along with his underwear, were shoved down his legs. He stepped out of them, then fully naked, he turned his attention to watching her. There was no disguising his state of arousal. His stomach muscles were pulled tight, and his erection was long and thick and throbbing.

She drew a shuddering breath. "Judd?"

"Go on, honey." When she still hesitated, he said, "You're doing fine, Em. Now, take off the dress."

His words hit her with the impact of a loud drumroll, and she couldn't swallow, her throat was so tight. She saw a slight smile hover on his mouth, and he said, "I've had some fantasies, too, babe. And seeing you strip is one of them."

"I can't."

"I'm not talking about doing it in front of an audience. It'll just be you and me." Then he lowered his gaze to where her hands knotted in the dress. "Take it off, Em."

She wanted to, she really did. But it wasn't in her to flaunt her body, not when she felt she had nothing to flaunt. She looked away, feeling like a failure, afraid she'd disappointed him. Tears of frustration gathered in her eyes, and just when she would have begun a stammering explanation, Judd touched her.

"Shh. It doesn't matter, honey." He pulled her close again. Emily kept her face averted.

Judd pushed the dress down her shoulders, then worked it lower. The soft material slid over her arms and caught, for just a heartbeat, on her narrow hips, then went smoothly to the floor.

Judd's breath left him in a whoosh as his gaze dropped to her black lace panties and stayed there. Emily suddenly didn't feel quite so awkward, not with the intense, heated way he watched her, as if she were the most fascinating woman he'd ever seen. She skimmed off her bra, then offered him a small, nervous smile.

"Incredible." His gaze finally lifted from her panties to her face. "If I'd known what you were wearing under that dress, I never would have lasted this long." He lowered his head for another long, heated kiss, and at the same time, slid his hands into her underwear, his large warm palms cradling her bottom. His fingers explored, probing and stroking, and Emily clung to him. Before the kiss was over, her panties had joined the rest of their clothes and then she urged Judd to sit on the side of the bed. She dropped gracefully to her knees before him, then reached out and encircled his erection with both hands. He was breathing hard, his thighs tensed, his hands fisted on the bed at his sides. Emily leaned forward, feeling her heart pound, and took a small, tentative lick. He jerked, and a rough broken groan escaped him.

Emily felt encouraged and anxious and excited. She leaned forward again, rubbing her breasts against his thighs, her nipples tingling against his hairy legs. Then she closed her mouth around him, gently suckling and sliding her tongue around him, feeling him shudder and stiffen. Judd gave a long, low, ragged groan and twined his fingers in her hair, leaning over her and holding her head between his large palms, urging her to the rhythm he liked. His hands trembled. So did his thighs.

For the first time in her life, Emily was able to indulge in her sensual nature. Judd encouraged her, praised her, pleaded with her. She loved the scent of his masculinity, the texture of his rigid flesh, so silky smooth and velvety. She gave him everything she could, and he gave her the most remarkable night of her life. She knew, if Judd left her now, she wouldn't regret a single minute she'd spent with him.

And she also knew she'd never love another man the way she loved Judd Sanders.

Chapter Nine

THE BAR WAS crowded as women waited for the show to begin. Emily felt a twinge of jealousy, thinking of all those women seeing Judd in his skimpy briefs, but she kept reminding herself it was necessary for him to perform.

She'd left John, still acting contrary and withdrawn, at her house. It seemed it only took one phone call from her father to destroy all the headway Judd had made with her brother. Judd told her not to worry, that he was certain John would work everything out. But John was her little brother, and she couldn't help worrying about him any more than she could stop worrying over Judd.

He was obsessed with catching Donner. Anytime Emily tried to discuss it with him, he went every bit as silent and sullen as John. She supposed he had to get into a certain mind-set to be able to work his cover. After all, not many men could pull off being a stripper. But she hated seeing him act so distant. Even now, as he lounged beside her sucking on an ice cube he'd fished from her cola, she wanted to touch him, to somehow reach him. But he ignored her.

"There aren't any men here tonight. It doesn't seem likely that Donner will come."

She knew Judd had heard her, despite her lowered voice. But he didn't look at her when he replied, "He'll come. I feel it. And there aren't any men because it isn't allowed. It's ladies' night. But Donner has free run of the place. He'll be here."

The look in his eyes, the way he held himself, was so different from the Judd she knew. She felt alone and almost sick to her stomach. She had wanted Donner so badly, but now, she only wanted to protect Judd. From himself. From his feelings. And most especially from his self-designed obligations to a dead man.

Before Emily could comment further, Judd glanced at the watch on his wrist, then said, "I have to go get ready."

He straightened, and Emily tried to think of something to say, anything, that would break his strange mood. Then Judd leaned down and lifted her chin with the edge of his fist. "Do me a favor, babe. Don't watch. If you do, I'll start thinking about last night, and I might not make it."

Emily blinked. "I thought you wanted everyone to believe we had an...intimate association."

"Oh, they'll believe." Then he kissed her. Emily heard the bartender hoot, and she heard a few of the women close by whistle. One particularly brazen woman offered to be next.

Judd practically lifted her from the bar stool, one hand anchored in her hair, the other wrapped around her waist. The kiss was long and thorough, and couldn't have left any doubts about their supposed relationship.

Pulling back by slow degrees, Judd said, "Damn, but I want to be home with you. Alone. Naked."

Emily hastily covered his mouth. "Hush. You'll have me so rattled, I won't remember what I'm doing here."

He kissed her fingers, then straightened again. "Stay out of trouble. And stay where I can see you."

"But don't watch?"

"You've got it." Then he flicked a finger over her cheek and walked away to his "dressing room." Emily couldn't hold back a smile. *He wasn't as indifferent as you thought, was he, Emily? Who knows, this may all work out yet. Maybe, if enough time passes without Donner showing, Judd will finally give up and let someone more objective handle the case.*

Emily was daydreaming about having a future with Judd, when Clayton Donner strolled in the front door, along with his bully boys. Emily sank back on her stool to avoid being noticed. Not that she was all that noticeable, with so many women in the room.

Donner stopped inside the door and spoke with one of his men. He checked his watch, smoothed a hand over his hair, then opened a door leading to a set of stairs. Mick, one of the men from the pool hall, stayed at the bottom. Minutes later, another man entered and spoke quietly with Mick. Emily sucked in a sharp breath as she realized he was the man from the photograph. Fear hit her first, knowing this man had deliberately sent someone to break into her home. But anger quickly followed.

Whoever he was, he could be no better than Donner. And Emily wanted to see them both put away—preferably without involving Judd.

Their heads were bent together in a conspiratorial way, and Emily wished she could hear what they were saying. When Mick led the other man upstairs, she decided she would follow. She felt a certain foreboding, not for herself, but for Judd. She had to protect him.

Her heart pounded with her decision.

Judd was probably the most capable man she'd ever met,

but his love for Max would make him vulnerable in ways that could endanger his life. If there was some way, any way, to help predict Donner's actions, she could use the information to help Judd.

With that thought in mind, she waited until Judd had been cued by his music and walked onto the dance floor, then she slipped away. Judd didn't notice since he seemed to be making every effort not to look her way. Women screamed in the background and the music blared. But above it all, Emily heard the rush of blood in her ears and her thundering heart. She tried to look inconspicuous as she made her way to the door.

It opened easily when she turned the knob, and she held her breath, waiting to see if anyone would be standing on the other side. She could always claim to be looking for the ladies' room. But once the door was open, she was faced with a narrow flight of stairs, with another door at the top.

Oh, Lord, Emily, don't lose your nerve now. And stop breathing so hard or they'll hear you. Each step seemed to echo as her weight caused the stairs to squeak. As she neared the top, she could make out faint voices and she strained to listen. Donner's tone was the most prominent, and not easy to miss. He had a distinctive sound of authority that grated on her ears.

Trying to draw a deep, calming breath, Emily leaned against the wall and concentrated on picking up the discussion, hoping she'd hear if anyone moved to open the door. Gradually, she calmed enough to hear complete sentences, and minutes later, she started back down the stairs.

Her hands shook horribly and she thought she might throw up. When she opened the door and stepped back into the loud atmosphere of the bar, her vision clouded over and she had to shake her head to clear it.

Nothing had ever scared her like eavesdropping on Clayton Donner. But she now had what she needed to protect Judd. She knew when, and where, the next shipment would be bought. A plan was forming, and she'd have a little more than a week to perfect it. She'd make it work, and best of all, it wouldn't include Judd.

Judd finished up his act just as Emily slid back onto her stool. She was stark white and her face seemed pinched in fear. He felt an immediate surge of anger. Something had upset her, and he wanted to know what.

Ignoring grasping hands as he left the floor, he strode to Emily and stopped in front of her. She met his gaze with wide brown eyes and a forced smile. A crush of women began to close in behind him and he took Emily's arm without a word, then started toward the room where he changed. As he walked, he glanced around, hoping to catch sight of Donner or one of his men. He saw only grinning women.

When he closed the door behind them, she began to chatter. "The crowd seemed especially enthusiastic tonight. It's a shame you're not really a performer. You're obviously very good at it."

Judd didn't offer a comment on that inane remark. He studied her face, saw her fear and wondered what had happened. "Where did you go, Em?"

"Where did I go?"

"That's what I asked." He tossed his props aside and picked up a towel to rub over his body. Emily watched his hands, as she always did, with feminine fascination. "You were gone the entire time I danced."

"Oh." She pulled her gaze up to peer into his face, then shrugged. "I went to the ladies' room."

"Uh-uh. Try again."

She tried to look appalled. "You don't believe me?"

"Not a bit." Maybe she had seen Donner. Maybe the bastard had even spoken to her. Judd felt his shoulders tense. "Where did you go, Em?"

She gave a long sigh, then looked down at her feet. "All right, if you must know, I was jealous."

That set him back. "Come again?"

She waved her hand airily. "All those women were ogling you as if they had the right. I couldn't bear to watch. I suppose I'm just a...a possessive woman."

Judd narrowed his eyes, mulling over what she'd said. She sounded convincing enough, but somehow, her explanation didn't ring true.

Emily gave him a defiant glare when he continued to study her. "How would you feel if the situation were reversed? What if that was me dancing, and other men...were ogling me?"

She blushed fire-red as she made that outrageous suggestion, and Judd felt a smile tug at his mouth, despite his belief she was keeping something from him. He pulled on his jeans and then said to her, "I suppose I'd have to take you home and tie you to the bed. I sure as hell wouldn't sit around while other men enjoyed the sight of you. I'm a little possessive, too."

"There! You see what I... You are?"

Shrugging into his shirt, Judd said, "Yes, I am. And because I'm so possessive, I'd like to know what you're up to."

She immediately tucked in her chin and frowned. Judd was just about ready to shake her, when a knock sounded on the door. He went still, his adrenaline beginning to flow, then he moved Emily out of the way and opened the door.

Mick stood there, an insolent look on his face.

"Yeah?" Judd forced himself not to show any interest.

Mick frowned. "Clay wants to talk to you."

"Tell Clay I'm busy." As he said it, he reached back and wrapped an arm around Emily. She seemed startled that he'd done so.

Mick's gaze slid over Emily, then came back to Judd. "He said to tell you he'd like to discuss a little venture with you."

"Ah. I suppose I can spare a few minutes, then. Where is he?"

"Upstairs. I'll take you there."

"I can take myself. Tell him I'll be there when I finish dressing." He shut the door in Mick's face.

Emily immediately started wringing her hands. "Don't go."

"What? Of course I'm going." He leaned down and jerked on his socks and shoes. His hands shook, the anticipation making simple tasks more difficult. He looked up at Emily. "This is what we've been waiting for. Don't go panicking on me now."

As he was trying to button his shirt, Emily threw herself against him. "It's too dangerous. You could get hurt."

"Em, honey." He didn't want to waste any time, but he couldn't walk out with her so upset. He drew a deep breath to try to collect himself. "Em, listen to me." When he lifted her chin, she reluctantly met his gaze with her own. "It'll be all right. Nothing's going to happen here in the bar. I'm only going to talk to him. I promise."

Her bottom lip quivered and she sank her teeth into it to stop the nervous reaction. Judd bent to kiss her, helping her to forget her worry. "I want you to wait at the bar for me. Stay by Freddie until I come back out. Promise me."

"I'll stay by Freddie."

"Good." He opened the door and urged her out. "Now, go. I won't be long."

Judd leaned out the doorway and watched until Emily had taken a stool in the center of the long Formica bar. He signaled Freddie, waited for his wave, then went back into the room, stuffed his props into his leather bag and hoisted it over his shoulder. He took the steps upstairs two at a time. He rapped sharply on the door. His jaw felt tight and there was a pounding in his temples.

Mick opened it, peeked out, then pulled it wide for him to enter.

Donner stood and came to greet him. "Well, if it isn't our friend, the stripper. Tell me, do the ladies ever follow you home?"

Judd forced his muscles to relax. "They try sometimes. But my calendar is full."

"Ah, yes. I almost forgot. The little bird from the pool hall."

Judd didn't reply. He wanted to smash his fist against Donner's smug, grinning face. Instead, he forced a negligent smile.

"Do you enjoy dancing...Sanders, isn't it?"

"That's right. And no, not particularly." Then he pulled a wad of money from his pocket, all of it bills that had been stuffed into his briefs. "But it pays well."

"I can see that it does. There are easier ways to make money, though."

Judd settled back against the wall and folded his arms across his chest. He was so anxious, his mouth was dry. But he kept his pose, and his tone, almost bored. He gave a slow, relaxed smile, then said, "Why don't you tell me about it?"

Judd was still trying to figure out how he was going to keep Emily out of the picture. He couldn't risk her by taking her along, but if she was told the truth, she'd insist on coming with him. They'd argue, and she'd end up with hurt feelings.

He couldn't bear the thought of that. Her feelings were fragile, and she was such a gentle woman, the thought of upsetting her made him feel like an ogre. But dammit all, he had to keep her safe. *Max was dead, but Emily was very much alive.* He had to make certain she would be okay.

Eight days. Not long enough, but then, no amount of time would be enough with Emily. The way he felt about her scared him silly, and it had been a long time since he'd felt fear. Growing up in the wrong part of town, with his father so drunk and angry and unpredictable, he'd gotten used to thinking fast and moving faster. Which was maybe why he'd never settled down with any one woman.

He wouldn't settle down now, either.

He couldn't. Not with Emily. She deserved so much more than he could ever give her, more than he'd ever imagined possessing. Not material things—she had those already, and he wasn't exactly a pauper. He could provide for her. But emotional things? Family and background and happy memories? He couldn't give her that. But he wanted to. So damn much.

She reached over and touched his shoulder as he drove through the dark, quiet streets of Springfield. "What happened, Judd? You've been so quiet since talking with Donner."

He couldn't tell her the truth, so he lied. And hated himself for it. "Nothing happened. He questioned me a little. Tried to feel me out. But he didn't give me a single concrete thing to go on."

"So..." She swallowed, looking wary and relieved. "So you don't know yet what his plans are?"

"No." He flicked her a look. The streetlights flashing by sent a steady rhythm of golden color over her features. She was so beautiful. "I guess we'll have to keep up the cover a little longer. I, ah, suppose I can let you out of it if you think it'll pose a problem. I mean, with John being home now and all."

"No!" She gripped his arm, then suddenly relaxed. "No. I don't mind continuing...as we have been."

A little of his tension eased. He desperately needed a few more days with her. Once it was over, he'd have no further hold on her, and he wouldn't be able to put off doing the right thing. But for now... He tugged on her hand. "Come here, babe."

Emily slid over on the seat until their thighs touched and her seat belt pinched her side. She laid her head on his shoulder. Judd felt a lump of emotion that nearly choked him, and he swallowed hard. For so long, he'd been driven to get Donner and to avenge Max's death. He'd thought doing so would give him peace and allow him to get on with his life. But he realized now, after claiming Emily as his own for such a short time, there would be no peace. His life would be just as empty after Donner was convicted as it had been before. Maybe even more so, because now, he knew what he was missing.

Emily felt like a thief. She was getting rather good at sneaking around. It still made her uneasy, but with Judd always watching her so closely, the subterfuge was necessary.

In order to "protect" her, he'd sort of moved in. It was a temporary situation, prompted by Judd's concern over the break-in. He'd never once made mention of any emotional involvement, but his concern for her was obvious. And though it made her plans that much more difficult to follow, she was glad to have him in her home.

During the day he teased her and talked with her; he made her feel special. And at night...the nights were endless and hot and carnal. Judd touched her in ways she'd never imagined, but now craved. The shocking suggestions he whispered in her ear, the things he did to her, and the greedy, anxious way she accepted it all, could only be described as wicked—deliciously wicked. She loved his touch, his scent, the taste of him. She loved him, more with every day.

They had to be discreet, with John in the house, slipping into bed together after he was asleep, and making certain to be up before him. But John seemed to take great pleasure in having Judd around, even trying to emulate him in several ways. The two men had become very close.

Emily had thought long and hard about her situation with Judd, and her main priority was to take every moment she could with him. She suspected John might be aware of their intimate relationship, but since she would never ask either man to leave, there was no help for it. And she simply couldn't feel any shame in loving Judd.

Now, as she slipped from the bedroom an hour before the sun was up, Emily thought of her plan. She knew Donner would be making his deal tomorrow at the abandoned produce warehouse on Fourth Street. She had her camera loaded and ready. If she could get a really good, incriminating picture, there would be no reason for Judd to continue his investigation. He would be safe.

Giving Judd the evidence he needed would be her gift to him, to help him put the past to rest. Then maybe he'd want her to be a part of his future.

She was at the kitchen table studying a map when she heard Judd start down the steps. Seconds later, when he entered the kitchen, she tried not to look guilty. The map, now a wadded, smashed ball of paper, was stuffed safely in a cabinet drawer.

"What are you doing up so early, babe?"

Emily drank in the sight of him, standing there with his hair on end and his eyes blurry. There was so little time left. After tomorrow, his case would be over, the threat would be gone and Judd would leave her. She rushed across the floor in her bare feet and hugged him.

Judd seemed startled for a moment, and then his arms came around her, squeezing tight. "What's wrong, Em?"

"Nothing. I just couldn't sleep."

He set her away from him. "Take a seat and I'll start some coffee."

She sat, and fiddled with the edge of a napkin. "Judd?"

"Hmm?"

"I have some stuff I have to do tomorrow. Around two."

His hand, searching for a coffee mug, stopped in midreach. When he turned around, he wore a cautious expression and his posture seemed too stiff. "Oh? What kind of stuff?"

"Nothing really important. I have a load of clothes to drop off at the shelter, and some packages to send to an aunt for her birthday." She held his gaze, striving for a look of innocence. "And I think I'll do a little grocery shopping, too."

All at once he seemed to relax and his breath escaped in a sigh, as if he'd been holding it. He gifted her with a small smile. "Well, don't worry about me. I'm sure I can find something to occupy my time. In fact, I should go check on my mail and maybe pay a few bills."

Emily congratulated herself on her performance. She'd been brilliant and he'd believed every word. Now, if she could only get him to leave before her so she wouldn't have to try to sneak out. He'd surely notice her clothes, dark slacks and a sweater, since he'd never seen her wear anything like them before. She liked the outfit. It made her feel like 007.

An hour later, all three of them were finishing breakfast. It was a relaxing atmosphere, casual and close, like that of a real family. Emily smiled, thinking how perfect it seemed.

That's when her parents arrived.

The introductions were strained and painful. Judd remembered now why he'd never done this. Meeting a mother, especially when you were barefoot and hadn't shaven yet could make the occasion doubly awkward. He thought about bowing out, letting Emily and John have time alone with their parents, but one look at their faces and he knew he wasn't going to budge.

"What is he doing here, Emily?"

"I told you, Mother, he's a friend."

"What kind of friend?"

"What kind do you think, Father?"

Judd winced. He'd never seen Emily act so cool, or so defensive. And her smart reply had Jonathan Sr. turning his way. "I think you should remove yourself."

Judd raised an eyebrow. Well, that was blunt. Before he could come up with a suitable reply, Emily fairly burst beside him.

"You overstep yourself. This is my house, and Judd is my guest."

That startled Judd, but evidently not as much as it did Emily's family. They all stared, and Emily glared back. "Uh, Em..."

"No." She raised one slim, imperious hand. "I want you to stay, Judd."

Evelyn Cooper stepped forth. She was an attractive woman, with hair as dark as Emily's and eyes just as big. For the briefest moment, Judd wondered if this was what Emily would look like when she got older—and he felt bereft that he'd never know.

"We have family business to discuss, Emily. It isn't proper for a stranger to be here."

John snorted. "He isn't a stranger, he's a very good friend. And he already knows all about me. I trust him."

Evelyn narrowed her eyes at her son. "I wasn't talking about your irresponsible behavior. You will, of course, return with us. We've found the perfect surgeon." Then her gaze traveled again to Judd. "I was speaking of Emily's...unseemly conduct."

Judd was still reeling over the way John had just defended him. He was a friend? A very good, trusted friend? He felt like smiling, even though he knew now wasn't the time. Then Evelyn's words sank in. *Unseemly?*

John had told him that Emily never stood up to her parents, that she took their insults and their politely veiled slurs without retaliating. Probably because she still felt guilty for misjudging her fiancé and causing her parents an embarrassment. But to put up with this? He didn't like it, but he also didn't think he should interfere between Emily and her parents. He drew a deep breath, and tried to remain silent.

Emily lifted her chin. "I'm not entirely certain John wants to see another surgeon, or that it's at all necessary."

"John will do as he's told."

"Despite what he wants?"

Jonathan Sr. harrumphed. "He's too young to know what he wants, and certainly too irrational at this point to make a sound decision. It's possible the scars can be completely removed. Appearances being what they are, I think we should explore every avenue."

Judd stood silently while a debate ensued. John made it clear he didn't want any further surgery. The last doctor had been very precise. The scars would diminish with time, and beyond that, nothing more could be done. Judd thought it was a sensible decision on the boy's part, but John's father disagreed. And though he'd told himself he wouldn't interfere, Judd couldn't stop himself from interrupting.

"Will you love your son any less with the scars?"

Both parents went rigid. Then Jonathan shook his head. "This has nothing to do with love!"

"Well, maybe that's the problem."

That brought a long moment of silence. Evelyn looked at her husband, and then at her son. "We only want what's best for you."

"*Then leave me alone.* I'm sick of being picked over by a bunch of doctors. I did a dumb thing, and now I have some scars. It's not great, but it's not the end of the world, either. They're just scars. I'd like to forget about what happened and get on with my life."

Jonathan frowned. "What life? Skulking around in the

slums and getting into more trouble? We won't tolerate any more nonsense."

"Is that why you wanted to keep me out of the country? Dad, I could find trouble anywhere if that's what I really wanted. But I don't." He looked at Judd, then sighed. "I'm sorry for the way I've acted. Really. But I want to stay here now. With Emmie."

Jonathan shared another look with his wife, then narrowed his eyes at Emily. "I'm not certain that's a good idea. Emily's always been a bad influence on you."

Judd waited, but still, Emily offered no defense. It frustrated him, the way she allowed her parents to verbally abuse her. Again, he spoke up, but he kept his tone gentle. "It seems to me Emily's been a great influence. Didn't you just hear your son apologize and promise to stay out of trouble? What more could you ask for?"

Evelyn squeezed her eyes shut as if in pain. "Good Lord, Emily. He's just like the other one, isn't he? How much will it cost us this time to get you out of this mess?"

Judd froze. They couldn't possibly mean what he thought they meant. He looked at Emily, saw her broken expression and lost any claim to calm. But Emily forestalled his show of outrage.

"How dare you?"

She'd said it so softly, he almost hadn't heard her. The way her parents stared, they must have doubted their ears, too.

"How dare you even think to compare them?" Her voice rose, gaining strength. She trembled in her anger. "You don't know him, you have no idea what kind of man he is."

Judd was appalled when he saw the tears in her eyes. He touched her arm. "Emily, honey, don't." She hadn't defended herself, but she was defending him? He couldn't bear to be the cause of dissension between her and her family. It seemed to him they had enough to get straight without his intrusion.

Emily acted as though he weren't there. She drew herself up into a militant stance and said, "I would like you both to leave."

Jonathan glared. "You're throwing us out?"

"Absolutely. I've listened long enough to your accusations and disapproval. I won't ever be the daughter you want, so I'm done trying."

Evelyn laid a hand to her chest. "But we just got here. We came all the way from Europe."

Emily blinked, then gave a short nod. "You may have ten minutes to refresh yourselves. Then I want you gone." And she turned and walked out of the room.

Judd started to go after her when he heard Jonathan say, "You're not good enough for her, you know."

He never slowed his pace. "Yeah, I know."

But before he'd completely left the room, he heard John whisper, his tone filled with disgust, "You're both wrong. They're perfect...for each other."

What did kids know? Judd asked himself that question again and again. So John liked him. That didn't mean he could step in and do something outrageous like ask Emily to marry him. No, he couldn't do that.

But he could let her know how special she was, how perfect...to him.

When he found her in the bedroom, she was no longer crying. She sat still and silent in a chair, her back to the door, staring out a window.

"You okay?"

"I'm fine."

She wasn't and he knew that. He made a quick decision,

then knelt beside her chair. After smoothing back her hair, he brushed his thumb over her soft temple. "Maybe you should go talk to them, babe. No yelling, no silent acceptance. Talk. Tell them how you feel, how they *make* you feel. They love you, you know. They don't mean to hurt you."

She didn't look at him. "How do you know they love me?"

Because I love you, and I can't imagine anyone not loving you. "You're a beautiful, giving, caring person. What's not to love?"

Her face tilted toward him, and he saw a fresh rush of tears. He kissed one away from her cheek. "Talk to them, Em. Don't let them leave like this." He stroked her cold fingers, then enfolded them in his own. "Anything can happen, I learned that with Max. Time is too short to waste, and there are too many needy people in the world to turn away those that love you."

She squeezed her eyes shut and tightened her lips, as if trying to silence herself. Judd stood, then pulled her to her feet. "Go. Talk to them. I'll get showered and dressed."

"In other words, you intend to stay out of the way?"

He grinned at her grumbling tone. "I think that might be best. But I'll be here if you need me."

She stared up at him, her eyes huge, her lashes wet with tears, and Judd couldn't stop himself from kissing her. He'd wanted to spend this last day with her, to fill himself with her because after tomorrow, he'd have no reason to be in her house, no reason to keep her close. No reason to love her. He pulled back slowly, but placed another kiss on the corner of her mouth, her chin, the tip of her nose.

"You'd better get a move on before they leave. The ten minutes you gave them is almost up."

She laughed. "If you knew my parents, you'd know how little that mattered. They think I'm on the road to ruin. I doubt they're about to budge one inch." Then she hugged him. "Thank you, Judd. You're the very best."

As she left the bedroom, he grinned, hoping she'd work things out, and wondering at the same time...the best of what?

Chapter Ten

UNFORTUNATELY, IT RAINED. Emily felt the dampness seep through her thick sweater and slacks. But she supposed the rain was good for one thing—it made her less conspicuous lurking around the back of abandoned warehouses.

Leaving today hadn't been too difficult. Judd had gone on his errands before her, and her parents, though they had stayed in town, hadn't remained at her house. They had talked a long time yesterday, and her mother had said they hoped to "work things out." They'd been apologetic, and they'd listened. Emily wondered at their change of heart, and if they'd still feel the same after she went against their wishes and brought charges against Clayton Donner.

This particular produce warehouse had several gates where a semi could have backed up to unload its goods. Three feet high and disgustingly dirty, the bottom of the gate proved to be a bit of a challenge as Emily tried to hoist herself up. The metal door was raised just enough for her to slip through, and although she still had time before Donner was due to arrive, she wanted to be inside, safely ensconced in her hiding place so there'd be no chance of her being detected.

The flesh of her palms stung as they scraped across the rough concrete ledge. Her feet pedaled air before finding something solid, and then she slid forward, wedging herself under the heavy, rusting door. She blinked several times to adjust her vision, then wrinkled her nose at the stale, fetid air. Donner had certainly picked an excellent place to do his business. It didn't appear as though anyone had been inside in ages.

Emily got to her feet, then hastily looked around for a place where she could hide, and still be able to take her pictures. The warehouse was wide open, so she should be able to capture the deal on film. The entire perimeter was framed with stacks of broken crates and rusted metal shelving, garbage and old machine parts. Not a glimpse of the vague light penetrating the dirty windows reached the corners, so that's where Emily headed. She shuddered with both fear and distaste. But she reminded herself that it could easily have been Judd here, risking his life. That thought proved to be all the incentive she needed.

Just as she neared the corner, she heard the screeching whine of unused pulleys and one of the gates started to move. With her heart in her throat, she ducked behind the crates and crouched as low as she could. She wondered, a little hysterically, if they would hear her heart thundering. She listened as footfalls sounded on the concrete floor, and voices raised and lowered in casual conversation. Then she forced herself to relax; no one was aware of her presence.

When Donner and the man from the picture came to stand directly in front of her, not twenty feet away, Emily silently fumbled for her camera. A van backed up to the gate, and the driver got out—Emily recognized him as Mick—and began unloading wooden cases. She almost smiled in anticipation, despite her nervousness.

Just a few more minutes and… A soft squeaking sounded near her. Emily didn't dare move, her heart once again starting on its wild dance. Then she heard it again. She very care-fully tilted her head to the side and peered around her. Then she saw the red eyes. *Oh my Lord, Emily!* A dark, long-bodied rat stared at her.

She drew a slow deep breath and tried to ignore the crea-ture. But it seemed persistent, inching closer behind her where she couldn't see it. She felt the touch of something, and tried not to jerk. The camera was in her hands, she had a clear shot between the crates where she hid, and Donner was winding up his business. All she needed was a single picture.

The rat tried to climb the crate beside her, using her leg as a ladder. Emily bit her lip to keep from breathing too hard. And she was good, very good. She didn't make a single sound.

But the damn rat did.

A broken crate collapsed when the rodent tried to jump to-ward her, and in a domino effect, other containers followed and Emily found herself exposed. She fell back, trying to hide, but not in time. Within a single heartbeat, she heard the click of a gun, then Donner's voice as he murmured in a silky tone, "Well, well. If it isn't the little bird. This should prove to be interesting."

Judd cursed, not quite believing what he'd just seen. How had she known? He'd been so damn careful, even going as far as faking frustration to make her believe that the deal had been called off. But somehow she had found out. And now she was inside, with Donner holding a gun on her. He lowered himself away from the window, then swiped at the mixture of rain and nervous sweat on his forehead. His stomach cramped.

Cold terror swelled through him, worse than anything he'd ever known, but he pushed it aside. He couldn't panic now, not if he hoped to get her out of there alive. His men were stationed around the warehouse, but at a necessary distance so they wouldn't be detected. Judd had planned to make the deal, recording it all through the wire he wore, then walk out just as his men arrived, making a clean bust. Now he'd have to improvise.

Speaking in a whisper so that Donner and the others wouldn't hear, he said into the wire, "Plans have changed. We'll have to move now, but cautiously. There's a woman inside, and I'll personally deal with anyone who endangers her." He allowed himself one calming breath, then said, "I'm going in."

With icy trickles of rain snaking down his neck, he took one final peek through the grimy window, then lowered himself and inched forward until it appeared he'd just arrived directly at the back entrance of the warehouse. His stance changed to one of nonchalance, and he walked through the door beside the gate.

Emily looked up at him in horror. Mick, his grin feral, held her tightly, with her arms pulled behind her back. Donner and the other man stood beside him. Judd feigned surprise, then annoyance. "What the hell is she doing here?"

Donner smiled, then inclined his head. "I'd thought to ask you that when you arrived. You're late."

With a casual flip of his wrist, Judd checked his watch. "Four o'clock exactly. I'm never late. Now, what's she doing here? I didn't want her involved."

"As you can see, she's very much involved." Donner held up a camera. "I believe she had some photography in mind."

"Damn." Then he stomped over to Emily. "I thought I told you to knock that crap off?"

He gave an apologetic grimace to Donner. "She's been thinking of doing a damn exposé on the east end. She's taken pictures of every ragtag kid, every gutter drunk or gang punk she can find. Annoys the hell out of me with that garbage."

Donner gave a lazy blink. "I think she's stepped a little over the line this time."

Judd lifted an eyebrow. "Got some interesting pictures, did she?" He turned to Emily, chiding her. "You just don't know when to quit, do you?"

"Actually," Donner persisted, "I don't think she took a single photo. But that's not the point, now, is it?"

Judd crossed his arms over his chest. "If you mean what I think you mean, forget it. I'm not done with her."

"Oh?"

"She promised to buy me a Porsche. I've been wanting one of those a long time."

Donner moved his gaze to Emily. With a nod from him, Mick pulled her arms a little tighter. The dark sweater stretched over her breasts and her back arched. Judd had to lock his jaw.

"After today, you won't need her. We can make plenty of money together." He dropped the small camera and ground it beneath his heel, then paced away from Emily. "Get it over with. We've been here too long already and there's plenty more to do." As he spoke, he watched Judd.

Knowing Donner was waiting for a reaction, Judd did his very best to maintain an air of disgust. But his mind raced and he tried to gauge his chances of taking on all three of them. He planned his move, his body tense, his mind clear.

The man from the picture grinned. He hefted an automatic weapon in his hand, the very same make that had been sold to Emily's brother. He held the gun high in his outstretched hand and aimed at Emily. Judd roared, lurching toward him, just as the gun exploded.

Emily squeezed her eyes shut, so many regrets going through her mind, all in a single second. She'd been a fool, a naive fool, thinking she could help, thinking she might make a difference. She'd ruined everything, and now Judd would die, because of her.

She heard the blast of the gun and jerked. But she felt no pain. A loud scream tore through the warehouse, echoing off the stark walls. She opened her eyes and realized the man who'd intended to shoot her was now crouching on the cold floor, his blackened face held in his hands. Blood oozed from between his fingers. The gun had backfired?

Judd reacted with enraged energy. His fist landed against Donner, who seemed shocked by what had just happened. She felt Mick loosen his hold and she threw herself forward, landing hard on her knees and palms, her shoulders jarring from the impact.

And then the room was flooded with men.

There was so much activity, it took Emily a moment to realize it was all over, that Donner and his men were being arrested. Judd appeared at her side, helping her to sit up.

"Are you all right?"

His voice sounded strange, very distant and cold. She brushed off her palms, trying to convince her heart that everything was now as it should be. Her throat ached and speaking proved difficult. "I'm fine. Just a little shaken."

Lifting her hands, Judd stared at her skinned palms, and his eyes narrowed. "I think you should go to the hospital to get checked over."

After flexing her shoulders, still sore from the way Mick had held her and the impact on the hard floor, Emily rubbed her knees. "No. That's not necessary—"

"Dammit! For once, will you just do as I tell you?"

Her heart finally slowed, in fact it almost stopped. He sounded so angry. She supposed he had the right. After all, she'd really messed things up and nearly gotten them both killed. *You might as well begin apologizing now, Emily. From the looks of him, it's going to take a lot to gain his forgiveness.* She reached out to take his hand. "Judd, I—"

He came to his feet in a rush and his eyes went over her, lingering on the dark slacks. He ground his jaw and looked away. An ambulance sounded in the distance, and when Emily looked around, she realized the man who'd been about to shoot her was very seriously wounded. Donner looked as though he wasn't feeling too well, either. He'd been close enough to receive some of the blast from the gun, and he bore a few bruises and bloody gashes from his struggle with Judd.

A passing officer caught Judd's eye, and he was suddenly hauled over to stand before Emily. Judd seemed filled with annoyance. "See that she gets to the hospital. I want her checked over."

"Yes, sir."

Remarkably, Judd started to walk away. Emily grabbed for him. Her hands shook and her heart ached. "Judd? Will I see you later at the house?"

He didn't look at her. "I already got my stuff out. Your house is your own again. Go home and rest, Em. We can question you later."

She watched him walk away, not quite believing her eyes, not wanting to believe it could end so easily. And then it didn't matter anymore. She wasn't giving up. She may have been a fool, but she refused to remain one. She wanted Judd, and she'd do whatever it took to get him.

He cut her cold. Emily tried numerous times to reach Judd. Three weeks had passed, and the police no longer needed her as a witness. Evidently, Judd no longer needed her...for anything.

She had no reason to seek him out, but she still tried. He'd remained at the small apartment. She'd been there several times, but he either didn't answer the door, or he was so distantly polite, asking her about her brother, wishing her well, that she couldn't bear it. They might have been mere acquaintances, except that Emily felt so much more. She loved him, and even though her parents tried to convince her not to make a fool of herself, she couldn't give up.

She had tried apologizing to him for mucking things up. That had made him angry all over again, so she'd refrained from mentioning it further. John had gone to him once, to see how he was doing. Judd received her brother much better than he'd received her, and Emily felt a touch of jealousy. It bothered her even more when John claimed Judd was "absolutely miserable."

"He wants you, Emmie. I know he does. He just doesn't realize you want him, too."

Much as she wanted to believe that, she couldn't allow herself false hope. "I've made it more than clear, John. I can't very well force the man to love me."

But John had shrugged, a wicked grin on his face. "Why not? At least then you'd settle things, one way or another."

She thought about that. How could she "force" a man who was nearly a foot taller and outweighed her by ninety pounds? She decided to try talking to him one more time, and went directly to his apartment. His old battered truck sat out front, and as Emily passed, something different caught her eye. At first, she had no idea what it was, and then it struck her.

She bent next to the driver's window and peered inside. The black lace that used to hang so garishly from his rearview mirror had been replaced by the tie from her dress. Emily vaguely remembered that night when Judd had shoved the pale strip of material into his back pocket moments before they'd made love.

And now it had a place of prominence in his truck.

It was ridiculous how flattered she felt by such a silly thing, but she suddenly knew, deep in her heart, that he did care. At least a little.

She remembered the day he'd allowed her to indulge her fantasies. He'd said he had fantasies of his own, and he'd whispered erotic suggestions to her while they made love, wicked things about her really stripping—performing for him. She had been mortified and excited at the same time. Some of the things he'd suggested had been sinfully arousing, and she'd promised herself, once she could gain the courage, she'd fulfill every single one of his fantasies.

But she hadn't. She'd let inhibitions get in her way, even though she knew how wild it would make him. But maybe it wasn't too late. Maybe she could still set things right between them, and show him how much she loved him by giving him everything she possibly could.

She started away from the truck, her confidence restored. But she stopped dead when a little old lady blocked her path.

"What were you doing there, girl?"

"I..." What should she say? That she was admiring an article of her clothing, strung from a rearview mirror like a masculine trophy? That she intended to seduce a man? *Get a grip, Emily.* "I was just about to call on my...brother. I see his truck is here, so I know he must be—"

"He ain't home. He's taken to walkin' in the park every evening. Usually picks up a few necessaries for me while he's out."

"I see." Emily's disappointment was obvious.

"I'm the landlady here. You want me to give him a message?"

"No. I had hoped to...surprise him." Her mind whirled. "It's his birthday today. And since he doesn't have any other family, I thought maybe I could make this day...special."

"His birthday, you say? Well, now we can't let it go by without a little fun, can we? I could let you into the apartment, if that's what you're wantin'."

Already Emily's pulse began racing. "Yes, that would be wonderful. And I promise, he'll be so surprised."

Judd dragged himself up the steps to his apartment. The weather had been considerably milder lately, and he wore only a T-shirt with his jeans. The early-evening air should have refreshed him, but he still felt hollow. He'd felt that way ever since Emily had been endangered—by his own design.

His drive, his need to see Clayton Donner sent to jail, had clouded his reason and cost him his heart. He'd thought losing Max had been the ultimate hurt, but knowing he'd endangered Emily, knowing he'd risked her life, used her, loved her, was slowly killing him. He couldn't bear to face himself in the mirror.

He also knew he'd love her forever, and it scared the hell out of him. Time and distance hadn't helped to diminish what he felt. But what could he do? Ask her to forgive him, to spend her life with him? How could he? She deserved better than him. Her grace was always with her, whether she was working at the soup kitchen, or sneaking into a warehouse full of danger. She was elegance personified, and he was a man who went to any extreme to get what he wanted, to see a job done, including stripping off his clothes for a pack of hungry women.

Self-disgust washed over him. He rubbed his face, wishing he could undo the past and be what Emily deserved.

Mrs. Cleary met him in the hallway, a huge smile spread over her timeworn features. Struck dumb for a moment, Judd stared.

"Did you fetch my bread and eggs?"

"Here you go, Mrs. Cleary. Are you sure you don't need anything else?" Judd had taken to the older woman with her

gruff complaints and constant gossip. He figured she was probably every bit as lonely as he was.

"No, I got all I need. Now you run on home. And happy
birthday."

Judd blinked. "But..." She winked at him, and he decided
against correcting her assumption. Age could be the very devil,
and if she wanted to believe it was his birthday, for whatever
reason, he'd let her. "Thanks."

When he reached his apartment and stepped inside, he knew
right away that something was different. He could feel it. All
his instincts kicked in, and he looked around with a slow, en-
compassing gaze. His bedroom door was shut.

That seemed odd. Then odder still, music began to play. He
recognized the slow, brassy rhythm as one of his favorite CDs,
and his instincts took over. Without real thought, he inched
his way to the cabinet where he kept his Beretta, slowly slid
it into his palm, and crept forward.

The beat of the music swelled and moaned, and Judd flattened himself beside the door. Then, with his left hand, he
slowly turned the knob and threw it open.

He waited, but no bodies came hurdling out, and he cautiously, quickly, dipped his head inside then jerked back to
flatten himself against the wall.

No. It took his mind a second to assimilate what he'd just
seen, and still, he didn't believe it. He blinked several times,
then peeked into the room again.

Yes. That was Emily.

Standing in the center of his rumpled bed.

He moved to block the doorway, his gun now held limply at
his side. The black leather jacket he'd used as part of his stripping costume hung around her shoulders, the sleeves dropping past her fingertips. It wasn't zipped, and he could see a
narrow strip of bare, pale flesh, from her black lace bra to her

skimpy lace panties. Her navel was a slight shadow framed by the zipper and black leather.

Max's hat sat at a rakish angle on her head. She grinned.

Sweat on his palms made it necessary for him to set the gun aside. He stumbled to the dresser, then took two steps toward her before he stopped, unsure of himself, unsure of her.

With her eyes closed, her hips swayed to the music. As he watched, her face blossomed with color—and the jacket fell away.

He licked his lips, trying to find some moisture in his suddenly dry mouth. It had been three long weeks, three *endless* weeks, since he'd made love to Emily. She lifted her arms over her head, her nipples almost escaping the sheer lace, and he felt his body harden. His erection grew long and full, pressing against his suddenly tight jeans.

She turned on the bed, not saying a single thing. Judd breathed through his mouth as his body pulsed, his eyes glued to the sight of her small bottom encased in black lace. Her hips swayed and his erection leaped, along with his heart.

Emily reached behind her back to unhook her bra. He took another step closer. He wanted to ask her what this meant, but he was afraid to speak, afraid she'd stop—afraid she wouldn't. When she turned around, she tossed the bra to him.

It hit him in the chest and fell to the floor. He couldn't move. He couldn't blink. He could barely force air past his restricted lungs.

The hat fell off when she bent slightly at the waist, hooking her thumbs in the waistband of her panties. The blush had spread to encompass her throat, her breasts. Her pointed nipples flushed a dark rose. The music picked up, hitting a crescendo and crashing into a final, raging beat.

Emily released the panties and they slid down her slender thighs, landing against his disheveled covers and pooling around her feet.

Judd stared at the triangle of dark glossy curls and his nostrils flared. He started toward her.

She raised one hand and he stopped. "We need to talk, Judd."

"Talk?" His mind felt like mush, his body, like fire.

"I realized desperate measures were necessary to get your attention."

"Believe me, Em. You have my attention." It was an effort, but he managed to force his gaze to her earnest face.

She lifted her chin. Her lips trembled for a moment. "I hope you'll understand. Sometimes we have to do outrageous things to meet our ends. Just as you had to strip to trap Donner, well, I had to strip to...trap you." She clenched her hands together, and then she blurted out, "I love you."

"You..." He'd been engrossed with her odd comparison, and the fact she'd evidently understood his motives all along. And she hadn't blamed him for doing whatever needed to be done. He'd been wrong about that.

But now his thoughts crashed down. She couldn't have said what he thought she'd said. "You...love me?"

"Yes. I love you. I want you. Forever. I realize I'm not quite what you had in mind for a...a woman."

"A wife?"

"Well, yes. That would probably be the most logical thing, considering how I feel."

"You love me?"

She made an exasperated sound and propped her fists on her naked hips. His body throbbed.

"Didn't I just say so? Twice?"

"I believe you did."

"Well? Do you think you can come to love me? I realize this is probably not very…fair of me. To try to seduce you—"

"You passed 'try' when the music began."

"Oh. I see. Well, then, you should know, I expect everything. Our…reactions to each other are…very satisfying, but I want more."

"You want me to marry you?"

She tromped over to the edge of the bed, bringing her breasts a mere foot from his face. He swallowed, then gave up trying to keep his gaze focused.

He put first one knee, then the other on the bed and wrapped his arms around her, pressing his mouth to her soft naked belly. "I love you, too, Em. God, I love you."

Her fingers clenched in his hair. "Really?"

"I was afraid to love you, but it happened, anyway."

"You were afraid?"

He nodded, then nuzzled one pointed nipple. "You deserve so much better."

Her fingers tightened and pulled. Wincing, he looked up at her. "Don't you ever say that again! You're the finest, the most caring man I've ever known."

He saw her intent expression, her anger, and felt himself begin to believe. "Our backgrounds—"

"Damn our backgrounds!"

Judd blinked. Cursing from Emily? He felt shocked, and ridiculously happy.

"You rose above your upbringing, Judd. Despite all your disadvantages, you're a hero." Her fingers tightened again and she brought his head against her. "You're my hero."

"No."

"Yes! I'm not giving you pity, because you don't need it. I'm only giving you the truth. I love everything about you." She swallowed hard, then gentled her hold on his hair, smoothing her hand over his crown. "And you make me feel loved. Nothing else matters. We can work out the rest."

"The rest?"

"I love my house, Judd. I'd like us to live there."

"I'd...I'd like that too. But Emily, I'm not a pauper. I've never had anything to spend my money on, so I have a hefty savings—"

Her fingers touched his mouth. "I never thought you were helpless, Judd. And we'll support each other, okay? That is, if you can tolerate my parents. They do seem to be trying."

He pulled her down until she knelt in front of him. "Marry me, Emily."

Her eyes, those huge, eat-a-man-alive eyes, fairly glowed with happiness. She kissed him, all over his face, his ear, his shoulder. "Yes," she shouted, "Oh, Judd, I love you."

As they both began trying to wrestle his clothes from his body, Judd said, "Promise me you'll strip for me again later. You took me so much by surprise, I think I might have missed something."

Her blush warmed him, and she smiled. "Whatever you say, Detective." And then he made love to her.

★ ★ ★ ★ ★